... OBViousLY you WERE SUPPOSED TO Fix :)

Flagpole

Neil Hall

This is a work of fiction. Unless otherwise indicated, all the names, characters, businesses, places, events and incidents in this book are either the product of the author's imagination or used in a fictitious manner. Any resemblance to actual persons, living or dead, or actual events is entirely coincidental.

For my wife and those that dream

1

Sleepaway America

I can't attest to being secure. Although, to me, I'm certain I am. Certainly. Positively. Perhaps. Fuck it. This is my chance to grow. I don't mean to be as cold-hearted as I too often appear. I'm not mentally ill. More just content with my own thoughts and confident with them. At least I think I am. I won't make any promises. I can't. Not that I won't keep.

This is the start of my adventure. That's how this whole working on a children's summer camp was sold to me. To all of us involved.

Off to America.

My name's Dylan Nemerov. I'm nineteen. Not sure how important that is. My parents named me after the bloke who built our extension on Lansdowne Road. I have this habit of telling people I was named after Bob Dylan. I'm lying. It carries more depth than a builder with a belly button like a dolphin's blowhole.

Now, when I mention camp, I mean summer camp. I'm English. So, not American. It's easy to confuse the concept. It's alien to me. The whole romanticism of a 'Sleepaway' camp and those summers distant from your parents is something I've never experienced before. This is new to me. The only exposure I've had is from films like Friday the 13th and Heavy Weights. The camp I'm going to isn't a fat camp and with any luck, I won't get slaughtered. Although, that would make things spicy.

I worry my thoughts of Laura will consume me. That stark realisation that I miss her touch. I'm scared too that my ability and freedom to roam will be taken from me. I need less drama in my life. I'm being independent. This is bigger than leaving for uni.

It's not the destination, it's the journey. That's bullshit. I wave goodbye to my Mother at Gatwick. She always hates it when I refer to her as 'Mother'. I find it hilarious; she flinches every time.

Shiny airport floors reflect my eyes. I feel youthful. I'm a little bean carrying a sixty-five litre backpack, too big for my spindly frame.

Last night, Laura shaved two parallel lines into my already short hair at an angle, two chicken talon swipes. I think I look cool, especially with my wooden rosary beads draped around my neck. I'm not religious but it makes me feel astute. That's what uni does to you; makes you a pretentious prick.

Check in, security, and duty free. I'm followed around by corporate signage for 'Sleepaway America'. Representatives sporting matching corporate T-shirts, holding clipboards. They're not even worth describing, more of a burden than noteworthy. They gave me a hand written name tag. I won't be wearing that shit.

So far, I've managed not to talk to anybody. I rely on the music I've brought with me. I have as many CDs as I could fit in my carry-on; in accordance with the weight limit.

They include, but not limited to:

Hot Hot Heat, 'Make Up the Breakdown', Tom Waits 'Mule Variations', The Stone Roses, 'The Complete Stone Roses', Bad Religion, 'The Process of Belief', Jimmy Eat World, 'Bleed

American' and Weezer, 'The Green Album'.

I'm now listening to Sean Paul's 'Dutty Rock' on my Bush CD player. I have the headphone wire threaded through a small hole in my backpack. It's designed that way; more than convenient. I don't have any of those tiny ear bud headphones, can't stand 'em. They just dig out my ears. Instead, I use the cover your ear foam ones. Puts me in a comfortable, safe place, shuts me off from this dreary world.

I'm not convinced, what with my neurosis, that I'm right for working on a children's summer camp. Am I even ready for what's likely to happen? What if it isn't as advertised, not the most enthralling experience of my life and not worth $580.00 for nine weeks' work?

I continue to tell myself it'll be worth it. It'll be worth the money for the flights, uniform, hotel accommodation and whatever else I forked out for to get here. The potential toll it may take on my relationship with Laura or losing it. Just keep repeating: 'it'll be worth it'.

I get to travel afterward from New York State. How the hell you're expected to see the whole of America on that wage afterward, is a mystery. The 'Sleepaway America' brochures and glossy information include images of elated young adults, enjoying camp life with twinkling, toothy smiles and giddy excitement. Pictures of the expansive Grand Canyon, the Manhattan skyline, open-mouthed faces, eyes sparkling with satisfaction. It's just masturbation.

It doesn't even hurt that I've left Laura. Not now with all these female distractions to indulge me. We had discussed this whole thing to death. I'm positive we'll cope. Over the past months, I've been an absolute bastard to her. I cheated on her with this girl, Zoe. I barely remember what she looks like. I called Laura soon after and confessed. It was over the phone. Who can blame me? I'm a pussy. I sat on my bedroom floor, leaning on my knees, Nokia 3210 to my ear. Sure, she was upset, hurt, and her voice wobbled and trembled. I cried, but almost laughed when she quoted lines from Justin Timberlake's 'Cry me a river'. She was trying to be vicious, but I couldn't get the song out of my head. She put the phone down, then silence.

Laura would eventually forgive me. There was the inevitable social stifling. I wasn't allowed out alone, my phone was suspect; she checked it constantly and I wouldn't dare talk to a girl. She'd forever peer over heads, shifting on the spot to gain a better vantage of our body language. Watching to see if eye contact was prolonged. It was worth it, it strengthened us. And, as much as she was apprehensive, she's now supportive of my travels. It helped that I laced on how special it was for me to experience this, that it was my childhood dream. Plus, I applied before we were a couple, so it was in motion. I wasn't about to ignore my predilection toward America and everything it represents for me. Those countless holidays as a child, which I'm more than grateful for. Now the opportunity to work there, I'll make the most of it.

Airport crowds, a captive adolescent audience. Just simmering white noise and stale shared air. Once you're inside, good luck getting out. I avoid eye contact with everyone at this plane gate. My fellow travellers stretch out across fixed chairs, reading flashy popular fiction. Spines on paperbacks and magazines are crushed by palpable concentration. Girls are already sharing contact information with new friends. Guys are standing, hands in pockets; talking in groups, rambling pointlessly about the impending journey to camp. It's my Sword of Damocles. The rabble of travellers stand out, what with the name tags and branded T-shirts. I'm happy remaining incognito. I threw my badge in the bin. I won't be touching any of these shared surfaces. It doesn't matter how vigorously I wipe my palms on my jeans after I've touched a handrail. I still need to wash them with steaming hot water. I just can't stand the smell of other people's shit, and on a plane. Well, I can't think about that right now. If I do, I won't be flying anywhere.

I'm ticked off a list of mumbled names by one of the braindead, branded 'Sleepaway America' staff. They guard the gate like the Special Forces, tactical positions with clipboards for guns.

Random people everywhere. I don't speak to them.
Everyone is being awkward. Empty sounding, uninteresting hogwash,
as I wait in line to board.

The Virgin Atlantic, Boeing 747 plane stands waiting, with the
name: 'Hot Lips' on the fuselage. It's got that woman in the red
swimsuit. The one bearing the Union flag, teasing us with escape. We
can't board until we find this guy Jimmy Wickwar. They've
announced his name over the airport loudspeakers. No one knows
him or where he is. The organisers are dashing back and forth from
the airline desk to other 'Sleepaway' staff, shaking their heads and
flapping their clipboards. He's nowhere to be seen.

It feels like hours. Arms are crossed and toes are tapping.
Then, a guy wearing a red Manchester United football shirt and black
jeans, carrying a pair of luminous yellow trainers in one hand, arrives
squinting his eyes and chomping on a triangle piece of buttered toast.
One of the female clipboard warriors runs over to him. She tracks her
finger down a list. Her exasperated, relieved face says she's found her
man. She nudges him in the back, ushering him forward. The crowd at
the gate erupts into loud cheers and whistling. This Jimmy Wickwar
guy, with no trainers on his feet and dirty white socks, raises his arms
in the air and high fives people as he struts closer, joining the end of
the queue. He's totally oblivious. I hope this Jimmy guy isn't traveling
to the same camp as me.

This seat is so dusty. There's a shared, stained safety card and in-
flight magazine in the seat in front, tray table stowed. I'm cramped in a
middle economy seat, between a kid who looks like Sid from Toy
Story and a pocket rocket dirty blonde. A sugary smell punctures my
nostrils. Sid, not his actual name, is placing Dolly mixture in size order
on his thigh. Only his right thigh, not the left. The off white and orange
cubes lined together, then the blackcurrant jelly ones. He's eating
them meticulously from his knee to his hip. He hasn't offered me or
pocket rocket girl any. We're not even speaking. I have nothing in
common with this lunatic.

I nudge pocket rocket to get her attention. She told me her name was Jenn. I'm not intimidated by her. When someone is out of this world, you can't string a word together. With her, I can be myself. Irrelevant if she likes me or not, I'm not bothered. She's nothing compared to Laura. Her hair is pinned up in the tightest bun. Gymnast hair, not flattering, designed only for performing a back handspring. I don't like it. I'd still do her.

I pretend to fall asleep and settle my head on pocket rocket, Jenn's shoulder, then slip my chin on her left breast. I nuzzle into her eighteen-year-old modesty and get away with it, bliss. She's a 'C' cup, that's my guess. She elbows my ribs to wake me up. I jump, acting like she's disturbed a deep sleep. She has flaky green nail polish, looks awful; cheap and chipped. She must have done that herself. Laura always has beautiful nails, professionally done. Jenn's are nothing.

The Statue of Liberty is an ant fleck on the horizon. The Twin Towers stretch above everything that surrounds them. The plane descends. JFK gets closer through the window. A speeding blur as we bump down on the runway. Arriving seventeen minutes early. Everyone stands, waiting to be let off. Usually, I'm patient, not now. It's every man for himself. This isn't two weeks in Cancun.

Gigantic coaches, parked up, plastered with 'Sleepaway America'. They load us and trundle to New York. The city that never sleeps. Another journey, JFK Airport to Port Authority, Manhattan. Never ending bus journeys. Get me to this fucking camp.

I'd like to be a part of this city and the life it breathes. Tall building after tall building, the sun reflecting off glass and steel. Road works, yellow cabs and silver smoke billowing from subway grates. I can imagine myself putting in a day's work, grabbing an Americano from Starbucks and cream cheese filled onion bagel. Then, catching a bus home, North to Yonkers or hopping on the train and pulling up in Tarrytown. It's a novelty in this moment. The daily grind would become monotonous. Life gets in the way.

The Port Authority resembles a mall, loads of shops, coffee places and escalators. I expected it to be busier. There are the herds of people heading to camp, but I thought more city dwellers would use it to commute. Could be the time of day. I don't know what the time is. I can't see a clock. Just like 'Hot Lips', everyone heading to camp needs to be together, in these groups and it's all by choice. No one wants to break away. Not interested in experiencing anything alone.

I have instructions to phone the camp and tell them I've arrived; they offer a pickup when we get to the town of Surrey. From the murmurs, we've all done exactly the same thing, each of us leaving a message to announce our arrival. I guess through fear we'd be stranded in Manhattan. Leave me here. I don't want to stand around in small groups of English people, chatting about Fray Bentos Meaty Puds, Bob the Builder and Rush Hour 2. Which are examples of actual conversations. I won't be hanging around to understand any of the contexts, I'm not interested. These people aren't my people. I've met none of them before and don't want to get to know them now.

"Can I get twenty Marlboro lights please?" I said, pointing over the newsstand at the rows of ciggies.

My first words to anyone in this city is to a guy, hidden by periodicals and magazines. His glasses rest on the tip of his runny nose. He's reading a folded magazine, slouching over the counter. He looks at me, confused, his face screwed.

"You want twenty?"

"What?"

I think we're both confused. I spoke my words clearly enough. He can understand, right?

"You want…" He flashes ten fingers twice "Twenty packs?" he said.

"Oh no," I said. "Sorry, I want one pack of twenty Marlboro lights."

Feels weird, having to justify that and providing an erect finger to explain I want just one. I guess asking for twenty is confusing. That's what we do at home. I don't think they do packs of ten here. Probably why he's perplexed. I wish he'd understand. The cigarettes haven't moved. I'm gasping for one, especially after that flight.

"I don't look old enough?" I said.

"No, my friend. No." He said, not looking up from his magazine.

I grab for my wallet, finger pluck my driver's licence and slide it across the counter toward him, under his eyeline.

"I can tell by your accent you're English." He said, standing erect with my licence in his hand, examining it. "I haven't seen a UK licence in a while." He flips it over. "You're cute in this picture."

No eye contact and now he's called me 'cute', that's unsettling.

He slides the cellophane wrapped treats to the middle of the counter. I grope for the cigarettes, exchange cash without physical contact. I'm polite, but get the hell out of there.

I haven't got time to explore. I smoke on 8th avenue, look up at the glass wonders, a patchwork of grey colours. I haven't noticed faces or even smelt obnoxious odours in the air. But navigating these roads is like a word search. Confusion curbing my enthusiasm. I'm skidding along the sidewalk with grit beneath my Converse trainers. I use my backpack as a seat, like a bewildered gnome, and suckle on the blissful nicotine.

I should have grabbed a copy of the U.S. version of 'Stuff'. The English magazine is about technology, gadgets and other shit. Their version is the equivalent to FHM. I couldn't buy it because of newsstand weirdo. It's a good job I made a mental image of the front cover; that Virginie Ledoyen, the French girl from The Beach. I'll need her face if I can't muster sordid sexual memories of Laura whilst in the shower. Thinking that, I bet they rob me of the ability to even stroke myself on this camp.

What am I gonna do?

2

The Silver Canine

Hideous orange tiled walls everywhere. The Port Authority bus terminal is like walking through a tunnel of the forgotten. It's so dated. The smell of burnt coffee beans and diesel exhaust fumes lingers in my throat.

There are guys and a few girls, still wearing 'Sleepaway America' name tags. I recognise them from the plane. They're waiting at the same bus stop. '77' spelt out in white tiles, making up the digits.

The guys lean against an orange metal barrier. Their hips thrust towards the three women, packages on display, concealed by a mix of mid thigh length chino shorts, Umbro joggers and Donnay three quarter length cargo trousers. English summer fashions.

The three girls stand together, one skinny blonde-haired, one black girl wearing a green trucker style baseball cap and matching green Chuck Taylor high top Converse trainers. Another girl that I've paid no attention to, and won't. I'm drawn to the black girl. Not because she's black, she looks heedless of her beauty, rock 'n roll. Reminds me of Moira. If I was to extend my right foot off the ground, she might notice me. I'm overwhelmed that we're sharing the same popular choice of footwear. She has no choice, she'll be mine. She's noticed my foot now, but hasn't continued up to my eyes, melting into my lust for her. Surely she'll be impressed by my rosary beads. I'm not even Catholic. It makes me think I'm Buddhist, in a perpetual state of clinging to life. I long for my nirvana but remain a creep.

My attention shifts to the English guys, now the high top queen has ignored me. They're standing together, still leaning. They've shared with each other where they're from and now it'll be my turn to face interrogation. Which I'll love every minute of.

"Hi, I'm Dylan." I said with fake confidence.

Normally, I wouldn't introduce myself. I know I'm better off getting in there first.

"Hi." They all said like the Children of the Corn.

"Where you from?" Asks a tall guy with a pudgy, stubbly face and short black hair.

"Bristol," I said.

With that, the Manchester United gormless fool, the guy who kept us waiting at the Gate. He steps forward, holding his hand out for me to shake. I respect that. He reminds me of one of those bucktooth bears from the Country Bear Jamboree.

"I'm Jimmy." He said, grinning.

He's not self-conscious of his hill billy ways, he'll fit right in with the hicks of the New York hills.

"Wickwar." I said, finishing his name for him.

His face shrivels with confusion.

"How you know that?" He said, in his thick Bristolian accent, his eyelids loose and heavy.

"You were late, back at Gatwick."

"Oh yeah." He said holding his gormless eyes on mine. He has one of those stupid-looking faces; his accent doesn't help either. He didn't display any guilt for keeping us waiting. I'll hold on to my grudge for a while.

"You said you were from Bristol," said Jimmy.

"I forgot who I was talking to." I said, shifting my bag off my back to the floor "I'm from Swindon."

"Not far from me then." Said Jimmy, smiling with his eyes shut.

Why am I on the same camp as this guy? I knew this shit would happen. I bet this black girl isn't going to the same camp, just my luck. Surrounded by retards, starved of Nubian princesses.

"Why d'ya say you were from Bristol, if you're from Swindon?" Said the tall guy with the receding bristly brush hair, his cheeks puffed.

"I think Americans don't have any idea where cities or towns in the UK are," I said. They each nod in agreement, with downturned mouths, "Some do, some don't."

More thoughtless, nodding. It's fake, this entire conversation. I'm nervous about talking to these guys. I'm worried the girls behind me are listening and thinking I'm a twat. Not sure why I care.

"I'm Daniel." Said the big guy leaning forward, offering his hand. "People call me Big D." His puffy cheeks flap like he was in a hurricane.

"Why do they call you that?" I said.

"Because I'm—," He doesn't finish his sentence. The girls overhear and snigger. Big D realises I'm joking.

He should know, I'm never going to call him 'Big D'. Not a chance. He will forever remain Daniel. Do people agree to use 'Big D', that's surely a joke? He's lanky, his head is so close to the top of the orange tiles.

"I'm Andy." Said a guy with short floppy bleached blond hair and a feminine heart-shaped face, clean shaven.

"I'm Mark. Mark Vizard. You can call me Vizard." Said a thick set guy in a white t-shirt, arms folded. He offers me his hand to shake too. Despite the handshake, this Mark guy is hostile. His grip on my hand is tight and firm.

"I'm from Oxford." He said, as if it should impress me.

Fuck me. It's only forty minutes up the A420. Not quite

Narnia. The prick.

"This your first time on camp?" said Oxford Mark.

Before I can answer, he interrupts my thoughtful hesitation.

"It's all our first time," he said.

He looks right, then left at the guys alongside him, their backs resting against the barrier. Who appointed him the voice of the people? I hope I survive these newfound fake friends and their questioning. Other than being on the same camp, me and my chums have nothing else in common.

A Greyhound bus pulls to a stop at 'Gate 77'. An ear piercing hiss of the brakes. 'America for me'. The driver opens the luggage doors; they rise like a Delorean. Bags taken and dashed, one by one. The fat driver flinging them into the underneath storage compartments, using his black leather boot to kick them into place. We all embark, single file, the polite and reserved English nobles we are.

On board this iconic 'Silver Canine'. In the storage flap of the seat in front is a leaflet, like the safety card on 'Hot Lips'. There's no real safety information, more the history of Greyhound; how it was founded in 1914 and a list of the major cities it services across the United States. It's a real piece of self-indulgent marketing material.

I have this aisle seat. Next to me is a petite brunette girl. Here I am, overwhelmed with being on an actual Greyhound that I didn't notice her. Maybe I'm losing my powers.

Bonita introduced herself in her loud Scottish accent, informing me her name, but that I can call her 'Boni'. When she speaks, she sounds like a frappuccino being drank, soft and warm, with a hint of cinnamon. Yummy. I lose myself in her narrowed eyes. We have no choice but sit in silence or learn about one another. She has a small chip on her top front tooth. You can only see it if she smiles. It won't put me off. She's a shorter, more compact version of Nelly Furtado, even with small, hooped earrings dangling.

All of my conversations with women are often stagnant but move quickly to subtle flirtation. Sometimes, it's fun to take a chance.

It's a long journey. The sexual tension between us igniting. I swear it's not just me.

"Bonita means pretty in Spanish," I said.

She stares at me, puzzled. "I haven't heard that," she said.

She maintains a perplexed face, relaxing to a slight smile, exposing her tooth again. She's attractive, I'm in trouble.

I have no idea where we are. I've barely looked out the window. It's all Boni's fault. The bus slows and stops. It could be a bus stop, there's no shelter or anything. Just a metal pole sticking up from the ground. The doors open, eight women get on. Middle-aged with no luggage or wedding rings. I didn't know we were stopping to collect more people. The bus is full. That's mad. I thought it was a bus straight from New York to our destination, evidently not.

Oxford Mark. Mark Vizard or Vizard to me, as he introduced himself, stands up.

"Please, you must take my seat." He said, with perfect diction and English eloquence, spoken with a plum like Oxfordshire accent.

The American woman he's addressing is holding a copy of Margaret Atwood's Bodily Harm. I haven't read it but the spiky sphere on the pale front cover attracts my eye. This woman, with good literary appreciation, accepts Oxford Mark's gesture, taking him up on his offer of chivalry. It's so trite. I can't oblige such perfection. He looks over head rests, as he's noticed another woman still standing. I'm not moving. If he wants to give up his seat, fair enough. Why he needs to involve me; I don't know.

"I'm sure someone else will be happy to give up their seat." He said, looking at me. Implying I should move. I'm not moving, never gonna happen.

"You can fuck right off." I mutter, dropping my head.

I don't feel guilty as Boni chuckles. That helps. I don't need her encouragement, but it's nice she's enjoying our conversation, too. She must want me. Who can tell where this is going? I long for exotic strangers in my life. For a sun-drenched naked experience. I so want this adventure to become my nomadic episode. I could be one of those smiling fools in the brochures. All my debauchery, despite having a girlfriend, waiting for me at home. Not to say Laura's waiting. Sat around pining for me. Nice if it were true. Camp may be the ideal opportunity to experience loads of other women. She'd never even know. Come to think of it, I've never been in the company of so many Scottish people in my life.

The bus cranks forward. I'm relaxing in my seat. That woman can stand. Oxford Mark can entertain her with stories of the Dewey Decimal System at Bodleian Library.

I'm learning about Boni, loving her accent. She has a vicious sense of humour. I wish Laura had a better sense of humour. It's a rare thing to find someone like Boni, who is as sardonic as me. I can see in her eyes that she wants to kiss. Laura can be so frigid in public. I've read a few books on body language. I can read someone well. I may push my luck, but we'll see how things go.

Boni excuses herself, patting me on the knee as she stands. I shift slightly. I won't make it too easy for her to get by without touching me. I assume she's going to the toilet. No need to stand up, but I do. If only to bow to her, bit of fun. She'll think of me as an attractive fiend. Her eyes pass below mine. Her stomach brushes against me. She squeezes past into the aisle. Nobody is stealing her seat. I'll remain bolt upright, open my legs wide and lean forward, limiting the optics of space next to me. No other bitch is sitting here. I conceal my semi-erect penis. The thought of our stomachs touching and the rhythmic rumble of this bus over potholes is enough to get his attention. I can't stop thinking of her graceful touch on my knee. I need to stop, otherwise I'm not concealing my wood before she gets back. I use my CD player as a shield. No one will be any the wiser. With my penis back to a bemused, nonchalant state, Boni has returned. Her hands brush mine as I stand to ease her back into her seat. I do that to Laura, place my hand in the small of her back. Boni's got clammy, moist fingers. She must have been in a rush. She too, thinking someone may steal her seat, didn't have time to dry her hands. I can't use a toilet on a coach. The people, on route would stare at me. There's no TV to entertain them. I'd become the distraction to the mundane. A feathered wand to a cat. I'm not sure I'm ready for that.

Oxford Mark stands in the aisle with his arms crossed, shuffling from one leg to the other. He must be gutted. Giving me nothing but the blacks of his eyes. I'm loving it, mate. All relaxed next to this beautiful Scottish girl, disguising the bulge in my jeans. My heart bleeds for you. Pays to be a gentleman, right. Why can't I have an exciting story? Why, for once, can't Boni lock eyes with me, shift her body and rub her index finger across my chin? She can touch whatever she likes. I wish Laura did more of that. On a postcard home, I'd love to write that I was close enough to this Scottish stranger that I could see my own eyes reflecting in hers. Her breath smelling of warm cinnamon, reminding me of Christmas. How she made a joke about it coming once a year and then fluttered her eyes, the tease. I'd love to do this girl.

I'm not exaggerating, and you won't understand the ellipsis of time. It's a long way from Manhattan to Surrey and we've stopped along the way. So, four hours of hard work, monotonous questions and agreements. Boni and I share my headphones and listen to 'Bandages' by Hot Hot Heat. I tell her stories of dancing to it during Freshers week, miming some of my moves in my seat. Laura skipped in and out of my mind. She always sings along to the song, changing the words to 'Bag of chips'. Perhaps now, thoughts of this song will kick into Boni mouthing along, as opposed to deep fried potatoes. It's an album that bookmarks my first year of uni. Now it'll be the soundtrack to this summer. Fingers crossed the soundtrack to bus sex.

The Greyhound trundles through the New York countryside. Boni's holding the CD player and keeps looking up at me, over her shoulder, smiling. The track now is 'This Town'. At the chorus, Boni continues to smile, in time to the music. Is that even possible? Whatever; it fits.

This is all comparable to a four month relationship. I'll subtly compliment her necklace or something, not drawing attention to the fact that I'm trying to glimpse her chest underneath her hoodie. She's a 34C. I may have added too much weight to her, she could be a 32C. I'd say they're bigger than Laura's. She nibbles her bottom lip. I can make out the chip on her tooth more clearly now, it's smooth. Should I ask how it happened? It might embarrass her and reduce the momentum of our brief encounter. I could romance her. Backed with the sound of Hot Hot Heat in my ears. Life strikes me as moving in slow motion. I lean in. Boni does too. We kiss. She must have chewed cinnamon flavoured gum; I can taste her smell. She's just slipped me her tongue. I close my eyes. Soft, wet and gentle; now it's over. Not the longest kiss, but it was new, different. She backs away and places her hoodie covered knuckles to her mouth, smiling cutely, as she curls her knees into her chest, staring out the window. How perfect to say to her: 'I have your gum.' I want one of those moments of playful intimacy. Maybe I am missing Laura. I want Boni to stick the tip of her tongue out at me with flirtatious cheekiness, or fall asleep in my lap. I want to hear her laugh from her heart.

She may well be sleeping now. But, to me, she's closed her eyes and smiling, her face reflected in the window. She drapes her right arm, over her left hip, contorting herself. Her hand floats, slender fingers rolling as if stroking the keys of a piano. That's an invitation to touch her. It has to be. She's resting her head against the glass. A solid white line on the road outside zipping past at speed. She exhales. It's the sound of frustration. Holy shit. She's arched her back and tilted her neck toward the air vents and that reading light. It's like she wants to be taken from behind. Something I'm never allowed to indulge in with Laura. She says it's too animalistic. I suffer because she's a prude. Laura's approach to intimacy is a guaranteed way to grow my sexual frustrations and breed my doggystyle fantasies. It's her fault I have a wandering eye. I run my two fingers around Boni's palm in a circle, like that children's nursery rhyme, with the bear going round and round, one step and a tickle under somewhere.

Boni's eyes are closed, her body propped against the window. She looks serene. I'm aroused. The thought of people watching drives me wild. Boni's legs have parted just enough that she's created a small gap, big enough that I can see the upholstery of the seat through her thighs, a bright maroon colour, big enough for my fingers over her jeans. I'm going for it; this might be my only chance. Her eyes ping open. The fun of seat 12C and 12D, is over. Heads turn at the sound of her slapping my cheek. There's no way to hide it. She's clobbered me. The coach stops. The driver's sunglass covered eyes stare back at me in the rear-view mirror. Perfect timing. We're here. Well, I got that all ways of wrong. Now for my hasty retreat.

3

Surrey, New York

This is it. Surrey, New York. The Upstate countryside is like
being in leafy England, reminiscent of Buckinghamshire, green and
dense. It goes on for miles. An expanse of nothingness. At home, you
can only travel a mile before you encroach on a housing estate or a
Tesco Metro.

A large white sign as we enter the condensed little town reads:

'Welcome to Surrey'. There's a concrete cenotaph in the
middle of the street, a traffic island of pride, surrounded by pristine
small hedges, delicately trimmed in the shadows of a pearly white
church steeple cutting into the blue sky. 'West 341'. The road sign
hangs down from overhead cables, alongside suspended traffic lights.
The bus pulls away. Boni has left with the bus, my cheek with her
imprinted hand. The windows are too tinted for me to see her
annoyed face. They're reflecting the green trees that line the road. It's
so white bright out here. There isn't even a distinctive country smell,
it's clean; crisp. The bus creeps forward at a 'Stop' sign. The
indicator blinks red, turning right. Gone.

Here we are, five disillusioned English guys, waiting by the side of the road, no pavement, just white lines and grass verges. Wooden telephone poles with rusted bolts stand tall like upturned pitch forks along this main road. We're on 'Candy Street' according to the sign ahead. There's a small fire station across the road, with big red doors wide open, a fire truck parked inside. Two bijou houses nearby; both painted matching parchment cream. The owners take care of them. We've been dropped on the outskirts of town, like Rambo. It's that kind of town too, everybody knows one another, and I imagine it would be cinematic as hell if it exploded.

On the bus, we passed houses lining 'Main Street' with wooden beam covered verandas and window shutters. We passed the inconsequential train station, a makeshift platform. I'm not clear why we couldn't've got a train from Grand Central to here. Perhaps it doesn't service the town, it looks small.

The 'Welcome to Surrey' sign as we entered, included:

'Population: 1,180'

The town is flat, only surrounded by hills like a salad bowl. I've already alienated myself from these English guys. I don't care, never have. I can't pretend to be interested in banal chatter with ugly men. I don't know why people bother. Why force me to get to know these people? I wouldn't, in the 'real' world, befriend any of them. I can see a soul in Andy. With his flamboyant disposition, he seems lovely. The others, they're buffoons. Tall Daniel or 'Big D' is gangly and keeps falling over things, a real idiot. I can't accommodate his blatant stupidity. I laugh more than anyone, but I can't laugh at rudimentary retards masquerading as enlightened individuals. I want so much to disassociate myself from them. I'm ashamed to call myself English. If I can't tolerate them, what will other nationalities think of their magical ways?

I'm afraid of letting these people in. If they were women, no problem. I get emotionally attached early on and I love their company. I'm not loyal, I don't know what that means. I wouldn't consider myself selfish. I do have Laura, but I was attracted to Boni. I don't know her, I still don't. But it was fun, and I wanted to be a part of it. I'm not sure that's selfish or not?

Despite four frantic phone calls from a nearby payphone to the camp for someone to collect us. None of us know where we're going. Three slow paced freight trains pass on the tracks, not stopping. I could run alongside and hop on board, see where it takes me and join a travelling circus. My life has never been that exciting. If I was braver, I'd achieve something.
The late morning sun is full, burning down on me. My head is hot. I'd be grateful for a hat. I'm not bothered to dig around in the bottom of my bag for it. I'm having to squint to help me see the town. I'm thankful, at least, to be here, I think.

Time has passed, we've stretched our arms, laid down, stood up and had a couple of playful races. Day by day, I live my life. Each hour fades into another.
      This road remains empty. We haven't seen one vehicle since the bus left. With that, a white people carrier turns in from the crossroads, pulling up to where we've dumped our bags and impatiently taken up our seated positions.
      The people carrier has 'Red Oak and Silver Wood Camp' written in a large red professional font down the side. No one is saying a word. The sliding door scrapes open. We jump in without confirming our names. No clipboard, no registration; no real hello. This is weird. The two men in the front seats could be anyone. Nothing but the backs of their heads.
I want a cigarette; I can't kick the sordid addiction. I've never considered it a fabled habit; I reminisce with affection when I'm not smoking. I even embrace how romantic it remains to me. I'm always hypnotised by smelling smoke in a club, the charred thickness of its lingering stench on my clothes the next morning. I cut back a while ago because of Laura, before she got caught up in the herb. Smoking allows me to escape outside when I'm cajoled into playing bullshit,

privately educated, student games at house parties. A party of 18-year-olds is supposed to include drinking, playing random records, arguing with the neighbours over noise and having sex in the back seat of your parent's Ford Fiesta. It isn't about standing around playing 'Names of, types of'. I'm not sure if it's Laura's circle of friends or her upper-class snobbery, but every party she's invited me to, includes competitive rowers from Henley-on-Thames. It's never enough to say: 'Henley'. It's forever and always 'Henley-on-Thames'. Laura is so impressed by rowers and their personas, their twisted egos as big as their turkey thighs. It could be my jealousy. She goes moist over a rower. I can't stand their fakery. In one breath, spouting esoteric lines from Hugo Dingler, the next taking fifteen-year-old girls into the back bedroom of their parent's yachts and giving them a finger.

I love to smoke. That familiar, warm, cocoa taste, the escape it gives me. I'm as big a fan of smoking as I am of Bill Hicks. I don't quite go through two lighters a day.

The door slides shut with a crunch, interrupting my smoke filled daydream. I don't know these people. It's safe to assume they don't want to know me. They're talking soft but remain excited. I can't even hear the words they speak, it's a load of distorted noise.

Am I going to survive this camp? I need to stimulate myself, get in the right mindset.

4

Red Oak And Silver Wood

We're travelling again for miles. Still, no one says anything. The two guys in the front seat have hardly said a word. They could have argued, I suppose. It's awkward between them. Both of their heads facing forward. The radio volume low. We drive deeper into the New York hills, ascending, descending, circling on and on. We're miles from that small Rambo town now. I'm not a nervous person, but they may take us to a remote location, make lamps out of our skin. They could be anyone.

Here, there're just trees, shrubs, and asphalt. We veer left, off the main road, and come to a break in the trees. On either side of the shingle road are two totem poles with red and white hand carved, sinister looking faces with creepy piercing eyes. Suspended between the poles is a wooden banner that reads:

'Red Oak and Silver Wood Camp'

The shadow silhouette of the sign runs across my eyes as we pass underneath it, the sun disappearing behind. We travel along a narrow single-track road, tall trees on either side, yellow triangular warning signs with the outline of children on them. Shafts of broken sunlight penetrate through the dark tree canopy. Massive grey rocks on the hillside, sloping from left to right.

Out of the darkness, we break into the sunlight. A wide expanse of green. The camp land is overwhelming; it blends like watercolours, as far as I can see. I never thought I'd fall in love with a location. I'm sitting up from my slouched, uninterested position, my face pressed, gazing out the van's windows, my head spinning from left to right, out the front and out the back.

"Look at that." I said, pointing at the massive lake to the right. Superlatives are being thrown around the place, even from me.

"Woah, check out that water slide," said Daniel. He's pointing at a long red and blue water slide attached to a tall wooden hut, reachable by a sloping ladder. The slide goes out and ends over the massive blue lake. Adults are using it, swooping down, their body shapes filling the flexible plastic, as they appear firing out the end, splashing into the crystal-clear lake.

The shoreline includes a man-made beach. There're so many people sunbathing on the clean white sand. Lifeguards stand on painted white jetties, men in pedalos wave at women. I'm referring to them as men. I mean, they're our age. Not sure I'd describe myself as a man yet, but these guys are enjoying the water, as are the girls, or women. These are the other counsellors we'll be working with. These girls have alluringly toned bodies, wearing skimpy bikinis.

"This is awesome," said Jimmy.

One blonde adjusts her swimsuit to cover her exposed right butt cheek.

"Awesome." I said, still gazing at her cheeks.

They're natural, toned and sexy. Girls next door. This isn't a scene from Porky's. Beautiful pert breasts. A girl wearing a full body swimsuit is hanging on to an inflatable water toy. Could be Shamu. She doesn't need to cover up; she looks in good shape. Girl, show me more, not less.

An American football arcs in front of the van. It makes me recoil, it's too close to the front. Hands smack on cowhide as a smiley guy catches the ball on the other side of the road. I can see the cabins we'll be staying in, painted bright white, sitting atop the hill that overlooks the rest of the camp. White picket fences and intricate decorations on the outside of the steps that create a landing for the two front doors. I can't make out the names that decorate the doors of each cabin, they're too far away.

The van crawls down the road, not exceeding the posted speed limit of ten miles per hour. Then, I see it, where I'll be working.

A large full-sized baseball field: ninety foot baseline, the centre field fence has got to be the full four hundred feet. It has metal bleachers, a dirt diamond, pitcher's mound, twenty foot fence back stop; everything. I'm entranced by the uninterrupted white chalk line around the edge encasing the perfect American splendour. I've seen a Pro baseball field before watching The Houston Astros play a practise game in Florida, whilst on holiday. This field though is the thing of Kevin Costner's dreams. I'm not thinking of smoking anymore. Laura flashes into my mind, but escapes with me wishing, longing to walk barefoot amongst the blades of grass of that field. Pounding my fist into a catcher's mitt and running the tips of my fingers over the morning dew covered grass. I used to practise baseball with my dad in the back garden. It was cinematic. Now, I'm here and I'm going to be teaching American children how to play their national sport, baseball. I'm excited again. I'm not taking my eyes off that field; we keep driving. The field even has floodlights, that's crazy, floodlights on a kids camp. They've pumped serious cash into this place. There's even an electronic score board below the trees.

We're driving past so many activity areas. I'm a caged bird. My wings are clipped. I'm a dog wanting to run free along the Kennett and Avon canal. Excitement and murmurs, pointing, joyful expressions and gesticulation from everyone in this van. I'm in awe, just as the others are. Now we're all connecting. I may have to question why I've been so negative. I know I'm still not ready to accept these new surroundings. I can't call this place home. This could be life affirming, but I've got anxiety building in me again. I need to listen to reassuring music, if only for my sanity.

Thank God. The van stops and the door slides open. The sun cuts through the darkness of the van's interior. My eyes adjust as I jump out, the last one to leave as ever. I kick up clouds of dust from the gritty pathway.

"Welcome to Red Oak and Silver Wood Camp." Said a man with a goatee.

"I'm Bill Chernobog, and this." Bill sweeps his hand, prompting the other man to speak.

"I'm Rod Desdemoni." He said, his handlebar moustache wriggling.

"Hi." We each respond.

We offer out our hands to be shaken. Both these guys are wearing red and white branded 'Red Oak and Silver Wood Camp' polo shirts, shorts and pristine white trainers, their pearly white socks pulled to their calves, stopping shy of their knees.

They're talking at us. I can't hear what they're saying. Sounds crackling through my head as everyone talks at once. Going over the formalities. Welcome and all that boring shit. Polite queries about the plane food, coach journey and small talk.

As these guys are the authority, there's arse kissing too, inevitable really. I'm not getting involved in brown nose boot licking. I'm more taken by the number of tennis courts on the hill. They're fenced in and professional. So much better than Delta Tennis Centre, back home.

I pick my bag up from the dirt, didn't even notice they'd offloaded it from the van. My catcher's mitt falls out and hits the ground, coughing up thick dust. Bill's baseball cap darts into my eyeline, he's bent over and picked it up for me.

"Oh. So, you're the catcher." Said Bill, chuckling "Little puny ain't cha?" He hands me my glove.

His goatee is black, matching what little hair I can see, exposing itself from under his branded cap. I grab my glove, disgruntled. Sure, I'm slight, I've got very little muscle and I'm not your typical catcher. I'm wearing glasses, which doesn't help. But, I was voted 'Player of the Year' two years in a row, 'Man of the Game' eleven times. They even selected me for the England try outs. I love baseball. If I was born in America, I'd be playing Little League. I'd probably be shot by now. It's my dream to be taken out with a . 44 Magnum, bloodied and in the arms of a lover. Beyond the Second Amendment, freedom of gun slinging. I'd have a great time playing ball, trying out for local teams, being pulled around in a Radio Flyer, going to Target and Walmart, munching on Moon Pies. The dream is my lost ambition.

My skin tingles with Bill's preconceived idea of me. It's made me think too much. Like when I used to get out of the shower. I'd revel in that feeling of my protruding hip bones, seeing my high cheeks poking through my face with that gaunt look in the mirror. I was getting over that. Now it's exposed again by a man that I've only spoken to over the phone. I can't believe Bill has ripped my world apart. My eyes water. How dare he assume anything based on my size? That's my problem. I let people get in my head and root around, tormenting my potential. Bill equals bastard. Simple as that. Twat.

They take our bags from us. I'm not happy with that. I have cigarettes in there. I'll have to let them go for now. If I protest too much, suspicion will arise. My blue sleeping bag flops as it's carried away. I wrapped my Sanyo 8mm video camera in there too; I don't intend to use it here. I brought it with me to capture my memories of travelling afterwards, prove to myself I've experienced something. I should get good footage. Out of sight, disappearing away from me, separated, for now.

"We're heading to orientation." Shouts Bill from up ahead. He waves, gesturing for us to follow. A walkie talkie gripped in his other hand. Most of these English guys nod and drop into line. I can't very well protest and stand here alone. I'm going to have to follow this impromptu convoy of fools.

I gaze around, taking in the grandiose location further. Trees everywhere, trees with giant pinecones dangling from branches, trees shaped like toothbrushes, trees shaped like rocket ships. Tree after tree after tree. There's three trampolines to our right with bungee cords hanging down. That looks cool. I guess you attach yourself and bounce like bellends. Beyond that is a soccer field, there's an elaborate skateboard park atop another hill. There's so much to explore here. I hope I get the time.

We, the English parade, arrive at a dining hall or canteen. However I should describe it. They're making us stand outside. We join a group of other mixed sex counsellors, kept outside by fly screened mesh double doors. We're too scared to converse with each other. There are subtle whispers among the more confident waiting, but no real talk. No one wants to draw attention to themselves. The mix of excitement and nervousness.

I'm stunned by these girls. This is wonderful. Women my age, slightly older, wearing tight red shorts and clean, pressed white T-shirts. Some plain shirts, others emblazoned with emblems and typography. There are 'Red Oak and Silver Wood Camp' branded shirts everywhere. I'm not interested in the fonts, more their breasts. Stacked, flat, curvy, voluptuous and a lovely bit of cleavage. There's one girl wearing glasses with auburn hair and handmade bracelets decorating her wrists, bits of string threaded together, she's got my attention. She has a tight arse, I've got a magnificent view. Her shorts are so tight, toned pale legs that go right up to that gap, a two fingers width up to her lips, fabulous. Oh. She's caught me staring. I dart my eyes up to the trees. She knows I was gawking at her. She's confused, now sort of flattered. She shoots me a smile. I reciprocate. It's the least I can do. I'm sceptical about camp but fascinated with the possibility of getting to know these women. Nipples embracing the cool air, shielded from the sun underneath these trees. This is great.

A tired-looking man arrives at the double doors. They swing open and everyone funnels into the dining hall. I'm not hungry, good job too; they've put no food on. This room is enormous enough to accommodate over two hundred people. A room full of large wooden tables that have smaller round tables on top that spin. I assume the reason for the spinning middle table is for condiments. There's an actual name for it, I can't think of it now. I, along with everyone else, sit at tables. It's like musical chairs. People rush to an empty seat as the last people filter into the room. I wouldn't want to be the last man standing. I sit down at the next available seat, right next to Oxford Mark.

Lazy Susan, I've remembered now. You spin it to share water or Grey Poupon with someone on the other side of the table. Pass the dutchie type thing.

"Dylan, this is gonna be great, mate, you excited?" Said Oxford Mark, in that clean accent of his.

For fuck's sake, why does he have to talk to me? Even calling me by my name. I know my own name. I hate it when anyone calls me 'mate'. I mean, he doesn't even know me and he's calling me 'mate'.

"Of course, I'm on the edge of my seat." I said. No eye contact, not just yet. He should sense my hate.

"At least you got a seat." He said, looking away, as if distracted by nakedness. "Don't worry, I won't suggest you give this one up." His face fills with a wry smile. He's handled my sarcasm well. A taste of my own, as they say. I appreciate his smirk. He must have read my mind, or I didn't hide my dissatisfaction with his earlier suggestion on the Greyhound. To try to get between Boni and me. How very dare he?

Now, I find myself strangely drawn to Oxford Mark. I hate to admit it, he's being as sarcastic as me. Funny with it. Maybe I judged him too soon; I'll have to see.

The entire room is bustling with resonating gurgles and echoes of human voices, bouncing off the cheap wooden interior walls. A group of four older men, early 60s, walk in through a side door, single file. They haven't spoken to one another or made a sound. They stand behind a long table at the back of the room. We're facing them. Everybody's eyes follow as if they're Led Zeppelin reforming with Jon Bonham on drums. The level of noise doesn't decrease. Instead, their movements spark more conversation and excited expectation. Not in me, they aren't getting my respect, not yet; they've done fuck all. The four men stand bolt upright with their hands behind their backs. Resembling Friday night, burly bouncers outside the Casbah. An unwelcome sight on our day of arrival. Who do they think they are? They're wearing a mix of white and polo shirts with 'Red Oak and Silver Wood Camp' printed across them, baseball caps and bright blood red shorts. They have facial hair. Bill from earlier is sporting his goatee. Rod, the second familiar face, has his handlebar moustache. Monte has five o'clock shadow, and Joe with his trimmed full-face beard and glasses stands gormless. I have no idea what they're doing, It's an attempt at asserting authority. It's unnatural and I'm not about to be quiet, although I'm not saying anything. But in an act of defiance, I decide it necessary to speak.

"You blame me for not wanting to move?" I said to Oxford Mark, whispering.

"No mate, she was cute," he said. "She was Scottish, right?"

"Yup." I said, nodding. I'm so pleased with myself. More pleased that he referred to her as 'cute'.

"You get her number?" he said.

"Of course. I'll call her later." I'm lying, he doesn't know that.

"What was her name?"

"Scottish Boni," I said.

"She didn't look like a Boni," said Oxford Mark.

"Did she look Scottish?"

Rod thrusts his stiff arm into the air. The room falls silent. I'm as confused as everyone else. I can't take my eyes off his arm. If that was the effect he wanted, it worked. I notice his moustache twitch. His arm is still up straight, like a Nazi salute; the similarity is incredible, almost laughable. The room rumbles back to the earlier level of distracted noise. The chipboard walls bowing under the chatter.

"Ladies and gentlemen," shouts Rod. "When my hand goes up, you go silent." He roars at the top of his cracking voice, adding unnatural bass from his throat.

Oxford Mark raises his eyebrows. I reciprocate his expression. My head jerks back, as if my eyebrows aren't enough to express my shock. Experience of a lifetime indeed. Have I stepped into some military ran death camp where they sterilise the kids and indoctrinate them with evil subversive ideologies or are they promoting the American dream? Will I be coaching the future President of the United States? Probably not. Hopefully though, I'll be corrupting them. I'll do my best. I can't wait for the 1940s propaganda to begin.

"You're expected to be leaders," said Rod. "When my hand's up. You're silent." He continues, looking around the room at the crowd of faces.

"What, no welcome?" I said. Thankfully, my sarcasm wasn't loud enough to expose me.

"Before meals, you will not sit until instructed to do so," he said.

I know we're young but I'm sure we get the idea behind the hand up gesture. Heil Hitler. Heil Hitler.

The counsellors who've attended camp before nod, without thinking. Everybody else in this packed room, including myself, stands like the compliant fools we are.

"Folks, there's no debate. In a matter of days, this year's session will begin," said Rod.

As if he wants to shock us into the realisation that this will be no easy-peasy Bacardi Breezie summer we dreamt of. The group of returning counsellors near the front table clap and whoop. I'm telling you, brainwashed.

"Every morning, without fail, the bugle will sound at 7.30am," said Rod.

Grunts of disapproval fill the air. That is early, and every day? I assume that doesn't include the weekends.

"You get up. It's your responsibility as counsellors, to get your bunk to breakfast and arrive at flagpole. That's morning and evening after dinner, with no exceptions, on time." Said Rod, with his arm still in the air. He grabs for a white mug and takes a swig from it, pursing his soured lips together. It's the same face I make when I sip absinthe. He plants the mug down with a clank.

Bill, standing next to Rod, follows the cup with judgemental eyes. That must be alcohol. Why would Bill be annoyed?

"You may be seated," said Rod. Lowering his arm as everyone sits down on his command, like we're hypnotised. He's sucked us in. Even Joe, the director, stands alongside Rod and sits at his instruction. His pointy nose raised to the ceiling, peering out at the crowd from under his glasses. It's as if we've fallen under their spell. They lean in and talk quietly amongst themselves for a second, like the top table at a wedding. Some counsellors do the same, soft voices audible throughout the room.

"Folks." Said Rod, his arm stretched into the air. "My hand remains up. You remain silent."

The room shudders to stillness. I'm not sure about this whole arm thing. Unnecessary to me and this guy is taking the edge off my excitement.

"We assign each of you activities. General counsellors, you'll supervise your bunk to and from each activity. Specialist counsellors, they will come to you." He said, clearing his throat.

See, even he can't keep up that roar. He takes another swig from his mug.

The rules of camp are extensive. No sexual interaction with any of them. Weird, they even had to mention it. It's a good reminder. No smoking, no drinking, and no drugs. Anyone who breaks the rules are fired on the spot. If you're a foreign counsellor, they take you to the train station serving Grand Central. You then have twenty-four hours to leave the country as they revoke your visa. That's official, not just scare mongering.

We learn everything, the location of the Health Centre, how to unpack and store each of the children's possessions and clothing. We're told we must perform the tasks on behalf of them. Weird, the kids can't do that themselves. Privileged little bastards. They even go over what they expect of the arriving children. We have to learn camp songs and sing them to the kids, making them learn them verbatim. The way days are organised, the camp activities; six per day, break times, lunch hours, snacks, and the evening activities. A whole heap of information I'm not interested in or I'm more scared by the sheer reality of it now.

Around this room, there are no black counsellors. Everyone is white, pale white. Weird. They're really forcing this; 'don't mess with the camper's thing', mentioning specifically the Seniors. I've learned the Seniors are the campers who are; for want of a better phrase, 'of age'. Presumably sexually active or more than close to it. I blame Hollywood. Short shorts, exposed navels, washing cars with soapy suds to the soundtrack of Meat Loaf's, Good Girls Go to Heaven. Naughty campers, such lascivious behaviour.

"No smoking on camp folks." Said Rod, clearing his throat again.

"Oh, a challenge," I said.

Oxford Mark laughs, drawing the attention of the room on us. He coughs and looks at his feet to mask his poorly timed outburst. My shoulders tremble as I do my best to hold back my own laughter. I keep my eyes closed to avoid eye contact with anyone, otherwise I'm gonna break.

Nothing here is funny so far.

5

Cabin Connecticut

After the drama of the orientation meeting, we're allowed to leave the confides of the dining hall. Breaking free to what will be our cabins, bunks of sleeping quarters. They'll be our homes for the next nine weeks. Strolling up the hill, in this massive crowd of guys, they're talking about nothing, pointless chatter. I have nothing to add. We pass a mass of tennis courts and yet another baseball field. That's three now I've seen. Not as well equipped as the first one by the entrance, but still grand. There's an open-air swimming pool surrounded by a metre-high chain-link fence. I know now where the medical centre is. It's supposed to service both the girls' and boys' but is on our side in terms of geography. The ideal place to bump into the female counsellors. I'll keep that in mind.

When I say cabin, a cabin to me, describes glamour, a luxurious mountain escape with an open fire, four poster bed, marble top island kitchen counter and a sheepskin rug with the finest vinyl records on hand, somewhere Chuck Palahniuk pens his memoirs and burns the words.

These aren't cabins, as I'd imagine. There's thirteen, they're shit. Made of wood, crap wood, chipboard. It's painted in a piss poor effort to cover up the age of the panels. They haven't been invested in for years. From a distance, they appear lovely, professional and liveable. They have two front doors up a shared set of steps. Inside, they're the same layout on each side. The steps approach from the left and right. You can then choose one of the two doors into the cabins. The right side of this cabin is named: 'Connecticut', hand painted on wood; next door is 'Georgia'. They're the thirteen colonies that created the declaration of independence. They've thought of everything. The cabin has two timber bunk beds, one inside, to the right of the door, and another opposite. There are ten single beds in rows, five along each wall, an exact mirror image on the other side. Smells like sweaty dampness in here. They cover the bare turquoise Mattresses in a thick plastic film, not plastic sheets, they're shiny and solid. They've designed the surface to be wipeable, I'm guessing for obvious reasons. I won't be cleaning up anyone's piss. They have no bed sheets or duvets, explains why we had to bring our own sleeping bags. The cabins are shit, graffiti on the wooden roof rafters, there's no luxury or difference, a communist wet dream. There's not even glass in the windows, just fly screens and wooden shutters, held back with a flimsy rusted latch. Each bed has a wooden open bedside table. Then there are the storage 'cubbies', that run down the middle, separating the cabins. Used for the storage of sports equipment and clothes. There are no doors, I guess, so nothing can be hidden. No room for contraband on a children's summer camp. At the rear of the cabin are the toilets and showers. American toilet doors, much like the toilets in The Karate Kid, you can see over the top, watch anyone taking a shit. I dread that because I wipe standing. I value my privacy. I don't know how I'll overcome the toilet setback. There's two urinals, two sinks and two showers with cream shower curtains that have thick black mildew in the bottom corners. Oh, joy.

After briefly becoming acquainted with the cabins. Without

conversation we're collected by the authority and frog marched to the linen cabin on the other side of camp. I haven't been introduced to any of these guys I'm with yet. Am I sharing a cabin with all of them? Out the backdoor, are more cabins, same as the others. We walk the same dirt track, a merry posse, past the swimming pool with other wooden buildings behind it. 'The Gym' building in the distance. Great if they have a treadmill. The medical centre in front of us. To the right is the skatepark. It has deep, purple-coloured ramps, a good size halfpipe, galvanised steel sides and a safety rail at the back. Everything is shiny, this is legit. There's a flat bank, handrail box and a grind rail. I know little about skateboarding. I won a board at The Litten Tree, in a pub raffle and since then grew more interested in the sport. I can ollie; just. I'd be keen to get on this park and kickflip. I built my passion for skating on the CKY video series and Tony Hawk's Pro skater 2 on the PlayStation.

We traipse past the dining hall; making our way to the off limits girls' side. Like the main entrance to camp with the totem poles, there are defined borders. They separate the two camps. Two tall totem poles reach up to the sky, as high as the surrounding trees. On top is a 'Silver Wood' sign painted in dagger grey to signify the entrance. They warned us, unless authorised, we, as counsellors, must stay on this side of camp, unless we're visiting the medical centre. That message is more for the girls, as the medical centre is our side of camp.

I'm not talking to anyone. A shit load of people. English and Australian voices mixed with American, and faces are familiar too. I'm not ready to get into a full-blown conversation with anyone. The girls' cabins are different to the boys. They have ten cabins, or that's what I've counted so far. They too, are named after States. The first to the left are 'Vermont' and 'Kentucky'. Beyond that, if I squint. I can make out 'Tennessee' and 'Ohio'. These cabins don't represent the colonies, so no idea the reference for that yet.

The girls' cabins are much bigger in lay out. They have one central set of steps up to a large grand porch with a covered, pitch roof. These cabins from the outside look pristine. The balustrades are beaming with fresh white paint. I bet though the inside is as nasty as ours.

Everyone from the boys' side of camp congregates at the bottom of steps to a hut marked: 'Linen Cabin'. Much of the male attention is drawn to the female counsellors, as they lay on the grass, flapping their golden legs and giggling. Playground humour, stealing footballs from the boys.

We're told to wait outside until called forward. This isn't fun, people have brought books to read, I didn't. I have my CD player with me, which I carry everywhere. It's my security blanket. I'm listening to Hot Hot Heat as loud as possible because the different accents around me are annoying and I'm losing my identity. It's too much at once. I lay on the grass, away from the masses, and shut my eyes. Good time to work on my tan and listen to one of my new favourite albums. I'm being told what to do at every moment. Give me my space.

I'm listening now to Talk to me, Dance with me. My lips are quivering along with the lyrics. My face is patchy warm from the sun. Then my eyes are shaded. Someone is standing over me. I open my eyes, squinting. I see the silhouette of a girl wearing a bright yellow bandana. I can't make out any of her features. The sun is beaming behind her head, creating darkness across her face. I can see her lips moving. I don't know what she's saying. Can she not see I'm wearing headphones? I sit up and get to my feet. This mysterious, brave and forward girl removes my headphones, resting them on my shoulders. Damn her confidence.

"How anti-social are you?" She said, with a chirpy American accent.

I'm not sure how to react. I'm filled with a hint of intrigue.

"Fan of Hot Hot Heat, I hear."

My eyes light up because she's recognised the band, impressive. I can't begin to hide it. Her bandana has a coiled snake on it with writing. I can't read it, it's obscured. I'm struck by her lips.

She has one of the most pronounced cupid's bows, if that's what it's called; you know that bit of your top lip, in the middle. A perfect 'V' shape. She has defined high cheek bones too, a well-shaped symmetrical face. She could be on the cover of a magazine or some shit.

"What's with the bandana?" I said. That's all I can muster. It's a weak choice of conversation, I know. I'm still trying to read the words printed on it. There's an apostrophe.

"You got alopecia?"

My jovial sarcasm, an attempt at flirtation. She rips the yellow bandana from her head, flinging it to the floor, revealing a spherical bald head.

"Sometimes I wear a wig, you asshole."

She turns, banging her feet away from me on the grass. She articulates the word 'ass'. She didn't say 'arse'. It was undeniable. My mouth always gets me into trouble. I pick up her bandana, it's opened out on the grass, revealing the design. It's a coiled rattlesnake in long grass. The words: 'Don't Tread On Me' written underneath, it's interesting. I hold it outstretched between my fingers. I watch for a moment as this girl stomps off, muttering something to herself. Damn. Buttery guilt filling my stomach. I skip forward, jogging to catch up with her.

"I apologise. I didn't mean to be a twat," I said.

She glares back at me with impatient eyes.

"I'm American. I don't know what a 'twat' is."

Body language wise, she's closed off, arms crossed, no eye contact. The whole thing. Text book.

"It doesn't matter, just know I'm sorry." I said, holding her bandana.

She stabs me with her eyes and snatches hold of the bandana, sliding it back to conceal her bald crown, ties a knot at the back of her head. I poke for the pause button on my CD player without looking. I think she deserves my full attention now and I can't very well go on getting distracted by breaking eye contact with her. I can hear the dull vocals of Steve Bay singing. Weird, it makes me think of Laura. I sing this song to her when she asks me to do something. Here I am falling into the sentiment of a first meeting with a beautiful American girl, albeit a bald one, and I'm thinking of my current girlfriend, the bitter irony.

"That's an interesting head piece," I said.

"You being a twat again?"

"No, I like it."

"It's a Gadsden flag." She said, standing with her hands on her narrow hips.

"I don't know what that is, but I am sorry for what I said."

She tilts her head, as if concentrating on what I'm saying.

"Now you understand why I was locked in my own world with Hot Hot Heat, " I said.

She cracked her vexed eyes and gave me a smirk, the slightest of side smiles. Her tongue rolls with a ripple. So cute. Is she trying to read me? I'm trying to read her. It takes silence to read someone. Too many words destroy discovery.

"It's for the colonies," she said.

That distracts my concentration from her smirk.

"What?" I said. She's lost me. I was listening, I swear.

"Don't tread on me. It's one of the earliest flags. A warning against violence to Americans," she said.

"You carry a gun?" I said.

"Lucky for you," she said. "Not right now. We've got guns at home, sure."

That doesn't surprise me. If only I, as an English person, was as proud of my country as they are. One day, when we experience freedom and an infrastructure to be proud of, I might be. I'm not one of these people that rejoice in the NHS. It's not that great. Don't believe the hype. I'd rather choose to pay for it like the Americans do. You use it; you pay for it. I like that way of governing. Can't afford it, you die. All about the money.

"Is it customary for me to invite you for a coffee or something?" I said.

"No harm in an invitation I guess," she said. "We could go for some caramels."

She's doing that little smirk thing again. I like it.

"Normally I would. But I'm in this queue to get sheets," I said.

"You're well behind then. You make sure you stay in this…" She stopped talking, lifted her hands in the air using the 'bunny' ear quotation gesture. "Queue." She shakes her head, mocking my use of the word.

A gust of wind comes in like a sneeze. She adjusts her bandana.

"I like your accent," she said.

"My accent?" I said, forcing deliberate received pronunciation, speaking the Queen's. I pretend to feign shock at her admiration. That's a performance on my part. I've heard that several times before from Americans. I have a strong accent, being as I am from the West country. It's not as bad as a Bristol accent. I mean Jimmy Wickwar, has a strong, broad accent. Proper retard.

"You could call me fat or bald again." She said, raising her eyebrows mocking me. "I'd still listen, if you said it in your accent."

Yeah, she wants me. Shit, does she want me.

"Oh, really." I said, without sounding like a deviant.

"Yeah, I'm a sucker for an English accent." She said, squinting to avoid the glare of the sun from over my shoulder. "Richard E. Grant in Withnail and I." She continued, shielding her eyes with her hand.

Right, wait, a minute. How has this girl heard of Richard E. Grant or seen Withnail and I?

"Sorry. Re-re-wind," I said.

Now, if she gets that pop reference, I'll marry her right here, right now. Although, she hasn't reacted, so no marriage yet then.

"You don't know what a twat is," I said. "But, you've seen

Withnail and I?"

"Of course. It's one of my faves."

I made a failed attempt at some Withnail quotes and impressions. She loved it. She was laughing. If only I could share them without getting sued.

What's her name, has she told me? I get that sinking feeling, as if I've forgotten to wear my tie at school. Should I know her name?

"What's your name?" I said.

"You wanna know?" She asked, teasing me. She flicks her left foot out, with a nervous reflex. I'm guessing it's nerves, could be Parkinson's. For now, I'll call it nerves.

"Otherwise, you'll forever be bald girl," I said.

"You bitch." She said with a crack in her voice, "Hazel."

What a beautiful name, like a chocolate bar. Her words, my thoughts are interrupted by a miserable sounding man on the porch of the linen cabin.

"You two," he said. "If you want sheets, you better get 'em now, we're closing."

Then, a girl with a tattoo of a white feather and writing on the inside of her arm. Looks like it says, 'White Russian'. She plants a kiss on the back of Hazel's bandana covered head, thrusting an armful of sheets into her bare torso.

"I already have some," said Hazel.

"You can never have enough." Said the girl with the tattoo. She glares at me, as if I've stolen away her best friend. She grimaces and bounces away. Not interested in knowing me then. Such a weird choice of tattoo. Does she enjoy the cocktail? She's white. Could be Russian? She doesn't look Russian. She's blonde with big, round doll eyes. I guess she has Russian lips, sharp and pointy. A Russian doll, loads of layers? I give up.

Hazel lowers the sheets to her side. I notice she has a pierced belly button, it's wonderful, delicious even. Not like a tied balloon, scrunched up or spilling out. It's a delicate tidy slit, narrow with a piece of white fluff caught in it, sitting idly staring back at me. I'm comfortable enough to remove it with my little finger, only a flick. It made the dream catcher navel decoration swing like a pendulum. It twinkles in the sunlight. I catch the flimsy metal feather with my finger and let it settle back into place, teasing me with its silver hypnotic shimmer. Hazel smiles. I smile. A lot of smiling. It's more than a smile. I'm getting lost in her. I now have time to scope out the rest of her body. I try not to make it too obvious. She's wearing a red, off the shoulder sports crop top and tight white shorts. I admire her shoulders; I can't help it. I imagine she's naked from the shoulders down. They're defined, her shoulders I mean. I wonder if she's a swimmer.

"Hazel, Let's go." Said the white Russian girl.

Hazel saunters toward her cabin. A sexy slow swagger.

"Valentine." She said turning, walking backwards on her heels, looking right at me.

"What's that?" I said.

"My name, Hazel Valentine."

"Dylan," I said. "Nemerov."

She smiles and turns away, scrunching up the bed sheets in her arms.

"See ya 'round Dylan Nemerov," she said. There's that smile again. She jogs up the slope to catch up with white Russian girl. Amazing arse. Hazel, not her friend, if I can call her that. She doesn't strike me as a friend, more of a jealous, insecure little bitch. She's wearing blue denim hot pants, her arse cheeks flopping under the ripped edges. There's nothing sexy about white Russian. I bet she's the type of girl who would sleep with her stepfather when her mum's out buying her a birthday present. I dislike her already. She rests her lazy, floppy head on Hazel's shoulder. She must have had the hardest day doing nothing that she needs to rest on Hazel. Am I jealous? I don't like her. I'm sticking with it.

Hazel looks back at me.

Now, I'm done for. So, she's a fan of Hot Hot Heat, Withnail and I, and she's funny as fuck. Well, funnier than Laura. Yeah, that's fair to say. Did I even think long enough to compare? Great shoulders, sparkling belly button and an arse like two M&M's pressed into melting white chocolate, with an abundance of allure.

"Hazel Valentine," I say out loud to myself. Her name escapes my lips. This is like I'm in a movie with Zooey Deschanel. I laugh to myself. "Hazel Valentine. Wow." I said, expelling a content breath of air. I feel content, for now. I approach the linen cabin in a daydream. Up the wooden steps, inside this now infamous storage cabin, my arms filled with a single white sheet and pillow. No trace of a pillowcase, savages. This cabin exists solely to store sheets. Some folded, others have never been washed. It's a mess.

I'm on my own again. There's nobody familiar in sight. No one that I recognise from the boys side. I slip my headphones over my ears and hit play.

Back I go to 'Connecticut'. The whole way, I'm listening to Aveda. I take the route back to the cabin, along the main road, in and out of camp. No cars come down here. I've seen a couple of golf carts ferrying around camp staff. Aside from that, it's an access road. I'm picturing Hazel walking away from me. I'm fixated on her. Laura's becoming a distant memory and it's only the first day. Not sure what that says about our relationship or what it says about me.

As I near the cabin, the door swings open and slams shut immediately. It has one of those massive springs on it, so snaps closed. I open the door and notice a stocky guy with his eyes closed on the bottom bunk closest to the door. He has a goatee and dark, Italian looking features. I'm not sure he's Italian, but he has dark olive skin and even darker hair. The door crunches shut behind me with the stiff spring, smacking it closed. His eyes open to see who's to blame for the noise. He must have seen me coming, and jumped back into bed. Who else could have opened the door? I can't see his chest raising as if he's trying to stifle his heavy heart rate. Anyway, he swings his feet round to the floor and jumps up from the bottom bunk bed.

"Wat up dawg." He said, in a thick Southern accent.

His accent throws me. I'm confused whether he's of Italian descent or he could have black heritage in him. He speaks with a smooth delivery of his words, a rhythm of soul. He stands up, outstretches both his arms to wake his slumbering body and offers out his right hand, open palmed for me to shake. I shuffle the sheets from one hand to the other and shake his hand.

"I'm Doug Trott. Good to meet c'ha," he said.

"You too," I said. The second that came out of my mouth, I question why I used 'Good to meet you'. I hate hearing it myself. Especially at a first meeting. I don't know him and I'm not convinced it is 'good to meet you'. It's a disingenuous thing to say to anyone.

"Where you from?" I said. My attention, feigning. I can't make it too obvious. I need to be more open to these people. Give it all a chance.

"Georgia," said Doug.

"I've never been. Well, I've been to Atlanta. Just to the airport, not outside it. It has that subway," I said.

"Yeah, that's right, it does. What cha say your name was dawg?" Said Doug, scratching his right nostril with his thumb.

"I didn't. It's Dylan," I said.

I'm never confident saying my name out loud to strangers, unless they're women. It's too easy to blame my parents. Still can't explain it.

"Cool, well I'm your bunk buddy," said Doug.

Now, let me set the record straight right now. I'm not keen on the expression 'bunk buddy'. I'll go with it for now without protesting. I still don't like it. This guy, Doug, is genuine and I'll let it go for now with little judgement. How long that lasts, time and telling comes to mind. Often, I create a picture of a person in my mind, way before I know them. I'm forever trying to avoid this; it continues to be something I'm working on. I'm not convinced I don't need professional help. My mind restricts authenticity.

The front door crashes open and a pudgy guy with red spotty, acne skin, wearing a purple Hawaiian buttoned up shirt with hibiscus flowers and a stupid blue striped bucket hat steps inside. He looks like a dick, throwing himself into the cabin.

"Hell-o," he said.

From his abrasive accent, he's South African. This guy will be the first South African I've ever met. I only know the accent because of Lethal Weapon 2. I can tell this guy is gonna irritate me. He's so loud. My worst fucking nightmare. At least I have more reason to befriend Greg. Wait, no. He said his name was Doug. Yeah, that's right. Doug Trott.

"I'm Benedict." He said in his brash accent, removing his hat. He says it loud, as if to get attention. As if Doug and I have our faces buried between the legs of virgins in an orgy of distraction. There's no reason to be as loud as he is. I won't be lifelong friends with this douche. Who has the name Benedict, for fuck's sake?

That's it. My cabin, my 'bunk buddies'. I'm including 'bunk buddies' facetiously. I'm not counting adverbs. Good luck if you are, they're words. I won't use it again, bunk buddies, I mean. Damn it.

So, here we are. The two people I'll share this space with and the ten-year-old boys. All set to arrive in a couple of days. The thought scares me shitless.

Until then, it's about orientation, setting things up and our freedoms being eroded before camp kicks off and these posh little bastards arrive. An ideal nuclear family, with parents working for Sony BMG, Goldman Sachs and Compaq Computers. They'll stand so proud, waving their little angels off for nine weeks. All for the paltry payment of $11,000. A measly price to pay for brain washing fun, conducted by individuals who are more interested in checking out the sixteen-year-old girls with flawless 'American breasts' and 'smooth pussies'. That's a direct quote I heard from one of the camp leaders speaking only earlier. Noble gentlemen here, noble indeed. I'm one of them, minus the beard.

Bring on the debauchery.

6

The Playhouse

The playhouse. If only it was as seedy as it sounds. It's the name given to yet another enormous building, lined with chipboard, behind the girls' dining hall. We're summoned to this so-called magical playhouse. Both male and female counsellors. Again, another opportunity to meet and check out as many attractive women as possible. I guess there'll be loads of competition from the other guy counsellors. Hopefully, most of them are in committed, loving and long-term relationships. Clearly, that doesn't stop me.

The sky is doing that mixing thing, fading to dusk, like adding milk to black coffee, swirling and curdling. The sun teasing us, poking over the trees beyond the camp entrance.

The entire camp, well us counsellors, are funnelling into this white painted rectangular building with a mix of impatience and eagerness, shielded under the canopy of hefty sized pine trees. Pinecones rest like misplaced footballs on the roofing felt. Yet another long line. It worries me I'm following everyone, no questions asked. I never used to be a follower.

Inside, row after row of solid wooden, red hand painted

benches, face the stage ahead, like church pews. I've never liked churches, it's where people go to die. It smells of boiled red cabbage in here, even with the doors open. I'm sure there'll be more rules. With my dictatorial rule summation now finished, any thoughts of my rebellion will be interrupted.

A bearded guy with a camera touched me on my arm with his ice cold fingertips. He's wearing dark brown, three quarter length cargo trousers. His pockets drooping with camera lenses. All the gear, no idea.

"I'm Max. Can I take your photo?" He said, in a deep American accent.

I'm gobsmacked. No one has ever asked to take my picture before. Max is brave. People are looking over, intrigued why he chose me to photograph. He must be early twenties. His massive, well-established, thick, bushy beard is distracting. He looks at me with intrigue, his scintillated eyes holding on mine. He sits on one of the church pews, shifting on the spot. I guess he's making sure the light is right.

"Put your arm up on the bench." He said, directing me "Don't smile."

I think he wants to get a picture of my tattoo. 'I am the Resurrection' inked on the inside of my right arm in Olde English font. A reference to The Stone Roses. It's not blasphemous.

Max holds his camera.

Click.

Tilts the lens.

Click.

Adjusts the lens again, twirling his fingers as if he was fingering a doorknob.

"What's your name?" He said, sounding interested, while he gyrates his body on the spot.

"Dylan." I answer, embarrassed.

Click.

More people sitting around us watch, raising their eyebrows at this impromptu photo shoot. My cheeks are getting warmer, more flush. Max stands up.

Click.

He slams his foot on the bench, his legs open, resting his elbow on his knee.

Click.

He exhales. Nothing but passion for his art.

"Thanks, Dylan. I have it." He said, as he lets his camera rest on his chest, relying on the strap around his neck. "I'll give you a copy when I develop them."

His words are noise created from his mouth without opening his lips, shielded by his bushy beard. I nod as he walks away. Strange fella. He's wearing a bright yellow t-shirt; on the back in black bubble font, it reads:'Soft Focus Hardcore'.

What a geek. He's designed it himself. As quickly as he's stolen my soul with a picture, he's disappeared.

The playhouse is full of counsellors now. Doug arrives and sits on one side of me, and Benedict on the other. Their legs are touching mine. For fuck's sake, everyone has gravitated to the people they're sharing their bunks with. Why do we do that, latch on to anyone that we have the slightest ounce of familiarity with? It's so boring.

A man and woman appear from behind the closed red velvet stage curtain. It's comedic. They poke their heads out, one above the other, disappearing again. The curtain opens, with the pair walking in separate directions, revealing the full expanse of the stage, with a TV screen and microphone on top of two large amplifiers. This is karaoke. Kara-fucking-oke. This will be our entertainment for the evening. How fabulous. I still don't understand it. How is that entertainment? Play me the original music. I'm not getting involved in this shit. I doubt very much they'd have The Stone Roses and they're the only songs I'm comfortable singing along too.

Benedict is looking far too excited, sitting up, peering over the heads of the people in front to get a better view of the stage. What a prick.

"I love karaoke." Said Benedict, with childish merriment in his voice.

"I thought you might," I said.

Yet another reason to hate him. He gets on my nerves, he has that dried wet smell of sweat on him, disgusting. Have a shower or douse yourself in Tommy Hilfiger. Don't burden me with your filthy skin odour, fat little shit bag.

The two on the stage. If I had to guess, I'd say they're husband and wife or at least in whatever relationship they regard as normal. They're comfortable with each other. The woman picks up a microphone from the top of an amplifier.

"Folks." Said the woman into the microphone. "Tonight, is your last free night before camp begins."

The room booms with cheers.

"We're here to have fun, get you enjoying karaoke." She said, in that annoying, cajoling American tone.

The room erupts with screams of appreciation, echoing off the hollow walls. I'm compelled to clap my hands together, just going along with the crowd, which I hate myself for. I don't indulge in the 'whoop whoop' though. It's karaoke. Have these retards never experienced the bullshit narcissism of karaoke before? Even the word does my head in. What the hell does it mean, karaoke, who came up with that? Even the word messes with phonetics.

"Who wants to be the first to take the chalice?" The woman screeches into the microphone.

A guy with a thinning hairline and goatee jumps to his feet at the open invitation. He runs up to the stage, beckoned forward by the woman's waggling hand gesture. Play your cards right. The way he's running, it's as if fifty grand is up for grabs. This guy is far too excited, clearly missing something in his life. A spotlight strikes his face as the rest of the room plunges into darkness. Embrace the atmosphere. This guy is the image of George Michael. Circa that album with Jesus to a

Child.

After he whispers in the guy's ear on stage. The first few bars of the song Faith ring out. He turns and shakes his bottom to the crowd, resulting in screams and cheers from the girls. I'm not getting involved in vocal appreciation for a male arse. He's holding his own, I'll give him that. He's reading the lyrics off the TV screen, imposed over a cloud background, as the black font words sweep across the screen. He's in time with the music and it's going well. He's performing the slower breakdown verse. His volume grows louder. The lyrics aren't George Michael's original. People near the front clap and shout louder encouragement. He rocks back and forth on the spot, dipping his shoulders. He shouts the lyrics from the version covered by Limp Bizkit. He throws himself in the air and screams into the mic, his voice cracking under the effort. The room cheers. Loose arms are being thrown in the air like it's a fucking Jay Z concert. The man and woman on stage glance at each other. The authority move away from their standing position against the side walls. Rod motions with his hand, sweeping across his neck to end the song. The room still filled with laughter, claps, and cheers as the music cuts off. The guy raises his arms in the air, accepting the appreciation from the crowd. He hands back the mic and waddles down the steps, laughing. He's welcomed back to his church pew seat with high fives and smacks on his back.

"OK." Said the woman, raising her eyebrows "That was," she pauses. "Great. Anyone else like to take on a track?"

Whoever that guy is, he did a good job. Not sure Rod or Bill enjoyed it as much as we did. Far too subversive. People are still going nuts. The woman uses her hand to shield her eyes from the lights illuminating the stage.

A girl hops up from her seat, as if raised by a higher power. This place is turning into an evangelical convention. She has on black-rimmed glasses, pristine blonde hair that resembles the Liberty Bell, minus the crack, curls up under her ears. She's wearing a black and white checked short skirt with a bright pink T-shirt. It's in the style of the movie poster for Clueless. She's cold, her skittle sized nipples poking through her shirt. It is fresh in here, the doors are wide open. The root vegetable smell still lingers. She walks with humble confidence, climbs the steps to the stage and stands with her knees touching. Her right arm draped over her waist, left arm dangling at her side. She's nervous, conscious of herself now, knowing a room full of strangers are staring at her, making judgements. She's confident enough to thrust herself forward into the limelight, but strikes me more of an introvert, a reader. Not just because of the glasses. She looks cultured. The smooth, faultless, Clueless T-shirt looks to me, to be worn with irony. The way she's standing makes her appear as if she walks with pigeon toes. That inward thing. I imagine her stood awkwardly like a schoolgirl reading aloud an essay. She's clutching the microphone like a penis. One hand clenched on top of the other. It's gagging for it. I need that myself. The music trickles out from the speakers. The girl shakes her hips, like no one is watching. I imagine her stood in front of her mirror at home. Bedroom door shut, music thumping. Her parents in the next room. Her hair wrapped in a terry cloth towel. Her body covered by a larger towel, exposing her naked shoulders and feet. Whatever she listens to allows her to explore herself. She's a girl that will tilt her head at her reflection, drop the damp towel to the floor, resting on her bony feet, stand naked for a second, looking herself over. Her eyes shifting to the door, with a look of hope that she's not disturbed, but excited by the possibility of being caught.

A crash of distorted guitar disturbs my speculative daydream, and the song begins. Sounds punk. Her voice is in tune. Wait, I recognise the song. She looks the part. It's No Doubt's, Just a girl. A near perfect rendition. Even I'm impressed, my jaw is slack. This girl looked geeky. Now, she's an icon. She's stood in the centre of the stage, shaking her head, Liberty Bell hair swishing across her face in time with the music. It makes her hair float, lifting at the bottom. Fair play to this mysterious girl, she's loving the music and being sexy with it. I've imagined her naked. It would be rude not to discover her name. I'll never talk to her, anyway. I'm filled with the best of intentions, crippled by fickle apathy.

The night goes on for the next couple of hours. People decide to show their nationalities. We've had four Australian guys stand up in yellow Australian football shirts and those outback cork hats singing, Men at Work. I've heard the purpose of those cork hats is that the corks hold the stench of alcohol, and you can suck them when lost in the outback. The real reason and less exciting, they're designed to fend off insects. The corks dingle and dangle when you walk, giving a protective force field from irritating critters. No sense to it. The guys must have known it was karaoke tonight. They dressed the part and even brought jars of Vegemite. They bent down, as if it was the closing number at the Royal Variety Show and held out the jars of yeast extract at arm's length; a unified symbol of pride, as the song ended. Who comes prepared for karaoke? Lord Jesus.

Hazel, six rows from the stage, Hazel Valentine. She's laughing and enjoying herself with that girl, White Russian. I'm not bothered with finding out her actual name. She'll forever remain the one that interrupted our first meeting.

The wig of choice tonight for Hazel is a short red one, malice red. It looks good. I wish I was more outgoing. I would relish nothing more than getting on stage. The spotlight casting my cheekbones with a favourable shadow. The soulful jive of Joe Tex banging out of the speakers. I'd command the stage, the audience in the palm of my hand, hanging off my delivery of melody. I'd sing in a way that creates a connection so profound. These people at first would assume I'd be shit. By the end, the room would be on their feet. I'd walk off the stage a hero. Never again able to fade into the background. My confliction is, I like the idea of being able to disappear. Do I need this room's approval? Some attention would be nice.

The end of the night comes. I'm thankful for that. I try to ease and squeeze myself through the crowd. Just to fulfil my want to get hold of Hazel, get her attention, have a simple conversation. She disappears, gone. Out of sight, beyond the 'Silver Wood' totem poles. The invisible barricade; my Laredo, The Berlin Wall. It separates me from her. The boys from the girls. I can't have that; it won't stop me. An urge of adventure takes over. The crowd congeals, stuck together like overcooked Farfalle pasta, as we stream out of the playhouse. The girls stroll toward their side of camp. The guys plod toward ours. This is so anti-climactic. We get an evening to socialise, to explore these beautiful creatures, my fellow female counsellors. We could sneak off and sit on tree branches, heads on shoulders, hand in hand, lips on lips. Instead, we watch a shitty sing song show and don't talk to one another. I need female attention. I'll slow down here, separate myself from the masses. No one will even notice. I wind myself around a clump of trees, circle behind them in the darkness. Guys are continuing flirtation with some of these girls. The attractive ones anyway. Damn it. I should hang with them. I could always approach and introduce myself. Instead, I'll stand here hiding and wish only for a new personality. I'll use the cover of these Christmas trees, they're not Christmas trees, but that's what they remind me of. I need to share myself with Hazel.

When it's quiet. I enter the girls' side of camp. Check me out, I'm so rebellious, super wild. I walk along the back of the girls' cabins. Is this really all worth it, what if I get caught, what if I don't?

I'm peering in through the back windows to spot Hazel. I can see into the bathroom areas. The cabins are set out differently to ours, I mean the boys' side. They have no back doors. Just a main entrance up the grand wooden stairs. Plus, they seem to have doors separating the sleeping quarters from the bathroom. A wall down the middle separates the two sides of the cabin. A hand painted 'Louisiana' sign on the outside. Why I think this is where Hazel is, no clue. I'll call it fate. I can't see her. I'll bowl up to the front steps and walk on in. I'm filled with adrenaline. If I'm caught, will they really kick me out? It's not like there are any campers here yet. I still have time before the actual rules kick in, I hope. I walk the entire length of the cabins and then make it to the front. I hear female voices; I can hear Hazel. I recognise her intonation. She's sitting on a rocking chair with White Russian and another girl.

"Can I help you, ay?" Said a girl with an Australian accent.

She leans forward over the bannister, looking down at me.

"Dylan?" Said Hazel, as she stands up, trying to make me out in the darkness.

"Hey, Miss Valentine." I said with deliberate nonchalance.

"Hazel." Said White Russian, her hand smooths along her forearm. "We should go in."

I thought she'd try to drag her away from me again.

"No. It's fine. Go in." Said Hazel, ushering the girls inside with a flap of her hand. One step at a time, this is perfection. She sweeps down, descending toward me, walking her fingertips down the wooden bannister.

"What are you doing here, you twat?" She asked with that smirk of hers.

"I wanted to say, I like your hair tonight."

Hazel twiddles her finger under a small, looped curl on her forehead.

"Thanks," she said.

"Now I've said that I can go." I'm nervous about smiling too much. I don't know why. Be cool.

"What?" She asks, shocked with no attempt to hide how incredulous she is.

"You never told me where you were from." I said, completely dismissing her shock. I could have made a joke. Now isn't the time to be funny, I must be poignant. This has to mean something to her, to me.

"You never asked," she said.

"I guess that's true. You gonna tell me then?"

There isn't much room for flirting in discovering the geographical origin of a person. Why do I care where she's from? She's here with me. It's like all that bullshit you might ask in an Internet chat room. Age, statistics and location, or 'A/S/L' for short. The international language for speedy analysis of a person's suitability for courtship. Based primarily on location, supported only by an up-to-date photograph.

"Sacramento. Well, Fair Oaks," said Hazel.

Why does that even Matter? We're in New York state. I'm not travelling to Sacramento.

"Good. Now I know more about you." I said. I'm being slightly sarcastic. All she needs to know is I want to know more.

"You're crazy." She said and let out a cute little chuckle.

"You have no idea." I said. Noises distract me from behind. "Hazel, I'd better go."

I look back over my shoulder.

"Yeah. I guess ya better had." She said, raising her eyebrows.

It's enough she's talking to me. White Russian girl stayed standing at the door like a mother, supervising a first date drop off, cramping our style. As if I was going to go in for a finger on the porch. I don't think Hazel knows she's there. She's right in my eye line.

"Now I know where you live, you can expect stones at the window and your name burning in the grass," I said. White Russian shakes her head. I thought that was funny, cute even. Hazel hasn't reacted. "I meant that to sound romantic, not creepy."

"Sounds fucking creepy." Said the White Russian girl, from inside the cabin.

"Sorry, can I help you?" I said.

Hazel looks back over her shoulder.

With that, White Russian goes back inside, shaking her head like the disapproving parent role she seems to have accepted.

Fuck her. That's better, she's gone. Hazel turns back and smiles at me.

"What's her problem?" I said.

"She's protective of me."

"Clearly. I better go. It was a joy to see you," I said.

Hazel nods. I haven't moved. She hasn't either.

"Night Hazel."

"G'night, Dylan."

The urge to have a cigarette pulses through me, right in this moment. I head beyond the boys' cabins and toward the woods. I get within the density of the matchstick tree trunks and open my packet. I let the cellophane drop to the floor beneath me. It might be found. Then again, there's no way I'd be linked to it. I pull out my purple lighter and place the tip of a luscious cigarette between my lips, spark it, concealing the bright flame from the view of any potential eyes from cabins in the distance. Difficult to hide illumination in darkness. I inhale, it's rough at first but tastes like smooth dark chocolate. It's good; the nicotine rolling through my veins, my temples throb. I relax, my chest tightens. It always amazes me how soon after inhaling, that my left leg, below the knee, aches. I've always had poor circulation. The number of times Laura has referred to my feet as ice boxes, I've lost count.

Having indulged myself and enjoyed this cigarette. I stub it out on the trunk of a nearby tree and amble my way toward the cabin lights of 'Connecticut'. I'm blindsided by golf cart head lights filling my peripherals. The cart grinds to a sudden stop. Thank God.

"Shit. Where did you come from?" Said Rod from over the steering wheel, readjusting his baseball cap. I can't see his face but recognise the voice.

"Dylan, right?" he said.

The lights are white, bright in my eyes.

"I had to use the toilet after the playhouse and got completely disorientated." I said without hesitation. That was a quick lie. I hate that ability in me. It's useful, but the battle I have with internal guilt often outweighs the smooth delivery of any lie laced utterances. Rod doesn't move or respond. I haven't filled the silence. Will he expose me if I continue this charade? Less is more. The yellow artificial battery-operated headlights are making my head pound.

"Get in. I'll make sure you get back to Connecticut. It's Connecticut bunk you're in, right?"

He knows exactly what bunk I'm in. He too is a seamless liar.

"Yeah, that's it. Connecticut," I said.

I get in the passenger side of the golf cart, sitting next to Rod. I'm leaning to the left, so not to sit too close to him. His left hand firmly gripping the steering wheel. He keeps shifting his baseball cap. His moustache twitches under his nose, it's like it doesn't belong to him. He sits staring ahead, not saying a word. Is he trying to intimidate me? It's working. He sniffs and stares right at me from underneath his hat. My eyes are forward, looking into the darkness. I know he's looking at me. I'm trying to focus on where the lights of this cart disappear into the grass. I won't look at him, I can't.

"I'll ask you this, just once," said Rod. "You been smoking?"

He knows, I know, we both know the answer.

"No, of course not." I said, pursing my lips together. My breath is still warm with that tarnished mahogany stench of tobacco.

"Strange, it smells as if you've been smoking," he said.

"Well, I had an Americano in the break room," I said, another lie.

Rod stares straight ahead. He bangs his foot on the accelerator. We zip forward with a whistle of the battery powered motor kicking in. We make it up the hill toward the cabin. The light is on. Doug is moving around up the steps, through the screen door. The golf cart comes to a stop.

"Thank you, Rod." I said, sliding out of the seat as quickly as I can. I need to get out of here.

"It's a bad idea to have coffee this late," he steadies his glasses on the bridge of his nose. "You'll be up all night. Get inside."

He stamps his foot down on the accelerator, circles the wheel and disappears into the darkness. I watch the taillights fade down the road. The whizz of the motor now out of earshot, like a fading boiling kettle. I'm under no illusion he knows I was out here smoking. I'll have to be more careful. If the days go by as slowly as they have, I'll be trying to escape to have a suckle more often. I just long to see Hazel again. I enjoy saying her full name out loud.

"Hazel Valentine. Hazel Valentine." I said. So good, she's lovely.

It's fucking cold out here. I'm going in.

7

The Bastards Are Here

I assume we'll have an element of privacy, or the ability to escape these kids when they get here. There's a counsellors' cabin. I call it a cabin, it's a second-floor room, not a cabin at all, above the social hut. The social hut is cool. There's a long counter that serves food and snacks. During supervised 'co-ed' meetups, as they call it. Each cabin has one night, every two weeks where you have a social event. I'm hoping I'll see Hazel again, Hazel Valentine. I like her name on my mind. Along the walls of the hut are old school arcade machines, they have the classic Pac Man and modern ones like NBA Jam and The Simpsons. There's an old flimsy ping pong table, two pool tables, and benches for the kids. If you leave the social cabin, around the corner is a hidden set of wooden stairs leading up to the counsellor cabin. There're signs all the way up, warning campers from going any further: 'Counsellors only', 'No Entry' and 'Staff Only'. If kids don't heed that warning, they've only got themselves to blame if they hear some depraved, vulgar language from the mouths of counsellors, relaxing on breaks and venting frustration. Not my problem.

The staff break room is dingy with its own pool table, cheeky you're expected to pay to use it. I don't carry change. There are three sagging mismatched sofas, arranged facing a large TV. Counsellors I don't know are sprawled out on them. Along the back wall are three Windows PCs, connected to the Internet. It's slow, but allows you to log on and check emails. I can read how happy Laura is without me or how she's been out at the weekend and met a guy with a pink mohawk, should have kept mine. All that heart-warming, reassuring relationship type of shit. Either side of the PCs are two wooden doors with graffiti scrawled all over the cheap pine wooden panels. It looks vibrant, and I guess they were going for that youthful urban vibe. Reminds me of Byker Grove. That deliberate, misguided attempt at inclusion through generational assumption. Behind the two pine doors are payphones and a single plastic chair, all very prison movie, Ernest Goes to Jail.

I've emailed Laura a few times already from my Hotmail account. She replied to the first, happy to hear I arrived safe, then she went on about meeting that pink mohawk guy. Why she has to tell me things, I don't know. King Kong balls. Like I said, heart-warming. Why she thinks it appropriate to mention how nice it was to meet a guy with a hairstyle, she creams her knickers over is beyond me. What does she think I can even do with that information? I didn't respond to it when I replied, why would I? I certainly won't ask his name. That would create a common ground for the two of them, common ground I can't walk on. I'm here, she's there.

In the last message I said how much I missed her. She hasn't replied to that. Shit like that makes me question how serious she is about me. I blame her in part for all my thoughts of sexual freedom. I'd be up for a threesome with Laura. She won't even consider the idea. I've floated it before, she's only ever offended. Bollocks to it, never gonna happen. Not with Laura, anyway. That's why people stray. If only she knew that. I'd much prefer to experience something with her as opposed to going behind her back. Does that mean I'm not happy if I want more? More is always what we all strive for, the next thing. The next word. The next chapter, next. Never happy with the now.

All that because I haven't received a response to my bloody email. I guess I'm being too impatient. I keep forgetting about the time difference. She should be waiting for my contact. Surely her life is on hold whilst I'm here. Call me delusional. With her lack of reply, I'm only ever going to destroy myself thinking about what she's getting up to. What friends is she seeing? She has too many male friends, far too many. It's not comfortable. She surrounds herself with them. Come to think of it, she's the insecure one, she must be. I'm not sure how else to explain her choices. Why else would you need that many men around you? I say men; I mean boys. I'm two years older than her. Half her friends can't even drive yet. I bet she'll be out with her ex-boyfriend, Charlie James. He's got a surname that can be a first name, you can never trust that. I still can't get out of my head when Laura told me; Charlie didn't have a bigger penis than me, but he had 'exceptionally large balls'. Why did she have to share that comparison of a pair of bollocks? Seriously, why, what was she expecting? I shook Charlie's hand the day I met him and immediately thought; the ex-boyfriend with 'exceptionally large balls.' Thanks again, Laura. It fucks me off they remain friends and he's always at the same parties as us. I mean move on, man. They share the same circle of friends and there's no escaping their intimate past. Buckinghamshire is a fucking large county, yet they all nestle sweetly together. All entitled, speaking with plums in their mouths. Laura enrages me. I put on a fake accent to fit in. I never thought I had an accent until I heard them speak. It's made worse when Laura and The Get Along Gang take the piss out of my Wiltshire accent.

Anyway, I deal with my mind running over these situations all the time. It should help when the kids arrive. I'm staring at a blank email. The cursor flashing, teasing me to write something. Without thinking, I stroke the keys and begin typing. I like how my fingers sound on this keyboard. I'm not looking at the screen to see what I'm writing, it's a stream of consciousness. I can't stop. My thumbs are striking at the space bar like a kick drum. I'm surprising myself with how fast I'm typing, it's become a challenge. I stop. Now, I'll explore what I've written:

'Welcome to my Neverland. Welcome to my nightmare. Welcome to my misunderstanding. Welcome to my slow-moving horror. Welcome to my insanity. Welcome!
No, really Laura.
You're welcome to it.
Fuck you and fuck you, world.
Fuck you all.
I will wash away my bitterness, I will walk alone.
Tormented.
I will implode.'

As quickly as I wrote that. My hand is on the mouse, select all, delete. A much safer choice to just make use of a simple 'X'. She'll respond to that. It'll make her think. I hope it worries her. If I received that, it would worry me, I'd reply. I'd want to know that I was OK. Only if she cares.

In this break room. No one talks to me. I don't talk to them. I may as well not be here.

"They're here." Said a guy in a Mancunian accent, running into the doorway of the staff room. He made me jump. He sounded almost frantic. The people on the phones stick their heads out the graffiti doors with the receiver still pressed against their ears.

The stocky, overweight Manc guy with a No.2 shaved haircut gestures for everyone to follow him as he skips out of the room, down the steps. All of us, those relaxing watching TV, even the phone users finish up, stop their conversations, get up, put phones down, and click send on emails. The TV left on, with no one watching. Counsellors running briskly to the door.

Here I am, on my own again. I begrudgingly hit send and sign out of my Hotmail account. No idea what I've written to Laura now. I swear I deleted that other shit. Seriously, do I have to log back in to check? No, I deleted it. My kiss of mystery, that's right. Safe. I can relax.

I follow the lost, questioning nothing. I too am herded. Step down the steps one at a time. I can't see much from here through the thick tall trees, reaching up skyway, covering the view over camp. I'm bursting for a piss. I circle round under the steps and go into the toilets below the break room. Open the door, grab on the top of the low cubicle. No privacy for a shit. The seat is down, but I don't have time to lift it. I'm pissing like a trooper. I could probably stroke myself now and come in this toilet bowl, romantic I know. I've got all this tension. I need to feel neutral, balanced. It won't take long for me to get hard. If I think of Hazel's belly button, that'll help. I'll start and it'll be over in no time.

Hazel's face lit only by candlelight. A room full of cushions, the floor, one soft bouncy surface, comfortable, cosy; Hazel laid open legged and pinching her nipples. Laura crawls in on her hands and knees. The feline she's become, swinging her naked hips, her breasts sitting proudly. She eyes up Hazel, lowers her head to the ground, as if performing yoga.

Shit. The door to the toilet behind me screeches open. The shame on my face should paint a thousand stories. The Mancunian guy who announced the kids arrival just entered. He's made me dribble piss on the seat. My fantasy is over. I wasn't even mid stroke. Lucky too, that could have been awkward.

"Come on, pal." He said, to rush me.

I shake my floppy dick dry. I can see nothing but three spots of my urine, probably mixed with pre-come on the toilet seat, glistening back at me. If this guy wasn't standing right behind me, looking at the back of my head with my penis in my hand, then I would certainly take a piece of tissue and wipe the seat clean. I can't now; that would look far too suspicious. Instead, I use my foot to flush the toilet, push on the door to open it. There's no reason to use the lock as he, like anyone, can see me standing up in the toilet, anyway. He rushes past me and relieves himself. The sound of cascading piss fills the room.

"You pissed on the seat, ya dirty bastard," he said.

Swear words sound better with a northern accent. I push through the main door to leave.

"It wasn't me," I said. That's all I can find as a response. I'm not hanging around. It's bad enough I can hear him pissing. I don't want to smell it too.

I should be more excited the kids are arriving, that camp has officially begun. Instead, I'm more focused on this guy from Manchester, thinking I'm a disgusting little shit not capable of pissing in a straight line. I can't go back and explain myself. Why should I have to? I could spark up a conversation about Affleck's Palace or my love for The Stone Roses. I think that may be a much too vulgar attempt to redeem myself. I could always go slam his head shut in the toilet seat. That way he might forget about the piss. I won't do any of that. I'll forever be indebted to his tone and ability not to share my lack of aim with anyone. I'm focusing on my feet as I walk, it's getting painful.

Around the corner of the dining hall, off in the distance, is an ever-growing string of single file cars, some expensive looking, others large. No shit ones in sight. Some cars are heading left to Silver Wood, some right to Red Oak. I count five large coaches. I was almost expecting those bright yellow school buses, none to be seen. Just hefty priced vehicles.

I can hear heavy thumping footsteps coming up from behind me, can't deny my intrigue. It's that Manc guy running toward me.

"Lick my piss." He said, rubbing his wet hands in my face.

I won't assume he's deliberately pissed on his palms to wipe them on my cheeks. I hope he washed his hands and didn't dry them. It's brave he could do that. Then again, what am I going to do?

As I approach the excitable crowd of arriving children and

counsellors, I wipe my face dry. Some guys from the break room are flirting with the girls they were sitting around with on the sofas. The guys are chasing a couple of them around in circles, playfully tugging on the bottom of their tight shorts, all very mature. Their shared laughter stops and they part ways to take up their roles. I walk alone toward the arriving cars and coaches. I arrive at a black hummer.

"Do you need any help?" I said.

The little kids exiting the car don't even acknowledge me. They run towards each other excited. Some of these children have been here before, others are less confident, almost how I'm feeling. The parents of these children throw bags from the boot, or trunk as they're referring to it as. The bags are scuffing along the grass. Some parents swing their expensive, new bags in the chests of any waiting counsellors.

"Shit dawg. Look at dem hummers." Said Doug with a smile as he slides alongside me.

I wander with him, almost deliberately unaffected by the kids. The number of exotic cars here is insane, a luminous, hideous green coloured Lamborghini, fourteen hummers; all of which are customised. The spinners on the oversized wheels are hypnotic, spinners spinning like a shining chrome filled kaleidoscope. It's like Daytona bike week.

Smiles and innocence. Waves, claps and cheering. Hugs for the returning campers, high fives for the new. Clutching at old friends and laughter from most. They all have name tags on with a flag of the state they originate from. More kids fall out of the doors of cars, their parents encouraging them to run free. They usher them toward gatherings of people, nudging them in the back with gleeful excitement. I'm guessing most of these parents look forward to having their kids out of the house for nine weeks. I must admit the break would be a beautiful thing for any parent. It provides these kids with misguided fake independence, which most of them don't require, as they appear to get whatever they can dream of.

Boys are grabbing at bags large enough to carry the body of a dead human. Perhaps some kids, even the counsellors, would end up in one of these bags. I wouldn't even mind if my body laid curled in a contorted mess inside, layered with baseball uniforms and American football pads. I can tell these little fuckers are going to be a dream come true.

There's no number of CDs that I own, books I can read, or even excerpts from Bill Hicks that are likely to provide enough sanity for me in this situation. I should elope, disappear into the bushes at night, smoke a cigarette, and saunter blissfully through this picturesque state of New York. I have New Found Glory in my head. Repeating over and over. One line that will rid my consciousness of bodies in holdalls. It's working.

Benedict, Doug and I are halfway down the hill taking up positions to welcome these little cunts. We stand here upright, straight, regimental soldiers, staring blankly into space.

"This is Dylan." Said Benedict on my behalf, pointing at me.

I must have missed all the introductions. There's a short, natural blond, almost white-haired boy standing before us with an expectant smile plastered on his face. He's accompanied by a pockmarked puny man, roughly the same height as him. Weird, given this kid must be ten years old.

"Hi, I'm Dylan." I said, repeating the previous introduction provided by Benedict, without his annoying South African accent.

"Hey, I'm Morgan's assistant." Said the dark-haired man with this kid, Morgan.

So not his dad. This is weird.

"Sorry?" I said. Did he really introduce himself as this little fucker's assistant, really?

"Unfortunately, Morgan's parents are away with work. So, I'm dropping him off." The assistant said.

"What is it that your parents do, Morgan?"

Morgan shrugs, looking around with wide-eyed amazement at his surroundings. More than bored with this adult conversation. It's obviously his first time at camp. It amazes me how excited these kids are to be here. Even the ones that have been here before. This is not somewhere I'd want to come as a kid, even if it meant that I would be free of my parents. I don't understand why you would want to stay in a draftee, shitty makeshift cabin. I swear if the parents investigated the living conditions, they wouldn't want their kids sleeping on a plastic covered mattress. I guess it goes full circle. Their parents experienced this, and they force it upon their own kids, under the pretence that it's character building.

I'm missing something here, I don't get it. It's not an English thing, even a cultural thing. I won't ever understand. Do we even have this type of thing? I went to a day camp once, and even then, I was happy to leave. That was only six hours.

"They're execs at Sony," said the assistant.

"Oh, right, busy putting out fires and saving lives." I said.

The assistant raises his eyebrows. Funny how money and lifestyle can clearly adjust your opinion of a subject. One day, this guy will realise his own passion and not continue to follow this kid around, picking up his shit and acting as a surrogate parent to a rich, privileged, spoilt little bugger. He's now passed over responsibility to us, his work here is done. He probably has a seven-hour drive back home. Home, which I assume is not his house, live-in assistant and all. He's off now to sing along to The Grateful Dead, arrive back at his staff annex, strip off his clothes, sit buck naked on a leather sofa and slobber down on cheese Doritos. Bet he enjoys a good wank. There's an air of perversion about him. I don't think my spirit has taken to him.

The kids stack their bags in a massive pile, a collection of personalities. I've never seen so much Gucci, Samsonite and Rimowa luggage in one place before. I used to love the sight of Jansport bags. It reminds me of American sitcoms. The kids here don't give a shit about their possessions. I'm guessing someone will have to go through that pile of shit and deliver them to the cabins. I sure as hell ain't being a postman, not getting paid enough for that bull hockey.

The kids are running around, greeting other kids they spent last summer with, hugging and high-fiving. It's a real music video. I can't find the most appropriate music to fit this scene in my head. Slow it down, black and white and boom bangarang, award winning. I'm far too disenchanted to explore my imagination. Fading as I struggle.

All the parents are told to stay with their children until they're called forward and then the boys move toward their assigned cabins, just up the hill from here. Counsellors work through a long list of children's names. The names I'm hearing are the traditional American wet dream of: Zack, Josh, Ethan, Cody, Seth, Chase, Jaiden, Carson, Ashton and even a Buffalo. The list goes on and on. I haven't got my headphones with me to drown this out, for fuck's sake.

These boys ranging from six to seventeen-years-old are marching forward. Some confidently, others nervously. They stand by their cabin counsellors. They called 'Connecticut' out and we soon have ten boys. All ten years old, standing around us, as if we're the three wise men, having all the answers. Doug and Benedict are trying to spark up conversations. I'm not interested. I'll get to know them, sure. I'm not in any rush. But isn't it right for them to at least try to settle my nerves? It's their fucking country. They're not talking to us, more talking quietly amongst themselves. If I was a kid, I'd do the same.

Their parents smile proudly and wave as they stand waiting. It strikes me that most of these parents are itching to escape, many already have. Some had organisers in their hands, as if they're already arranging their next meeting. Never has it been more apparent to me that for most of these kids they're a burden to their parents. Now, a burden to me. I have no sympathy. They decided to have them. Now I'm responsible for them. The joys of life, the fucking joys of life. I wanna be aborted.

"OK. Parents," said Rod. "Thank you for being here. It's now time for you to leave. Your children are in safe hands and the fun begins."

All the children shout and scream with excitement. The parents get in their cars, doors slam with thunderous conclusion. Mother's blow kisses, father's salute and nod with a subtle subversion, maintaining masculinity, obviously. One father, I assume he's his father, is hugging his son. It appears natural, heartfelt. He pauses as he's holding on for too long. He seems almost embarrassed.

Engines start, horns toot. Cars back out in single file and slowly disappear back up the dirt road, waving their arms from open windows, disappearing into the tree-lined distance as fast as they appeared.

All the boys run up the hill to the cabins. For the ones this is new to, they slowly and tentatively enter the cabins through the front doors. I, along with Doug and Benedict, enter the cabin behind our newly assigned little angels. Some boys are putting away lacrosse rackets in their cubbies. Others stay outside, and play catch with baseball mitts, soon cajoled into the cabins by Rod and the other senior counsellors.

You are free to do as we tell you.

I reach my bunk bed. Unlike Doug, I've chosen the top bunk. Josh, a small ten-year-old boy, his face lost in his pillows on the lower bunk. He isn't talking to me or anyone or making any noise. Everyone else, the other nine kids are crashing around, being excited and exploring the cabin. I'm not naturally paternal. It's not nice to see this kid alienated, albeit self-inflicted, but still.

"Josh." I said as I continue to rearrange my sleeping bag. There's really no way of making this hard mattress more comfortable.

"Josh." I said, louder.

He hasn't moved.

I lean back further on my heels and bend down, touching him on the shoulder. I'm not comfortable touching these kids or any kid. There are so many horror stories of being blamed for stuff. I want nothing to be misinterpreted. I don't know him, he doesn't know me. As I touch him on his back, he raises up, shuddering uncontrollably. Clearly, he's crying. Doug's eyes are shut tight with his headphones on. Benedict is sitting with his back to me, chatting with two boys at the end of the cabin. Shit; I'm on my own with this then. Fucking hell, just what I need. Here I am, trying to get my head back to normality, slowly ridding my mind of Laura. Now I must be all responsible and try to console a miserable, crying ten-year-old.

"Josh," I said again. Nothing. Not a sound from him, "You OK mate?"

Most people hear 'mate' and for whatever reason assume it immediately means the speaker is their friend, it's complete bollocks. Although Josh has now turned his head, clearly worked on him. He's a kid, kids are stupid. His cheeks are magenta, eyes soaked. I'd say he's been crying for some time. His lashes are congealed and thick.

"Red eyes and tears, no more love for you, my dear," I said.

Why I said that, I don't know. He won't get the reference. If he does, he's the coolest kid in the world.

"What's the matter mate, you miss home?"

What a stupid question. But come on, what a pussy. He's been here all of five minutes. It's like pull yourself together, man. I should at least try to be slightly more empathetic.

"Hey, think about what it's like for me. My girlfriend is over four thousand miles away," I said.

I won't go into detail about my insecurities. They form into one blotch of tedium.

Josh sits bolt upright, wiping his mouth with his wrist.

"Can you get me a towel down from my cubby?" He said, snivelling.

That shocks me, I'll oblige. I get up and retrieve him a white towel from his wooden storage area or 'cubby'. That name for a wooden shelf is laughable. I won't be heard adopting that shit. It makes no fucking sense. The towel has 'Josh' professionally embroidered on it with blue thread, every towel. My towel is rough tarmac. I only have one. These kids seem to have five each. Josh grabs the towel from me. He swings his legs round, placing his bare feet on the cold wooden floorboards.

"Thank you." He said, getting up, wiping his eyes with the towel, and walks toward the bathroom, disappearing out of sight.

"No problem." I said, laying on the sarcasm. I can't help it.

A loud bugle sounds.

I look at Doug, he looks at Benedict. We all look at each other.

The boys jump up.

"Flagpole." They shout.

We're all summoned. They didn't put us through a test run of this. That four horsemen of the apocalypse bugle sound blares out across the camp again.

To flagpole it is then.

8

Allegiance

Standing in awe of a naked white flagpole. I'm so vulnerable, like I've reverted to being a kid myself. The golden shimmering bulbous ball atop it glistens with pride. We're all standing within our assigned camp cabins in disorganised lines. We'll become more regimented. Its early days. All the kids standing in front of us; as we, the counsellors, act like responsible parents behind them, hands crossed behind our backs, shoulders upright. I'm not paternal. Nor do I intend to be whilst I'm here, I can assure you of that.

The murmurs of childish speculation, high-pitched excitement, rudely penetrate my ear drums. Disney World this isn't. A golf cart zips toward us in the distance, whizzing with electric bliss. It darts between the many wooden cabins, approaching on the dusty track behind. The men from the canteen appear like a calvary and drift with indignation. It doesn't seem fitting for this environment. They stomp to the base of the flagpole. They're here again. The big boss men, the ones we all fear, for no real reason, except their enforced authority. Why we cast power on others, those who don't deserve it, still puzzles me. I have Rage Against the Machine in my head. It's more entertaining to believe I'm filled with juvenile defiance. Instead, in the realms of this, my reality. I'm just an English teenage coward.

This will be my first experience of a real-life flag raising. I've seen it on TV, taking place at sports events and schools, real pomp and ceremony. It's always made out to be a big deal. I'm excited and nervous at the same time.

"Gentlemen." Screams Rod. "Welcome. Some of your faces are familiar. Others we don't know yet. Over the next fun packed weeks. You will all become part of the Red Oak and Silver Wood family. Today is activity day one!"

All the boys jump up, screaming with tangible excitement. The ground shudders with the collective weight shift. It's hard to be negative about this. A part of me wants to find the villainous machinations in it. I can't, I can't yet, anyway. I'll keep looking for the evil. I'm not buying into anything just yet; never blindly. I can't believe how unquestionably excited everyone is. No thought. I'm clapping my hands and going along with all this too. I'm not sure if this is mob mentality or what, where has my mind gone?

"Gentlemen. It's already a hot one." Said Rod, using his cap to waft air across his face. "The forecast is for it to get hotter. We're hitting the middle of the day and it's getting spicy."

Rod shifts as boys laugh. He scolds them with the whites of his eyes.

"Drink plenty of water." He said, as he lifts a half empty bottle of water with a red carabiner clip on it, clanking against the plastic. As the water sloshes, I'm comfortable to refer to his bottle as half empty, he's clearly drank half of it. The operative word being drank. It's only half full while filling the bottle to full capacity. It has nothing to do with optimism, pessimism or communism. I won't be psychoanalysed with pseudo-science bullshit. It's half empty.

"You should all have your own water bottles. Take them to every activity without exception. I don't want anyone suffering from dehydration." He said, instructing with a commanding finger poke in the air. "Drink. The water from all faucets is filtered and safe." He takes a deep breath. "Gentlemen. There is no excuse."

The prepubescent clueless boys hang off his every word. His speech sounds practiced. He must say the same thing every year.

Rod stands back into line with the other authoritative looking men, no longer centre stage.

Bill, with his dark black goatee, touches Rod gently on the shoulder. Rod looks to his right, as if not happy being touched.

"I just want to add to that." Said Bill, stepping forward. "If you're feeling faint, have some water. I want all counsellors to set an example. It's vitally important, as Rod said. Hydrate your bodies. We want you all to have as much fun as possible. In this heat, you need to drink." Bill mumbled on, in his soft southern unassuming accent.

"Yeah, hydrate your bodies." I shout, in a mocking American accent. My hands cupped over my lips. I even surprise myself. I'm not one for unnecessary attention, but I share my sarcastic addition for the benefit of this crowd.

Everyone looks up and around at me, all the kids, counsellors, and the spooks. My face is hot, going red with embarrassment. I stay standing proud, smiling, despite my comfort zone fading beyond my outburst. I maintain my stupid smile. Some counsellors chuckle.

Mark, a small red-headed kid with freckles on his cheeks. I think he's from our cabin. He looks up at me from under his oversized navy-blue New York Yankees baseball cap. He's stepped back and loads his entire bodyweight on my right toe. I wince. He hasn't taken his eyes off me and nor has he removed his fucking foot from my big toe. It's killing me. The little fucker. He's heavy for a ten-year-old. I shove him on the shoulder to make him get off. It feels like I have the early stages of an ingrowing toenail. So, his fat arse won't help. His body jerks forward with my shove, his head flops, as if he's a crash test dummy being catapulted into a brick wall. I think he's milking it. He drops his head in apparent shame. I didn't mean to push him that hard. Eyes are still on me.

Bill uses the corner of his clipboard to scratch the side of his right temple. The crowd's attention spears back from me to impatient Bill.

"Dylan." Said Bill, his shoulders rounding like a raging wrestler.

He's shocked me, and the others. He just flipped to anger, and then returned to his soft, relaxed demeanour. That's the scary thing. Good to evil in response to unruly subordinates.

"Thank you for your enthusiasm," he said.

It amazes me he's even remembered my name. It's impressive how he remembers any of our names.

"You're welcome Bill," I said.

I need him to know he can't growl at me. Plus, I've taken everything too far already, to crawl up my jacksie.

Bill moves back and forth, sweeping his eyes across the entire crowd, allowing his voice to be heard.

"Activities start today," he said. "If you're unsure about which activities you signed up for, come to either me or Rod. Better still, ask your counsellors. That's what they're here for."

I have no idea what any of the boys in our cabin are doing in terms of any activities, no clue.

"I need to see all specialist counsellors after flagpole," said Bill. "Every day, morning and evening we'll all meet here to raise and lower the flag and to make any daily announcements. Attendance is mandatory. All health centre visits are after flagpole, not before. I'll hand over to Monte to raise the flag."

Monte, a broad-shouldered, military looking man with a short crew haircut and a slight back hunch shifts forward. He's been standing quiet. He coughs without covering his mouth. A neatly folded American flag is draped over his left arm, an almost perfect right angle. Monte points at three boys to his left. It even intimidates me, a real jabbing air poke. They must be scared shitless. I would be too. He extends his index and middle finger in a 'come-hither' motion. That's disturbing. It reminds me of just one thing. As hard as I try, or as sensual as my motion, I still can't get anyone to squirt. Laura enters

74

my mind. Nothing but red raw chafing, horny desperation.

The three boys reluctantly step forward from the supportive surrounds of the other boys crowded behind them. They move closer toward Monte. He passes the first approaching boy wearing oversized red shorts, beyond his knees, held up with a black leather belt. The folded American flag is in the boy's arms. He's holding it like a baby. He pensively approaches the base of the tall white metal flagpole and ties one end of the flag to a long rope attached at the top with a pulley system. Monte helps with the knot. He slaps his banana hands down on the shoulders of the middle boy and guides him toward the rope, using his hands over the boy's to help him raise the flag, pulling on the rope cord. The flag ascends. It hangs saggy until it reaches the very top and begins flicking erratically, playing with its position of flaccidity to rigid vigour in the breeze. A perfect flying American flag. Red, white and blue. White stars blinking. This is so Hollywood.

"We raise and pledge allegiance to the flag. We ask everybody to do this as a sign of respect." Said Monte, grunting in an English accent.

This is the first time I've heard him speak. I didn't know he was English. Monte's words are half-arsed. It doesn't carry as much impact or passion as the other American guys. Our accent just doesn't push forthrightness. He sounds too proper.

Rod steps toward Monte, whispering in his ear. I'm slowly learning the hierarchy here. Rod places his full open palm on Monte's shoulder. He's become subservient. He moves like a scolded child being told off by its parents and falls back into line like a little bitch.

"Gentlemen, hats please." Said Rod in his thick Texan accent.

The American members of staff and kids remove their hats. I'm not wearing one. Everyone is submissive. I'm dumbfounded by this spectacle. For years, I dreamt about growing up in an American school and being part of the pledge of allegiance. Now I'm here, I'm not ready to partake in mass conditioning. This whole camp experience is going to be harder than I thought. Rod must have sensed my indignation.

"Gentlemen." He said, whilst glaring at me. "It's the first day of camp. Begin as we mean to go on. Respect our country. We ask you to remove your hats as we pledge allegiance to our flag."

The remaining hats swipe off counsellors heads. It's mostly the English and foreign members of staff that are unaware of the etiquette. There's no choice involved in any of this, it's all a false choice.

"Salute my shorts. I thought this was the land of the free." I said under my breath. No one heard me. Lucky I suppose.

Rod moves his right hand from his side in a deliberate and stiffened motion, covering his heart on the left side of his chest. His palm flat. I can't get over just how surreal this all feels.

"I pledge allegiance," said Rod.

Everyone joins in, shouting, becoming one mass droning murmur.

"To the flag of the United States, and to the Republic for which it stands, one nation under God, indivisible with liberty and justice for all."

Rod is the first to nod agreeably, placing his baseball cap back on his thinning hair to shield his glasses from the sun. All the removed hats return to reddening scalps. One boy, about eleven years old, puts his baseball cap on. Takes it off quickly and investigates the peak. He replaces it. Then removes it, dusts it with his left hand nervously and puts it back to his head. He then licks his left little finger and runs it over the white stitching. It's a DC branded hat, pretty nice, and it's new. I'd put money on either his mother or father purposefully buying that hat for him to bring to camp and if for any reason he lost that hat, he'd be devastated. It isn't just a hat of practicality, it represents his parents for the time he's here. It's their love.
Doug shifts from his left leg to his right. We've been standing out here for ages now. I'm a little stiff too.

"I've done that for twenty years, dawg." Said Doug in his seemingly thicker Georgia accent.

"You serious?" I said.

Yeah, really astute. What a fucking way to prolong a conversation. Doug acknowledges my non-question with a downward turn of his lips and rubs his goatee. Might have to keep count of how often he does that.

"Lower camp, back to cabins for your morning clean up. Upper Camp to lunch. Activities will begin at two thirty," said Rod.

"Chinese dentist time." I said.

I'll do my best to undermine his authority, obviously. I'm not sure about the instruction to clean up the cabins, the kids have only just arrived. What do they have to clean up? They haven't even settled in yet. But whatever, I'll play the game, go along with it. Just enjoy this fucking experience. It'll get better. I swear it has to.

Joe, the shy-looking man, also with a beard, steps forward. When did facial hair come back into fashion? Most of these guys look the same. It's hot too. I can't think of anything worse than carrying a blanket around with me on my face. Like I said, I can't grow a whisker. I thought they were for wizards and paedophiles. Not the best advertisement for a children's summer camp.

"I just want to say, have a great day. Have fun," said Joe.

Given this guy is the camp director. I expected him to have more about him than that. Perhaps bang his chest or hold the crowd more. He's vanilla, bit of a hippie. His beard is neat. I imagine he'd surround himself with loose women, puffing the herb and performing forward facing dog, with his bollocks resting on a worthy handmade thumb piano. He wanders casually back into his original position, pushing his glasses up the bridge of his nose with his little finger. He clasps his hands behind his back, then gazes up. I look at the sky myself, to see if he's gazing at anything specific. He isn't. He's just stood still, squinting with a fixed smile. His beaky nose protruding. My heels are throbbing from all this flagpole fakery. My toe is still burning me. Just when I thought I could escape, Bill bounces forward toward me, stopping dead in his tracks, gripping his clipboard, gently scratching his temples with the corner, as he waits for us to stop muttering amongst ourselves. He stops scratching his head and looks down at the clipboard, reflecting the glare from the sun into my eyes, from the piece of white paper.

"Dylan," said Bill.

"Yes?" I said. Nervous is an understatement.

"Can I see you for a moment?" Said Bill, looking back down at his paper.

Some counsellors look at me with smirks over his shoulder, as if they know I'm in trouble. They all walk back toward the cabins. The specialist counsellor for skateboarding is practicing his ollies on the grass. I don't know his name yet either, but he's caught my eye, as much to say, 'oh shit, what have you done?'

As soon as the other guys are out of earshot and there are no kids around. Bill starts. "I know this is your first time at camp and your first time at flagpole. I have no doubt that was your first experience of the pledge of allegiance," he said.

Bill has a weird birth mark in the colour of his eyes, the pupil sort of bleeds into the brown. I swallow and clear my throat. I'm intimidated. I almost cuss myself having to do that. I mean come on. I can't make it obvious he's unsettled me.

"Yes, first time." I said, swallowing.

"I don't need your confirmation. I know it is." He said, almost belching out the words.

Wow. He is serious.

"When I ask you to pay respect to the flag," he said.

I quickly interrupt him in an attempt at self-defence. "I wasn't wearing a hat."

He doesn't like my interruption, I get the distinct impression he doesn't like me assuming what he's going to say. Just a face full of stone. He's locked his eyes on mine.

"There's a hierarchy here. I don't know what you're used to in England. But the raising of our flag is a big deal. One stoked in tradition, in history. I find it utterly disrespectful to my brother," Bill said.

"Your brother?"

What is he talking about?

"My brother died in the gulf war in '91."

"Oh, yeah, the invasion," I said.

Bill's face turns a pale colour and his eyes are wide, like hard boiled eggs. He steps forward, almost touching my nose with his. He bites down on his bottom lip, his face grimacing.

"I'll forgive you for that. But, know this, you're in my country now. You fuck with me and you're gonna wish you died in Iraq," he said through gritted teeth.

"You can't talk to me like that." I said, somewhat defeated. "Look, I apologise if you thought I was disrespecting you or your flag. But, it's just that, it's a flag,"

"You must be special, boy. Don't make me assert myself. That flag symbolises our freedom. I swear to God, I will lay you on your back, if I so much as hear you talking out of line." He said, hissing the words. The hairs in his nostrils fluttering, he is so close to me.

"Wait, I'm not that guy. I haven't come here to shake stuff up. That's not my intention," I said.

"All you need to know is whilst you're here. There's a hierarchy. When I talk, you don't. When that flag rises. Talking shit, you ain't." He changes his hardened facial expression, softening it like butter and with a caricature smile, he said. "Here at Red Oak and Silver Wood camps. We encourage diversity. For over fifty years we've been providing innovative programmes set amongst an environment created specifically for the safety, education, and growth of our campers."

He spouted it like a sickly corporate promotional video. The words falling from his lips with ease and familiarity. A flash darts through my mind. Shall I punch him, shall I head butt him? Now Laura's standing before me, shaking her head and smiling, her cheeks dimple. My vision of her is enough to rid my mind of violence. What about me, my dream, my American Adventure? Everything I've built this experience up to be in my mind. Every moment, finding my passport, buying a brand-new backpack. My mother suggesting different sizes. Buying plain white T-shirts, red shorts with no branding as per the list of uniform rules. I don't want to throw this experience away on what is the first official day of camp. Besides, what else am I supposed to do?

"Bill, I apologise," I said. "We got off on the wrong foot." By apologising, I'm submitting. I think he's trying to scare me. It sort of works, but he's showed me who he really is. Evil when backed into a corner.

"We've had no problems up to this point. I need you to be responsible and set an example for these kids. You're with ten-year-olds and that's an impressionable age," He said.

I nod my head in agreement. I'm relieved I didn't do anything stupid and lash out.

"I know, Bill, you can rely on me. I'll do the best job possible," I said.

Bill scratches his temple with the corner of his red clipboard, his ritualistic scratching movement. "You're here for nine weeks," he said. "So, you're gonna have to do as the Romans do, as they say."

That's such a strange idiom for him to make use of at this point. It's playfully dictatorial. I'm not one to accept that sort of language from anyone. I'm not a kid. Now is not the time. "I'll be quiet at flagpole!" I said. Now, I've become submissive. It'll be worth it. It'll be worth it.

Bill turns on his heel. I have no choice but to remain standing here, still. Just for a moment as I watch him casually walk away. I take a sharp intake of breath, hold it for a while, and push it free from my lungs. My lips quiver. I cry. I try to force myself not to. Something changes within me. There's disappointment, anger, an abyss. I never expected this kind of treatment. I thought I was an adult. I thought I had experienced a lot so far in my life. I've been in a few fights, but never broken down emotionally like this. I just feel alone. I keep hearing Bill's voice in my head; 'Don't be late for your first activity.' I can hear the drone of the pledge of allegiance, rambling over and over. Eerie childrens' voices. The same tone repeating. I jerk my finger into my eye to rid my cheeks of tears. I can't let anyone see this.

"I love Laura. I love her to death. I love you, Laura." I say it aloud. I need to hear it just to settle me. No one has heard me. I shake my head. Knowing deep within myself, this isn't normal behaviour. Well, at least it isn't for me. I play through the interaction with Bill again in my head. I could have said so much. I should have. I should have sparked him out. I notice the flag. I need to pull myself together. I look out from the flagpole, down over the expanse of camp. It truly is beautiful. I'm lost in the possibilities of exploration but imprisoned with passivity. I turn, scorned. I feel sulky. I head back toward the cabin, shaking my head. With each step I compose myself mentally, for what I imagine will be questions about my encounter with Bill.

I have to stop second guessing myself. There's nothing I can do now.

It'll be worth it.

9

Flagpole Resentment

My copy of 'Malcolm X' slides down from its vertical position, lying flat with a soft thud. As if the pages were trying to get my attention. Some form of divine intervention. The book by Alex Haley is in my 'cubby', also known as a fucking bookshelf in English. I stand it back up. I'm not sure why I brought it with me, but I did. I've read it once before, I thought it might be a conversation starter. No one has even noticed it yet. See, pretentious.

I notice the sacred sought-after cabin broom; it seems this is a tool to alleviate boredom. It's resting against my bunk, perched the wrong end up, bristles like spiky hair. I swing it around, clapping it down on the floor, disturbing Doug. He opens his eyes. I sweep the floor, uninterested in the world around me.

"Dawg, they've done that already," said Doug. He nods toward the boys at the back of the cabin.

"That's fine, I'm thinking." I said, digging the bristles into the wooden floor. Sweeping the brush back and forth across the clean surface. In fact, there are large bits of fluff. So, if they have cleaned this floor, they've done a shit job at it.   Doug stands up from his flat-out, laid position and rests his elbows on the top bunk. He looks to be daydreaming.

"Doug." I said, getting his attention.

"Wat up Dawg?"

His accent makes me smile. The way he greets people with 'dawg'. My assumption is, it's a term of endearment. He says it a lot.

"How much you getting paid?" I said.

"I think 'bout twelve hundred, just short of that." He said, drawing out his words with his southern drawl.

I nod in vague acceptance, though I'm not entirely happy by his response. My silence motivates him to continue.

"We get three hundred travel allowance too."

"What?" I said.

How can he expect me to believe that? I need more details than that.

"Yeah, to get here," he said.

"Really? I got nothing like that."

"The thing is, Landon, my buddy from Bama. He's gettin' eighteen hundred."

I stop sweeping and stare at him. He gives me a comedic double take, his head jerking.

"Are you taking the piss?"

"Nah-uh. What 'cha mean, takin' the piss?" he said.

I find it hard to believe he's never heard that expression before. Where has he been living? I mean, come on. He's from Georgia, not Jupiter. "Are you serious?" I said.

"Nah-uh, for real. Landon's been here before. If you're a returning counsellor, they pay you more, kinda like a retainer," He said.

"Fuck off."

Doug smacks his hand to his mouth, shocked, glancing around the cabin at the kids, checking that none of them have reacted to what I said. Good, they didn't hear. Like I give a shit, anyway. I'm not being paid enough to care.

"You gotta watch that 'round these guys." Doug said, raising his eyebrows. "They'll kick you out, if any of these dudes complain."

I stand holding my hands wrapped around the top of the broomstick. I can see Andy through the fly screen window. I prop the broom up against the bed, right way up, bristles on the floor, like any normal person.

"Hold on a sec." I said to Doug, walking to the door. "Hey Andy." I beckon him inside.

Andy with his feminine looking, soft mozzarella face and good cheekbones. He's quite a beautiful guy. He has a spring in his step, light and excited. I've not noticed him flounce before, he's flouncing now, a feathery flamboyance. He's always smiling. He shows me nothing but pearly teeth, as he bounds up the steps toward me.

"Hey Dylan," he said.

I notice Doug raise his eyebrows, shocked by how flamboyant he is too. Not entirely sure they've met before.

"Andy, how much you getting paid?" I said.

"Same as you and everybody else, I guess." He said with suspicion, looking between the two of us.

"OK. So, how much is that?" I said. Why do I have to instigate everything?

"Five hundred and sixty dollars," Andy said.

"Doug, tell Andy how much you're getting paid." Now, I'm fully aware of how infuriating that sounds to encourage someone else to speak. It does my head in too. But, I consider myself a revolutionary, fighting for the rights of the nobleman and cleaning up the system. Fuck Authority. I'm still punk through and through, right to the core. Despite the mohawk missing.

Doug looks at me, then back at Andy, following my instruction to divulge the information I'm hungry to hear. Although, I'm not sure I really want to hear it now. Doug shares it. Andy is shocked, just as I was. It sickens me to hear of the disparity. It's hard to come to terms with the fact I'm effectively working for nothing. Like slave labour. Doug and Andy may argue that I chose to come here. I thought they both might think the same way as me, clearly not. I can't stand placating tones. That's all they both give me, diplomacy. I sweep again. I need the fucking distraction from this shit. I used to think I was positive. I find all the negative in everything now. I'm not interested in hearing the romanticism of their dreams. I've had to scrimp and save to be here. Lost in thoughts of what could have been. I could be at a free party with Moira. Sharing a blunt with Laura, although she should slow down.

Andy shares how much he enjoys university. Takes it all at face value. No real brains. He's studying drama, of course he is. I'm getting enraged by him, by this place. I want to hurt him, for no real reason. I still have the broom in my hand. I could easily slam it into his Mona Lisa nose, have him swallow his own blood and choke. That would be one hell of a way to go. My knuckles click as I squeeze the broom harder. My eyes explore around the cabin for a second. The boys are laughing and joking with each other. It makes me adjust my mind. For a moment, it seems to help. It seems ages since Andy disturbed me with his moronic chatter. I'm not inspired to begin a lengthy diatribe about shallow people and how there's no integrity anymore. Andy and Doug don't want to hear it. They just don't care. When I get locked in my own thoughts and my distractions browbeat to destroy me. Laura knows how to deal with it. She always cuts me off when I start. It bores her. She'll refer to me as 'far too political'. Cynicism really puts things into context, especially when things get a bit too serious. It's about educating yourself to realise that life isn't all about campfires and fucking s'mores. Tell me again why I came here, why have I done this to myself?

Andy's queer laugh is interrupted by the front cabin door swinging open. He jumps back from the entrance. He plants his right hand, limp and loose on his chest, inhaling sharply. If it wasn't clear before, that Andy is acting camp. I don't mean acting summer camp. I mean gay, chichi, homo, completely gay. Whatever flowery alternative exists, forget political correctness. 'Mi nah business', as Sean Paul would say. Get busy.

Rod staggers through the front door, bumping each of his shoulders on the door frame. He takes his cap off and clenches it in his fist. It's fair to say he looks drunk and out of breath. He is drunk, I can smell the putrid metallic warmth of cheap red wine in the air. He can't have showered. A balmy sweat laced, almost crisp urine smell lingers. Party after flagpole, was it?

"Gen-tle-men, we're supposed to be at Flagpole now, aren't we?" he said, stuttering whilst concentrating on his words.

I look down at my wrist. I'm not wearing a watch. It's an excuse to avoid Rod's circling pupils.

"Activities, Rod, we have plenty of time." I said, looking down at my fleshy wrist.

"Excuse me?" He said, stepping forward.

His trainers are untied and dirty, all scuffed up, still almost white, but browning around the toes. I can't look him in the eye. I know he's trying to unnerve me. Why else would he shift forward?

"Look at me, boy." He said. It was more of a command.

I have no choice. A small bubble of white spit forms on his bottom lip. I can see his moustache is grey, he hasn't tried to dye it. His top lip looks like a badger's snout. My eyes fixated on the sparkling bubble of saliva. He pinches his lips together and what was one small globule of spit turns into two delicate spheres.

"We've already done the pledge. I thought we had time before the activities started." I said, to avoid further facial space invasion. Hopefully that'll satisfy his ego.

"Well, Dyl-an." He said, with a hiss in his voice, "I'm telling you, ya need to go right now."

I'm nervous, I won't argue. I want to laugh, let out one of those defensive, uncomfortable chuckles. I can't pursue my initial reaction to tell him to kiss my arse.

"Yes, sir." I said, like an inexperienced territorial army recruit. I like the way 'sir' sounds. When I say it, I mean it ironically. There's no respect there, none at all. He doesn't deserve it.

Rod looks from me to Andy. Andy steps back, intimidated again. Proper pussy.

"That's you too." Said Rod, clearing his throat.

Andy nervously looks at Rod, then down at the floor, back up at Doug. His eyes swiftly dance over mine. He shuffles out of the front door, holding on to it with his fingertips as he exits, so it doesn't slam shut. He disappears out of sight, down the steps. Poor guy, can't fight back.

"Where d'ya want me, Rod?" Said Doug, as he suppresses a yawn.

"Well, Dougray." Said Rod, using a version of Doug's name that has never been uttered before. Rod is looking past both Doug and me, around the cabin, still clutching his hat, making it obvious that he's looking for something or someone. Could be searching for another bottle.

"I have a question; where are all the boys?" He said.

Doug looks out through the fly screened windows. "Outside," he said. Pointing at the boys sat on the grass in a semi-circle.

"Outside?" Said Rod, sounding appalled. "As a general counsellor. It's your responsibility to know where the boys are. Get them to their activities now."

Doug paces past Rod, dropping his head. He slips his bare feet into a pair of flip flops from under his bunk. As he reaches the doorway, he rotates his shoulders backward. In what I assume is an attempt to ease tension. The sound of the door springs open, it snaps shut with that double tap of wood on wood.

"Dylan, move it. Where did that faggot go?" said Rod.

I stand wide-eyed in shock that he's referred to Andy as a *'faggot'*.

"Don't act surprised. He's in denial." He Said, pulling his cap back on. It's lopsided; the peak below his eyes. Sure, I think the same thing about Andy, he's effeminate and flamboyant but, he's never said he was gay. It's OK to think, different to share it with the world.

"I'm pretty sure he's got a girlfriend," I said. I need to defend him or something.

"He's here to teach arts and crafts," said Rod.

He turns and struts toward the front door, pushing it open, as if he was trying to move a bouncer out the way. He doesn't stifle the front door slamming shut. The force thuds in my chest. Rod bangs his feet down the front porch steps. Too much thudding bass, slamming doors and percussion everywhere. A golf cart begins humming, with that familiar battery whizz as it pulls off, disappearing into the distance. I need a moment, just to settle myself. This place is fucking crazy. What have I done, are they treating everyone like this? I need to pull myself together.

Doug comes back into the cabin with Mark and Liam, two of our kids. Mark with his red hair and toe crushing mass. He goes on about his hometown, Atherton, in California all the time. Not sure I like him. He only wants to talk about himself. Liam doesn't seem to have any clothes that fit, talks about being a child star. He wears basketball shorts and a vest, literally all the time. He's not loyal to any team either. He was wearing a Chicago Bulls strip when he arrived. Now it's The Knicks. I don't even know where he's from, I don't care. I haven't asked. There's nobody on this camp that I'd trust to tell what Rod just said to. What if they all think the same? They could all hate gays.

Doug nods at me without smiling. Should I share it with him, what would I achieve by it if I did? I don't want to ruin this experience for him too. I mean, we don't really know each other. Would he even believe me? I think he would, he should. Don't think me precious, I've used 'faggot' a lot in the past. It was the thing to call your mates. 'Hey faggot, what you saying?' But Rod's expression was derogatory. I'll hold on to this burden and see what happens. I'm not gonna let Andy know.

Where the hell am I, who are these fucking people? This place is mental.

10

Excalibur

Ginger Mark runs over to me, pointing at his cubby. How spoilt is he? He's just pointing. He can talk, lazy fuck.

"Dyl, I need my baseball glove." Mark said, pointing.

"Dyl?" I said, shocked.

The brazen little bastard. When did I say he could call me 'Dyl'? I hate that. Makes me think of a dildo.

"Sorry Dy-lan." He said, with a real sarcastic effort to pronounce my full name. "I need my baseball glove." He said again, almost frantic. His round head bobbing to reach the top shelf of his cubby. His hair is cut so short, a No.1. Like his parents are trying to hide the fact he's ginger. It makes him look like a thug.

"Do you have baseball first then?"

"Yeah." He said, bouncing on the spot. Looking up at his cubby, he's packed well, or his parents have. He has a clean catcher's mitt, an outfielder's mitt that has never been used, even a pair of brand-new cleats, shiny red leather ones. They haven't ever seen a field; the studded bottoms are like cut diamonds. Fuck off, he even has his own set of Wilson protective catcher pads. All of it is brand spanking new, pristine black. Straight off the shelves of Academy Sports. All these trainers, sorry sneakers, as they call them. It's like a fucking Foot Locker in here, puts my soiled trainers to shame.

"I'm going down to baseball now, too. I'll walk with you," I said. That'll be the nicest thing I'll do today.

"OK, just hurry." He said, snatching for his glove as I pass it down to him. With it in hand, he's gone, running out the back door. He's sliding his left hand in the glove and punches it on with his right fist. The door bangs shut. I should probably get my stuff together too.

"Dylan, come on." He said from outside, circling back like an excited dog.

I guess he might be a cool kid. He reminds me of the kid from Problem Child. He hasn't been mischievous yet, but he's cheeky. He doesn't seem to care if you're an adult, he does what he wants. For a ten-year-old, he's brave. One day, I'll research where Atherton is. I've been to Los Angeles, stayed in Anaheim for like a week. Did all the Disneyland stuff. Walked around it in a daze, surprised at how much smaller the park is compared to Orlando. Guess we won't be having any more family holidays, that's all over. I'm too old for all that shit now.

Mark, despite all the shiny new shit, seems well adjusted. I wouldn't immediately say he's spoilt. He's got all this brand-new equipment, and he's quiet whenever asked about how he arrived on camp. I didn't see or meet his parents. That's all a blurred memory now. The backdoor pings open again, Mark's being impatient with me.

"Come on," he said. "I want to warm up." He's ushering me along. He's so serious about baseball, I'll give him that, he'd better be good.

I get my stuff together and follow him to the back door. He's left his baseball bat behind. Evidently, not that serious, if he can forget his pristine bat. I grab it by the handle and drag it up out of his cubby, swinging it and resting it on my shoulder. It has a thick end to it, the size of a milk bottle. This will be my second nice feat of the day.

Mark is almost at the end of the cabins, thumping his fist into his mitt. The customary warm up. He's waiting for me. He really doesn't want to.

"Mark, you forgot your bat." I said after him.

He looks up with canine recognition and comes running up the hill toward me. Making a deal with god.

"Shit." He said, panting.

I laugh. I've not heard him swear before. In fact, that's the first time I've heard any of these boys swear. I won't reprimand him or warn him. He hasn't heard that from me. It sounded funny, the way it fell from his childish lips.

"Excalibur," He said, snatching it.

"You've named it Excalibur?"

"My dad named it." He said, swinging the bat. "I've already hit twelve home runs with him."

"I could slay a dragon with that thing too," I said.

"What?" He said, shaking his head.

"The legend of King Arthur."

"Oh yeah, my Dad likes all that stuff." He runs off. "I just wanna play ball."

I watch him get smaller off in the distance. It reminds me that, this kid, all these kids have personalities and minds of their own. It'll take time and effort to understand them. I assume he must always use that sort of language. I'm not even sure why I'm that surprised. I don't know where my boundaries are. Now, if he had blurted 'cunt', I may have reproached him for that. So, I'm seen to be taking this shit seriously. This experience may expose me to how kids normally speak when they're not around adults. I can't remember how I used to behave, whether I swore or not. I don't think I did, through fear of being whipped by a garden cane. As kids, the mere threat was enough to make us second guess the use of inappropriate language. Fear derived from expression.

Mark, clutched Excalibur. He's a mere speck ahead, far into the distance. He's raising the bat, straight into the air with a stiff right arm. As if he's running into battle. Now he's stopped. I think he's waiting for me. The baseball field, or one of them, isn't even that far from our cabin, down the hill past the tennis courts. That's at least where the first baseball session is being held. As I understand it, we change up the use of fields based on age groups. Mark has now turned, glaring at me. Members of the senior staff are sitting on golf carts, watching us come down the hill. I must appear lackadaisical, as they haven't taken their eyes off me, their arms folded tight. I want to act out a little, like I need to convince them I'm committed to this whole premise of camp.

"Hey, wait up." I said, down at Mark. I even jog in his direction. Surely they'd be impressed. Play the game, we all have to play the game.

"Hurry, we're gonna be late." He said. Well, he shouted it. Nothing calm about his delivery.

He makes me wanna laugh, he's like Dennis the Menace in a way. Not sure what he thinks we're gonna be late for. I'm one of the baseball counsellors, the bellend. They aren't gonna start without me. They might. They shouldn't. Who knows? We pass the tennis courts, that session in full motion. Are we late then? The tennis counsellors are demonstrating a swing. All the young boys are standing along the baseline of one of the professional sized courts. Some kids have tennis rackets gripped in their hands, emulating what's being shown. Some of the other kids don't give a shit, they're balancing their rackets on their fingertips. One kid, I recognise from flagpole, is using the handle as a phallus, simulating a thrusting motion with his hips. These kids, oh so innocent. Dirty bastards.

Bobby Oppenheimer, a bulky guy with a curtain like haircut, side swiping across his forehead in the wind. I don't know where this whole 90s hair style thing comes from, but it seems more than popular in a lot of these guys, a preppy look. I'm not confident in saying it's an

American thing but most of them seem to sport that privileged Ivy league college persona. He's yet another one holding a fucking clipboard. These Americans and their clipboards. No pen or pencil, just a clipboard and one sheet of paper, flapping back and forth in the breeze. The floppy haired guy rolls his hand over it each time it tries to escape, enthusiastically smoothing it down. This guy's walking towards me. He doesn't look pleased. No smile for me then.

"You're late." He said. It was almost like a bark, as he takes a baseball cap out of his shorts waist band, unfolds it, pulling it down on his head, immediately turning it round, the peak facing backwards. Such a dude, yeah right. I can see his face again now. His forehead is framed by loose, escaping hair. His body size makes him seem older than his fashion sense. He looks about thirty. I can only think his favourite pastime is hanging upside down, drowning in a beer keg, pissed up with the boys, his frat bros. That astute mention of sharing his buddies girlfriend on the backseat of a Prius, driving south on the A1A, Beachfront Avenue. All because she gives good head and swallows.

"Hi," I said.

This guy Bobby looks down at Mark. "Go find a partner little man and warm up, we're gonna run drills," he said.

Mark nods, slams a clenched fist into his mitt and skips off toward the other twenty odd, ten-year-old boys.

"This is the first day," said Bobby. "Make some fucking effort."

What is it with all this effort, bollocks? I'm making loads of effort. Here, everyone assumes I'm late. I've never been late in my life. One person says one thing, someone else says another, I'm not sure who to believe. I'm over all this bullshit. It'll be worth it. Play the game. I'll ignore my instinct and placate him for now.

"Sincere apologies." I said with a smile. I always think the utterance, sincere is a good start with most people. It really grabs them by the ears. Who can argue with an apology, and sincere apologies at that? I challenge anyone to stay irate. Especially from an

American to an Englishman.

"Won't happen again," I said. "I thought we had to be here at two-thirty."

"Whatever." He said, his cheeks turning red. He's really giving it the berries. I've heard his name banded about, but what a warm welcome this is.

"Sorry," I said.

He's the baseball director. I have nothing but arrogance from him and a knowing smile. He's offering me his hand to shake now. Is this a joke, is he likely to crush it? His smile isn't a friendly one, he knows he holds the power. I didn't know he was the boss man. Two guys stand behind him, leaning against the fence.

"I want this to be successful," said Bobby. "I'm quite embarrassed that this camp." He circled his finger in the air. "Decided to hire an English guy to teach an American Sport. You won't have a clue."

"Hold on," I said. "I've been playing for years. I represented the South of England."

Bobby shakes his head. He's dismissing my defence.

"Whatever, little man. Actions speak louder than words," he said. He turns his back on me.

If Excalibur was in my hand, I'd lift it above my head like a fairground mallet and slam it right into the crown of his soft little shit for brains head. But, with no Excalibur in my grasp, I'll just stand still for a moment and watch him scuttle away to a metal fence that protects spectators sitting on the bleachers behind home plate. He stands in between the two other guys, raises his right foot up and rests it against the fence, leaning back into it, bastard. What an actual bastard.

All the boys on the field are throwing balls, the silence punctuated with the snap of leather gloves.

"Everyone." Said Bobby, to the boys on the field, as he pushes himself upright, off the fence. "Let me tell you a bit about what we'll be doing this session."

The boys run toward him, circling around. Why does everyone have to shout? There's so much of it. Should I be speaking at volume too, just to be heard?

"We gonna play a game?" A young boy said, sat on the bleachers. There's a rumble of voices from the main field, as if agreeing.

"Well, if that's what you all wanna do?" Said Bobby, searching for the consensus.

They all scream, hopping up and down, chattering amongst themselves. Everyone is so loud. I'm not sensitive to sound, but this is ridiculous. They're pounding their gloves with fists and twiddling the handles of baseball bats between their fingers, cracking them off the heal of their trainers.

"Game it is," said Bobby. "First, let me introduce you to your coaches."

One kid drops his baseball bat and stands still without retrieving it. His shoulders drop like he's intimidated. I bend down and pick it up for him, stand it on its end. He grabs it with his open palm and smiles with appreciation. Another good deed for the day.

Arnold, with a curly Afro hair style moves forward, rearranging his shirt, plucking the collar with his two fingers. He clears his throat as if he's going to deliver a life-changing speech. This isn't the reflecting pool. I'm so excited to hear what he has to say, if only he had a microphone.

"Hi, I'm Arnold from Nova Scotia, Canada. I love the Toronto Blue Jays and well, I'm looking forward to playing with you." He said in his Canadian accent.

Some boys snigger, others have no clue what's so funny. Don't get the euphemism. Arnold stands back against the fence, embarrassment on his face from the laughter, he realised. "Baseball, that is." He quickly adds. "Looking forward to playing baseball with you, I mean." He nods his head, happy with his own introduction.

Carl Lee steps forward, small in stature with Elvis sideburns and a quiff. A rockabilly look with a name like a serial killer.

"Hey guys, I'm Carl Lee, from Oklahoma City. I've been playing baseball for well…" He pauses. "Years now, like eleven, anyway, and it's my life."

Now, anyone that says that sort of shit, needs to get another hobby. I get being passionate and I certainly own my shit, but you say that kind of crap, you're a nob. A kid raises his hand. Bobby points at him, indicating he can speak. They have these fucked up rules for speaking here. I haven't come across that 'hold the stick' sensibility yet, but, I know there'll be a newfangled way to allow you to speak, such bollocks. Freedom, I won't let you down.

"Where they had the bombing?" said the boy.

I scoff, as it's such an outlandish but funny question to ask. Everyone seems to take it seriously. I'm not trivialising the act of terror, don't get me wrong. But, it happened a while ago. Their reaction is as if it happened yesterday. I'm impressed this kid even knows about it. What would he have been, five or something?

"Yeah, my dad was like four blocks away." Said Carl Lee with concealed pride.

"Cool," Said one kid.

That could be the best response so far. I guess now it's my turn to speak. I'm not that fussed. I hate being the last to speak. Anxiety builds within me. As others are finishing their sentences, it makes me clench my butt cheeks with anticipation. I step forward. Bobby blocks me, holding me back. Even if I wanted to speak, he isn't letting me. That's that then.

"And finally, this is Dylan." Said Bobby, pointing with his finger. "He's from England. I have it under the best authority, he can play ball, even though he's from England."

The boys laugh, Arnold and Carl Lee get involved, producing slight condescending smiles, joining in with the chuckles. Just a bunch of impressionable bullies. I'm embarrassed again. I feel like I'm being paraded like a second-rate citizen.

"Right, now that's over," said Bobby. "Game time. We'll pick teams. I'm gonna pitch and umpire. Each team can have a counsellor.

I'll decide who gets the Queen of England." He stabbed his finger into my back.

I don't like public speaking as it is. I would have liked to have introduced myself. Forever stifled, forever forgotten. Forever, forever and many more. O say, can you see.

All the boys separate, half remain seated on the bleachers and the others grab their baseball gloves, running out onto the field. It's like they're a tube of Smarties rolling free across a desk. Different coloured shirts and shorts breaking off in different directions. Strange, when there's supposed to be a camp uniform. I guess if the parents are paying, wear what the fuck you want. As counsellors, we don't have a choice. Slave to the system.

Some boys take up the position on each plate, first base, second, third and a nominated catcher. The others move out to the field and stand expectantly for the first batter to take up his position. A skinny boy gets up from the bleachers, grabs for a navy-blue plastic helmet. The ones with that donut shaped plastic piece that comes down and covers your ear. He picks up a metal bat, walks to home plate, steps with a gay briskness and awaits the ball to be pitched. Bobby throws it soft and considerate. The boy swings, connecting with a crack, scuffing it low across the grass. He tosses the bat and runs toward first base, the top of his thighs rubbing.

Let the games begin. Remember, it'll be worth it. Oh, it'll be worth it.

11

Noggin′

To me, I'm always present. I'm here on this camp. This first baseball game is a joke, albeit branded as practice. I've forgotten most of these kids names. They're not bothered about knowing me, either. Mark is running around aimlessly, a darting ginger blur. I have no genuine interest in getting to know these people. I'm happy to stand here, let my life pass by and watch these spoilt kids swing a baseball bat three times and miss the ball. It doesn't matter because every time they swing the bat, even if they miss, they provide a cheer of encouragement. It's all very American in the strictest of stereotypes.

"Good job."

I hear all that shit banded about here, despite most of these kids efforts being completely lacklustre and crap. I watch in surprise as one boy hits the ball, it sails into the air. Two kids in the outfield run to catch the loose ball, both completely fuck it up. They drop their heads in shame, rightly so. It was an easy catch, should have had it, they should be embarrassed.

There's excited bustle and fervour when the boys switch. The boys on the bleachers pop to their feet, like bread from a toaster. They run full pelt out on to the field, gloves clutched in their hands. The fielding boys begrudgingly leave the field, step by step they make their way to the bleachers. Everything's becoming a manifestation of stereotypes. The catcher, wearing all black padded safety equipment, catches the ball as a boy swings the bat. I'm bored watching the game play out. A boy runs from third plate to home with a smile on his face, odd when he's trying to run as fast as he can.

My mind leaves the present, my body in place of this boy's. I'm running to home plate, being scouted to represent England. The all-star game, representing the South West. There I was, on third base. Home plate seemed so close; I can smell the gravel dust. Phil, a teammate, was up to bat. I had the coach from the Reading team standing beside me, his mouth near my ear, providing me with instruction. As Phil warmed up his swing, standing outside the batter's box. This coach with a dirty chin, leaned into me closer and said:

"Listen, when I say run, you run."

I remember looking up at him. It was an intimidating piece of direction. I was so nervous, unnecessarily so. Not only could I see my parents watching me with pride and reclining on two sun loungers, holding a packed lunch. There was a lot of pressure on me at that point. Baseball coaches and parents living vicariously. Phil hit the ball. It wasn't the most powerful of hits. I knew I'd never make it to home plate. I don't believe that my nervousness or hesitation meant I couldn't make it before the ball reached the catcher.

"Run. Go. Go. Go." Coach shouted in my ear, droplets of spit firing across my right cheek. He could have said it in slow motion, low bass, thumping. As soon as I heard those words screamed at me. I ran as fast as I could. It wasn't fast enough. My hips were too heavy, too fat. I always knew my baseball gear was tight, but I honestly didn't know until that day, through one man's disapproving words, that I was a failure. He approached me after they called me 'out'. That one word cut through me, felt like I was falling. I didn't make it.

The coach sauntered over to me, disappointed with my honest effort. I was thirteen.

"I didn't realise you couldn't run that fast. I knew you were chunky, but that shocked me." He said, with raised eyebrows.

His words hurt. It's such an easy, fleeting comment for an adult to make. It's stayed with me; I even hear it now. I'm not sure adults consider how powerful their words can be. At that moment, the coach made me question my worth. I was at the mercy of his words.

I had that fear in mind when I applied for 'Sleepaway America'. I can't be one of those hurtful adults, leading these kids down a path of self-harm or negative thoughts. I didn't represent England in the end. I was too fat, too slow.

How did I get here? The heat of the afternoon sun brings me back to camp. I'm a 19-year-old man. If you can consider me a man, I'm masquerading as a man. This place reminds me I'm not a grownup. I'm expected to teach these fucking kids a sport I don't really give two shits about anymore. All I can think about is crazy fucked up shit from my past. I muddle through my days, playing at life as it ticks on by without me. I'm on my own here, lost. If I concentrate hard enough, I can almost hear Hot Hot Heat playing in my ears. It'll let me escape into some form of tranquillity. Music does that for me. If I think about Hot Hot Heat, it leads me to Hazel.

I need to teach these kids all the wonders of baseball. I'm like a fraud, standing here in red Umbro shorts from Soccer Sports, with a semi-erect penis, all because I'm thinking of Hazel Valentine's bald fucking head. Shorts are not the clothing of choice to conceal a hard-on. Jeans would be better. I need to concentrate. I turn back to the game.

"Heads Up." Shouts Bobby through cupped hands from the batter's box.

I turn around to avoid getting clouted. Bobby provided the warning; he tosses a ball up in the air and clocks it with a wooden bat. The sound of the ball on bat, a thunderous crack follows, the baseball smashes into the side of little Mark's head. I bet he won't be complaining about being late now. He lies on the thick carpet like grass, pawing at his throbbing head. Everyone running over to him as he continues to roll around on the grass. He's wailing and screaming, a disturbing noise coming from his mouth that doesn't seem like it's even possible for him to make. A kind of terror filled scream, like a pig going to slaughter, dead inside, knowing the inevitable. Some boys from the outfield and baseman are already standing over Mark. Bobby bends down and touches him on his head. Mark lets out a torturous yelp. The only positive from this is, it's given me enough time to adjust my underwear to conceal my aroused state.

"I'll take him to the medical centre," I said.

Bobby leaning over him, his palm face up, signalling for the kids to give Mark some space. I lean down to offer my hand; Bobby slaps it away. The dickhead.

"There's no need. He'll be fine," He said.

"I think it's probably best if he gets checked out," I insist.

Bobby stands up and grits his teeth.

"He's fine. It's just a knock on the noggin'." He said, locking his eyes on mine.

What is it with all these staring contests? He's obviously shitting himself, he's the one who crunched Mark in the head. He for damn sure doesn't want him going to the medical centre. Instead, Bobby clicks his fingers and gestures for the Gatorade tub on the bleachers. Three lean boys run to retrieve it. Between them, they carry it back, shuffling their feet across the grass as if they're skating on ice, becoming more hurried as they get closer. All the activities here have orange Gatorade tanks full of iced water. There's that big push to optimise hydration, not a bad thing. The boys place the tub next to Mark's head. Bobby kneels and picks Mark off the grass in his arms, like he's cradling a baby. Mark, still writhing in pain, kicking out his legs. Bobby, being the stocky, tall man he is, kicks off the white lid of the Gatorade tub. It flies off. He flips Mark upside down at the waist, as if he's a bottle of ketchup. Headfirst, Mark is thrust downward into the iced cold water. Mark screams. He's now become calm, probably from the shock. Mark now supporting his own weight with his arms on the rim of the tub.

"Gotta say this is some weird first aid," I said.

Carl Lee curls his lips in agreement.

"Pretty fuckin' clever though," He said.

Really, is that what he thinks? Clever, this isn't.

"What are we gonna drink now?" Said a tiny boy with a Green Bay Packers hat on.

"It's fine, it's filtered water." Bobby responds, cutting his eye at the boy.

That explains that then. Dunk some kids head in the water cooler and expect these kids to drink from it. This place is getting crazier by the minute. I won't be drinking that ginger infused water, even if they do filter it.

Bobby lifts Mark higher, his hair dripping wet. He swings him around like a Ferris wheel and plants Mark's feet on the ground, steadying him as he finds his feet. At least he's stopped crying now. He's still holding his head. His face is red, eyes streaming with tears. Difficult to tell the tears as they mix with the water dripping down from his soaked head.

"Come on, big man. Let's go take a seat. We might have to call you Noggin' from now on." Said Bobby , chuckling. He leads Mark to the bleachers. "Right, Let's see what you've got, Mrs England. Hit some fly balls to 'em." He said to me, marching with Mark.

This guy is such a twat, like a proper prick. What is his problem? I hold my eyes on him. Make him feel uncomfortable. He's leaning forward on the bleachers, attempting to console Mark. Yeah, good luck with that, dickhead. The boy should be in the medical centre. Still, what the actual fuck do I know? I need to show this prick how capable I am. I walk toward home plate, the boys behind separate and return to their fielding positions. This is more than hitting baseballs, this is about honour. Home plate never seemed so far away. I look toward Bobby, like an expectant child. I'm trying not to make eye contact. I need to shut this guy up. I kick up dust as I stand in the batter's box. My feet fit perfectly beside the white plate. I lurch forward for a solitary baseball. Here goes. I toss the ball into the air and crack it perfectly with the baseball bat. It's a beautiful hit, truly. The ball sails into the air, far beyond what would have been a home run. All the boys stand in awe, like they've witnessed a UFO flying overhead. Not bad for an English chap.

"I said fly balls, not home runs." Said Bobby from behind me.

Perfect, not even impressed. Whatever. I pick up another ball, toss it in the air. The bat makes a plonk noise. A perfect fly ball into left field. Bobby isn't even looking, fabulous.

Bobby taps Mark on the shoulder, stands up, leaving him on the bleachers and walks toward the pitcher's mound. A slight duck like walk in his steps. He's not stopping. He's gonna pitch to me. He hasn't looked up at me yet. I swear he's going to pitch. It'll be a mental one. He'll give it everything he has. He stands on the white pitcher's plate, the white hyphen in the middle of the field.

"OK, England-shire," he said.

I can only assume that was his best attempt at an English accent. He's going to take a run up, aim for my head.

"See if you can hit my fast ball." Said Bobby, as he grabs the baseball from his mitt. He's gonna make this impossible for me to hit. I'm expecting it to skim the plate, probably close to my body. He kicks out his left leg, jerks his body forward. The ball is a blur, fast, aggressive. Bobby's face is grimacing. He's holding no prisoners. My heartbeat flutters in my chest. I need to exhale. I focus on the ball. Everything else is a blur. The ball fires past my eyes, a white fleck in my vision. That was dangerously close to hitting me. I drop the bat from off my right shoulder and take a step back out of the chalk rectangular batter's box. I need to take a breath. If there was an umpire here, he would have let me walk to first. Seriously, I had to shift to avoid being hit by that last one. I tap the bat on my heels, all very Major League. I step back into the box, as soon as I do, another ball comes swooping toward me, crashing into the fence behind, rattling it violently.

"I wasn't even ready for that one." I said at Bobby, dropping the bat again.

Bobby shrugs. My words wasted. I understand now, this is a Mexican standoff. I have my eyes on his and his on mine. I can't see his pupils. I'm not sure there's any good in him, nothing to find. He wants to prove to me he's amazing and I should stand idly beneath him. I'll prove that I can handle anything he throws at me, anything: a ball, intimidation, mental games, everything he's got.

Bobby kicks his left leg out and up, his right arm flings back, springing forward. The ball flies perfectly. It's coming down the middle of the plate. This is a wonderful pitch, it almost makes you stand to attention. I swing, I have no choice; the bat takes over. My vision blurred. The resistance from the bat is like a punch to my liver. The force in my wrists. I've scuffed it. The ball spins backwards, swooping over the chain-link fence behind. I barely caught the underside of the ball. It's heading right toward the medical centre. I feel sick. I know it's going to hit the building. My shoulders tense up into my neck. I wince and close my eyes. We all know what's following.

Smash.

The ball crashes through the large front window of the medical centre.

"Oops," I said.

All the boys gasp. Some laugh nervously and run to hide behind the bleachers, thankful it wasn't them to blame. Bobby and I remain on the field, both looking at the destruction. I stare at the shards of glass. I'll take responsibility for this, it's my fault. I drop the bat to the dusty dirt below. If you think about it, the bat is as much to blame as I am. Bobby too; he threw it. It's just a game, a game. This probably happens all the time. The building is close to the field, poor design.

I sheepishly walk to the medical centre. As I do, three

women, wearing white nurses uniforms. Well, white jackets anyway. Not nurses uniforms like I try to encourage Laura to wear. She has none of it. The nurses or doctors, whatever they are, tentatively exit through the opened main door, looking through the fresh hole, carefully avoiding splinters of glass scattered across the ground.

"I'm sorry. That's my fault." I said, raising my finger, owning up. It's the right thing to do. I try to put on my most humble, apologetic face. A face your dog might make when it chews your vinyl collection, looks at you with those sorry eyes, deep down knowing you'll forgive.

Holy shit. Hazel just walked out through the front door, too. I try to maintain a straight face to these nurses, but now I've seen Hazel, Hazel Valentine. I beam with a smile. She smiles back. There she is, all beautiful and different.

"Hi," I said.

Hazel blushes, looking at the ground, and glass, then back up at me.

"This your handy work?" She said, nodding down toward the destruction. She's amused, now knowing it was me who caused the damage. It's like I've somehow become cooler to her. A bad boy hooligan, worthy of knowing. I'm certain the nurses and some kids behind me are making noise, saying something. Probably asking me how it happened. I'm not paying attention to any of their words. All I can see is Hazel, Hazel Valentine. There she stands. There she goes, there she goes again. I can't be sure if I said her name out loud or not. I don't think I did, no guarantee.

She has blonde hair today. Obviously, it's a blonde wig, it suits her. She does well to expose her scalp with a centre parting. It looks so real, natural. I really don't think you'd know she was wearing a wig. She has her magical belly button covered up today. I wonder when I might see that again. It's almost too easy to refer to her as beautiful. I'm not sure she is beautiful, she's alluring. Is that beauty? Whatever it is, she has something about her I like. She's so different to Laura, not just in terms of looks. She also appears harder in disposition. I get the impression she won't take any shit from anyone. Could the lack of hair do that in her? I really want to know more.

"You have to be more careful." Said an overweight, scraggy haired nurse. A true matron frump.

"I wasn't the one who put the baseball field there," I said. I won't apologise again, there's no need, anything more would be disingenuous. It would have been a good hit and shut Bobby up if I had hit that clean on. He must have put some weird backspin on it. Not sure, I don't care. I want to talk to Hazel.

All I do is smile at her. A petite girl, about eight-years-old, walks out of the medical centre with her hand over a patched eye. She's got an oversized bright pink plastic replica pearl necklace on. She stands in front of Hazel. Hazel places her hands on the girl's shoulders, she's almost maternal. Hazel has a ring on her wedding finger. Hold up, she's married? She's no older than nineteen, twenty at a push and she's married? Why is she at a children's summer camp for nine weeks if she's fucking married? That trust in action. It's hard enough leaving Laura, and she's just a girlfriend. Isn't marriage supposed to mean so much more to people? She must have noticed me looking at her finger. She, too, looks down at the shining ring and smirks. She kneels in front of the girl and whispers in her ear. The girl squints her one eye and smiles, she's cute. As Hazel bends down, she's wearing cloth shorts, a grey colour. The material accentuates the curvature of her bottom cheeks, it's amazing. I bet she's not wearing any underwear. I can't take my focus off it.

Wait, she's fucking married, how is she married? That dream is over. We can still have a sordid affair. That would be an experience. She smiles again as she stands up and mouths to me.

'Bye.'

Such a pleasant smile. She bites her bottom lip. She bit her fucking lip. That drives me wild. Girls know exactly what they're doing when they bite their lip. She wants me. That to me says she wants my lips all over her body. Why the fuck did I agree to go on a summer camp that isn't mixed? This whole separation thing is gonna kill me, it'll kill me dead. I'm a sexual being. I need interaction with women, I really do. Seriously, this is unnatural.

Bobby and the nurses are standing together, with serious sounding murmurs. Yeah, that's right, you deal with it, bitch. You're the Baseball Director. I'll leave that to him. Thank you, please.

As I clear up some of the equipment, that's been left behind, spare baseball gloves, a couple of helmets and a few bats that haven't been put away. The general counsellors left hanging around, supervising the children, gather the boys up, herding them towards the canteen. Some head toward flagpole. It must be snack time. No, it can't be. No idea what's going on. Which is good, I guess. Not sure we're eating again until dinner. The food so far is nasty, it's all right. Nothing that appetising, it's a means to an end. I pick up a red plastic baseball helmet with a worn emblem of the camp stuck to it. Some words are cracked, peeling off, but it's 'Red Oak and Silver Wood Camp'. I place it on top of other red helmets in the netted storage bag.

"Great job." Said Bobby, as he approaches me.

He's slowly clapping. I can't help it; I need to smirk. A slow hand clap. Come on, dickhead, really?

"OK, that's it. You can all go. Take any left gloves to the shed," he said.

The remaining boys and counsellors grab and collect their stuff and run as fast as they can back up the hill toward the cabins. Others walk toward the canteen. I pick up the catchers equipment: a black helmet, chest protector and leg guards. I toss them in the storage shed with my best underarm, callous lob.

Bobby slams the sliding doors shut. Just as I move my hands outta the way, good timing too, otherwise he would have severed my hands clean off. I think that was the intention. Bobby clasps the padlock, pinching it shut. He looks around over my shoulder, making sure no kids are in earshot, glaring down at me, his hat pulled down over his forehead.

"Don't embarrass me in front of these kids." He said, pointing his stiff finger, prodding me in the chest. His fingernails are long with embedded brown dirt.

"I didn't mean to embarrass you, it was an accident. It was a good pitch, unlucky it went through the window," I said.

"I don't mean the fucking window." He Said, moving his blushed cheeks closer into mine.

"What do you mean then?"

"I'm well known on this camp. I have a reputation and I won't have some English jerk. Come here and fuck with me." He said, glaring at me.

I scratch my head. It's natural to scratch my head, a little contrite, but natural.

"Bobby. I respect you. I sincerely apologise for the window. I mean it's the first day, I wanna enjoy myself. I want to teach these kids about my culture and learn about yours," I said.

Bobby stands still. I see his eyebrows raise as the peak of his hat rises in the middle. He doesn't break a smile, not once.

"I'm here for these kids." He said, pointing his finger at the distant boys.

He's clenching his biceps. I nod my head. Another battle I won't win. I can only try to ignore his masculinity.

"You and I are not gonna be friends," he said.

"Well, if that's the way you want it, that's the way it has to be, so be it. But, I'm here for nine weeks. We have to work together. It would help, if we get on or at least try to," I said.

Why am I being the responsible, mature adult here? I'm acting, yet again.

"Get to wherever it is you should be right now."

I guess that's the end of our conversation then. He turns his back to me, swaggering off, up the dusty road toward the infamous flagpole. We won't be walking anywhere together. Which is a good thing. What would we even talk about? I could always learn about his life, whatever mental hick town he's from.

I scuff my feet up the road to flagpole, leaving the drama of the medical centre behind me. I've deliberately left a big enough gap between us. That way there's no chance of forced conversation.

All I know is, I wanna taste a piece of Hazel.

12

Kryptonite

I hear footsteps behind me, crunching on the gravel path. Please be Hazel, please be Hazel. I turn around. A beautiful blonde girl, so many blondes here. Unfortunately, it isn't Hazel. This girl must be twenty-one. She looks older than me, walking toward me with a tiny little girl, probably no older than seven, she's short, not like a dwarf. Just a tiny seven-year-old.

The blonde girl is having to lean down to one side, to maintain her hand holding. The little girl stumbles and staggers. The blonde girl trying her best to hold her up. This is my chance to act as the hero. I walk toward them. She puts her hands under the little girl's armpits. My god, she's so beautiful. My feet jog in her direction. I've got no actual choice in this. Women have such a strange effect on me, they're my Kryptonite. I want all of them; they destroy me when I reveal myself. I'm getting closer. From somewhere, unbeknown to me, I have the confidence to approach her, an out-of-body experience.

"Can I help?" I said. I don't wait for her to respond. "I'm Dylan." I said, going straight to bamboozling her with my name.

She's struggling to hold the little girl up, she exhales

frustrated. She doesn't seem all that interested in what I said, or at least doesn't seem to be interested in my name. Sure, it's not the greatest of names.

"Can you get her legs?" she said.

I drop immediately, like the good little boy I am, grabbing for the girl's ankles. I should probably be more delicate. The blonde girl leans back, and we lift the little girl up. Why hasn't she told me her name? She's not even making eye contact with me. Why can't she see me? I'm smiling and everything, she's not even paying any attention to me. She could have a weird name, like Moira, bless her. No choice for me but to follow her lead. We walk toward the medical centre. The little girl is secondary to me. She has flushed cheeks and her eyes are closed. I really don't care. She looks tired. I'm not a doctor. She isn't going to die or anything. Too much drama. She's probably dehydrated or some shit. We'll get her to the medical centre, and all will be fine.

Alyssa tells me her name in a whisper, filling the silence as we walk, still carrying this girl in our arms. I like the idea of her being slightly older than me. She's thin, no, athletic; yeah, she's more toned than thin. Rounded shoulders. She's wearing the required camp uniform, red shorts and a white T-shirt. The sleeves and her plunging neckline have a red trim. She must have customised the shirt, it's roughly cut all the way around her body, clearly by hand, quite short revealing her navel. I have never seen this many belly buttons on show before. I like it. A soft looking 'inny', perfect. She has a tattoo on her hip of a white feather, random. Wait, that's the second white feather tattoo I've seen here, I think. It's the same design, I swear. A delicate white feather intricately inked with perfection. I've never encouraged feathers or stars as tattoos. Too easy, too common. Be original, think of something. Not just what's recommended to you. For too many people, it's a case of picking a 'number forty-four', paying fifty quid, and you're part of the club. Creatively lazy.

If I was a nice guy, I'd care more about this little girl. I should have asked her name. Teased her or something. Made light of the situation. She's limp and gasping for water. I assume that's what she wants. Her lips are white and cracked. She won't be interested in me trying to dilly dally with her. I won't add anything to her life.

This Alyssa girl, I can fuck her. I couldn't care less if this dwarf girl collapsed in the dirt and was left to frazzle in the afternoon sun, like a discarded, lifeless Capuchin monkey. Alyssa gives off an air of sex about her. If I could eat her pussy, I'd be happy. I'd do a magnificent job too. She can see I have no heartfelt interest in helping her and I'm a product of typical sin. I bet she gets this all the time. Guys picturing her naked and submissive, half listening, hearing the sound of her climaxing every time she laughs. She's holding her gaze on the girl as she moves her hands from her head to her stomach. She makes no noise, laying still as we carry her. Good job too. I'm trying my best to hold her. If she wriggles, she could fall from my grasp and that would be utterly terrible, apparently. I need to try harder. Surely empathy shouldn't be this hard.

"Hey cutie, what's your name?" I said, stroking her foot with my thumb. Cutie. I swear, I've never used that in my life, and never will again. It's the first thing that came to mind. I wish it hadn't, but I'm committed to it now. I'm not convinced of what I was thinking, stroking her feet, either. Is that even appropriate? I meant for it to be sincere, not creepy. I can't manufacture or muster a legitimate American accent. Everything sounds softer in caramel tones. The little girl squints up at me through pained eyes, complete disregard. She hasn't answered me. This girl knows I'm only offering my help because I hope to explore Alyssa's wet warmth.

"Megan." Said Alyssa answering on her behalf.

"Of course," I said.

Alyssa looks at me, surprised.

Yet another stereotypical American name. I would have been happier if my response had remained in my steely mind. Alyssa's face says it all. Some things are better left unsaid. The epitome of every American stereotype going. In fact, the entire camp is. I should have known from the start. I shouldn't be surprised. This is an American camp for American children after all.

The bastard medical centre, my second time here. They're going to know me by name at this rate. We reach that flimsy loud set of double doors. Thank God we're here. Although Megan is light, my arms are aching now. I grab at the door handle and swing it open. We manoeuvre inside, Megan still floppy in our arms. It seems melodramatic. Weird, there's no one else here, oddly quiet. No noise except the limp weight of Megan's body, causing the blue plastic chair legs to scrape across the vinyl floor under her weight. The plastic chairs you get in school canteens, cheap spindly metal legs, no consideration for comfort. Some parts of this camp are so dank and dreary. I wouldn't have expected such cheap crap. It reminds me of my youth club, as a kid, the one on Southbrook Street, filled with haunted spirits, jaded dreams and spoilt aspirations for the future. A no hope life of failed ambition.

A woman with husky like, pale blue sunken eyes appears from an open doorway and approaches us. Megan still flopped in the chair, only held up by Alyssa's lose free hand. I gave up trying to support her ages ago.

Here I am, stood in this makeshift reception area. Old black and white pictures of previous camp years plaster the walls. I look at this attractive, albeit shifty, doctor. She raises her eyebrows, stretching her eyes wide as if experiencing the Ludovico technique. She must be tired. The skin under her eyes is like the crust of a pasty, purple and puffy.

"I'm Doctor Dumbarton." She said, squinting her eyes wider, as if to focus on us. Her forehead scrunched like paper.

I don't recognise her from earlier. Although, I'm sure a smashed window isn't that big a deal if you're tending to a sick child. That's the hope. She's quite young looking, young enough to get away with wearing red shorts. She's probably got a cracking belly button under her white jacket too. She looks serious. Stockard Channing in Six Degrees of Separation comes to mind. Her hair is all tied up and swept from her face. I'm looking her over. Every woman I meet, I'm interested. She doesn't really do anything for me. Well, she does a little. Doctor patient scenario wouldn't go amiss.

"Hi y'all, too hot for her?" she said. She looks down at Megan, limp in the chair, her feet dangling over the edge.

"She's been vomiting." Said Alyssa, her hand to her mouth "She's really weak."

"Have you seen her vomit?"

Alyssa screws her face up, almost insulted by the question.

"Yeah, I was there the second time," said Alyssa.

"What colour was it?"

"Clear," said Alyssa.

The doctor kneels down in front of Megan, looking up into her vacant eyes.

"She's dehydrated," I said. As if I know what I'm talking about.

The doctor looks at me, then eyes Alyssa.

Not sure she agrees with that.

"What activities has she done?" said the Doctor.

"I don't know. We did ropes, then gymnastics." Said Alyssa.

"Has she had a bump on the head?" The doctor, jabs her finger and thumb onto Megan's eyelids, opening them wide.

"Not that I'm aware of," said Alyssa.

Megan's eyelids fight to stay open.

"She looks to be concussed. She wasn't knocked out?" said the doctor, turning her head back to the two of us, her eyes prompting a response.

"No," said Alyssa.

Megan groans, sounding like a distant bumble bee.

"Right, I think it's time we get you to hospital."

Doctor Dumbarton stands up, grabbing for a set of car keys. She quickly sweeps down and shoves her hands under Megan's arms and takes her off the chair, out the main doors in one swift, flashing movement.

Alyssa jolts forward to hold the doors open, following her out. I guess that means I'd better follow too. I jump forward to stop the door from slamming against the frame and get out of the medical centre, right behind Alyssa.

"She'll be fine." Doctor Dumbarton says, reaching out for the passenger car door.

Alyssa gets alongside and holds the door open as wide as it will go on the hinges.

Doctor Dumbarton wrestles with the seat belt, clicking it into place. As she does, she rubs her finger and thumb across Megan's chin.

"You'll be OK, button face." She said, pulling the door closed, wrenching it from Alyssa's fingers, slamming it shut.

"What hospital you taking her to?" said Alyssa.

"Harlem Valley. It's the closet."

"Hopefully she's all right," I said.

I'm so going to console Alyssa. Slow back rubs, slow in the small of her back will help. Nice.

"I hope so." Said Alyssa, tears threatening to escape.

I wrap my arms around her and give her a hug, a subtle squeeze. She accepts my advances and falls into my arms.

"She's OK," I said.

Her shoulders tremble. She's not making much noise. She turns away from me, my arms thrown to my sides. Doctor Dumbarton runs around the car.

"Don't worry." She said, propelling herself around the bonnet. "You've been a huge help."

She propels herself to the driver's side and winds down the window. The car engine erupts with a vibrating roar. The Doctor grapples with the steering wheel as she speeds off, kicking up dust from the tyres, soon disappearing out the back road, past all the staff and catering quarters concealed by the dense treeline.

* * *

Back inside the medical centre. Alyssa picks up a phone receiver.

"What's the admin office number?" she said.

"I have no idea," I said.

She looks for anything that could resemble a directory on the front reception desk.

"There must be a number here somewhere." She said, as she rifles through papers, her eyes caught by pictures of doctors who have previously served in the Medical Centre. The picture she's fixated on dated: 'Summer 1983'.

"What is it?" I said.

Alyssa hasn't reacted. She's staring ahead at the picture on the wall. We both stand in silence, she sniffs.

I've only just noticed they've boarded up the broken window with a piece of cardboard and duct tape.

"This picture," said Alyssa, like she's in a trance.

"What about it?"

"Doesn't this girl." She points, pausing. "Look like that, doctor?"

The front doors open with a crash.

A woman shoves herself inside. She jumps at the sight of us. She's clutching a large bowl in the shape of a dog's head, a Bassett hound, spooning what looks to be pale yellow custard into her mouth. She slurps and makes a clanging noise with her teeth as they crack against the metal spoon.

"Can I help you guys?" She asks, wiping her mouth with her sleeve.

"I think we're all good now, thanks," I said.

Alyssa turns around, sniffing again. Her eyes are red. She puts the phone receiver down.

"Megan went to hospital," said Alyssa.

The woman stares for a second. She bolts forward, shoving her dog shaped bowl on the corner of the front desk.

"Megan?" She asks, reaching for the phone. "Megan

McKenzie?"

"Yeah, how d'ya know that?" said Alyssa, surprised.

"Who took her to the hospital?"

"Doctor Dumbarton," I said.

"OK, you two need to leave." The woman jams numbers into the phone with her stubby index finger. "Did she say which hospital?"

"Harlem Valley," said Alyssa.

The woman spins on the spot.

"What?"

She knocks her bowl off the edge of the desk. It crashes to the floor. Shards of ceramic basset hound fly up, splatters of custard spread across the floor near my feet. Alyssa jumps back to avoid the yellow gloppy mess.

"What's up, is she OK?" asks Alyssa.

"There's no hospital in Harlem Valley. That's a veterinarian," said the woman, as her face turns milky white.

"What?" Alyssa shakes her head. "What are you saying?" Her trembling hand pressed against her mouth.

"She's fine." Said the woman, shuffling the phone in her hand, putting it to her ear. "Don't worry."

One ring.

"You can both go."

Two rings.

"Get to flagpole."

The phone connects.

"You need to…" Said the woman ushering us out through the front doors, we skate on the slippery custard. "Get here now." She said into the phone. Her palm pushed into my shoulder, her other hand grips the back of Alyssa's arm.

We're outside. Back over my shoulder, with the woman gone. She's talking inside. I can't hear what she's saying.

Alyssa stands for a second, shaking her head and tries to

listen in. I place my hand affectionately on her forearm, that's genuine. I do care now. Well, I'm trying to. I lead her away from the veranda of the medical centre. She sobs uncontrollably, her shoulders rattling, as if she's riding a horse's cart.

"What the fuck?" she said, with an inability to breathe properly.

I search myself for an answer. I can't answer that. I honestly have no idea what just happened in there. What did just happen?

"We did the right thing," I said.

I'm trying to reassure Alyssa. I don't know this girl, but I know within myself I don't want to see her upset. I have no interest in that.

"Seriously, she wasn't well." Said Alyssa lifting her wrist to her nose, to hide her embarrassment as she continues to cry.

I pull her into me again to console her. For once, I don't have the feeling I want to manipulate her or make an advance. I'm genuinely concerned for her. I think she did the right thing. In fact, we both did. A little girl was ill. Sure, I thought she was being a bit of a malingerer and playing up.

"It's OK." I place my palm on the back of her head. "Seriously, she's in expert hands," I said.

As we're standing here in the shadow of the medical centre, lost in confusion. A golf cart comes towards us at speed. It's spraying up dust along the dirt track. Three men running at full pelt too, their feet clipping their backsides. Something's going on here. They're all followed by a cloud of dust. I won't draw attention to them. I'll pretend I haven't seen them. The dilemma now is how the hell Ilm gonna make sure she doesn't see the commotion behind us. It could be too late. You can hear the audible battery powered golf cart getting closer.

Alyssa pushes me away.

Bill and Monte arrive in a golf cart, red faced and sweating. The cart comes skidding to a halt on the grass. They disappear into the medical centre. The door slamming shut behind them.

"What's happening?" Said Alyssa, throwing her arms in the air.

Three more senior counsellors come running behind them. Alyssa drops to her knees, sobbing. It's disturbing to see how scared and emotional she is. Megan's not her kid.

I approach one of the guys

"What's going on?" I said.

Whoever this guy is, he's about a centimetre from my nose.

"You don't need to know." He said through gritted teeth.

This place is a fucking joke. I'm no longer able to react how I ordinarily would, fractured rationality. I mean, if someone got in my face at home, out on the street. I swear I'd at least say something. I'm at the mercy of this place. If I kick off, I'll be kicked out. That would be far worse than swallowing my pride and keeping my head down. I'm not likely to win with these people. This isn't Deliverance or The Hills Have Eyes. These are normal people, normal in that they aren't disturbed. They're here to be supervising responsible adults. I've seen little that I'd ever want to aspire to from any of these fucking people.

Alyssa's going crazy, still crying.

The entire atmosphere has changed. She needs to suck it up.

I take her by the arm as she continues to flail. I pull her to the side of the Medical Centre, having to yank her up. She's being resistant, it's for her own good.

"You need to calm down, seriously." I said, looking her right in her concerned wet eyes.

"What's the matter with her, where is she?" She said, in a tone that begs only for reassurance. The tone of a mother-to-be. Unrequited love; lost only in guilt.

"She's in the best hands," I said.

The medical centre front door slams shut, Bobby comes running out. I didn't even see him go in. He jumps in a golf cart, zips past us and stops.

"Nothing to worry about, she's OK. Go get some food." He said, pointing in the canteen's direction. His foot slams on the pedal of the golf cart, he jerks off into the distance. Odd he's being nice.

"See, she's fine," I said.

I lean into Alyssa and give her the corner of my T-shirt sleeve to wipe her eyes on. She manages to chuckle and sniffs. She takes me up on the offer, wiping her eyes.

"Don't blow your nose on it," I said.

That should hopefully lighten the mood. Everyone likes a bit of levity.

Alyssa sniffs, a small saliva bubble rolls out of her mouth, caught by the wind.

She notices it float away and sniggers to herself.

We begin to walk away from the medical centre, following the path to wherever it takes us. I'm listening to everything she's saying to me. She seems distracted, looking back over her shoulder as if she's hoping Megan will magical reappear.

Our conversation is poignant, at least to me. We aren't talking about other people. We're not speculating or gossiping. It's us being ourselves. Insignificant minute details about life and living. Existentialism shalt rear its head. She's confident in Kierkegaard and Jean-Paul Sartre. Books that I only explored because they were a pound in a charity shop.

I found Hazel, Hazel Valentine agreeable too. Her name still gets me. I'm weak. All these people, the women. The free advice, the American Dream. So many choices in life. I've never been so disorientated, even having attended orientation for a week. No more orientated with life in my head.

Alyssa will become another distraction. I need distractions to cope with life. What am I searching for? I have thoughts of emptiness, then I'm filled with conflict, guilt, and excitement all rolled into one blonde, body beautiful girl of Alyssa.

Through silence, my potentially misinterpreted romance and introspection. We're getting to know each other. We near the entrance to the boys' side of the canteen. The boys from lower camp are running up and down the steps outside, some rolling on the grass with excitement, waiting to eat.

"Have I made you miss getting something?" said Alyssa, pointing up to the double doors of the canteen.

"Nah, I don't think so. No more than I have you. I'll walk you," I said. I need to drop her off. Not right for me not to offer to walk her. Thankfully, she accepts. We walk in sync, our feet mirrored in pace. I always love it when that happens.

"Try not to worry about Megan." I said, touching her forearm.

"I want to know she's OK," she said.

"I know you do, she's fine," I said. "Trust me. Like I said she's in the best hands." I give her arm a gentle squeeze.

She tickles her hand on mine, then let's go. She uses her index finger to brush her right nostril in a controlled, and I must admit not entirely sexy way. I think she's more comfortable with me. Anyway, it doesn't matter. I still find her a pure soul. Although, I hope she doesn't wipe her nose like that again. Unless that means she's going to friend zone me. No, not possible. Too many good signs.

"It was nice to meet you, Derek. I better go," she said.

"Derek?"

"That was a joke," she said.

Does she know my real name? She didn't correct it. No, she knows it. Of course she does. She was joking. She knows my name. I could test her. No need, she's smiling. She was joking. Damn, I'm not sure.

Alyssa turns and walks up the wooden steps to the girls' canteen. She's pensive in her steps. I really hope she turns around and does that whole over the shoulder looking back thing.

One. Two. Three.

Score. She looked back at me, a gentle goodbye gesture.

I nod my head in acknowledgement. I can't go crazy and have her thinking I want her naked on the salad bar.

The canteen doors open. The raucous noise of a room full of girls talking, laughing, and eating crashes out. Almost destroying my ears, Alyssa walks in. The noise then reduces like a lid closing on the rumbling bubbles of boiling water on a stove. Damn, she's fine.

I'm a little offended she would rather eat grilled cheese sandwiches than talk to me. Should I be hurt? I'm hungry myself. I could have forgone a snack. I'll have to convince myself it's less about me and more about the little girl they entrusted her to take care of. Still, wasn't our fault. We could have carried on our chat. A grilled cheese sandwich over a nice English spoken chat.

My feet step up on the bottom rung of the stairs to the boys' canteen. I'm not even sure why grilled cheese is even a thing over here. We have cheese on toast. But grilled cheese? Most of the time it's done in a frying pan, so not even grilled. It's fried bread. I get the cultural significance of it. I was brought up on films like Mr. Mom and the suggestion that the most convenient food source would be a lovingly prepared grilled cheese sandwich. In fact, he uses an iron to prepare it. It's a funny scene, still doesn't make me want to eat grilled cheese fucking sandwiches.

13

Laura

I don't worry about Laura, I'm not concerned with hurting her. I don't she cares about hurting me. That may say a lot more about me and even more about our relationship. But then again, I'm young. This is an opportunity of a lifetime, to experience a bit of the world and meet new people. I may even meet someone that I genuinely fall in love with. Not that I don't love Laura, I do. But, we've been together for about a year. I'm not sure I'm gonna marry her, she's beautiful and I miss her sometimes. I miss the physicality of our relationship, more than anything. I enjoy it, I miss it, I want it.

It would be wholly inappropriate if I were to enter the cabin with an erection. I'll avoid lingering thoughts of being inside Laura, as I imagine her nibbling her lip and clenching my buttocks in her hands.

It confuses me how my mind works, as vivid as that thought is in my head. Bang, it's gone. I enjoyed that.

I can't ever get my pants off fast enough. I live for the initial inhalation from a girl when I enter her, the warm breath followed by ravenous kissing. Really gets me, that fingertip entwined passion.

Shit. I'm almost at the cabin. Right, seriously, get this out of my head. The more I think about it, my stiffness is going nowhere, perfect.

The cabin door swings open. I raise my palm to stop it slapping me in the face. My reaction speed surprises me. Any arousal I was experiencing disappears.

"Oh, shit." Said Doug poking his head around the door. "Sorry Dawg, wassup?"

"Not much man, had a late snack, I've been putting out fires all over the place." I said with deliberate exaggeration.

"Nah-uh, what 'appened? I've been up in here with these guys." Doug said, shuffling on the spot. "I'm dying for a shit and can't leave 'em."

"Where's Benedict?" I said.

"I have no idea, dawg. You good with them?" He rocks on his feet. "I got to concentrate for this one."

He holds open the door as I follow him inside the cabin. He wiggles in desperation and rushes toward the toilet. The door slams shut, followed by the click of the lock. His flip flop feet poke out from under the door, he's wearing white socks. His shorts peeled down over his ankles. Pretty safe to say, he's having a shit.

I'm now alone in here with these kids, that's scary. I've had very little engagement with them so far. I'm not scared of them, but what the fuck are we going to talk about? I mean, really? They all appear independent. I could always jump up on my bunk and read a book. I haven't touched Malcolm X yet, accept to stand it back upright.

Josh is sat on his bed. He looks upset again. Jesus. Why me? His body hunched and mangled with worry. It's best to ignore him. If he cries again, I don't know what I'll do. He'll be fine. Shit, now I feel guilty. For fuck's sake, his shoulders are shuddering again. I'm getting used to this. Thing is, he was fine a second ago. He wipes his nose with the tip of his erect finger, more like a flick, so awkward. What is my problem with people and wiping their noses? Freaks me out. The movement always seems premeditated. Not that he's faking it. It's an odd way to wipe a tear away or dab at your nose.

"Hey Joshy, what's up fella?" I said, cheerfully.

No idea why I said 'fella' either. Don't know why I called him 'Joshy'. I'm overthinking all this. I'm not good with kids. Why on earth am I here on this friggin' camp? I'm so uncomfortable with all this. His shoulders keep doing that irritating thing, up and down shudder, shudder, shudder. He doesn't want to talk. Trust me, nor do I, kid. He keeps looking off into the distance. I'll give him sympathy with my eyes. I sit down beside him. Our shoulders almost touching, I'm having to hold my weight awkwardly so not to touch his resting arm with my thigh. I'm not sure how convincing I'll be with sympathy. I don't think he cares either way.

"So, you don't want to talk to me?" I said, watching his bottom lip quiver.

Not sure I'm cut out for this bullshit, I can get him to talk. I should try.

"I know it's hard for you to understand me." I said, leaning my shoulder into his playfully. "What with the accent and everything," I said.

No reaction. I'll try to be funnier.

"What if I was to speak like y'all." I said, plastering on my best Southern accent, like I'm a bean eating cowboy, yeeha.

Still nothing from him.

"Come now, cowboy, this town ain't big enough for the both of us."

Honestly, no idea what I'm doing. A Woody impression?

Didn't work anyway, he's still crying. Wouldn't work on me either.

"I just wanna go home," he said.

His words are music to me. I know that feeling, brother. I know exactly what you mean. Shit, tell me about it. I would much rather be at home than dealing with your shit. It's so uncomfortable to have someone cry incessantly, especially a kid. This isn't fun, can't be fun for him either.

"Its early days. Give it a chance, mate," I said.

Perhaps I should tell myself that too. My god, if I could, I'd leave with Alyssa or Hazel right now. It'll be like we escaped this fucking hell hole together. That would be romance right there. I want to share an experience with someone. For now, anyone will do.

Josh sniffles. "I miss my mum," he said. "I hate this camp." His bottom lip vibrates. "I told 'em last year. I said, I didn't want to come." He pauses and makes a wailing noise. "They made me come, anyway!"

Big tears now. Oh joy, some of the other boys look round at Josh crying. It's hard to ignore.

"Why do you think they made you come back a second year, didn't you like anything?" I said, waving my hands at the onlookers, shooing them away. Their heads spin back to their card game.

Josh didn't notice. His head is down. The last thing he wants is an audience as he bawls like a baby.

"My dad came here. It's a family thing." He said, sobbing.

"Red Oak family for generations," he said.

"I know how you feel. I'm away from home for months too. I miss my family. I miss my girlfriend, lord." I look up, "Do I miss her?" I stab my finger into my chest "Think about me when you're chilling at home in a few weeks. I'll still be stuck here." I said, nudging him again with my shoulder.

He sniffs and chuckles, humouring me.

"Yeah, I guess. How you gonna do it?" He said, looking up at me with soaked eyelashes.

"I have no clue mate." I shake my head "I'm gonna keep my head down. try to have some fun, not take things too seriously," I said.

"Good luck." He said, looking right at me. "You're gonna need it."

He's being oversensitive. It can't be that bad.

"When this camp gets going. You'll wanna leave too," he said.

Whatever. I'm not taking him seriously, he's a kid. What does he know? He can't tell me shit. This little miserable bastard is trying to educate me.

It's so difficult to maintain this palaver of professionalism, act like I care. If he wants to go, fucking let him go. Here comes the fakery.

"You ain't got long. Then you're free. If you can try to have fun." I think for a second and spot my baseball glove. "I'll give you my catcher's mitt at the end," I said.

I'm not entirely sure I mean that, but it'll cheer him up a little. Even if it is a false promise, he'll forget anyway.

"You serious?" he said.

He's turned far too excited. I might have to give it to him, damn it.

I nod my head. That's my glove gone then, it'll lighten the load. I can always buy another one.

"I don't want to carry it with me afterward. I wanna travel light, ya know." I said, smiling.

He nods, "Deal."

In any other story, this kid would have got up, smiled with some cheesy grin, and hugged me. This, though, is reality. Instead, he gets up and fucks off. He picked up a pack of cards, shuffling them.

As fast as that, all the drama, all the tears now over. All off the promise of a catcher's mitt. I'll have to remember that.

The toilet door bangs shut, the spring on it is as strong as the spring on the back door. I swear it's dangerous, fingers and kids, all that slamming. Obviously, they're trusted enough to avoid death by door.

Doug glides into the room. I assume he's washed his hands. I won't ask. He's cupping his slight belly over his shirt, as if he's delivered a baby with satisfied relief plastered all over his face.

"Woah, damn. I needed that." He said, letting air out of his mouth as if he was inflating a tyre.

"So, dawg, you were saying, what happened, where were

you?" Said Doug, in one breath as he neared his bed, sitting down on the edge. He kicks off his flip flops and lays down, forearm behind his head, looking expectantly at me for a response. I sit parallel to him.

"Well, I met this girl," I said.

"Right, go on. Was she hot?" he said.

"Well, I met a couple of girls."

"Shit. Go on." His eyes now wider.

"She kind of reminds me of my girlfriend Laura, so yeah, pretty hot," I said.

I'm lying again. I didn't consider Laura once, I rarely do.

"Dawg, you missed us for a girl?" He said. "She had better be hot. I wouldn't miss eating for no one." Doug said and pulled on a baseball cap.

"We had a good chat, but something kicked off at the medical centre," I said.

Doug frowns, he's intrigued. Much like I am with the whole situation. How am I going to explain it? It was weird. It really was. The whole thing was different. Even if I relive it in my head. It still makes little sense.

As I explain, Doug lost interest. He didn't consider it a big deal. He isn't bothered. Should I be?

The boys in the bunk do their own thing as we talk.

I keep thinking about my loneliness. I can see Doug's mouth moving, but everything else is a blur. It's a strange sensation to be talking to someone face to face, but still be utterly alone. I like and respect Doug, but can I call him a friend? We've only been in each other's company for a few days. Can I trust this guy? It's hard to see the good in anyone when you're left to fend for yourself. I've been thrown into this situation, and they expect everyone to think the same way. I can't do that, it's not even a possibility. I keep telling myself the only reason I'm here; is to live my dream and travel after all this is done. If I can do that with someone that looks better than Laura. Then I'll take that opportunity. I'm gagging for the chance to feel someone again, to feel anything.

Why is life so hard?
It's the wild west, a fucking wilderness.

14

Salacious Guilt

I'm committed now, cigarettes in my back pocket, lighter in hand. Doug and Benedict can entertain themselves. I'm going for a smoke; I owe it to myself. My addiction clawing at me. I won't be able to think straight until I'm having to clear my throat for the rest of the evening.

In the dark depths of the woods. I embrace these moments of freedom. I shouldn't be out of the cabin. I got away with it before. What if I'm not as lucky this time?

I have four and a half cigarettes left in this pack. Shrouded in the shadows of these trees, cigarette now in hand. I delicately navigate through the woods, planting my palm on the dry trees, to avoid making noise. It's too dark to be seen. I shield the sparking flash from the lighter through cupped hands. That first intake is, as ever, the best. Always get past that wooded smoke flavour. Even when I don't smoke for ages, I love that first taste; it never puts me off. It's not torturous, just familiar. Cigarettes always taste different in America. No idea what that is or even what causes it?

The woods have made me lose all sense of direction, I'm

disorientated. There's the main baseball field. I'll walk that way, it'll give me a chance to have another smoke. If I'm caught out here, I'll have to come up with some excuse. I was out looking for my baseball shed keys, or I thought I heard a noise. Bridge and I shall cross when questions arise.

I've finished that fag off in about three pulls. I was enjoying it that much. Smoking a cigarette is almost like meditation. I'm consciously considering every breath. Arguably fucking bad for you, but it allows me to explore myself. I really think I should do it more often. I stub the dog end out on a narrow tree trunk.

There's a dull thud of a noise behind the baseball field. Sounds like it came from the store shed.

Crash.

Again, as if someone dropped a ten ton barbell to the floor. It looks from here as if the door is wide open. No one would rob from the baseball shed, there's fuck all in there worth stealing, a stack of mats, bins of gloves, baseballs and helmets. Baseball shit, that's it.

I roam the perimeter of the field, dodging between spindly trees. I can hear a much louder, audible commotion. Hushed voices and the shuffling of feet on grit covered metal. Orgasmic sounds come from the shed. A female releasing a fuck noise. Now I'm intrigued. There's certainly a girl in there, and based on the repetitive rhythmic rattling, metal on metal, she isn't alone either, unless she's pleasuring herself with a baseball bat.

"Arghhhhhh."

Confirmed, she's not alone. A male, deep sounding groan, another fuck noise. A breathy grunt. I'll stay here in the shadows of the woods, sidestep along until I'm in line with the opening of the shed. Sex noises being stifled and shushed.

The silhouette of a naked, smooth back gyrates, straddling two thick, hairy legs, stiff under her bare bottom, shorts pulled down to his ankles, white trainers with high socks still on.

I can't see who it is, but my dick doesn't care. I'm not even in control. Immediately, I have a hard-on. More female gasping noises, as the thumping rhythm gets quicker. I flip my shorts over, and like the pages of a children's pop-up book, my hard dick is throbbing, begging me to clasp my fingers and thumb around its veiny shaft. I indulge myself.

How lucky am I to be seeing this shit?

I defy anyone not to be intrigued by this. Could be anyone in there, I don't care. This is hot. If only I had a camera, better still my video camera, 8mm Sanyo sex tape.

I need to keep this vision with me, always. I have my cigarette squeezing between my lips. I roll my palm and stroke in time with the rhythm from inside the shed. I don't need to imagine it's me in there, feeling the tight, warming constriction of that woman. I'm happy with watching. I inhale nicotine, indulging my voyeurism. The fact that this girl is on top, riding, naked. The moonlight reflecting off pale skin. Now she's shifting. That's right baby, turn around, reverse cowgirl.

Laura does none of this shit.

Their faces remain in the darkness. The shafts of light enhance her areola. I imagine rolling her nipples between my thumb and forefinger. The face is irrelevant at this stage, just that warm moistness around my dick is enough. It seems watching wasn't enough. My imagination always wants to get involved.

"Yes, Yes. Yes." She squeaks.

Some wild noises. It sounds to me like she's close to climaxing. I hope she is. I'm gonna come in a second. She could be acting. If she is, she's doing a superb job. Yet again, here I am being a deviant. This is my first experience into actual voyeurism, and I really like it. The fact I can hear her noises too is sending me delirious. I want to prolong this, but I need to come. I like to hear everything. This is real.

The noise stops.

"Can you smell cigarettes?" Said the female voice in an American accent.

"Shut the fuck up," said a male voice.

Shit. I'm too close.

A slapping noise crackles out, followed by a loud intake of shocked breath.

"Again," she said. "Come on."

Another slap, like boxing gloves on a cow's carcass.

I squint as the cigarette smoke blows in my eyes. I have my left hand cupping my testicles and the other hand maintaining a breathy rhythm.

They keep going. I keep going. The point of no return reached in me. Smoke making my eyes itch. Burnt ash drops from the tip, showering ash over my white shirt.

"Shit," I said.

My only reaction, I want to cuss myself for saying it aloud. They could have heard me. Luckily, based on the volume of their moans, they've heard nothing. I'm so close to coming, she's making all the right noises.

The mystery guy in there releases a strained whistling noise. I think he's done. No, he isn't. Still going, expulsions of grunts and deep breathing. She's so close.

"Wait for me," I whisper. "Wait for me."

My body stiffens with tension, my hand gripping tighter.

"Ohhhhh," she moans.

Her noise stifled, he must have put his hand over her mouth, smothered yelps of climax.

My body jerks forward, my back arches, I'm coming. I roll forward on the balls of my feet, heels off the ground, my eyes rolling back in my head as I grit my teeth. I continue to jerk, breathing deeply, only through my nose. If I open my mouth, I'm going to make too much noise. It hurts to come, like all the blood in my body has rushed to my head.

That was awesome. I have myself all over my hands, trickling like warm egg white through my fingers. Twigs crackle beneath my heels.

"What was that?" she said.

"No idea, I heard it too."

They nervously turn around, looking out from the doorway. They can't see me, it's too dark. They scrabble for their clothes. I bolt to the left and edge behind an enormous tree trunk. Big enough to hide me. They didn't hear anything. I pull my shorts over my weeping nob, wiping my palms on my thighs. I need to catch my breath.

The male voice blurts. "I forgot how tight you are."

How grotesque do you have to be, man?

Just be grateful. Dirty bastard. Fair comment though.

They can't see me. I'm intrigued to know who I wanked off to.

"What did you expect, it's only been a year?" She said, with a high-pitched, immature voice.

"A year is a long time to wait," he said.

That male voice is deep, imposing, and I swear familiar. Who is that?

"Amped." The girl says. "I missed you. I thought you might ignore me."

I edge my head from behind this tree. I see a bandaged arm pulling on a white blouse, almost like a Dutch looking top, all frilly around the sleeves. The blouse drops down over a flat, toned navel with a pierced belly button. She flicks her hair from under her collar.

"Seriously," she said. "I can still smell smoke."

"Let's get out of here." He said, pulling a baseball hat over his head as he ducks down out from inside the shed. Tall stature. I can't see his face or her face.

I need to hide.

This guy is much larger than the girl.

"Abyssina," he said.

Their fingertips touch as they part ways, at arm's length. They may as well be on the ceiling of the Sistine Chapel. The girl strides toward Silver Wood, and he heads off up the hill toward Red Oak.

Holy shit. I can't believe I've seen two people having sex. I want to crash my head against a tree. What did I just do?

I'm disappointed in myself.

It'll be worth it.

But, for now, my salacious guilt.

15

Monotony

One day merges and moulds into the next. Today, outside, it smells like maple syrup, sometimes Mickey Mouse cookies, other times horse manure. Here goes:

Bugle.

Shower.

Breakfast.

Flagpole.

Cabin chores.

Activity.

Lunch.

Rest.

Activity.

Snack.

Activity.

Dinner.

Evening Social.

Lights out. Sleep. Thank the lord. That's every day.

I teach little bastards stuff they know better than me. Fucking ungrateful kids. I listen to their shit. I'm surrounded by so many confusing accents. It's a muddle of misunderstandings.

Loud voices, loud kids voices, everywhere. There's all the shouting from authoritative figures. Light rain, hot sun. It's windy more than I thought. Then I miss Laura. The word 'Gentlemen' makes me cringe. I miss my family. I drink water that tastes of stale ice cubes. I swig water from a plastic shared jug. I miss my bed at home. Usually, that happens on a Thursday. I still don't understand why. The cabin smells of Deet and coconut sunscreen. I don't enjoy showers anymore. I rush to get dressed. I spend most of my time in queues, for everything, food, drink, the toilet and I hate every time I hear a queue referred to as a 'line'. Being locked in this place, the world gets smaller.

My body is in the canteen again. Surrounded by kids and counsellors. I think it's dinnertime. I can't be sure as it's always light outside until late in the evening.

Noise. Noise. Noise all around me. It's like a chicken coup, warm gobbles. I stare into the empty reverb of lost voices. A group of senior adult counsellors are all standing around a table in the centre of the room. We filled the seats at each table with the children of the cabins. The room is loud, the raw sound of young children talking, laughing, and joking.

Loud, Loud and louder.

The dazzling female Polish kitchen staff are standing quiet, subservient, with towels draped over their arms, ready to remove the metal lids off the buffet style containers. I don't feel like I'm present. I wish I wasn't.

Rod, with his thick rat like moustache, walks from his stationary position behind the table, with his arm pointed at an angle into the air. The laughable salute.

Several of the other senior staff members raise their hands, emulating Rod.

"Gentlemen." Said Rod at the top of his voice, so loud it's intimidating.

You can see it coming. He digs down deep. His shoulders raise and his neck becomes red. When you see that, time to brace yourself.

The room stops silent. I swear I can hear heartbeats. His voice is booming. Ridiculously loud. Still quiet. The entire room still. Even all the caterers and the Polish twin sisters are all observing his demands. Everybody around the room, I swear, must be holding their breath. I am too.

Most of the kids have their heads down to avoid any wrath or alienation from Rod. He's slowly walking around. Step by step, his arm still flat palmed and raised high into the air. He's circling round the centre table like a crazed bobcat glaring through the frames of his glasses.

"Gentlemen, let me remind you. As soon as my hand goes up." He said, pauses and slowly steps around in the little area he's created under his feet. Put him in a courtroom drama and he'd be delivering his closing statement right about now.

"That means you shut your damn mouths." He said, erupting.

The word 'Damn' sounds better coming from the mouths of Americans. There's more life in the words, a real damnation.

Doug is standing opposite me, his eyes are closed. He hasn't been sleeping well, he won't get much sleep standing up though.

He's opened his eyes and noticed my smirk. He hasn't reacted. Doug is hard to read. He's so chilled. I want to like him, he seems genuine.

"Gentlemen. I do not want to repeat myself. If we must, we'll go outside and come back in again. My hand is up, your mouths are shut." Said Rod, again. His voice cracking, laced with phlegm. He must smoke, he really must, he needs to have a good clear out, get rid of all that debris.

The room is quiet, so still.

He's got our attention. Speak for fuck's sake, speak. I wish I was brave enough to scream that. He's deliberately deciding not to say anything. He's looking for an excuse to kick us out. He'll keep us waiting. It's like a game. We're his cat toy and he wants to bat us about the head like an injured blue tit.

"Now gentlemen, we say Grace," said Rod. He extends three fingers in the air.

"Three." He lowers one finger. "Two." Lowers a second finger. "One." Clenched fist. "We thank."

The boys and counsellors join in with Rod and mutter along:

"God for the food we're about to receive."

I've never got that, having to say Grace. There seems to be no choice in it. Who are we talking to, anyway? I know it's supposed to be God, but I thought we were all past that. We know too much now. Apparently not. Still got people believing in magic.

As soon as Rod's last words are spoken, boys run towards the serving tables jostling for plates, the first ones to fill them and stuff their faces. Food glorious food, cold jelly and custard.

A queue forms. The boys help themselves to everything on offer, big patties piled up, they don't look appetising. There's pasta, it's not macaroni cheese, just Fusilli pasta with black olives thrown in. Next to that is some simmering tomato sauce, could be more of that aubergine with marinara sauce. I've been having that a lot. Slices of pizza. Some kind of charred fish, no idea what fish, it's skin down but fleshy, could be cod. I can read the label now, 'Tilapia'. Whatever that is, never heard of it. Fish anyway. Not really interested in any of that shit.

I'm struck by the salad bar today. It looks fresh as a dandelion. There's iceberg lettuce, tomatoes, radishes and pumpkin seeds. I'll probably have some of that. There's a small aluminium table pushed up against it with wrapped loaves of bread. White bread, brown bread and what looks to be a combination of the two, all wrapped in unbranded clear plastic. There's even that plastic cheese, the manufactured excuse for cheese, anyway. Far too orange to be natural, completely processed, resembling cartoon cheese not suitable for human consumption. Only the best for these kids.

After what is a melodramatic palaver, to get a couple of salad leaves, a piece of ham between brown bread and a cup of ice. I can comfortably sit around this table. We don't have to stand up and listen to Rod being a plank now.

I'm eating. The boys are eating. The room is distracted with the noise of clunking and clattering cutlery. Screeches of knives across plate surfaces, water jugs bashed down on pine. It's a real Tom Waits percussive fantasy.

It's hard to talk to anyone, it's so loud. The room is full of these children making noise as they eat, vying for the attention of their respective counsellors. Then, you have counsellors pontificating on world views, politics, history and sport.

I'm no braggart, it really meddles with my head when people try to assert themselves over others. There are so many vapid, banal conversations going on its hard to enjoy this fucking salad, which isn't all that great.

See, this is what this place is doing to me, it's making me a self-obsessed maniac. Narcissistic or desperate for any and every form of attention. I'm no better than one of these kids. I'm not inspired to have a conversation with any of them. I'm bored talking about baseball with Mark. I'm scared of saying the wrong thing to Josh, in case he cries. I can't stand Benedict, he eats like a pig, never wipes his mouth clean, talks with his mouth full. He slathers mayonnaise on everything too, so I can't get into a conversation with him. I can chat to Doug, although he's opposite me, starting a conversation would invite everyone sat around to get involved, which they always inevitably do.

I can't be bothered to explain everything. Sometimes, it's nice to say ass or titties out loud. I don't want to worry about the repercussions or these kids repeating it.

Without thoughtful conversation, my mind drifts all the time, all the livelong day. I know I read too much into everything. I'm becoming a victim of my obsession. Surely this isn't healthy. Is this environment making me see sex and sexuality in everything, or is this place merely exposing my hunger for debauchery and rebellion?

I'm surrounded by these kids, every minute of every day. Do you know how difficult that is? Perhaps it's because I'm having to perform like a Disney cast member, squeaky clean. No abrasion. I can't reveal my true personality. Through fear they'll realise I'm not the poster boy of sanctity that I'm presenting. I'm not the confident guy they interviewed over the phone anymore. I've got a voice like everyone else, I've become too afraid to use it. It's like I'm losing who I once was, or at least who I thought I was. I don't know what's acceptable. Any grasp on my reality is becoming deliberate, jaded and sarcastic for the sake of it.

Sometimes, I find the evenings so long here. The camp puts on activities, but not tonight. So, back to the fucking cabin for monotony, to our wooden prison.

Doug is laying on his bed, his normal position now, laying on his back. Baseball cap tilted down over his eyes, his right arm like a makeshift pillow, left hand resting on his chest. He must be one of those that have to take a nap after he eats, he sleeps a lot. Could be boredom. I've never understood that. It seems like such a waste of time.

Benedict, with his South African twat like ways, is laying on his bunk above Doug. I'm not sure I've seen them both in bed at the same time before. Not together, but they are both resting. What is that boredom? I never just want to lie down. I won't do it. Such a waste of valuable time. Soon we'll be old as balls. There has to be something we can do. All the other boys are laying on their beds, some chatting and messing about, almost whispering.

I need to brush my teeth after that bread. I have a weird taste in my mouth, kind of like when you take a multivitamin, that metallic dusty taste. I'm not entirely sure how most of these kids, despite constant encouragement, can't brush their teeth. I'm obsessed with cleaning my teeth. I can't sleep without that cool freshness hitting my throat. I feel repugnant with fiery breath when trying to sleep. You never know who you might run into. Clean teeth, clean bellend, simple rule.

The front door cranks open with a sudden jerk. Rod stomps inside the cabin. I think out of courtesy, I would have knocked. He never seems to follow etiquette. I understand it's a camp and they're in charge here, but I query how you can instil manners and politeness in anyone if you, yourself aren't showing how to enter a room nicely. Practise what you preach. That always gets my back up. You can see us through the front door fly screen.

Rod just bowls on in.

I don't want to give him my attention. That fucking nobhead wants to always be heard.

In the mirror, I focus my attention back to brushing my teeth. I can't see anything behind my eyes anymore. Toothpaste doing its best to escape my mouth. I'm staring at myself in the mirror, using my fingers to pull down on the puffy bags under my eyes. Rough, I look rough as balls. I've been sleeping OK and eating whatever it is I can muster.

Rod never attempts to lower his tone, even at night. All the kids are winding down and he enters like a Tasmanian devil.

"Gentlemen," said Rod.

All the boys look up with nerves from their individual peaceful activities. The cabin was quiet. The boys were entertaining themselves, 'were' being the operative word. Most with books. I haven't taken the time to understand what each of them likes to read, probably should. All I keep seeing are copies of Harry Potter strewn all over the place and it's annoying to see its been renamed over here. I love how they assume American's aren't intelligent enough to know what a philosopher is.

Let's just say, if one of them was rocking out a copy of anything by Noam Chomsky. I might then become interested in their personalities. Otherwise, when camp is finished. I'm never gonna see or communicate with any of these little people. Rightly so, surely that would be inappropriate. I wouldn't be surprised if email addresses are exchanged between counsellors and campers. That would be a weird one to explain to anyone.

I'm taking a lot of pictures, but it's weird to think when going through them, there will be random pictures of ten-year-old boys that I was at camp with. That's a hard one to explain out of context without the back story of Sleepaway America. 'Yup, that's flagpole, random kid. Me looking bored. Another random kid'. Too weird.

Some boys are wearing headphones, listening to personal CD players. I know Will has my Stone Roses CD. I'm listening to Bleed American. I'm seriously loving Authority Song. It's a great album. I keep going back to track ten all the time. Music here is my saviour.

No one was being boisterous before Rod entered. Our cabin was respectfully relaxed. He's made them all nervous, all before they go to sleep too. Don't have nightmares, kids. What a great way to interact with, what will one day be adults. When they themselves look back on this experience, I have no doubt they'll realise just how fucked up it was.

"Gentlemen. Lights out at nine o'clock. It's nine eleven," said Rod.

It's becoming so boring, it makes my skin crawl with impatience, a sizzling anger every time he uses that fucking word.

As he's burdened us with his stringent time keeping, I spit loudly into the sink. One that comes thick from the back of my throat.

"Goodnight, gentlemen." He said, more shouting it.

He walks toward the cabin door, lurches forward for the handle and pushes it open. Everything is performed with such aggression with him. His actions are forever bullish. He switches out the light with a snap of his index finger and the door slams, crashing shut with hate filled punctuation.

It's almost completely dark outside.

Still in this communal bathroom, I can hear the boys stirring for a couple more minutes. I rinse my toothbrush with the obsession it deserves. The mirror steams up. I don't store mine with the rest of these kids. I'm not leaving it in amongst that festival of bacteria. They've got them all stood up together in a shared, hand painted tin, a tin that once contained catering sized baked beans, a fun project for arts and crafts, a bit of upcycling, but not for me. I merrily store mine safely in a zip-lock bag hidden behind Malcolm X. I snap off the bathroom light, the cabin now dark, only lit from the moonlight outside. It teases me with its perennial possibilities.

There's some gentle whispering from one end of the cabin. I won't say anything, just kids being kids and they can talk as much as they want. As soon as my head hits the pillow. I'm out like the snap of that light switch. I quickly remove my T-shirt and shorts. When the sun goes down, it can get cold in here. It's one of those chilly nights tonight. I climb up onto the top bunk. I've manged to get this down to a fine art. I can jam my foot on the third ladder rung. As quick as that, I'm in bed, in one movement. I'm like Tom Hanks in *Big*. I need a glow in the dark compass ring. Mastering the movement of getting into bed helps me. I don't want my half-naked body to be seen by any of these boys. It disturbs me to think that any of them could peer wide-eyed from the opening of their sleeping bag. It's something I can half imagine myself doing if I was one of them. The intrigue of having a glance at my counsellor's bulge. It's probably just me, but as a kid I liked to imagine how my body might be shaped as an adult. I don't think you can go by your father's body, as he performs sit-ups in his underpants. A stranger's body provides more truth.

I slide down into my sleeping bag. I'm not too proud or embarrassed to have to climb up into a bunk bed. It's kind of weird how both Benedict and I are the ones having to sleep on the top bunk. All the kids have got their ground level beds. It gives a good supervisory view of everybody. I can see everyone except Josh. But then again, I can usually hear him whimpering into his pillow. At least I know he's in the cabin and not roaming about the woods, trying to escape, like I wish I could.

The moonlight illuminates my eyes. I can't close them, I almost don't want to. We have the wooden window shutters open again, to let the air flow through. We don't get many moths in here, which is good. I would have preferred it if the shutters were closed, because that moonlight usually shines in my eyes, if it's a clear night. The disadvantage of having a top bunk, I guess.

The cabin is quiet again. I've stopped fidgeting. I can hear my mind chugging around. It continues to race. What am I doing here? I grapple with guilt constantly. I tightly squeezed my arms into the side of my body, tucked up like a hibernating hedgehog. I move my right hand down over my hip bone and cup my testicles, squeeze them gently with a familiar titillation, massaging gently between my middle and third finger. With every extension of my fingers, my motion is silent. I can't indulge in real masturbation, the damn trappings of this sleeping bag material, too much rustling noise. It comforts me to feel myself, albeit over my underwear. It would be so good, a relaxing relief to touch the velvet texture of my testicle skin again.

I'll wake up tomorrow and do all this shit again. Sometimes I wish my eyes never opened.

16

Wet 'n Wild

In the morning shadow of this fucking white flagpole. Again, every day the same thing. I'm getting away with having my headphones on, listening to Bad Religion, Broken from the album The Process of Belief. I've always seen the cool kids wearing Bad Religion T-shirts, but never took the time to listen to their music. It's like those hot girls who throw on an AC/DC T-shirt, never actually realising they're a band. They don't even know what alternating current is. I have punk sensibilities in my ears. I am anarchy. With raw vocals and guitar chords thrashing in my ears. Here I am, dazed and confused. All right, all right, all right. Not had breakfast. I've had no time for any original thought, forever following orders. That's all I do now; stand, forever looking up. That expectation from ruling adults I should be submissive. Ask no questions.

That prick Rod and all the other senior counsellors stand in their usual customary spot; all in a line. They get to stand in the shade. It's early, still the sun is getting hot. I'm not sure what time it is, time is irrelevant. It keeps moving, that's all I know.

Rod steps in front of us, his cap shielding devilish eyes. The man can't be trusted. My spirit doesn't take to him. I better pause my musical escapism and take my headphones off. I don't want to draw attention to myself, unnecessarily.

"Gentlemen, activity day eleven," Said Rod.

That 'Gentlemen' thing again. I know it's coming, it's the not knowing when. I'm always shocked nowadays. Shocked because most of these boys, like a mob of hooligans, clap their hands automatically. There's no authentic emotion. Just this night of the living dead, a circle of dreary eyed kids. Most of the counsellors follow the lead of others like a braindead collective.

Only day eleven? This is dragging like a motherfucker. Seriously, come on now. I'm counting the days, not far off etching lines into my bed post. I'll be making a papier mâché head soon and stitching raincoats together to escape across the lake.

"Gentlemen," said Rod.

He said it again. He's already got our fucking attention. It's losing all impact. It no longer means English nobility or chivalry, like it once did. Now it sounds like a scornful way of harnessing attention through passive aggression. In fact, I'm uncertain it's passive, always aggressive. They're just kids.

"Next week, we'll be holding the boy of the bunk competition." He said in his raspy monotone.

The boys whoop. Some of them clearly know all about this. I don't even care. Boy of the bunk indeed, they're all pricks. "You have a few days left to show your counsellors and division leaders that you deserve this prestigious award."

Prestigious award, really? It's hardly an Oscar.

I turn looking at Doug, he's staring vacantly with his mouth wide open. I hope he isn't becoming one of them. His baseball hat tilted upward, sitting awkwardly on the crown of his head. He looks gormless. He's trimmed his goatee again, I never see him doing it. He must get up early.

I exhale air from my nostrils with a shocked, subtle laugh. I'm exasperated. Yet again, disbelief.

"Doug, mate, how much favouritism is encouraged here, how are we supposed to pick?" I said with my arms crossed.

"It's more about rewarding them." Said Doug, adjusting his baseball hat. "The other day, Rod came over at Lacrosse and picked out Kieran, gave him a pass to get as much candy as he wanted." He rubs his chin hair with the back of his knuckles.

"What a reward, a Mr Goodbar." I said, rolling my eyes.

"I know, right." Doug said, giggling. "They were three Musketeer bars." He clears his throat.

"Whatever. If we have to pick. I'd go with Josh."

"Josh?" Doug shrugged, as if he doesn't know who I'm talking about.

I thought he would be the obvious choice. Apparently not in Doug's book. Josh is whiny. Doug knows him better than I do. I guess we're almost like divorced parents, sharing custody at the weekends. Kind of like my life. I defy anyone to argue that, as a child of divorce, you always end up picking sides, my side is never fleeting. My mother knows that.

I can see Rod's lips flapping. I'm not hearing his voice. I'm uninterested in everything he has to say. I don't give a fuck anymore.

"Yeah. The way Josh has turned everything around, he's cool. Everyone else doesn't deserve shit. Little bastards," I said.

Doug swings round to face me, as if I interrupted his thoughts.

"Cool Dawg, I guess Josh has my vote too."

He's not a robot too, is he? He didn't put up much of a fight to suggest another kid. That was too easy. Quite the impressionable fellow is our Doug.

"The others are too entitled," I said.

They are posh little rich fuckers. At least Josh clears his own plate. Most of these kids have never lived hardship. I'm not saying I have, I've struggled a bit at uni, for money, having to sell VHS tapes at cash converters to buy a packet of super noodles and some fags. These kids haven't lived in the real world. They provide everything they could ever dream of to them. They don't even say thank you. It's all so trivial, life is a fairground to most of these kids. A stranger has not photographed them on a beach in their speedos. Never been followed as they search the shore for eroded glass chippings. The stranger with a lens, his hand rubbing under his lime green Bermuda shorts. Snapping away, capturing pictures of my childish shock and intrigue. I remember that man's face. He enters my mind whenever I hear the word 'tickle'. He kept saying it as he snapped photographs of me. The experience shaped me. I'm voyeuristically charged.

There it goes again, the flag rising to the top of the fucking flagpole. How it poetically dances in the wind. I can't continue to be enthusiastic about this cult bullshit, bowing down every day, twice a day even.

The flag is up. I think we proclaimed the pledge of allegiance. I can't be sure.

"Don't forget your water bottles. It's gonna be a hot one." Said Rod, as we all disperse. "Oh. Deet. Make sure you use Deet."

There's a rumble of distant murmurs of acceptance from us counsellors.

They've given me the opportunity between baseball sessions to check out some of the other camp activities. I have a free couple of periods, I need to try harder to socialise. So, I agreed to the offer. It's far easier to distract myself from my ever-growing apathy to get involved a little more. The camp is on the edge of a massive lake, the one I intend to escape across like Frank Morris. The water sports facilities are epic, I can admit that much. Most of the kids rave about each session they've had at the lake. That's often all I hear about at the dining table.

Sitting on the sandy shore, looking across the blue beauty. It really is stunning. Tree lined all the way around, a couple of gigantic houses set amongst them. The backyards stretch out into the water to jetties with small boats moored. One yacht named 'Guinevere'. I wonder who owns it. They can't live here year round, there's nothing

for miles. Where do they work? Manhattan, or across state lines in
Connecticut, New Haven or Hartford? Perhaps the institutes of
education and wealth, who knows? That's one hell of a daily
commute. I bet their jobs allow them to work from home, attending
meetings via satellite phone.

A speed boat skims across the lake, pulling in its white bubbly
trail, Geoff a thirteen-year-old boy. I recognise him from baseball, a
pretty good player. Good second base man. He doesn't suit the name
Geoff, that's an old man's name, but then it's the name he's been
given. His face is beaming, all teeth. I'm a proud parent. Am I wrong
about this place? Geoff is having the time of his life. Am I not
appreciating it? Am I going to revisit this in my memory and be
thankful for being here, for feeling lost? That feeling empty, so
restricted. I wrestle with being happy and then hate myself. Not truly
knowing who I am, wishing my time away and praying for my release,
I'm conflicted, my own worst enemy.

Some kids from our cabin run to me and check in, telling me
about what they're up to. They quickly shoot off after Doug and
Benedict. They're more used to their company than mine. Doug is
always getting involved. I need conversation more stimulating than,
'did you see that?' and 'were you watching?' These kids expect me
to act like their parent, act like I care. In fact, I'm a stranger. I'll never
see these kids again in the future and won't be putting any of their
finger paintings on my fucking fridge.

We move around between different activities, watch the boys
take part in golf and even I get involved. Even when swinging a golf
club and striking a ball, always a spectator. I'm never present. I'm
trying, I'm really trying to experience this and get involved. White golf
balls are being smacked down a straight driving range, swooping
across the grass and bouncing with playful innocence.

Lots of high fives and handshakes. I get encouragement, but
too much seems fake. High five after every stroke. Like saying 'thank
you' to a supermarket assistant every time they bag an item.

* * *

Water is where I'm complete. We move on to swimming. But, I don't want to get wet. Too much like hard work, having to get dry and change and all that shit. I think for most of these boys, being ten, they really enjoy being taught by the female swimming coaches. I would too. This one's fit and blonde, her hair drawn up in a tight bun, wearing a purple shimmering full-bodied bathing suit, she's very curvy. Her swimsuit stretches around her bosoms, there's a fair amount of cleavage on show, enough to make me look twice. Each time her back is turned, the boys simulate on their own pigeon chests, miming the curvature of her breasts. They all giggle uncontrollably. I'm appreciating the sight too. Body off Baywatch, face off Crimewatch. The hair being that tight doesn't do much for her either, not flattering. These kids aren't paying any attention to swimming techniques, perhaps only breaststroke.

We pass an American football field, twenty boys, half wearing yellow ribbons and the others wearing red are playing touch football. The sheepskin ball thrown by a bouncy overweight boy to a stick thin little kid as he runs to receive it. Boys tug on the ribbons from around waistbands, stopping dead in their tracks. Like a spoilt little bitch, the ones tagged out, stamp their feet in disappointment. Another example that these kids expect to win everything, no room for losing here.

Instead of touch football. I would love to see the female counsellors running around in hot pants, stamping their feet as their nipples slip from braless tank tops. Too many fantasies lost in my frustration, all this pent-up sexual energy. We're not in direct contact with the female counsellors, wise too. Our cabin, being ten-year-old boys, are too immature to walk past a group of girls, as they bounce on trampolines, attached by bungee cords. They can't help themselves.

"You can bounce on this." Said Mark, slapping his thighs.

Roars of laughter, Doug does his best to conceal his urge to laugh, Benedict fails, clapping his hands together mindlessly. These are ten-year-olds, where did he get that from?

"Move it." I said, shoving Mark in the back to make him

keep walking along. The squirming prepubescent sex fiend. I nod apologetically to the supervising female counsellors. Wow, their legs. I study their navels. I'm no better than Mark, although I'm not shouting it. There are so many girls that tie their shirts up in a knot at the front. Fine with me. Thank God the trampolines are on the boys' side of camp. Every activity we've walked past so far has involved the girls. Female counsellors on the grass, trainers removed, white frilly socks stuffed down inside, bare feet. Legs resting on knees, as they elevate them aloft and lower them down. I've clocked a very nice arch of a foot, teasing me in the sun. Three counsellors peer over the top of their sunglasses and smile at Doug, Benedict and me. Hopefully, they're looking at me. I'd be directing my attention at Doug over me, if I were them. Mark's jeers could have offended them. I guess they weren't that impressed. They pay no more attention to us as they chat. Sometimes, I wish I had a six-pack, bigger arms, a perkier chest. That way I could remove my shirt and they'd flock on over. They wouldn't have a choice. I want to be more appealing. I want to be inside them, their feet ready for toe sucking. I don't know where we're going now. I need to forget all the navels and feet. They make me crazy. We're on our way to go-carts. This camp has full on go-carts. Not cheap ones, proper ones. Honda G200 petrol go-karts. The track winds through a clearing in the trees, with some good hair-pin bends. I need to accompany Doug and the others before I go back to baseball. The raging engines of go-carts rip through the silence. They buzz round, kicking out dirty fumes.

A golf cart zips along the track toward us. Max, the guy with the beard, the photographer, is driving.

"Panning Shot." He shouts, directing three boys with a video camera hanging precariously off the back of the cart. They teeter on the back seat.

Max handles all the camp photography and end of session video, we all get a copy. I should have been a Video Production specialist counsellor, worked with Max instead of the brute, Bobby. I probably know more about that than I do baseball, thanks to my degree. I certainly wouldn't have boys holding on to the back of a golf cart for dear life.

In the evenings, Max seems to disappear into the editing studio on his own. Must be a dark room in there. I imagine him perving over his four by six black and white prints of girls. Licking his lips as he pegs the shots on a washing line, shadows created by a red light. I bet he's got shots that are just for him, that's what I'd do.

Max stops the golf cart in front of us. The kids continue to film, aiming the camera at us. Mark performs energetic star jumps, sticking his tongue out. Max is staring out at Doug and me, he's unsettling me. He should concentrate on supervising these kids. Looks like he's checking us out.

"You want a picture of your bunk over by the bleachers?" Asks Max, lifting his camera from his chest, as if ready to pap us.

"Nah Dawg, we gotta get to the carts." Doug said, pointing off toward the trees, the spit of go-cart exhaust blaring out from the distance.

Max nods politely, still looking at us, and then smiles. He's so socially awkward, odd. It's that weird, vacant look he gives people.

The golf cart whizzes away, the camera boys grapple to hold on as they almost fly out, off the back. They seem to enjoy it, laughing the entire time. They've gone, that's a relief. There's always too much activity going on around me, I'm not invested in this experience.

A group of seven boys are running through a tree lined dirt track. Their legs covered in caked on mud, dripping with sweat. I didn't know they do long distance running here, is that even an activity? I like a bit of cross-country myself, it's the stamina involved.

I need to get back to baseball, my free time is up. I leave Doug and the kids at go-carts. Josh and Mark are the only two boys from our bunk to wave goodbye, I reciprocate. Benedict doesn't give a shit. They've all fucked off to bag a go-cart. Doug nods at me, too.

I dart in the direction of the field, jogging. I can't be late for that prick, Bobby. Three guys in a golf cart drop off an orange Gatorade water cooler for the session. I nod to them as I continue to run. I'm the first one here. I grab an upturned plastic cup from the bleachers and fill it with ice cold water from the cooler. I down it and try to get my breath back.

I'm now waiting. It's weird how no one else is here. I fill my cup with water again, swallowing it down in a massive gulp. Bobby, Arnold and Carl Lee appear together in a line on the horizon, walking heavy footed down the road as if they're accompanied by the opening music to Reservoir Dogs. Odd how they're all together. Looks ominous to me, as if they're scheming. I'm not involved, alienated as ever. An Englishman, lonely in the outfield.

"Good to see you, Dylan." Said Bobby, being sarcastic. His face plastered with a dirty smile. I really don't like this guy, not one bit.

"Oh, and you." I said.

I can give as good as I get. He doesn't scare me.

Bobby casually drops his worn, floppy baseball glove down at my feet. It's a Wilson mitt, it's nice. My catcher's mitt is a Mizuno, nowhere near the quality of his; he knows it too, bastard.

Bobby grabs for a plastic cup, filling it with water. Carl Lee and Arnold saunter over to the chain-link fence behind home plate and stand leaning against it, staring over at me. Bully boys. They're not smiling, they're not laughing. Nothing, lifeless. There's nothing there in them. The atmosphere here is getting unsavoury. Bobby is silent, not even looking at me. Just resting his foot on the bleachers, looking up at the hill behind me.

"Alright?" I said.

He hasn't responded. I nod my head at Arnold and Carl Lee. I thought we were getting on all OK, but their lack of response, implies otherwise. They're looking at each other. They're maintaining their expressionless faces. They don't even appear human. They both walk off onto the baseball field and lob a ball between each other, catching it with a thud in their gloves. They carry their gloves everywhere with them, it's the American, done thing. Always have your glove with you, because you never know when you might play.

Bobby stands level with my eyes. He has his cup of water up to his lips, he flicks his baseball cap up with his index finger. He's clutching on to that cup, his grip getting tighter. He moves in closer to me. I can see threads of spit from his lips to his teeth like guitar strings. He could do with another drink. I wonder what these guys have been up to. His mouth is so dry. His eyes are even blood shot. If I had to guess, they've been off smoking weed.

"Dylan, I have some news for you." He said, taking another swig of his water.

"Oh yeah, what's that?" I said. I need to look away from his face. He's too close for comfort.

"You'll be happy to hear, you get to take the girls softball session today." He said, taking yet another long swig of water.

Imagine as I am, he's spitting tobacco at my feet. The balance of power is clear now. This is our High Noon. All that is news to me. There was never a discussion, no intimation that this would ever happen. When did I volunteer for that? It might be cool to be around the girls for a bit.

"Ya see, we drew straws." Said Bobby, smiling.

"Of course, you did." I said, knowing full well they considered no one else but me.

Bobby looks deep into the bottom of his empty cup. He's searching to find the last drop. It's like he's got rabies.

"Look, one of us has to do it. You were unlucky." He said, smirking.

He's loving every minute of this.

"What a shock," I said. I can't now take my eyes off his slimy grin. My protest comes as a sigh. I have nothing else to offer. I can't muster the energy to argue with him. I know I'm not wanted here so why attempt to contest this, there's no point.

"Off you go then." He motions with his limp hand flapping from his wrist, as if he's a Broadway showgirl. He lets the crinkled cup fall to the grass beside me.

I swipe at my baseball mitt, snatching it from the bleachers. I would love to explode into his eyes, deep into his browbeaten soul. I step down from the bleachers, walk up the hill to the roadway.

"Put that in the bin." He said, nodding down at the cup he dropped.

I shove the tip of my tongue into the crevice in my back tooth. It won't be long before I need a filling. I'm not sure why I bend down and pick the cup up. I grab it, crunch it in my hand, clearly imagining it's Bobby's skull, and throw it in a nearby bin.

I've become far too subservient. I should never have given him power over me, it'll only get worse.

"Good boy," he said.

Keep walking, just keep walking. My task is to take the girls softball session. I'm going to do it. Show it hasn't bothered me, at least pretend it hasn't.

I get to the brow of the hill. It drops down a large slope to the larger of the main baseball fields. As I make heavy steps down the slope. There are teenage girls performing handstands. Most of the girls wearing the standard camp uniform of red and white. Some girls have black armbands with the letter 'N' printed on them in white. The 'Seniors'. The 'N' apparently means 'Nephilim'. The guy seniors wear black armbands with 'CV' on them, meaning 'Cardinal virtues'.

Until now I've had no contact with the senior age groups. Most of these girls may as well be the same age as some counsellors. The only way you'd tell them apart is by the branding on their shirts.

I could get into some serious trouble here. Eyes up, professional. Behave.

17

Softball Jailbait

A baseball field of teenage girls, using their camp uniforms, hair and trainers to express themselves individually. Many have modified their red T-shirts, cutting them short, revealing the peak of their Adonis belts. That V-shaped, lean look over their hips. Flat belly buttons, a plethora of 'inny' and 'outey' ones. Some tanned, some pale, all of them tight and toned. It really is a sight to behold. There are tight shorts, cycling shorts, shorts that only just cover butt cheeks, they may as well be hot pants.

Some groups finish performing handstands, crumbling to the grass as they wait for the softball session to begin. Although their breasts are snug in sports bras, I'm in awe of some of those wearing loose fitting T-shirts. On some, the drastic homemade cuts are enough to be able to see the bottom of their bras.

With a heavy exhalation of nervous breath, a firestorm of twisted thoughts. I step down the steep hill, into the fray I go. I should warn myself to remain locked in chastity. All these girls, they're off limits.

I check I'm not aroused. My Umbro shorts will never conceal

shaft movement. I'm certain these girls wouldn't let me live that down if I were to rock up with a hard-on. I only imagine the trouble I'd be in. I'm good though, thank God. I've managed to stave that off.

There's a female counsellor already here, sitting off on the metal bleachers with her back to me, her knees resting perpendicular to the seats below, a clipboard on her lap.

I won't be alone with the girls. Probably a good thing too, for my sake and theirs. Who's to say what could happen. It could always turn into a scene from Caligula.

Some girls have noticed me. Hells yeah, I feel like a celebrity. They're talking amongst themselves, looking up at me, approaching as I reach the bottom of the hill. I'm the new kid in school. They snigger, hands at their mouths, so mischievous. I like the attention. This is the welcome I'd prefer over incurious boys.

I'm here to teach softball. Softball. It's all about the game. Just the game. Softball.

The female counsellor is writing on her clipboard. I hope to Jesus she's not drawing a cock.

"Alyssa," I said. I'm delighted to see her. I didn't recognise her at first, "What are you doing here?"

Her shoulders tense as she turns. I'm so happy to see her. I love how some people have that effect, the ones who draw your focus at a party. Finally, someone that I can really to chat with. She smiles when she sees me. She looks happy too, smiling with her perfect Hollywood incisors, pearly white. These Americans all have perfect teeth.

Alyssa uses her pen to scratch the inside of her ponytail bun. I give her a full toothed smile, even with my crooked imperfections. In life, it's best to share your weaknesses.

Alyssa says, "What are you doing here?"

"I'm the lucky fella, sent to help you."

"You've come from baseball?" She said, her pen now resting between her lips.

"Yeah, I didn't know you took softball." I said, shaking my

head.

"Are we gonna waste time with this trivial shit or talk for real?"

Her face transforms into a soft cheeky smile, dimples and all. Her eyebrows raised, she's playing with me. I'll find out the rules. Alyssa intrigues me, that's always dangerous. It means I'm interested, I'll exploit that interest to find out more at any cost, even loyalty, despite all the repercussions. To cure my inevitable guilt, I'll try to forget Laura. I'm attracted to Alyssa's dismissive persona, I see a little of myself in her. I hope to see all of myself deep in her soon.

"Have you ever felt the need to coordinate denim outfits with a girlfriend? Said Alyssa, twiddling the pen between her teeth. The click of plastic on teeth distracts me.

"Not something I'd do," I said.

"The answer I was hoping for," she said. "Sit, sit." She tapped the seat next to her.

"Thanks." I said, sitting down.

"I'm thinking about getting Kiefer Sutherland's face tattooed on my forearm, ya know."

"OK."

"Yeah, right about here."Said Alyssa, covering her right forearm with the palm of her left hand, opening out her slight fingers to show where she wants this celebrity tattoo.

"Why Kiefer Sutherland?"

"Not Kiefer Sutherland, well yeah, Kiefer, but as David from The Lost Boys."

"Great movie," I said.

"I know, right. Well, that's what I want right here. I love weird tattoos." She slaps her arm with her hand.

"Evidently. Garlic don't work," I said.

Alyssa slaps my knee, "That's it," she said.

Sure, It's a great film, but I wouldn't get a tattoo on my arm. Kiefer Sutherland even has that bleach blond mullet in it, too.

"I hope you like sixteen-year-old girls," said Alyssa.

"What?"

Is she reading my mind? There's no way she knows I was looking at ripe breasts and fruitful bottoms.

"Why, are you sixteen?" I said in jest.

Alyssa smiles bashfully. She makes me so nervous; this girl breaks my powers of flirtation. I hope she's enjoying our saucy glances; she looks down at her clipboard. I'll call it nerves.

"Rest assured." I said, touching her on the wrist, as she goes over the same circular squiggles with her pen on the page. "I like girls like you, whatever age that might be."

She looks at my hand, touching her, distracted. The circles stop.

I can hear girls talking amongst themselves and giggling again. This is all about Alyssa and me. I'm enjoying this moment. I hope to see her heart beating in her chest for me.

"You might have a chance with me then." She said, jumping up from her seat.

She peels her shorts away from her buttocks with her fingers, hitting me on the shoulder with her clipboard.

"Oi, eyes up, dirty boy." She said, flapping for me to stop looking at her bottom. Cupping her hands around her mouth, she shouts, "Right, girls." Getting their attention. "Come take a seat on the bleachers." She jumps down to the grass from the bleachers. "We'll get started."

Alyssa steps with delicate precision, as the girls begin to sit down. She grabs me by the hand, pulling me forward to join her off the bleachers.

I'm so uncomfortable now, looking at these teenage porcelain faces. I shield myself behind Alyssa. I know these girls are judging me, just as I am them.

"These girls are sixteen and seventeen, be prepared." Said Alyssa, whispering in my ear.

That's right, scare the shit out of me. The girls sit like an expectant audience on the bleachers, waiting for us to perform.

"Some of 'em can get very handsy. Plus, you're English and not bad looking." Said Alyssa, shielding her mouth with the back of the clipboard. I guess she doesn't want any of the 'Nephilim' to read her lips.

"Not bad looking?" I said. "Thanks, I think."

Note to self: Try harder with the flirtation.

"I'm here though," she said.

Her words help me momentarily. I remain drawn by these girls. Maybe she meant she was here, as a warning to me too, that she'll be watching.

Some of these girls though, seriously. Some of them are so beautiful. They don't look their ages; far older. These girls could easily pass as the same age as Laura. I'm telling myself they're off limits, no step. What am I, though, three years older? That's not much of an age gap. They're all so shiny. They're looking at me with gigantic eyes and smiles. It's like I'm going to perform tap, or dance naked for them. I have their full attention, I love it. It's making me feel amazing. Eyes on me, all eyes on me.

With the looks, come the nudges. An elbow in the ribs from one girl to another in row two. Similar flashes flit into my eyeline from the back row. Only this time it was a finger tap on a shoulder. Each girl is pestering the girl next to them, laughing and whispering. They keep looking me up and down. Are they thinking of me naked? I'm self-conscious. If I had the choice, I wouldn't be wearing these stupid shorts and white socks. I'd have made more of an effort. I mean they deserve it. How do they perceive me? I can't care. But they're people after all; and I, like anyone, have my insecurities. All this female attention is my most favourite part of camp. Should I include that detail on a postcard home?

"Get a glove each from the storage shed." Said Alyssa, waving her hand toward the shed. "You'll need balls and bats too, please. Bring 'em on down here."

Some of the girls chuckle at the mention of the word balls.

"Can't we just use his balls, Alyssa." Said one girl, shoulder barging her friend, unbalancing the girl walking next to her.

Their laughter interrupted by Alyssa's scowl.

"You should have had all this prepared for us." Said a lanky girl, as she stays sat still on the bleachers, not moving with her arms firmly crossed. She's determined not to move from those bleachers, anchored to the spot.

"Sharley, don't give me your back talk." Said Alyssa, fanning her clipboard, encouraging her to get up and go to the shed.

Sharley stands with a sour face. She flicks her body round on the spot and skulks off up the hill, trailing along behind the other girls. She jogs to catch up with a uninterested group of other girls, they're all walking painfully slow, scuffing their trainers across the grass toward the storage shed. The scene of the sex, the night of mystery, horny silhouettes. I can't dwell on that right now. I watch the girls as they walk, pushing and shoving. Some run, some dawdle. I'm in awe of their pert little bums. They all have pronounced strong solid calf muscles, like defined racehorses. So distracting.

Alyssa has a white feather tattoo on her hip too that catches my eye protruding from her shorts. I can only see the tip of it, but it's enough.

"I like that." I said, poking her. My finger behaving without my consent. I should have kept it as a verbal observation, instead of jabbing her. She grabs for her hip, recoiling back, as if I've winded her.

"Sorry," I said. "It's subtle. I like it." I pause again, "Your tattoo."

"Thank you. It was probably ostentation. I'm not sure." She said, examining it with her fingertips.

"Ostentation? Not sure that's right. That's a display of wealth," I said.

"Oh shit, excuse me." She said, not happy that I've corrected her. She looks kind of angry. "Can you do me a favour and correct my speech again? It's so sexy." She said, with brimming sarcasm.

I may have really pissed her off with that one. With that tattoo, she's not as original as I first thought.

The girls are returning to the bleachers. Some girls have their softball gloves on their heads, covering their hair like spatchcock chicken. Others carry them with nonchalant apathy, not motivated by the session ahead of them. A little blonde girl walks toward both Alyssa and me, she's looking at me, but walking toward Alyssa.

"Alyssa I can't play today. I hurt my wrist, playing soccer," she said.

She hasn't taken her eyes off mine. I'm admiring her, scoping her from head to toe and back up again. Her sultry stance tells me she knows how life works. She's short, physically mature. Looking at her I would say she was in her twenties. She has a peachy mature face, wearing a tight pink T-shirt. Her breasts are hard not to notice. She's standing with her right wrist bandaged. It's like I've seen that before, shrouded in midnight silhouettes. Her arm wrapped across her waist. It drags her shirt down, making her breasts even more delightful than they perhaps normally would be. She knows too that her breasts are impressive, she's trying to get my attention with them, it's working. Now for my concerted effort to look nowhere else but into her eyes. In fact, I'll sweep back and forth to Alyssa. Focus on the clipboard, focus on the sky, focus on anything other than her tits, the torture.

"Thanks Lacey, I guess you'll be spectating today then," said Alyssa.

Lacey smiles, relieved, raising her eyebrows at me. That was suggestive, I swear.

"You can help Dylan Score," said Alyssa.

What? Did I hear that right? Lacey heard it, too. She leers at me. She may as well be licking her lips, her eyes undressing me. I'm fucked.

She turns and swaggers to the first step of the bleachers, sitting down like an agent provocateur, a femme fatale. She crosses her legs, right thigh over her left knee, leans back and arches herself like a stretching feline, resting her elbows against the seat behind her.

Her eyes closed tight as she exhales, flicking her hair. It flows down behind her as she pushes out her chest, her neck growing longer. She sinks into her seat, the sun bounces off her already tanned, golden skin. Lacey knows exactly what she's doing and exactly how to do it. She's a mirage of sexual teasing.

I snap out of it with Alyssa's voice loudly announcing:

"OK ladies, we're going to be playing a game."

The girls on the bleachers flop forward, lifeless with boredom at the thought of a game, huffing and puffing.

"More enthusiasm please, ladies." Said Alyssa, clapping with encouragement.

The girls whoop with fake excitement.

Am I honestly expected to score this, are the rules to Softball the same as Baseball?

"If you're wondering who our guest is today." Alyssa said, pointing at me.

I wave. I'm so stupid, must look like a right geek.

"This is Dylan," she said.

"Hello," I said. I wave again. No clue what I'm doing.

Lacey's eyes ping open. I try my best to curb my accent. A girl sits down next to Lacey, slapping her on the forehead. Lacey huffs and sits up.

"Are you British?" Said Lacey, as she sits forward on the bleachers, resting her elbows on her knees. Her face perched in her open palms. A girl sitting directly behind her, on the upper bleachers step, removes her hat and places it on Lacey's head, covering her eyes, pushing it down tight. Lacey bats her hands away, removing the hat. She dashes it on the grass.

I wonder if Alyssa can see what I'm seeing. Lacey is wiggling her legs slight, but obvious to me. Opening and closing them, with only the tiniest of movements, like slow motion wings.

"I consider myself English. But yeah, I'm British. It's the same thing," I said.

Lacey smiles. I know what that smile means. I want her to

smile more. Why am I trying to make her smile? This is wrong, but it's so right.

"Do I have to play? I think I need to learn English." Said a red-haired girl, sniggering.

"Everyone is playing. The only exception is Lacey." Said Alyssa, holding her clipboard close to her chest. "Hit the field, ladies."

Most of the girls moan and groan in disappointed displeasure. They push themselves up from the bleachers, walking toward the field, dragging their feet. Some girls launch their gloves in the air like graduation hats.

"I'll set this up and be back with you in a minute. Take a seat." Said Alyssa, nodding toward the bleachers.

She doesn't have to tell me. I'll go. I know exactly what awaits me there. Lacey hasn't moved, she's still staring at me, head in her hands. The bleachers never looked so small. Be cool. I'm the adult here. She's the one who should be uncomfortable. I step forward one step, conscious of my feet. My toes hurt. Wow, my toes really hurt. Like they're burning again. I take a seat on the same step of the bleachers as Lacey, with her leaning over and tilting her head, still looking at me. There's a good metre between us, maybe less, but we must be at arm's length. A safe, professional distance. I could always move along. Why would I move? I'll sit here in silence, if I must. I can't be seen to be getting into full conversation with this girl, everything professional. She's looking at me. As hard as I'm trying my best to be entertained and distracted by the game. This is so weird now, I need to confront her. I turn, she's sat looking at me with a crooked smile. She looks younger now. I'd still go with seventeen or eighteen at least.

"So, you're English?" She said without taking her eyes off me.

How do I answer that? She knows I am. I nod my head. This girl is precocious.

"That's so cool." She slides closer toward me, as if she's sat atop a luggage conveyor belt, floating along.

"I'm elated to hear you think so, cheers." I said. I'm trying

165

not to speak in my natural accent. I'm making myself sound more posh, forcing it.

"Cheers." She said, imitating me.

That is kind of cute. The way she says it still sounds American, but deliberate and funny. She can say that again.

"I love your accent. The way you say every word," she said.

"You mean enunciate."

"Listen, honey," she said. "No clue what that means, but the way you talk. I'm loving it." She whispers, looking down at my thighs.

She makes no effort to hide it. I'm now more self-conscious of my accent than I've ever been before, like it's a nuclear weapon.

Alyssa is on the softball field directing the girls to run around, she's being larger than life, so passionate about the game and encouraging the girls to enjoy it too. Most act like it's a struggle. They limply lob balls, dragging their bodies around like Neanderthals, gloves tickling the grass, dangling from hunched shoulders.

"You met the queen?" said Lacey.

"It might surprise you. But no, I haven't," I said.

Lacey looks disappointed. Her eyes fade, waning attention.

"I drink tea though, that's basically royal." I said, her disappointment turning to a smile.

"Nice, you ever been to DC?" she said.

"I have actually, yeah, I love Georgetown." I said.

"Shut up," she said. I feel her silk fingertips touch me on the forearm. "No kidding? I live in Georgetown. Oh, my god." She said, gripping my arm.

OK, so now she has my attention. Not necessarily because of the arm contact, but Georgetown I love. It, to me, is the most beautiful place in the world, especially in Autumn, all the cherry blossoms loosing their leaves. All the history, the culture. I Love it. There's something about the brickwork, too.

"Now that's cool. When I'm finished here. I'm going to DC," I said. "Get on a greyhound. Do the whole thing."

"Like an American adventure." She said, placing her left hand over her heart, "Greyhound is scuzzy though."

"Yeah, I guess. Needs must and all that." I said. "I can't rent a car yet."

Lacey places her left hand, full palm, on top of mine.

"Amped," she said.

Her hand is soft and warm, like kneaded bread dough or lava fudge.

"What does that mean?" I said.

"Ya know, like cool. That's the best," she said. "I can teach you so much."

Wait, I've heard that before, haven't I. I can't think, she's touching my knee cap. I thought her hand on mine was bad enough. No one else has seen this. Only me and her know. This isn't right. I stare down at her hand. I like the secrecy, it's just between me and her. This is inappropriate though, it's wrong. Still exciting. I could go to Washington and see her. What? I'm a counsellor. It's not right, I know it's wrong. I'm fighting with myself.

"You can stay with me. My parents are never in. My dad's a general or something," She said.

This has taken a dangerous and dramatic shift. I need to knock it on the head right now. My wide-eye shock should say it all. She needs to understand that a subtle, polite English rejection is on its way.

"I'm very flattered Lacey, that won't be happening. What would your father say?"

"Like I said, he's a general; he's away a lot," she said.

"Lacey. I don't know you and it's not right. You could ruin me."

"You better believe it," she said. "My name's Lacey Lane. I live at two two six three Dumbarton Street, Georgetown, Washington District of Columbia." She pauses, looking at me with sarcasm. "Now, you know me." She stops. "I really like you."

I could get lost in those green eyes. I believe her, I think she probably does like me. She means it, she believes it. I'm confused, there's something wrong with me. I suppose I'd always have a story to tell when I get back home, a sordid affair with a sixteen-year-old. Then again, come to think of it. At home, in the UK, I could be sexually intimate with a girl of sixteen. They can't vote but you can fuck 'em. It's not illegal anything, is it illegal here? Why am I considering the legalities of this, I don't need to justify it, it's never gonna happen. What if we're meant for each other? This is ridiculous. I can't be contemplating any of this. I sure as hell can't do anything with her. I'm in a position of power, of responsibility. Then again, happens all the time.

"Miss Lane, we've only just met," I said. "You know I'm not gonna stay with you in DC. I'm nineteen. It's not right."

She has nice eyes, really sea green, clear and mesmerising. Look away, you dumb arse.

"Love knows no age." She said, dipping her eyes, "Plus, I'm two weeks away from my seventeenth. No one has to know."

She makes a good point. I can't argue with that. No. Not right. Stop it. Stop it now. I stand up, moving away from her. I hope by moving, it'll tell her I have no intention of pursuing any of her advances.

"Lacey." I said, looking out to the field, "You can't say things like that. You'll get me into serious trouble."

"Well, you're single right?" she said.

I shake my head. I want to lie and nod. I can't be doing that. I'd have no excuse then.

"No. I'm not. I have a girlfriend," I said.

She shakes her head as if I've told her I fucked her mother, she looks so upset. Devastated.

"Fuck yo," she said. You're gonna regret that." She jumps from the bleachers.

"Lacey, you'll have to get over it." I said as she stands with her arms crossed, tapping her foot on the grass.

"I don't get over, I get under." She said, pushing her tongue to the side of her mouth "And I always get what I want."

"Not this time, you don't." I said.

I feel proud of myself. She can't hypnotise me with the promise of oral sex. I'm flattered by the drama, but if this turns into something darker, I'm not ready for that.

She turns and runs toward the girls side of camp. I feel fluttering fear in my stomach, that heavy ash in the back of my throat, for the first time, fear. All she'd have to do is accuse me, and I'm sure I won't be here for much longer. They would never believe me over her. My word is already suspect.

As Lacey disappears into the distance, I feel empathy for her. Perhaps, I've just broken her heart. I can't be a story she tells her friends ten years from now, detailing how she lost her virginity to an English counsellor on the bleachers at summer camp. I can't be that guy. Assuming she's even a virgin. I think from her forwardness, she's probably not. I bet she's been fingered at the rodeo.

Alyssa's looking over at me, inquisitive why Lacey has gone. Some girls waiting to bat, peep from under their oversized helmets, having to tilt their heads back to see under the peak. They've seen her run off.

Alyssa walks over to me, still carrying her clip board.

"You OK. What happened?" she said.

"She invited me to her parents' house." I said. I need to wipe my top lip, it's wet with my sweat. It was enjoyable articulating the beginnings of this drama to Alyssa. I feel wanted, finally. I want Alyssa to feel an ounce of jealousy.

"I told you. You gotta be careful with these girls. They'll eat you alive, no shit." Said Alyssa, clutching her clipboard into her chest again.

Lacey would have done anything I'd ask of her. She's probably more willing than Laura.

"I told her I was in a relationship," I said.

Alyssa jerks back in shock at the mere mention of my relationship.

"I didn't know that," she said.

I like that she's surprised, I can't hide my smile. I'm touched, she's shocked. I can almost save this and bottle it up. I don't need Lacey to make her jealous. I'll mention the existence of Laura instead.

"I'm not really. That's what I told her, so she'd leave me alone." I said. I've taken a real chance with that. I want Alyssa to keep hold of her interest in me. If I'd realistically mentioned Laura, that would have been that. She wouldn't have wanted to pursue me. There'd be no jealousy to have.

"Good, watch yourself. She's that kind of girl to tell the world you hit on her," she said.

"If that happens, will you vouch for me?" I said.

"Of course, I know what she's like. Her sister used to be a counsellor here. She got involved with a few of the guys too and it got real messy."

Alyssa places her warm fingertips on mine. There's a lot of hand touching today. I've been here for weeks now, it's taken this long to get any real physical contact. Now, I've got young girls touching me, girls I'm attracted to all over me. I pray I take softball again. Fuck Bobby. If only he knew I was relishing life, physical contact with women, there's more eye contact here than Specsavers.

"I'm not going to hide the fact; I really like you." I said, trying to hold my eyes on Alyssa. There's a touch of irony here. I just had Lacey; she may be sixteen, but she was declaring her attraction for me. Here I am now, telling this girl, an appropriate, socially acceptable age, that I've only met twice. I really like her.

I may well be missing Laura too much. I can't remember what she even looks like. I've put her picture next to my bed, but day to day she escapes me. I know she's blonde. I can sometimes hear her laughing. I need to phone her again. I have a phonecard. I read her old words in emails, but I still don't get the sense of her. I feel it in her words that she loves me, at least she says so. She signs the older ones off with a kiss. The distance makes me forget. Out of sight, out of mind. I really challenge anyone to maintain a long-distance relationship. At least one half of them, at one point, will be unfaithful.

"I like you to,." Said Alyssa.

The girls are still playing softball. The ball is erratically launched all over the place, backed up by distracted giggles. This whole thing would be topped off perfectly if Alyssa was to rub my thigh or curl her bottom lip and slowly bite down with lust for me. That would make this day special. We could sneak off somewhere and turn our subtle touching into passionate penetration.

We both edge closer together as if we're about to kiss, anticipation growing in my tongue.

"Excuse me." Said an exasperated, familiar young female voice.

Alyssa and I turn. There she is, a red faced Lacey, her arms folded. Thanks then, for interrupting our almost kiss, you little bitch.

"The session has ended." Said Lacey, glaring at us.

I feel guilty. I'm holding Alyssa's hand, am I betraying Lacey? It's like being caught in the act, unsettling, a compromising situation. She's not my mother.

"Watch your mouth." Said Alyssa, poking her finger at Lacey.

"Or what?" Lacey counters.

She's now more like a petulant child, only with childbearing hips.

Alyssa stares, shaking her head. I found that intimidating. She maintains her subtle authority without raising her voice.

"Ladies. It's time to end it there," said Alyssa.

She hasn't moved her eyes from staring down Lacey. The girls run off the field. Far more excited to get off than they were to get on. They're throwing their softball gloves in the air, jumping to the side to avoid being hit on the head, as they land. No attempts to catch them.

"Return any equipment not belonging to you, back to the shed." Alyssa barks. Still, she hasn't stopped staring at Lacey, it's getting intense now.

"Then, you're free to go," she said.

The stare down continues. Lacey still standing there, arms crossed, staring back at Alyssa.

I offer a smile to ease the tension. Lacey cuts her eyes at me, no body movement, just piercing pupils. She turns around on the spot, her heel ripping up grass. She jogs after a group of girls, now walking up the sloping hill toward the tarmac road that leads back to Silver Wood.

That girl Lacey is dangerous, she's too obsessive, beyond Fatal Attraction. Alyssa picks up some of the left-over equipment the girls have failed to collect. I'm obliged to help her. I probably wouldn't have helped, but it's all about providing context that I'm not a bad guy. In fact, it's like we've been through so much drama already. I'm concentrating on self-preservation. I don't want any accusations coming my way.

Alyssa, with her red face, seems to concentrate on not losing her shit. I'm closer to her. Although short-lived, this session was fulfilling. I'll now be looking forward to coming to Softball. I think I may even raise my hand and volunteer.

Alyssa and I stand in relative silence, in front of this storage shed, looking with what I consider fondness for one another. I hope she'll drag me inside and we'll live out what I gleefully witnessed the other night. I don't want to count the seconds, but it's nice gazing at her. She drops the equipment she's holding in her arms to the grass, it clanks with metal clips locking together and thumps like an empty drum as the helmets roll free.

She grips me by my T-shirt with one hand, pulling me closer into her. I can feel her lips on mine, soft and warm. She's forceful with it. Our teeth almost meet. I drop the gloves to the ground. Kissing deep, I'm lost for a moment. Our bodies touch. I desperately paw my hands all over her body, clutching at her toned back and gripping at her little waist.

We stop kissing, our heavy breathing gets all too loud. I was conscious of it. Trust me, if we were anywhere else we'd be having sex right now. I know she's self-conscious. We're out in the open, only trees behind us. I can't hide my desperate lust for her.

"When will I see you again?" I said.

"As soon as possible. We have softball again tomorrow."

"Good, well I'll see you then."

"You know we have to keep this to ourselves right." She said, picking up some of the loose helmets. "I mean, we're not allowed to have an obvious, open relationship, not on camp."

"There's an element of excitement." I said, as I readjust my T-shirt.

"Joe would go crazy, if he knew," she said.

We stand looking at each other with transfixed, giddy, stupid smiles. It's all very predictable. She's the one who referred to this, whatever this is, as a relationship. That might be a bit too much. I can't be smothered with commitment. I have all that at home.

Why does life have to be so serious, can't I just enjoy a kiss?

18

Chicken Choke

Another moment in time, another ounce of boredom. Time spent in the confides of this fucking chipboard cabin, more time off my life. I've returned once again from a tedious session of baseball. Stood in a field trying to be engaged all day, shuffling my feet, getting the blood flow to my numb throbbing toes.

All the kids are here, thankfully doing their own thing. I'm not having to get involved with them. For me, it's now time to lay on my top bunk, staring into space. I study the only pictures I have of Laura, almost like a ritual now. It hurts to know she hasn't been in contact with me yet. I might try meditation, get my crazed mind on to cleansing. I can't close my eyes. If I do, I'd rather not wake up.

The days, evenings and nights creep up on me, that orange glow of the sun, once again piercing through the mesh fly screens. The late afternoon breeze teasing my freedom. We haven't had dinner yet, at least I have that to look forward to.

Doug's laid on his bed again, same position, arm behind his head, hand on his chest. He looks asleep, can't be, he's wearing his headphones, I can hear the dull roar of whatever music it is that he's listening to over the chatter of the boys of the bunk. He's got an intense liking of hip hop, CD copies of De La Soul's: 3 Feet High and Rising and Licensed to Ill. He doesn't have much of an open mind for music. I offered Mule Variations when it was raining, and he couldn't get into it. I should have started with something slightly more accessible, Closing Time, perhaps.

I really want something to do. I've had a shower, I don't need another one. They're like a waste of time now, my only opportunity to relieve my frustrations and have a quick wank. I can never do it. Someone, usually Tyrese, comes into the bathroom, every time. He must follow me. I can hear him using the toilet or I can smell it. Whatever he's up to when I'm trying to knock one out, it's enough to put me off. In fact, I can't even see him. I sit up, we seem to be missing a couple of 'em. I can't see Josh either, that's weird. He's always here, moping about. He wants to be close to us. Mark, I can't see either or Morgan. I should probably pay more attention. Where have they gone? I'm past caring at this point. I could call their names like a parent, it's not worth disrupting my mind. I should go find them, damn it.

Doug might know where they are.

"Doug," I said.

My legs dangling off the top of my bunk. He can't hear me, or he's deciding to ignore me. I need to find out where these kids are. I jump down, bare foot on the wooden floor, cold. I wander over to his bedside, tapping him on the shoulder. His eyes pop open like he's possessed. He wasn't sleeping. He slides his headphones off in a seamless motion, smooth. It sounds like he's listening to a country song. I haven't seen any country CDs. Unless he hides them. All his hip hop albums are out in the open, for all to see. Not as proud of his love for Kenny Rogers.

"Sup Dawg?"

"Where is everyone?" I said.

He looks around bewildered, forcing his eyes wider as if to help with his disorientation.

"Next door with Nate and Andy." He said, as if he's received divine intervention.

Nate is Nathan, from Sacramento, California. It's the way he introduces himself. It's normal for him to say his name is Nathan, but he encourages you to call him 'Nate', he's more than proud to be from Sacramento too. He thinks it makes him more admired, he always behaves almost untouchable. His whole introduction sounds scripted.

Andy is Australian. He does a similar thing to me, in that he tells people he's from Perth, but as the conversation continues, and if you pay him the time he feels deserving, he explains he's from a town called Bunbury, East Bunbury. He'll go into detail that he can see Forrest Park. Andy is a real loose cannon, he's funny but up for anything, easily led. Full of energy, like a kid. You'll be talking to him one second, then he'll be out of sight, climbing up a tree, he's spontaneous, proper mad.

"Where's Benedict?" I said.

"Nah-uh. You haven't heard?" Said Doug, chuckling to himself.

"Heard what?" I look at an empty bed, bare mattress. "Wait, where's his stuff?"

Doug swings his legs off the bed and stands beside me.

"All gone, Dawg." He said, laughing with his clenched fist covering his mouth.

"What?"

"Boy, only gone and got his ass fired." Doug's face mirrors mine, complete elation.

"Marvellous," I said.

We're both practically dancing, acting like little kids, giggling and bouncing on the spot. I'm so happy that twat has gone. We both didn't like him. Now, I won't have to use his name. Doug agrees with me, only he's more diplomatic. He tried his best to get on with him. I let him know I didn't like him. I rarely entertained his bullshit and made no effort. Why bother to be nice to people when you see no good in them?

Some of the boys are looking over at us, laughing. They've rarely seen me this happy before. Trust me, Benedict was such a prick. I'm more than pleased he's gone.

"What the fuck did he do?" I said, excited with wide-eyed wonderment. "Why didn't you tell me this before?"

Doug laughs again, a real belly laugh, he's holding his lower abdomen.

"He told them." He points at the kids in the cabin. "What a blow job was." He said, chuckling, lifting his clenched fist back to his mouth to suppress his own noise.

It doesn't surprise me he told these kids what fellatio was. I know he would have only told them to be popular. I shudder to think if he provided visual gestation of the actions involved, I bet he did. He's that obscene and stupid. The minute he gets a laugh from anyone, he'll then butcher the point until the laughter stops and embarrassment falls upon his audience.

It's scary how quick they get rid of you. One minute you're here, next you're gone. No announcement, no goodbyes. They discreetly make you gather up your stuff when the cabin is empty. Then you're out on your arse.

Doug folds up his headphones, placing his CD player meticulously on the bed beside him. He rarely uses his own bedside table, always the bed to his right.

"Yeah, well, it's kinda our fault," said Doug. "Josh knows we don't like him, so he told John about the blow job thing. He really hammed it up too." He motions with his right hand and jabs his tongue into the side of his mouth. He even adds a realistic gagging noise, gargling from his dry throat.

"Sick." I said, watching Doug finish his demonstration.

I could do with a bit of sucky suck myself right now. I'm getting so desperate I'd let Doug perform a Lewinsky on me. I think I'm joking, it's been so long though.

"Bless Josh," I said. "Not sure how you ham up a blow job,

but more fool Benedict for being a nobber."

"Good riddance I say, dawg." Said Doug, stretching his arms.

Doug smiles a cartoon smile, his face becomes like plasticine for a moment. He raises his hand in the air, the internationally accepted gesture to receive a high five. Usually I wouldn't, as I can't stand high fives, but on this occasion, I accept his invitation, and our hands clap together with a resonating fleshy kick drum. I really do like Doug, he's good.

"We'd better get the guys, dinners in like twenty minutes," said Doug.

"All the blow job news," I said. "I almost forgot." I follow Doug's cue as we walk toward the bathroom. "I'll round these guys up, you get Jake and that lot,"

Doug nods, clapping as he approaches the four boys at the end of our cabin. They're playing Top Trumps.

I walk into the cabin next door. The layout is the same as ours, ten beds, two of them bunks, cubbies, windows with shutters, fly screens, graffiti on the chip board, same shit.

Nate, with his tall, broad-shouldered frame and spiked up hair, is standing in front of all the kids, circled around him. I can see Josh, Mark, Tyrese and Morgan. That's a relief at least, they're not lost. There must be fourteen kids entranced by whatever's taking place. I don't know what he's up to.

I walk over to the kid filled crowd. I'm more intrigued, also a little nervous. Weird that he's commanding all their attention. What's going on, is he handing out sweets?

"Nah, I was in college and it was done to me." Said Nate to the crowd.

His audience of kids, with faces transfixed, appear like an audience of bewildered villagers at a travelling freak show. They're ready to part with their hard-earned crops or the little silver they've scrounged in exchange for escapist entertainment.

Jordan, a tiny, thin looking boy with a scraggy hair cut stands up from his kneeling position. Jordan never wears a T-shirt. You can always hear him arguing with Nate and Andy over it. Trying to get him to dinner with a shirt on sounds painful. It happens most evenings. I'm thankful he's not in our cabin. Jordan really needs to eat more, I can see his collar bone protruding like bone scaffolding.

"Would you do it to one of us?" said Jordan.

No idea what's going on here.

"What you guys doing?" I said.

I'm honestly intrigued. How has Nate got all their attention?

Josh turns to look up at me with a chuffed, brief smile.

"Nate's gonna make us pass out?" said Josh. You can always rely on Josh, he's like the teacher's pet.

"That explains it. Is that a good idea?" I said, my voice laced with hesitation at this proposed action of entertainment. Only ever gonna end badly.

"Go on Dylan, let him do it to us." Said Jordan.

All the boys' eyes now on me, hoping I won't ruin their fun.

"Jordie boy." I said, in a deliberate Geordie accent. "I'm not gonna stop you. I don't think it's a great idea. But whatever, be my guest."

I shake my head disapprovingly. I must at least appear like I'm a responsible adult, and care. I don't care. How can it end well? Up to Nate. If he does this, it's on him.

"Don't worry, it's safe. I've done it loads before. We call it 'Chicken Choke'." Said Nate.

"Chicken Choke?" I said.

What the fuck is chicken choke? The name's no better. It hasn't allayed my fears. Sounds like tossing someone off to me.

"You clutch their neck and choke 'em out." Said Nate, miming a choking action of his hands clasped around a neck. "Not up for it. Then you're chicken."

"Crystal clear," I said. "You've done this to ten-year-olds?" That's a fair question.

"Sure. I've had it done to me loads of times," said Nate.

That doesn't really surprise me. Clearly oxygen has been suppressed from his grey matter for too long. If he thinks this is a wise decision, he's mental.

"Who wants to go first?"

The rascal of ten-year-old arms fly up, as if they're an audience at a theme park being invited to dance on stage with Goofy. Put your hands up in the air, shake around like you just don't care.

Jordan, the most excited of the funky bunch, throws his arms up first. He's far too excited about this. He jumps forward toward Nate, like he's fearful he's gonna lose the opportunity of a lifetime. Dead man walking, if you ask me. This may be Nate's worst moment, he could let himself down here.

"I do. I do," said Jordan. "I want it done on me."

Nate takes hold of Jordan by the shoulders and stands him up in front of the rest of the boys, like a Christmas nutcracker, his arms stiff, straight by his side. The boys all move forward, circling much like they do at the base of flagpole.

"Right," said Nate. "What you have to do is lean forward like this." Nate demonstrates. Leaning forward with his head between his legs, he bolts up quick. "Then, you breathe in like real deep and fast."

Jordan follows his instruction without question. He bends over at his hips, like a door hinge, and breathes in deep, loud and gusty. His back expanding and contracting with each breath he takes. Nate then rests his hands on Jordan's back, looking at the second hand of his wristwatch.

"OK, keep going. Only a few more seconds. When I tell you to stop, take one more deep breath and stand, like up straight, real quick." Nate continues with his instruction, concentrating on his timepiece.

Jordan breaths in deep, still bent over.

"Deep breath, now stand up." Said Nate, grabbing Jordan by the shoulders to swing him up like a medieval catapult. He pulls Jordan toward him, spins him around on the spot with a flick of his shoulders, his face a blur. He pushes him against the chipboard cabin wall, grabs him by the neck, strangling him. Jordan reaches up over the top of Nate's hands. His face swells red. He doesn't struggle. Nate then concentrates, as if this is tantamount to keyhole surgery. Jordan's arms and shoulders drop limp and lifeless at his side, his eyes closed. Nate lowers him to the floor. Jordan lays still between two beds on the cold wooden floorboards.

"Cool," said Tyrese.

"Nate, man, is he OK?" I said.

I'm a little more concerned than I was before. He could be dead.

"Sure, he's havin' the best time of his life," said Nate.

I step toward Jordan. He's laid out with his eyes shut, tight. He isn't moving. Just a floppy bag of shite at the edge of the cabin wall, in this narrow claustrophobic space.

"Nate. Seriously, how long do we leave him?"

I'm genuinely worried about him now. All the kids eyeball Nate, we're all hoping he has the answers. Nate steps back, bumping shoulders with me, as he bends down and back slaps Jordan across the cheek. He isn't moving, his cheeks flush raspberry red from the slap, his lips turning blue.

"Jordan, time to wake up buddy." Said Nate, hitting him across the face again, back and forth. He looks more panicked now, too. I know I am, this isn't right. What if he's killed him?

Nate bundles Jordan up in his arms in one swoop, barging past me and the onlooking kids, parting them like drapes. He darts toward the back door, kicks it open with his foot. He's only wearing socks. I run after him. Most of the boys follow. Nate is running, tiny little steps with his back arched, Jordan isn't that heavy, but he's like a dead weight, limp and floppy.

I'm confused where we're running, we're heading in the opposite direction to the medical centre. Where's he going? Nate runs up to the chain-link fence surrounding the twenty-five metre outdoor swimming pool. He isn't going to do what I think he is?

He jerks forward with a jolt, launching Jordan's flaccid body into the air, freeing him from his arms. Jordan, now airborne flings over the fence, crashing down with a tremendous crunch onto the surface of the pool water. A splash erupts around him, and showers chlorinated water in every direction. The sound may as well have been him hitting concrete. Nate vaults over the fence. Jordan emerges, flailing, trying to take a breath, I swear he's swallowing water. Nate dives into the pool headfirst. He grabs Jordan, drags him to the edge of the pool under his chin. He pushes him out of the water, like a piece of poached cod folding off a spatula. Jordan lays on his side, coughing as he takes panicked breaths. He must be scared shitless. A lot of the freak show spectators are now alongside me, gawping on like I am. This is completely nuts. Jordan appears fine, wet, but fine.

"You OK Jordie?" I said.

Jordan rolls over in the crowds direction, nodding his breathless head at our puzzled faces. He flicks his head loose, signifying there was something or someone of interest approaching behind. He's trying to warn us.

"Everything OK here?"

The inquisitive voice of John, our illustrious long haired division leader with his trusty keys around his neck jangling toward us. I don't think you have to be a genius to assume something other than swimming is going on here. We shouldn't be by the pool, anyway. So, questions are gonna be asked.

Nate sits up on the side of the pool, fully clothed, dripping wet. He pushes himself up as water flows down off his drenched camp clothes, water squelches free from the holes in his socks. He helps Jordan to his feet.

"He's fine," said Nate. "He fell and like slipped in. He's fine now though, ain't cha buddy?" He rubs his fingers through his wet head and pats Jordan on both shoulders. Droplets of water expel with the pressure.

I can't believe what I'm hearing. Nate has performed an act of desperation to cover his own arse. Chicken choke was bad enough, dashing him in the pool, fucking insane.

John walks conservative and slow around the whole length of the chain-link fence to the entrance gate into the pool area. His steps are deliberate. John isn't stupid, he knows exactly what's gone on. He certainly doesn't believe the story he's been fed from Nate. I mean, who the fuck would? The gate slams shut. Another spring-loaded joy. As he approaches, Jordan shakes his arms like a dog. His face looks as if he wants a hug. John doesn't give him a hug, I won't either. John squats down, meeting Jordan's eye level.

"Let's get you checked out, little buddy." Said John, taking him by the hand. He lifts him up and over the fence from under his arms. I take hold of him from the other side, supporting him by his armpits. He helps by swinging his legs over the fence, still soaking wet. The pool water always smells of old socks and toilet bleach. I place Jordan on his feet. John vaults over the fence, grunting, like he might when pulling on his socks. His feet pound on the grass, he isn't athletic. He steadies himself, breathless, leaning back on the fence and grasps for my shoulders for support.

"Dylan, take 'em all back to the cabin. Then get to dinner," said John.

There's no need to respond to him. I know what I need to do. Everybody seems to follow me without question anyway, even Nate.

"Where d'ya think you're going?" said John.

"Who me?" I said, as I turn round to face him. It's got nothing to do with me.

"No, not you," said John. "Nate."

I can't be sure what's gonna happen. Whatever it is, I'm not sure it was worth all this.

All in the name of 'Chicken Choke'.

19

Golf Cart Frog Match

I'm too sensitive. I am tired today. I'm warming up with Alyssa for softball. We haven't gone as far as warming up our bodies by bumping uglies, not yet. Our time will come. We both will too, I hope. Room for some sweaty romance.

Alyssa's standing opposite me on the softball field. This place is like a second home now. I'm concentrating on the thumps created by large softballs smacking into gloves. I clutch the ball, toss it back at her, under arm. Every time I do, I smile as she catches it. Every time she throws it back to me, my smile seems to fade. Alyssa's laughing at my mercurial reaction. I've noticed, she's always somewhere else in her head, distracted. Laura does that too. It's yet another thing I focus my attention on, I think I have a problem. All these insignificant details consume me.

All the girls or 'Seniors' warm up around us, paired up, throwing and catching softballs. Most of the balls are hitting the ground. These girls don't give a shit. Lacey's standing close to me. She's throwing the ball, still wearing a bandage sleeve. I'll ignore her. She keeps laughing to get my attention. She does have an infectious laugh, although it's beginning to irritate me now, because it sounds so fake. Laugh away, bitch, laugh it up. I find it hard to ignore how vacuous she is. I need to remember she's only sixteen and I'm here to mentor, inspire, and be responsible. It's not only confusing because she looks older, but because she's getting in my head.

There's a lot of noise around. It seems noisy in my thoughts. A golf cart grinds to a halt on the road, up on the ridge. Bill is driving, his face filled with vexation as he casts his eyes on me. He cranks on the steering wheel, driving the cart down the hillside, looks dangerous given the angle. He's bossing it, must have done that a few times before. He's driving it at me. I catch the ball from Alyssa and hold on to it for a second in my glove. Bill parks the golf cart alongside me. He beckons me over, pushing the peak of his baseball cap up off his forehead to reveal more of his eyes. Vex eyes, no less. All very spaghetti western. His invitation looks ominous.

I throw the ball underarm back to Alyssa. I muster a wink at her. I don't intend to make a habit of winking. She looks worried, worried for me, that is. I nod to reassure her. Who's going to reassure me?

"Looks like you're in trouble." Said a chuffed Lacey.

"Lacey." Said Alyssa, tossing the ball from her glove into her empty throwing hand.

I get in the passenger seat of the golf cart. Bill puts the cart into reverse and backs it away from the softball field, the girls shrinking smaller as we zip away.

"I'd like to get your side of the story," said Bill. The cart stops with a jerk "Tell me what happened yesterday." He grips the golf cart steering wheel. His facial hair thick, behaving independent of his lip, the breeze pulling on it.

"I don't know what you're talking about," I said.

"I've spoken to the kids and Nate and Doug. I wanna get your side," said Bill.

"Well, respectfully. If you've spoken to everyone already. Why d'ya need to talk to me?" I said, shaking my head. I'll try to keep this pretence of innocence up for as long as I can.

Bill removes his hat, wiping his brow with the back of his hand.

"Am I being fired?"

"No, you're not gettin' fired," said Bill.

Thank God for that. After everything so far, I can't leave now.

"Nate might be," he said. "I wanna hear the truth from you."

I still have my baseball glove on for some reason. I remove it, place it on my lap. I pat it down like it was a Dachshund, it's comforting.

"I don't wanna see him get fired. He wouldn't deliberately hurt any of the guys," I said.

He may be from California and think he's from NSYNC but he shouldn't get fired for horseplay. Albeit stupid, dangerous horseplay.

"OK, so tell me what he did."

"You know what he did," I said.

This is just some bullshit power game for him, I swear.

"So, you're confirming it?" said Bill.

I almost react with defiance. Instead, I reject my rationality and nod my pathetic little head. It's like I've betrayed myself. I've done Nate an injustice. I'm such a pussy.

"Thank you," said Bill. "I now, on behalf of Red Oak, have to call every one of these kids' parents and explain exactly what happened. Otherwise, they won't attend next year."

"So, are you worried about the kids welfare or that you won't have their parents' money next year?"

I'm taking a chance with him, I know that. But, this is all getting on my tits now.

"Spare me your politics." Said Bill, placing his hat on his head "Tell me what happened."

Without hesitation, I go into detail. Calling out the name of the game; *'Chicken Choke'*. Nate's hands warpping around Jordan's neck. Bill even asked me to demonstrate on him. I should have squeezed harder in my re-enactment. I didn't want to make it appear worse. As much as I wanted to throttle Bill blue.

"That's news to me," said Bill.

What, hold on. Has he just got me to drop Nate in it? Maybe I'm the only one that said anything. But I can't defend him. From the way Bill was talking, this is it for him. I can't create a story to defend him for launching Jordan in the pool. I still don't know what he was thinking with that.

"You can get back to it. I'm watching you," said Bill.

I'm half expecting him to do the whole two finger eyeball gesture. He hasn't. I may have laughed if he threw that one in. I step off the golf cart, holding my glove.

"I don't want Nate to get fired." I said, clutching the cart to steady myself, peering at Bill.

He turns, looking straight at me with a patronising smile.

"If he does. He's got you to thank," he said.

His head flicks round like a robot as he slams his foot on the accelerator. I jerk my head back outta the way to avoid being struck by the cart. He zips away, disappearing in the direction he came. I know now Nate's fate. The story Bill fed me was complete bollocks. I gave him everything he needed. Should I feel guilty?

I stand motionless for a while, my toes aching. I can only contemplate my manipulation. I hear Alyssa's sweet voice from behind me. Her face becoming ever clearer. She's so beautiful, American and poster girl perfection.

"Everything OK, sweetie?" she said.

She tosses me the ball. Luckily, I react fast enough and catch it in one hand. Her face is concerned, a minute frown, the subtlest of furrows. That's the first time she's called me sweetie too.

I've never been a fan of predictable pet names. I always get playfully pissed off with Laura when she calls me, babe. I can't stand it. If you're gonna call me anything. Make it random or atleast original. Call me; Captain Carousel', Donkey Kong, even Gwin.

Anything but Babe. I'm far too preoccupied with all this pet name annoyance.

"I think I just got Nate fired," I said.

"I'm sure you didn't. They won't fire him," said Alyssa.

"Even after choking out the kids, I'd fire him."

"Everybody does it in High School. It's part of growing up. It's not that shocking," said Alyssa.

She walks toward me, planting her arms around my shoulders. It's what I need, a well-timed, sincere hug. I stare lifeless over her shoulder. It's not contrived. She pulls away, still maintaining a hold on me.

"You wanna umpire this game for me?" She said, rubbing the back of my arm.

Is she being condescending? I pray she's being sweet again.

"Sure, might take my mind off all this shit." I said. She's being lovely to me. I kiss her on her moist lips. Her warmth soothes me. She has slim lips compared to Laura. Laura's are far more voluptuous, especially for a white girl. You can't beat Moira's. They're just wow. Maybe, I'm too familiar with Laura and taking everything for granted, but Alyssa's kisses are far better.

"What you doing?" Said Alyssa, looking around. "Someone will see."

"Little lady." I said, holding on to her hips and pulling her back into me. "I don't care anymore. I won't let bad people tell me what good is."

She smiles, although she seems embarrassed, squirming. I can see that she likes me acting dominant. I'm happy to oblige. She expects me to kiss her again. It would be a travesty if I wasn't to act on my instincts. Sometimes, it's right to take a chance. A kiss will do it. I'm reading this all right.

The softball game is well under way. I'm standing behind the female pitcher, Louise, with pink dyed hair. I'm the Umpire, this way I can still see home plate and I don't have to put all the pads on, that's all too involved. I'll use Louise as a human shield.

Alyssa is standing at the side of the field, marking down the score with her trusty clipboard. She seems to use that clipboard as a security blanket, almost to hide a weakness, albeit a cute one. I keep looking at her every time the ball is thrown. She reciprocates my glances, putting the end of her pen in her mouth. I'll read into that what I will, this game is already shit. It's a pussy excuse for a watered-down, safe version of Baseball. It's a girls game, in every sense of the word.

Louise, the short blonde-haired girl with pink dyed tips, is pitching. I say pitching, I mean doing that whole underarm projectile throw thing that looks completely retarded, there's no class to it. The ball fires over the plate with surprising accuracy. The pitch is far from ladylike.

"Dylan, are you calling this?" Said Louise. Little mouthy bitch, barking at me. Now, she's glaring at me from under her cap.

"Of course. Ball." I said, providing a much needed and all too familiar American southern twang. Louise shoots me another glare. Why is it these girls are all so bloody brave?

"You weren't even paying attention, that was a strike." She said.

"I called it. Ball." I said, again.

I'm so stern these days, all confident and direct for no reason. No idea where it's coming from.

"You were looking at your girlfriend, ya pussy." She said with this humorous vexation. I'm not surprised by her vulgar use of language, it's well-timed. Most of these girls are ratchet hoes anyway, completely entitled, not original, and none of 'em can think for themselves.

"Sorry," I said. "You're right, I was looking at my Mrs." I made sure Alyssa would hear. She heard it all right. She lowers her head, not even laughing. There's nothing sweet in that reaction. She looks ashamed, her head staring straight down at the grass. I swear she's gone red. This is the first time I've publicly alluded to the fact we might be an item. We haven't had that conversation, it's too late now. I took a chance, it may backfire. I'll find out. She doesn't impressed. I would have preferred her to smirk sweetly, chuckled coyly, or shifted her weight from hip to hip. Instead, she's staring at the floor. I should try to ease off on all this love and relationship stuff a little. I mean, I have a girlfriend. At least I think I still do. It's been so long since I've heard from her, heard her voice. In fact, I still haven't really thought about her in real terms. I've been far too distracted. I need to make more of an effort and just be Laura's boyfriend. That all sounds far too adult and full of unnecessary commitment to me. I should probably grow up.

Louise looks disgusted, as if she's gonna vomit at our public display of affection. Well, mine, I suppose. Alyssa hasn't given me shit, all very one sided. She's gone from hot to stony cold.

Oh, joy. Lacey, of all people is up to bat next. She removes her helmet, flicks free her lush blonde hair, scoops it up, tying it in a loose ponytail, before popping her helmet back on her head. Despite her bandaged wrist she looks committed to hitting this softball as hard as she can. Why it's referred to as a softball, I'll never know, it's hard as fuck.

"I'd hate to break this up but throw the damn ball." Said Lacey. Forever disapproving, nothing but teenage jealousy. She sticks her arse out.

Louise lobs the oversized ball. Lacey swings wild and misses. Her body spins on the spot with reckless momentum.

I gesture to the side, "Strike." I shout as loud as I can. Almost too enthusiastic. I'm smug she missed. That'll teach her.

Lacey's not happy with that call, she's shooting me a look of death. This one more scathing and disapproving than the one before. The catcher throws the ball back at Louise; she catches it with arrogance, smirking at Lacey. She's swinging the bat in preparation to hit the next pitched ball.

Louise winds up and pitches. Lacey swings. The ball clips off the bat, flying high into the air. I don't think she was even ready for that. All eyes are on the ball as it floats. It's returning, back down to earth.

The catcher holds out her mitt to catch it, crack. The ball lands with a thud in her glove. Although a foul ball, Lacey's out. She's failed. See, she doesn't get everything.

I see a flash of Lacey's red angry face in mine. It's all so quick. I'm on my knees. An empty, heavy, earthy pressure in my stomach. My balls are throbbing. I flop to my side.

Louise standing over me, sniggering. My vision's dark. I can make out her pink hair. Alyssa's running over. I can't hear anything. She grabs a bat from the clutches of Lacey, throws it to the ground. From everyone's reaction and my crippling pain. I know now Lacey's made her way from Home plate, stomped across the field and launched her bat into my groin. I didn't even see it coming. I can only see her back now as she's being marched away by Alyssa. She hit me square in the bollocks. Like a hard, empty air jolting right up through my body. I can't even think about standing.

Time seems to pass so painfully. I'm being helped to my feet by teenage girls. I'm so embarrassed as I clutch myself. It makes it worse that these girls know that I've been compromised. Alyssa is crouched over, giving Lacey an animated talking to, pointing and jabbing her index finger into her shoulder.

Off on the horizon, Bill's golf cart whistles along, kicking up dust as it travels the brow of the hill. Nate's sitting on the back, feet dangling with a large duffel bag across his lap, a tan leather suitcase by his side. He's holding on tight as his body rocks. He's noticed me and winks. I know, and he knows we'll never see each other again. I provide a subtle salute. Nate and the golf cart disappear into the darkness of the trees.

Alyssa sees the golf cart too. She stops berating Lacey, following the cart with her eyes. She's looking over at me and mouths. *'I'm sorry.'*

That's that. Nate's gone, he's out. I can't think about all that right now. I need to breathe; my balls are fucking burning.

"Ice. I need ice," I said.

20

Photo Sensitivity

No sanctuary. No time to myself. I think about Laura when I'm laying here on this top bunk. I need to tuck my arms behind my head to add some elevation. These pillows are crap. How are we expected to sleep on these?

If I was anywhere else, feeling as I do, I would certainly have a wank. It would never beat my last piece of voyeurism. I could get it done all before anyone was to return. Just not in the mood. I lean over, grab Malcolm X, I pluck for my picture of Laura. I've been using her as a bookmark. She's more than a bookmark obviously, but her picture provides perfect page separation. Plus, I can see her when I want. Usually, the mere sight of her appeases me. I grapple with tormented thoughts of what she's doing and who she's doing it with, Charlie, no doubt. Whether she suspects I'm exploring other women, who knows. I try to read some of Malcolm, at least once a day, for mental stimulation, call it my escape.

This picture of Laura, is one of her flicking her blonde hair from the collar of her beige corduroy jacket. Because our student house was always so cold, she's wearing a thick black jumper too.

Then another coat over the top, a Parker with a fluffy Liam Gallagher type hood. She always smells so good. She reminds me of lychees. I miss that. This picture is slightly out of focus. I rest it on my chest for a moment. I'm trying to see life in her eyes. The picture almost transports me back to that moment. As I was standing in front of her, holding the camera, taking this picture, trying to get her to laugh with stupid voices, so I could capture the moment. They can't take my memories.

The front door swings open. It almost makes me shit myself and no sooner have I realised it's Doug with the kids. As the boys come spilling in the cabin, Doug shuffles behind them.

"Why have you done that?" I said. I can't hide my shock. Doug's face is bald. He looks completely different, his face is clean.

He's shaking his head, not making eye contact with anyone. He's looks fucking angry.

"They made him do it." Said Josh, jumping on his bed.

Doug's shaven his goatee off, all gone. Nothing, he's still shaking his head. I've never seen him like this before. He looks close to tears. It's odd to see his chin. You can even see his teeth better now. They're glistening white, they're really set off by his olive skin

"I was told I had to," he said. "I'm not allowed facial hair."

"Who said that, Rod or Bill?"

"Both of 'em, dawg. They don't approve."

"They've both got facial hair," I said.

Doug's pacing up and down. Mark appears to my right, on my bunk ladder. He's holding on to the top of my bed, peering over at me.

"You have to get involved don't ya," I said.

Mark shrugs his shoulders, leaning back, outstretched. I can't have ginger Mark looking at me, being weird. I'm trying to talk to Doug. Now, Mark's all up in my face space. I forgot Laura's picture is on my chest. I grab it, placing it inside the pages of Malcolm X.

"What's that?" Said Mark, in that annoying, inquisitive childish way.

"None of your business." I said, trying to enforce my authority.

Doug carries on stomping his feet, removing his baseball cap and wagging his head, like the Ultimate Warrior, ready for a fight.

Mark snatches my book.

"Oi," I said.

He jumps down off the ladder with Malcolm X in hand and my picture of Laura. The one I was trying to shield him from. I don't wanna let him into my life. He doesn't need to know who Laura is, and by seeing her it's like an invasion of us. Of who we are as a couple. I have to get it back. I jump off the bed without using the ladder. He isn't getting away from me. I'm getting my picture.

"One sec, Doug." I said, waving my hand at him, distracted. "Mark, stop being a dick." I said. I really do wanna carry on my conversation with Doug, but I'm having to plead with this kid to give me back my shit.

"Mark, seriously. Give me the picture." I said, flapping my open hand.

Mark pulls the picture from the book. The movement may as well be the screeches of violin strings in my head. It's painful to see his eyes widened with excitement at the sight of Laura.

"She's sexy." He said, laughing and jumping between beds. Trampling over sleeping bags and pillows. The rest of the boys aren't really paying attention. The last thing he needs is encouragement.

"I'd do her." He shouts as he throws his body against the wall and dry humps the photo.

"Mark." I said, yanking him by his arm. He drops to the bed and rolls on the floor. I grab for the picture and pull it close to me. Mark's cowering at my feet. I really want to punch him in the face, I wanna lay into him, really hurt him. My cheeks are hot, back teeth clenching. I need to calm down. He looks scared. He should be. I can't hurt him though. I won't. He does need to learn some manners. I replace Laura back inside Malcolm X.

"I'm sorry, Mark." I said, offering my hand to help him to his feet.

"I was only playing," he said.

"I know you were mate."

"Is she your girlfriend?" He said, adjusting his shirt from his neckline.

That's kind of a stupid question, but he's trying to apologise. He's paying attention now. I should probably give him a chance.

"Yeah, that's Laura." I said, looking down at her picture, opening out the page of Malcolm X, to see her blonde hair and beige jacket again. I'm happy for a moment seeing her, pride. So much contentment, I like the familiar, it's grand.

"Can I see?" Said Josh, getting up from his bed.

I like Josh. I'm happy for him to see her with no argument. I turn the photo round in my fingertips, he doesn't touch it. Instead, leans forward as if he's trying to read an in-memorandum plaque on a park bench, too afraid to sit.

"She's pretty." He said, nodding and just walks back to his bed. No drama, true gent.

I put Laura back in the book again and sit opposite Doug.

"They said they'd fire me if I didn't do it."

"They can't do that," I said. "It looks all right though." I scope out his smooth face again.

"I hate it." He said, pinching his nose between his finger and thumb, looks like he wants to cry.

"You'll get used to it, I am already."

"Maybe." He said, looking around the cabin and then back at me. "You see Nate leave?"

"Yeah, with Bill."

"He may have had a lucky escape. I can't take much more of this shit, dawg."

"I'm just happy I have tonight off."

"Nah-uh, shit. I forgot about that," he said.

"Boy of the bunk, mate, after that I'm getting pissed up."

I owe it to myself, after all this shit I've been through. I haven't had a drink for so long. We're obviously not allowed to talk about it or discuss it. I haven't seen or heard of anyone having any alcohol on camp, not yet anyway. No one surreptitiously hiding bottles in the rafters or burying Jack Daniel's in the woods. I'm really looking forward to this night of freedom. I'm not sure I'll get served, but I'll do my best at drinking something, anything. Even if that means sneaking swigs from other peoples' empties.

Alyssa mentioned this bar in town, Chillingsworth's or something like that. So, balls to my fear of crowds. I'll get seriously lubricated. Plus, it'll be nice to hang out with her and have a drink. I won't be touching absinthe. Hopefully I can take whatever this is between us too, to the next level. That'll be cool. I may have to suck up my introverted traits and be the most affable of all people you'll ever know in all the living world. Chin chin.

I only have to survive another hour before I can escape. Just need to get these guys to the rec hall for the damn awards. Fucking hell, how boring.

Deep joy.

21

Boy of The Bunk

The rec hall is packed out with kids and counsellors. The entire room is roaring with the noise of almost two hundred boys, talking, shouting, singing, and screaming.

All the boys and counsellors are sitting on rows of the familiar solid wooden benches, all facing the stage, where Rod is sitting dead centre on a collapsible sun chair. In his hand, he's holding a cabled microphone. He looks like a dick, Elton John he ain't.

I'm perching on the edge of the bench; my bare leg touching Doug's. I don't mind all that much. The surrounding noise is getting louder. Rod jumps up from his reclining relaxed position. The microphone rolls off his lap and hits the floor. The distorted feedback screeches around the hall through the speakers. His stiff hand now in the air. We all know what that means. Heil Hitler. He wants a bit of library silence. As he wishes, it is granted. Rod eventually lowers his arm. Only when he wants, Big man Rod. He steps around the stage in front of a table covered in several shiny plaques. I hadn't even noticed the table.

"Gentlemen." Rod shouts into the microphone. "Tonight, is the night you've all been waiting for." His voice too close, the bass booming, making the speakers rumble. The boys stamp their feet and shout, excited.

"Boy of the bunk awards," said Rod.

The room gets louder. I'm not sure how that's possible. But, Lord Jesus, the room erupted. The kids are bashing, crashing and stomping their feet, clapping their hands like crazed felons. This is all too much for me. Now this son of a prick, Rod raises his hand again. He's just caused the fucking raucous and now he's asking for quiet. His hand stays in the air. He trudges around, holding the microphone wire out to the side like some televangelist.

"Balls." Shouted from behind me. Everyone turns round and laughs. Doug and I laugh. We both know. The room knows, Alabama Landon has burst out with a perfectly timed addition to the silence.

"Thank you, Landon." Said Rod chuckling into the microphone. Rod's laughing encourages some of the younger boys on the front benches to chortle uncontrollably.

"Settle down." He said, flapping his hand. "As I was saying, boy of the bunk. The one lucky boy from each bunk that receives this award, has shown a level of maturity and willing. Impressing both your counsellors and division leaders alike."

He holds up a cheap looking small plaque. It's shaped like a shield with a flimsy little plastic hinge on the back. I can't see what's inscribed on the gold-plated centrepiece, but it's probably some bullshit.

"The winner should be extremely proud of themselves," He said.

Josh is sitting on his hands, looking over the kids' heads in front of him. He pivots on the spot and looks up at me.

"Dyl, d'ya know who's gonna get it for Connecticut?" He said, as he straightens his little back.

"I can't tell you that, mate." I said, smirking at him, raising my eyebrows. I hope my subtle face will be enough to non-verbally confirm that I did in fact vote for him and so too did Doug. In other words, 'you got it, mate'.

Josh smiles. I can see then he's interpreted my words as they were intended. I was blatant about it. His happiness is tangible. I feel so good for him. He's had a tough time of it. He's done well and deserves to win.

"OK gentlemen. The moment you've all be waiting for," said Rod.

He's got a microphone, but he's still shouting. Anyone would think we couldn't hear him. The entire room goes silent in anticipation. The silence is disturbed with the clearing of throats, and high pitch screech of trainers on wood, like a squash game. The room is hanging off Rod's every word. Not me, fat chance of that.

"The boy of the bunk for Delaware is." Rod pauses for dramatic effect. "Brian Woodley."

The room is filled with clapping appreciation. Brian, a tiny eight-year-old boy, gets up from his seat, down the front and sheepishly walks toward the stage, stepping up. Rod takes Brian by the hand and shakes it with adult vigour. From here it looks as though he's imparting his authority again, like a salesman, strong and determined. Sale of the century. Rod hands Brian one of the small pathetic little plaques. Brian looks happy with it, a genuine open-mouthed smile. If he's faking it, he's convinced me.

One after another, same thing. Working through most of the East Coast states, in chronological order of joining the colonies. Time ticks on. I'm looking forward to getting the fuck out of here. I can't wait to have this evening off. Sooner we get this done, the better.

Rod turns and grabs one of the last plaques off the table and holds it up like gold.

Josh swivels and looks at me again. His excitement is palpable.

"It's me next. I can't wait." He said, clasping his hands together with expectation.

"You deserve it mate." I said, tapping him on the shoulder.

Rod walks to the edge of the stage, microphone in hand. The

wire trailing behind him.

"Now, that brings us to the award for Connecticut Cabin," said Rod.

His voice now horse, gravelly, struggling through his words. In predictable and now tiresome fashion, the room claps, going quiet in anticipation for Rod to announce the winner.

"Well done to," Rod pauses, scoping out the crowd, doing his best to build tension in his childish audience. "Mark Clarendon."

The room booms with noise. No thought involved. Brainwashed fools join in mindlessly.

Josh is sat mouth wide open, looking vacant toward the stage. I can't believe it either. That's not right. Doug looks at me, confused. I shake my head. Josh's face is white. I'm not sure he'll come back from this. Perhaps I shouldn't have got his hopes up. It should have been based on Doug and my vote. Doug is as surprised as me. I cut back with the same look, baffled.

Mark jumps up, running toward the stage. His trainers banging on the back of his hamstrings. Of all the boys to have received that award, Mark is an arrogant twat. I hoped he would have behaved more humble.

Josh taps me on the shoulder. He looks heartbroken. His soft face, almost velvet, his eyes loose and watery.

"You said it was me," he said.

I look at him with sympathy. How can I explain this? I can't provide poetry. I'll have to be honest with him. I'm angry, but I need to be strong for Josh. I need to act for him.

"I'm sorry Josh, Doug and I will have a word with Rod," I said. "There must be some mistake. We both voted for you." I place my hand on his shoulder. I'm being genuine. I don't wanna see this kid affected negatively by this, something so unimportant. It shouldn't now define him for the rest of his life. Josh at least smiles. He's being good about it. I hope he appreciates our respect for him, more than he could for a plaque. He isn't the type of kid to enjoy the attention anyway, he's never given me that impression. He may well have been happy with knowing within himself he was meant to win, as opposed to standing in the spotlight on a stage.

With the pomp and ceremony over. The crowd filters out of the rec hall through the back doors. It's still light outside, only just. I'm itching to get out of here. Doug and I, closer together after making sure everyone exits and is heading back toward our cabin. We both hang back in the hope to catch up with Rod.

"This motherfucker better hurry up," I said. "I'm meeting Alyssa at the bus. I need a drink, man."

Doug smiles and nods beyond me, off over my shoulder as he spots Rod leaving the rec hall.

I bet he's got a packet of fags under his hat. Addiction fills the wrinkles on his face. He wants a smoke, as much as I do. I've never smelt it on him, but I'm telling you, he's a smoker. His yellow teeth give it away.

Rod's spotted us, our heads peeking over passing heads like floating birds on the peaks of drifting waves. His eyes flit from me, then on Doug. He must know what we wanna say. He doesn't deserve polite salutation, but I'll provide it, anyway. I still have that submission in my unconscious. They have a strange hold over me here, on all of us.

"Excuse me, Rod. May we have a word?"

See, that's polite. Not overly, but it'll do.

"Gentlemen," he said.

He uses the same old condescending tone. It doesn't matter what context or even the audience. It's a visceral explosion of syllables. Exasperated and impatient. It has an edge of intimidation to it. This though remains the best time to approach this injustice. At summer camp, everything becomes a drama.

"Well," I said. "Doug and I have a question. We both told John that Josh was our choice for boy of the bunk. Why didn't he get it?"

Rod stares at me. Not only now is he silent, but his eyes are doing the intimidating.

"Josh was a pain in my ass," he said.

I certainly didn't expect that response. I don't think Doug did either, considering his shocked expression. Pretty much the same as mine.

"I was on the phone to his parents all the damn time, reassuring them," he said.

"Yeah, but he turned it around. Now he's having a great time. Plus, he's a cool kid," I said.

Rod scratched the back of his neck with his fingertips, it was almost aggressive convulsion.

"That's the reason we wanted him to get boy of the bunk, right Doug."

Doug's positioned himself behind me, past my shoulder. He does though, to be fair to him when I sort of prompt him with my intonation, steps forward, alongside me. Shoulder to shoulder.

"Yeah," he said. "We both saw he was putting a lot of effort in and—,"

"You threw that hard work in his face," I said.

I had to interrupt him. I won't apologise. Doug's being far too submissive. I can't be listening to more of this shit.

Rod squares up to me, right in my face. My vision filled with nothing but meandering tiny veins trickling through is blotchy cheeks under his red baseball cap. He crosses his arms in front of himself and inflates his chest. I'm not gonna flinch. If I close myself off and cross my arms too, he'll know his position is intimidating me. If he hits me, there's very little I can do. If worse comes to worse, I'm willing to fucking head butt him. I think the angle would clip the peak of his baseball hat too. I'd have to strike upward. It would reveal if he has got fags under there. Might be worth it, just for that.

"Dylan, you're pushing it."

I put the tip of my tongue over the front of my teeth. I don't have a dry mouth, but my jaw has become tight again.

"I'm livid," I said. "Because the boy who should've got that award, Josh, was snubbed for missing his parents." I'm very deliberate in my use of language. I think it sounds more convincing, ya know. That's the hope.

"Who d'ya think your talking to," said Rod. "You don't get to argue with me. That boy pissed me off. If you continue to cause my blood pressure to rise, I'll drag you off this camp by your hair."

We stare at each other. I know he's never gonna back down. I'm seeing myself almost in the third person, as if I'm witnessing this encounter. A weird sensation, what is that, fear? I can smell Rod's dry mouth, he's definitely a smoker. I would say he's an avid coffee drinker too. His breath is thick with self-loathing. I have to back down now. I don't stand a chance. I believe it when he says he'd drag me off. Not sure about by my hair, but that would be it, I'd be out all the same. Selfishly, I need to consider my own time on this camp. He can't beat me. I wanna get out of here alive. I think having the night off will certainly help with that. If I can have a drink and see Alyssa, then that's all I need for now. As I'm sniffing Rod's breath. There she is, Laura engulfs me. It's her turn to have her head massaged. With that, she's gone. That safe thought is enough to have my rational mind take over again and drag me away from all this before it gets outta hand. I wanna avoid that place where there's no going back. It would've been a brawl. I'll walk away, I'll be the bigger man. I imagine Rod is as relieved as I am. He wouldn't back down if I didn't. How could he ever show his face again? If the kids deemed him weaker than a teenage camp counsellor from England, a scrawny one at that. He'd lose all respect. I storm off, my heart still racing. The pulse beating up in my neck, my cheeks are burning hot.

"You OK, dawg?" Said Doug, jogging to keep up with me. He placed his hand on the back of my neck. I stop and glare at him.

"Sorry dawg." He flinches, removing his loose grip as fast as he applied it.

His hands are damp. He must have been as nervous as me.

"I'm sorry, Doug. Shit, man. I was ready to knock him out."

As those words left my lips, I'm cold. I was so scared. I need to stop myself from crying. A wave of shock takes over. I've never experienced shock like this before, it's an intense gush of emotion in my stomach. I wanna shake. The top half of my body quivers. A shiver of relief.

Doug and I continue to wander back to the cabin. I don't really know what he's saying, I can't even hear my own responses. It's a flood of words, a lot of noise. We get to the cabin. Doug opens the door and lets me enter first.

"Shit, Dawg," he said. "I gotta round the kids up. They're out front."

"Cheers," I said. I'm in no state to deal with all their shit. Rounding up kids with a stick.

"Enjoy tonight, get some." Said Doug, smiling. He jogs around the cabin, out of sight.

I really like Doug, he's cool. If I didn't know better, it's like I'll never see him again. Even though I'm coming back.

It's so strange to see the cabin empty, on both sides. I can hear the familiar voices of all the boys outside. It's almost comforting to hear them laughing. I'm not getting soft or soppy, but that reassurance is nice. I pull off my shorts and grab for my folded jeans. I make a point to slowly zip up my fly. I'm almost living a scene from a Diet Coke advert. My imagination flashes to Alyssa unzipping them for me, using her teeth. I remove my white stained T-shirt and run my left hand over my torso. I don't have abs, but I'm defined. I starve myself, rather than crank out oblique sit-ups. I shove my feet into my black and white Converse trainers and pull a black T-shirt over my head. As basic as jeans and a black T-shirt looks. There's no actual time or choice involved in what I wear. I didn't really pack for going out on the pull or impressing anyone. If I had brought a button-down plaid shirt, I would have worn that, but I didn't, so plain Jane it is. I grab for my wallet. I don't have that much money with me, enough though to have a drink or two. I could always put a request in for additional funds, at the admin office, pain in the arse process, so what I've got will have to do.

I push the front door open and run my palm across my head to flatten what little hair I have to be more presentable. If I had more time, I would've had a shower. I'm out. Down the wooden front steps I go. I'm receiving claps and encouragement from the boys of the cabin. They're even offering out their hands for low fives. I walk amongst them like I'm on the red carpet. They're sending me off for the inevitable courtship that I'm hoping to be involved in. It's strange to be encouraged by them like this. I clear the crowd.

Doug shoots me a subtle nod and smile. He too, without speaking, articulates his good wishes. He knows that Alyssa and I are potentially building on a mutual appreciation of each other. I guess that's rare. There are already stories existing around camp of people getting involved with each other. But for obvious reasons, no real confirmation. I'm thankful that something finally seems to be going right.

Now I need to find Alyssa.

22

Tree Rubbing

I'm so excited. I kind of wish I had my headphones with me. I always have this innate urge to accompany, even a short walk like this, with some banging music. Not sure what that music would be. A bouncy number, Santeria by Sublime. Can't beat a bit of chirpy up strumming, cool and slow. I even call the English teacher daddio. I want a tune that will fit nicely with my happiness. Finally, some freedom.

There are yellow school buses in the distance. It's so American. I'm going to be like Forrest Gump on my first day at school. There are two, no, three buses. Apparently, we have the choice of where we wanna go for the evening. It's a bus to the movie theatre. Still doesn't sound right to me movie. Everyone, even the English guys, have adopted that use of an Americanism. To me, it's still the cinema. Anyway, I can either get a bus to the pictures or a bus to town to explore. It's everyone's intention to get on the second bus and get into a bar called Chillingworth's, have a drink. If the rumours are true, we're all likely to get served. Even me with my baby face. That's my intention, anyway. Get me a JD and coke.

There's a crowd of people standing outside the buses. I can see some of the English crew. I'm not hanging about with them, trust me.

"Dylan, you heading to town or the movies?" said Big D.

Big D, shit, I've just used the name I've managed not to, so far. These guys blindly go along with it. Daniel, as I call him is leaning against the bus with his arms crossed, looking at me gormless, as ever.

"I think I'm heading to town," I said.

I really hope they're all going to the cinema. Please say the cinema.

"We're undecided yet." Said Oxford Mark, stepping forward from behind Jimmy.

Jimmy's wearing that Manchester United football shirt again. The only thing these guys have in common are they're all English. I'm not including myself in that because I for one am nothing like these guys. They're so weak minded.

"Oh right." I said, uninterested. Why do they feel the need to tell me this shit? I don't care what they do. I'm going to town with or without them. Without, is the favourable option. Chatting amongst themselves about bollocks. They seem to hang on every word from Oxford Mark.

It's always hard to get involved when conversations are in full flow. Even more difficult because I scream bullshit to what they've got to say. I wanna find Alyssa. These guys can do whatever the fuck they want. I sidle away from them. I'm not listening to their noise, anyway.

Most of the people standing out here are clustered in groups of five or six. Few are moving around on their own. I try not to cling to people. You always become too reliant on them. I like my company most of the time or at least being with one other person. When there's too many people chatting, I'm not comfortable in interrupting, if it's well underway. I mean, what do you say? I can't nod along, I'd be thought of a fool.

No one seems to be getting on the buses, they're standing

around flapping gums. There's a lot of fakery. A lot of soppy laughs. The third bus is a quarter full of people sat in seats waiting to depart. There's Hazel. Feels like I haven't seen her for so long. She's leaning over the back of the seats, talking to two girls behind her. Yet another two girls I don't know the names of. It's almost perfect timing. As if the gods have spoken, she's looking at me through the window. It seems to take her a long time to realise it's me. She hasn't smiled. I smile. She then smiles back. She's waving now. She's even beckoning me to join her on the bus. The two girls, who remain nameless are now looking over too. They must have asked who I was because Hazel turns from looking at them to back at me. I don't know what she's saying.

"I'm going on that one." I said, pointing to the bus for the bar.

Hazel's giving me the thumbs down gesture. Her face, an exaggerated sad clown, she still looks good. I really like her eyes. Her eyes are doing something to me, churning. Even though I'm looking at her through a window. I have this thunderous doubt come over me. I should join her, that would be cool. We could kiss in the back row of the movies on a Saturday night. I don't even think it is a Saturday, but the choices. No, I'm going to Town. That's what I said to Alyssa. As amazing as Hazel looks with a purple wig. She's staring back at me. She looks confused. I point at her and run my fingers through my hair. I think I'm trying to signify I like hers. It may be lost on her, it's almost lost on me. She obviously knows what I'm trying to say. As she flicks her palm through the ends of her hair like a L'Oréal advert, she's laughing. I wave.

I need to find Alyssa. I can't see her anywhere. I hope she doesn't stitch me up. Perhaps I should've got on the bus with Hazel. I'll find her. I need to.

"Are you Dylan?" Said a tall, thin girl with glasses. She's almost leaning over me to get her head down closer to mine. She'd be perfect for Daniel. You know, Big D. Damn close to being the same height. She's a giant of a woman. I give her my full attention, avoiding looking at the length of her legs.

"If you're looking for Alyssa, she said to tell ya she's held up by the lake, she'll be here though." She said with a smile.

"Thanks very much," I said. I still can't get over her height. I couldn't with a cherry picker.

"She's right. You do have a cute accent." She said as she lifted the arm of her glasses up and peers at me from underneath.

I blush. I can't ever hide my blushing. But that means Alyssa's been talking about me. That's a good sign. I like that. Nice.

"What's your name?" I said, leaning back to get a better vantage of her.

"Toni," she said.

Then, like a gazelle, she skips off.

I'll wander down and wait for Alyssa by the water. I walk past a whole crowd of people, they're all talking. No one acknowledges me. Either that or I'm not really paying attention. I've only got Alyssa on my mind.

It's a nice pathway down to the lakeside, a little winding tarmac road, only suitable for a golf cart. The sun is slowly edging toward the horizon. Won't be too long until it sets. Darkness will be a nice backdrop to a night of merriment.

I'm stood with my feet almost in the lake water, distracted by the sun. I feel light, like I've shaken all the tension from my shoulders. I'm ready to 'ave it. Drink and dance, come on. Where the hell is Alyssa? There's no one down here. The water's still, no noise. Just the occasional distant laugh from the crowd of people behind me, up on the road. A bus has started up, the engine rattling loud. Gotta be a diesel. I'm not happy with that sound though, here comes my panic. What if this is a cruel joke and Alyssa's already on the bus? She and Toni laughing at me from afar. This could be karma for not wanting to stay around the English hoodlums. No, that Toni tall girl, it felt like I could trust her. Alyssa's not here though, nothing. My trainers three inches from the still water of the lake, only a tiny ripple lapping graceful over the sand. This is fucking stupid, she isn't here.

Crack.

The sound of twigs. I hope that's all it is.

Crack.

There it is again, beyond the tree line. I stand fixed to the spot.

Snap.

It's coming from the trees. I can't see anything.

Snap.

Again. This time a violent rustling among leaves.

Shit.

What if it's a bear? They warned us about ticks, but not fucking bears. I swear they have black bears in this state. If this is a bear, I'm literally gonna shit myself. Why my feet are still inching closer to the trees, I'll never know. I should bolt in the opposite direction. Then I hear it.

"Aggggggh."

It's female, human. She yelps with intensity. My stomach floods with what feels like acid. My head empty, brimming with vulnerability. My chest tightens. I know that sound. That's the sound of sexual enthusiasm, a heavy growl, like a bear releasing wrath into the air.

I can see it now. Alyssa has her arm extended, palm flat against the trunk of a tree. She's clasping her white laced top in her hand, scrunching it up at the collar. Head down, jerked back by her tight ponytail. Her jeans down around her ankles. Then, hairy defined calf muscles. My eyes fixed on a white male bottom with tan lines. Jeans rolled down to white socks, trainers still on. The hairy arse ripples, clenching and relaxing with every thrust. I try to look beyond his arse. It's the fucking swimming instructor. The one with the dodgy tattoo of the Three Little Pigs on his lower back in colour. He's penetrating Alyssa. Doing her up against a fucking tree, doggy style, hard. She's loving every minute, too.

Heat in my jaw, a tremble in my cheeks, my eyes are dry like I've got glass in them. I almost need to see this. I need betrayal. I need to feel what I've inflicted on Laura. I need to know what she felt when I told her about Zoe.

Neither of them turn around. Not sure I would either. They haven't noticed me. I bet he's not even wearing a fucking condom. He's gonna come inside her, isn't he?

What I need to do is take a rock and split this fucking guy's head open, like how he's separating her labia. I think I'd take genuine pleasure in knocking him to the floor. What's likely to happen when he collapses? I'll see his hard dick. Surely it won't turn flaccid straight away. He could be bigger than me. How would I explain my reaction to Alyssa? Fuck Alyssa. I could bash her head in too, leave them both out here to bleed, naked. I could put this rock in one of their hands, and you don't need to be Columbo to speculate on motive. Surely, it'll be like rape with self-defence thrown in. No one would think I did it. Wait, that Toni tall girl, with her glasses, she knows. I told her I was coming down here. I can't murder them, prime suspect.

Too many thoughts. So many considerations. Tunnel vision. They haven't seen me. I want her to lie to me. The whole thing is done now. It could be fun to test her, see how she deals with this, how she deals with me. Why I'm thinking we even have an allegiance? Clearly, we don't. Yeah, we kissed, we talked some shit. I gave her nothing, she's given me nothing. I have to learn not to be so trusting. Maybe she'll ignore me. I should stop being such a fucking pussy and end them both. The Three little pigs tattoo guy has put his hands on her shoulders. She leans her shoulder into the tree bark as if she's entering a scrum. The bastard convulses, tugging on her ponytail again, he's so rough with her.

That's it. He's done. Finished. He's come.

I'm not convinced she's finished, but I'm not about to intervene and suggest he eats her pussy. Heavy breathing follows, getting their breath back. I can't see any rubber on his flapping cock. I bet there was no debate. Lust took over. Laura always makes me wrap him, sometimes double. She's too nervous she's gonna bloat and put on weight if she goes on the pill. Sometimes, I can't feel anything.

With the click of his belt clasping closed, they both scramble to pull on their clothes. I bolt from the pathway. They could've heard me. I'm not hanging around to find out. I don't care. I run up the hill. My Converse clipping the tarmac, my toes smarting again. Alyssa was providing me with some form of solace, some hope in life. An excuse to continue to be here. Is travelling after this experience enough motivation now? I'm so hot, I can't shake this off. I'm out of breath.

The loud blaring honk of a horn in my ears. I turn, my eyes blur to the piercing, overwhelming sight of two bright yellow circular head lights coming toward me.

Shit. It's the bus. I leap backwards off the road and watch it belt past me, the burning white in my eyes fading. If it hadn't swerved. Well, there's no telling. That was close, too close. I watch it pass. The driver's face pressed against the window, he isn't happy. I then catch Hazel's eyes as she passes. She follows me as the bus drives off. I think I tried to ask for her help without saying a word. I hope she feels it from me. It's strange that the bus driver hasn't stopped. I think if I was driving, that would have shit me up, I would've stopped and at least shouted at me or something. He hasn't. The bus disappears into the treelined darkness. Only its red tail lights illuminating the trunks of trees.

It may have been an escape if it had hit me. Perhaps then Alyssa would be remorseful, blame herself. Fuck it. I have no thoughts. Nothing in me now.

The crowd around the entrance to the bus is growing smaller as they step up and embark. I'll join the queue, like the passive little fake I am. I'll remain silent, not speaking to anyone. The vision of what I just saw plaguing me, a handful of her hair pulling. His orange peel bottom thrusting, her knees bending, her foot off the ground. That flat palmed pressure of hers against the tree, her fingers extending and spreading as she yelps with pleasure.

I step up the first step, then on to the second. My shoelaces could do with a clean. I nod with a fake smile at the female bus driver, she smells like a heavy smoker, her wild grey knotted hair fills my vision. She's got blackened plaque between her teeth and trumpet shaped earrings in. I must have walked past a load of people without acknowledging them. I'm not concerned if I'm perceived as rude. The bus may as well be empty right now. I sit down on my own by the window.

Alyssa's head appears in the stairwell of the bus. She steps up from the road. The bitch is on the bus. I can see her from here. She's looking around for an empty seat. There's one next to me. She hasn't even noticed me. I'm almost thankful for that. I'd probably punch her in the tit. She's sat down next to a chubby girl with a fat neck. I think that's Mary, I don't care. Alyssa rests her head on fat Mary's shoulder, she's exhaled. If I didn't know any better, I'd say she was trying to catch her breath. She doesn't even look round. She hasn't looked for me, not once. OK, now she's turned her head and looked back. Yeah, she's seen me now. She smiles. There's guilt within her. I refuse to smile for a second. I don't want her to know that I know. I shoot her a fake smirk. It comes from the side of my mouth. Why did I ever invest so much in this girl? I was almost willing to leave my girlfriend, forget about Laura, the one person who has said she loved me, and I've reciprocated. Who the hell is Alyssa, anyway? Can that Mary girl smell sex on her, sweat with fromage? Alyssa is a girl that has led me on and likes to be fucked from behind against a tree. Perhaps not someone I was ever gonna marry. I'll continue to torture myself with this thinking far beyond the bus engine kicks over.

The door shuts with that manual operation of the driver pulling on that weird lever. The bus jerks forward. Out of the window, I can see that prick, with his pig scene tattoo, standing in the centre of a group of other waterside counsellors. I imagine he's detailing the experience he just had with Alyssa. How long he lasted, the noises of satisfaction, the wetness of her pussy. I'm sickened with jealousy, filled with hate. The bus falls dark as it drives into the woods.

* * *

The journey must be fifty minutes. I'm obviously alone here within my own thoughts. Alyssa hasn't turned around once. The bus travels over a large, long steel constructed bridge, with an arch in the middle. The girders painted a pale blue. In places it's rusting, the paint peeling like flaky pastry on sausage rolls. The river beneath flows slow. Nothing but trees to the right, a load of baseball fields to the left. Along the road is a closed shop, an illuminated neon sign inside reads: 'Antiques'. It all looks typically American with an old Coke machine outside. This is small-town America. There's a general store down a minor road, with brooms stacked against the closed entrance doors. The bus wobbles over a level crossing, crunching over the railroad tracks. All the roads are named literally. We go over 'River Bridge', turn left on 'Railroad Street', to the right is 'Bank Street'.

The bus pulls into a car park next to the railroad tracks. It jolts to a stop and the doors chuckle open. All of us clamber off. The female bus driver is eager to join us as we all filter off down the steps. She takes out a packet of cigarettes from her top pocket, grapples to open it and plummets her impatient chunky potato fingers inside. She lobs it into her mouth and lights the tip. She inhales deep and exhales in relative satisfaction with her eyes closed. I step down and immerse myself in her cloud of nicotine wonder. It's like I haven't had a cigarette for such a long time. It's a welcoming smell. I take it in, take it in deep.

"Be back on the bus by twelve-thirty," said the bus driver. "Or, I'm leaving without ya'll." She exhales another cloud of smoke, it puffs from her cheeks. Another cloud obscures the shape of her head.

Everyone seems to wander. I've never been to this town before. Clearly these others have. They all seem to know exactly where they're going. I hang back. I thought Alyssa would approach me or something, she hasn't. She's walked off with her friends. Well, if I can call them her friends.

Yet again, I'm alone in a car park. Is it my fault that I don't seem to be included in anything? I'm really affable most of the time, it must be my fault. I should ingratiate myself with everyone, get in with some of these people. I'm not sure that I even want that. It's all these confused thoughts that seem to orchestrate my loneliness.

Where's this bar, what's it called, Chillingworth's?

23

Chillingworth's

With the thought of Laura cascading through my mind, hindered only by my lack of self-confidence.

Over by the Bank, Megan, the little girl from camp, is weaving in and out of grand stone columns. Alongside her is that woman from the medical centre, the doctor. What was her name? Doctor, Doctor Dumbarton. They both look happy. They walk up the street, out of sight.

I wanna tell Alyssa, she'd be happy to know she's OK. I can't even see where she went. Why should I tell her? She can suffer. "Dylan dawg." Said a deep sounding, Southern accent from behind me. It made me jump. Everything sounds southern to me, all prolonged and drawled. I turn around. Three massive guys, stood before me. I recognise them, they're always together. We haven't been introduced. I've seen them around. They've each got impressive facial hair, all matching full faced lumberjack beards. They're huge guys, overweight and tall. Bodies, like strongmen, bulky. Wearing the same style clothes, dark-coloured baseball caps, pulled down about an inch above their eyes. They give off a sort of intimidating comedy, imposing but loose. I know they'd have my back in a bar fight. It's like, now they've spoken my name, I'm protected. Weird. These guys certainly are outdoorsy. You know, like real men, woodcutters or farm hands, men carrying heavy shit. I imagine them lighting fires in the woods with no matches, hunting Bison with their bare hands; ripping at meat without cutlery. Brutish. I'm shocked they know my name.

"Hey," I said.

"We're gonna hit up that bar across the street." The guy in the middle points. "Chillingworth's, you wanna come?"

I'm excited by the invitation. I'm still shocked at how much taller they are than me, and wider. So much of me is excited. Now I'm confused, suspicious even. Why would they want me to come? They could plan on leaving me here. I may never get back to camp. Hey, that might not be a bad thing. This could be fun, I should go. This is what camp is all about, apparently, experiences, fresh adventures and new people, all that marketing shit.

"Yeah sure, why not?" I said. My head nods, not sure I'm in control of it.

"We haven't been introduced, I'm Carter." Said the middle guy, the voice of the group. "This is Bedford." Carter indicates to the guy on his right with his thumb. "He's Herold." He continues, using his other hand to waggle to his left at Herold. I acknowledge them all with a concerted nod, more like a bow. It's like I should respect them for being nice.

"I'm Dylan."

"We know." They all said in their deep southern accents.

"That's Herold with an E." Said Herold, shaking my hand.

"You're like Mike and the Mechanics." I said in jest, smiling. They don't react. I bet they're into the music of George Jones. I can't think of any other stereotypical country music artists. Other than Dolly Parton or Kenny Loggins. No, I mean that guy Kenny Rogers. How judgemental of me. At least they're trying. They, no exaggeration, all look the same, like brothers. Levi jeans, hiking boots, and plaid shirts. I'm not sure I'll remember who's who. The Three Stooges seem cool though. I won't be calling them that to their faces. It's the red neck vibe in them. Bubbling below their charcoal-stained fingertips.

'Chillingworth's' written in red neon lights shines out from the brown tinted front window. The four of us stand outside. It's a grand red brick building with full windows across the front. Only a single black wooden door with a small brick shaped window that stands between us and booze.

    'Budweiser; King of Beers' illuminates the other window to the right in a closely matched red neon, a slightly pinker shade. Above the door is a faded, poorly painted coverup job of the old name. It looks through my squinted eyes, like it was once, 'Locofoco's'.

    Carter is the first to push on the black iron finger plate to enter. The door swings inward. He's the first to speak, he's the first to move, he's the boss here. Herold then follows behind. Bedford, being polite lets me ahead of him with a subtle hand tilt.

    It's so much darker in here than it is outside. The place is small and square. Bare brickwork. Smells like sawdust and cigarettes. Tables are dotted at random around the place. The bar counter fills the entire back wall with a mirror behind it, glass shelves lined with liquor bottles. I'm trying to look around Carter and Herold. They keep shifting and obscuring my view. There are a couple of guys sitting at the bar and a woman behind, serving. My exploring eyes are interrupted by a skinny man in a matching black tracksuit sitting on a stool in the doorway. He's wearing a red New York Yankees baseball hat with the white stitched iconic 'N' and 'Y'. One eye on the TV in the corner, watching a baseball game.

    There are more men than I first noticed. All sat at the bar on stools, clutching beer bottles and smoking cigarettes. Most of the tables are empty. If I had to guess I would say these are locals. Music is playing at a low volume, a slow number. One of those quintessential country songs about love, life and loss. This scrawny guy sat on the stool breaks his attention from the television and his eyes widen at the sight of us coming into the bar. He's leaning on his thigh with his elbow.

"Welcome fellas. I'm Dan. Where y'all from?" He said, looking us up and down.

"We're from all over," said Carter.

Clearly, we aren't known to him. It's odd to have this guy sat on a stool, manning the front door.

"Good going, good going." Said Dan, nodding. "You have a good night, brother." He waves Carter in.

"Sup," said Bedford.

"Good going, good going. Sup." Said Dan, waving Bedford in with two fingers.

Dan turns his attention back to the TV in the corner. It's now my turn to pass the gatekeeper. He knows I'm playing at this, I don't fit in with these guys, they could have jobs down a mine. He knows I'm fresh out of immaturity. I stand up straight and do that shoulder drop walk thing. Drag and slide, drag and slide, dip the shoulder. He'll see my attitude, be convinced I should be here too.

"You got any ID, boy?" Said Dan, asked from the corner of his mouth, not taking his eyes off the TV. He takes a single cigarette from behind his left ear and places it in between his dry lips, lighting the tip with a lighter from underneath his legs. His stubbled face illuminated by the yellow flame of the cigarette lighter. I can see he has piercing puffy blue eyes. It looks as if he's recovering from a heavy night. In fact, I'd hazard a guess that his means of recovery from every night is to indulge in more drinking. He has tired dry skin, like the leather wrist strap on an aged watch.

"Hey, you like the Yankees?" I said.

That's my lame way of potentially distracting him from asking to see my ID. He sucks deep on the cigarette, holds it for far too long, and then exhales, his face obscured by thick white smoke. He points at the TV with the same cigarette clutching fingers, not once taking his eyes off the action.

"Yup," he said.

This guy will not fall for my obvious mind games. He's far too street for all that business, he looks like a Beastie Boy.

"How d'ya know about baseball, you Australian?" He said, smirking to himself.

"It's what I'm teaching on camp. I'm a baseball counsellor. I'm English. My team's the Braves." I said, looking up at the TV.

"Well Mister, Mister. This line is building up behind you," he said.

The only person behind me is Bedford, he's not bothered, just watching the baseball too.

The front door then cracks open, the light rips into the room and more people from camp file in. Some of them are wearing branded camp hoodies. Why would you wear that on a night out? You're free from the torment. I don't want to be reminded of it.

"ID and we'll chat over a beer later." Said Dan, looking up at me from under his cap. "You need to know, you got yer head up your ass with the Braves."

I haven't been this nervous being asked for ID for a long time. I have my driver's license, but I can't show this guy, Dan, that. It clearly has my date of birth on it. The only other form of ID I have is my Student Union card. It's really the only thing I can flash at him. I pull the card out of my wallet. The picture of me with a crazy bushy haircut before I cut it all off for Laura. I used to have it like Ian Brown's, very Beatles-esque, mop top style. I've clearly since trimmed it right down. It still resembles me though, I was carrying more weight then too.

"This is my student ID card," I said.

Dan hasn't looked away from the TV. He waves me inside. His eyes transfixed on the TV again. I look to see if it's an interesting play, it isn't, it's a camera shot of people in the crowd. Sweet, well that worked. Easy, I'm surprised.

"Good going, good going, I don't give a shit. Drink as much beer as you like." Said Dan.

"Thanks Dan, Thanks very much." I said. Grateful, that could have been embarrassing.

"Tell Amanda to fix ya'll up with a free round of drinks." He said, waving Bedford in behind me.

The female bartender, a halogen lightbulb blonde. I can see her better now, I'd hope she's over twenty-one. She could be Dan's daughter, she looks young enough. Her hair is cut into a bob, she's wearing a cleavage enhancing tight camo vest top. I can't see what the emblem is on the front of it, but the words are fluorescent pink. She has masterful breasts; they're being helped and pushed up. I'm not complaining, they're perfect, all natural. She has a constant smile on her face. She's flashing it to all the men sitting at the bar on their stools. I doubt they're paying attention to her smile. This Amanda girl keeps this bar open. I assume this town doesn't have a Hooters. She'd be better placed there, serving up original style chicken wings. She could be saving for college or aspiring for things much greater than her current job role. I'd like to find out.

I join Carter and the other guys standing at the bar. I'm not confident enough to push my way forward. Carter looks down at me, given his huge stature. He smirks and raises his eyebrows to draw my attention to Amanda behind the bar. I nod with appreciation. Carter's already ordered drinks.

"Here ya go guys." Said Amanda, placing four bottles of beer down on the bar in front of him.

"What can I get you, sweetie?" She said, flashing her bright white teeth at me.

Carter slides a bottle of beer along the bar in my direction. I grab it. Amanda realises I'm with them.

"You're all set, I see," she said.

"Thank you. I don't need a drink yet, Amanda." I said, not taking my eyes off hers, she's so sparkly.

"Wait," she said. "How did you—, Oh Dan, OK. When you're ready, sugar, you come to me."

I'm impressed with myself that I haven't lost my eyes on her nipples. I'm being such a gentleman.

"I was hoping you'd be able to put my mind at rest." I said.

"Go on." Said Amanda, throwing beer bottle tops into a distant bin.

"I heard bartenders with blonde hair and pristine nails like yours, they inherently enjoy conversation, they're more open to projecting personality on to others. Is that right?" I said, aware of how convoluted it sounds.

Amanda chuckled. My three new buddies look at each other, confused.

"I haven't heard that," she said. "s'pose it could be true." Her breasts jiggle as she chuckles.

"Well, you're talking to me," I said. "It must be true. I'm rarely wrong about these things.

"Careful fellas," said a guy at the bar. "We've got a charmer here." He sipped on his beer, cigarette ash dropping in his lap.

"You're cute, sweetie." She said, leaning on the bar. "What's your name?" Her breasts hoist up with her arms pressed against her side.

"Dylan." I said, trying my best not to allow my eyes to stare down at her cleavage. If I was to glance down, I'd be consumed. Call me Neil Armstrong, because her tits remind me of the surface of the moon. One step for Dylan, one step closer to coming in her face.

"I'll be watching you," she said.

She shows me all her teeth, big smile. She taps the bar and walks away, looking back over her shoulder at me, as she gestures to another customer and pours a drink. She moves well behind the bar. I need to check her arse out. Yup, confirmed, it's a fine one, nestled tightly in hand cut denim shorts.

"Shit, bro," said Carter. "Check you out, ya little heartbreaker." He offers the neck of his beer bottle for me to clank in cheers.

I must admit, I impressed myself there. It comes in from leftfield sometimes, without warning. The thought of alcohol, even when I'm not drunk, gives me a confidence with words. It's probably unfounded but I become more creative with my language. If only I didn't need to drink to feel it. I've read somewhere about how to talk to female bartenders. I assume it applies to male ones too, but that's not important. The article said something about not considering them as regular women, out on the street, explaining they're likely to hear the same lines all night long and they plaster on a fake smile to get tips. I'm under no illusion she'll be working this room, a girl has to eat. If I can get inside her head for all of two seconds, she'll at least remember my face. At a push, she might, if she's interested, remember my name, only time will tell. All I can say is, Alyssa's far from my head. I'm so shallow, so fleeting. Amanda, her teeth, arse, and titties. Finger looking good.

"Let's get a table." Said Carter, looking around the bar.

Free tables everywhere. This is a local bar for local people. Carter's maintaining the role of leader of this tryst. Bedford and Herold rarely speak, all very subservient. That's strange how equal men will succumb to the authority of the alpha in a group. I've never been that way inclined. I'm not interested in such a demographic constraint. I'd much rather not compete with such trivial social interactions. That's another reason I keep myself so distant from large groups of people. If a group of people exceeds four, that's too many for me. I don't think you're engaging with each person in that situation, there'll be internal fractions of people who want to be 'top dog', I can't be bothered with all that shit.

We sit down at a vacant table, against a wall. The bar now, except for the locals and a few others from camp, is empty. That surprises me. I'm guessing Dan isn't sat at the door to get a better vantage of the TV, there are TV's all over the place, in every corner. All playing the same Yankees game. One is showing Nascar. I only imagine he's expecting the bar to become busy. I thought they would cram this place with Red Oak employees, all trying to forget their repression and lubricating their inhibitions. I can't hear the music now. I would imagine that's purely down to Dan watching baseball. He must want to hear the commentary. If they ramped up whatever this music is, sounds like country, they'd sell more beer. They need to get this place banging to get the liquor flowing. It gives the four of us at this cramped little table the chance to talk. They may well have been friends for years before attending. From how this conversation is flowing, I would say they're close, old friends.

"Mazel tov." Said Carter, holding up his bottle for us to tap the necks. We clink the bottles together.

I've got the perfect view of the bar and ample opportunity to smile at Amanda. Unbeknown to her, study her face, teeth, tits, navel and her peachy bum. We each take turns in looking at her cleavage, trying our best to point to the ceiling in a ridiculous attempt at disguising our ogling.

"One night with me, is all she'll need." Said Carter, rubbing the base of his beard with his open hand.

"Two and half minutes, would do for me," I said.

"We could all get involved," said Bedford.

We all sit silent, awkward at the suggestion.

"What's the Matter with you, man?" Said Carter scowling at Bedford.

"What?" he said.

"The last thing I wanna see, is your hairy bobbin' ass pumping a girl." Said Carter, laughing to himself.

With the clanking of shot glasses, the scrunching of red plastic cups in our bare hands. The type you always see at frat parties in films. We laugh rapturously. The bar is filling with more patrons. The front door opens. Every time it does, everyone already here looks expectant at the new customers. We scope them out with interest. Who the fuck just walked in? None other than Alyssa.

"I've seen you around with her." Said Herold, nodding in her direction as she stands at the door, dolled up like a whore.

"Yeah, what's the deal with that?" Said Carter.

"Fuck all, I've helped her out with Softball."

"Softball, boring." Said Bedford, taking a swig of his beer.

Alyssa walks straight past our table. She must have seen me. You can't miss these guys. Everyone knows 'em from camp, even if not by name. She's seductively walking toward the bar with a group of girls from camp. Dan notices her, hard not to with her sweeping hips. He's diverted his gaze from the TV for a moment and winks at her. The slut has only smiled back. No surprise there.

"Let's turn these tunes up," said Dan.

Amanda looks up from behind the bar, smiling, and leans down out of sight. The volume of the music is increased as she shakes her shoulders. Dan reaches into the pocket of his tracksuit, removing the TV control, muting the baseball game. It's like he now knows his bar is about to become a darkened music filled cauldron of drunken stupor. It signals dollar bills in the cash register.

Dan follows behind Alyssa and the crowd of camp girls. He reaches out for her arm. I can't hear what they're saying, but Alyssa places her flat palm like a flirt on his chest and laughs out loud in complete fakery. Her head back, mouth wide open. Makes her a bigger cunt. She must have sensed my dissatisfaction, she's noticed me now. She shakes off her behaviour. You think you know someone until they throw it all away. She's reaching into her clutch bag. I didn't think she'd be the type of person to be comfortable with such an accessory. Dan must want to see her ID. She pulls it from her bag. A small twig caught in her fingers, drops to the floor, she hasn't seen it, I have. Where else would that come from but the woods, the woods of venereal nightmares.

It's time for another drink. That'll make me forget. I stand up from the table, circling my finger, indicating I'm purchasing another round for The Three Musketeers. No words are necessary. They know what I'm saying and agree to my offer with emphatic nods. I'm having to concentrate on my movements. I'm relaxed, warm but relaxed. I hear none other than Tom Waits booming from the jukebox in the corner. What a beautiful coincidence. That thing of music or films being played only for you, all for your personal benefit. I move towards the bar in what could be slow motion, with the music booming. I'm avoiding Alyssa, but we've caught each other's eyes. Not sure how I'm going to negotiate around her without having to speak. My thoughts punctuated by Tom Waits's distinctive voice. It makes me happy. I smirk. Alyssa thinks I'm smiling at her, she's now reciprocating with a nervous twinge of a smile. This is awkward. I can't maintain my hatred toward her for too long. She has a face like the sensation of joy, she embodies happiness. I at least know she doesn't consider doggystyle 'too animalistic'. She's more than happy to indulge in a bit of penetration out in the openness of nature and that's always fabulous. What a fucking whore. I'm more annoyed Laura never wants to have sex outside.

"Hey Dyl," said Alyssa.

Her voice interrupts my visual torture of her hand pressed against that tree, her distant moans cutting through Tom Waits creative genius. The music falls silent, the bar rowdy with the gaggle of voices. The refurbished jukebox extends its aged arm and selects the next track, it isn't a jukebox selecting seven-inch records, the arm still works but it's entirely digital. Still looks good.

"Don't call me Dyl." I said, shaking my head. "My name's Dylan."

The first notes of Staind, 'Outside' rattle over the speakers. Whoever is choosing this music is a fucking genius, and it's getting me riled up. The times I've spent in front of the mirror at home, screaming into my reflection along to this, never able to bring myself to slice my arms open with a blunt disposable razor, just so I could feel, I can't begin to count.

"Everything OK?" She squints, trying to examine my eyes. "How much you had to drink?"

That annoys me. How dare she ask me shit like that? It's my fucking night off. I'm staring at her lips. I'm still in control, for now. Sure, I've been drinking, but I know what I'm doing. I resist the urge to lean on into her. I wanna kiss her. Her tongue tickles her bottom lip. I need to shake that from my mind. I should revisit the sight of her being fucked from behind. Seeing that guy's arse wobble and stiffen as he came. Is this the right time to make her aware that I saw her having a bit of the old in out, in out? Or, should I let it build and fester in me until I can't resist the urge to bottle her. I think I would happily fling an elbow across her face, really spread her nose out.

"I need to drown my sorrows," I said. I pretty much cough the words at her in complete contempt.

"Your sorrows?"

"I won't drag this out anymore," I said.

"Drag what out?"

"Well, if you'd let me fucking finish." I said, with considered effort to articulate the profanity in an East End accent.

"Excuse me?"

"I'm interested to hear," I said. " I think I deserve to know, what were you doing before you got on the bus?"

"Before I got on the bus?"

"Are you just gonna repeat my question?" I said. "If you need more thinking time to make up a beautiful story. Don't bother."

"Thinking time? I don't need time to think about anything. What have you heard?"

"I haven't heard shit."

"Well, explain what you're talking about."

"It's not what I've been told, sweetness." I said, leaning in close to her face. "It's what I saw."

She contorts. Nothing but a lifeless expression falls across her shallow face. She knows I know.

"Look, Dylan—,"

"Oh, don't bother. It was fun while it lasted, love."

"We should talk," she said.

"Fuck that." I said, throwing my hands up, flapping the bitch away. "I'm gettin' a drink."

"Let me get 'em."

"Piss off. It's like New Year's eve up in 'ere. I'm gonna get wasted. To the bar, darling."

Hopefully, I won't see her again tonight, dirty bitch. How dare she look me in my face, giving it the innocent. I'm liberated. This is my emancipation. Just what I needed.

Amanda in her subservient position, leans forward on the bar again. Lucky for me, I can see damn near straight down her top, it's fucking lush. If I saw nipple, it would ruin it. With the way Amanda pours drinks, all loose with no measures. I'm going to be off my titties and hopefully sucking on hers in no time.

"Hey Manda, can I have another round please?" I said, taking a chance calling her 'Manda'. She doesn't seem to mind.

"Sure, you can, cutie," she said.

I check her out again, with one eyed closed. She has a small-town arse, impressive to the locals and me obviously, but take her out from behind that bar and she'd be lost amongst the culture of Manhattan bottoms.

At the end of the bar, I've noticed a slight, blonde woman sitting on her own. No one's paying her attention, weird. I thought she'd be top of the pops being on her own, in a place like this. She has a delicate, beautiful face, her nose pierced with a small shiny, ruby red stone. I suspect her face isn't as delicate as I first thought. I blame the Whiskey. Seriously, the way they measure their shots here, they just grab the bottle and pour. I wander over to her and take my chances.

"Evening," I said.

I'm completely relaxed. I don't really care if she responds positively or not. I have nothing to lose.

"Hi." She said, twitching her nose, accentuating the ruby stud as it flickers in the light.

"You having a good night?" I said, as I shuffle on the stool next to her. I'm having to make more of an effort to support myself on my elbow. The drinks are having an effect.

"It's early." She said, with a side eye glance.

Small talk has never been my favourite thing. This introduction could go on for some time. Time I can't spare. I'm on top of the world, rebellious and imprudent to anything that may happen, not only with this girl, but for the rest of camp. I don't care anymore. Don't give a shit. It's liberating.

I won't be able to compete with Alyssa and bend this girl over the bar, spread her cheeks and sniff her. I'd hope Alyssa would be jealous. I'm disappointed she left. It would be joyous if she returned and sees me with my tongue down this girl's throat. I can't even remember her name. Has she told me yet? Whatever, she's beautiful. I'm still surprised why this girl is alone, there's no competition. Not that I enjoy competition when it comes to women. I'd much rather skip on to someone else who isn't that typical of a beauty. Often more attracted to the girl in the corner reading a book, dog earring all the pages or sat alone with headphones on, eyes closed, comfortable in her own skin.

I'm checking this woman out, looking her up and down. She has relatively small breasts, she's a delicate lady. I can see she has great firm thighs and even her knees are well proportioned. I follow her thighs up to the beginnings of her short red dress. It has a strange floral design, it's out of place in a bar, certainly in a bar like this. Wait, she has a deformed right arm. How did I not see that? She's doing well to hide it. Looks like a thalidomide arm, short, fused and well, deformed. I'm overcome with sympathy. I assume the main reason she isn't as popular in this bar as I originally thought she should be is because of her unfortunate arm. I'll hide the fact I've noticed it. I don't wanna make her feel bad. Then again, why would she? I can't abandon her now. That would be too obvious. I swear she'll realise I saw the arm and bolted. It's probably what every man does. I'm not being unsympathetic. I was enjoying talking to her. Have we spoken? I can't remember. I have no intention of taking this any further. I mean, how would we even negotiate the discussion around her arm, how it happened, why it happened, was it a vitamin deficiency? She's looking at me, in my face. She knows I've clocked it. I consider her arm like Amanda's spilling cleavage, yet another thing I can't look directly at. I must maintain unbroken eye contact with her, eye contact, eye contact. My eyes grow wider and disappear into the green lake of her pupils. That way she'll be none the wiser that I've been looking at her arm. I want to though, such a tumultuous thought to avoid.

"You seem like a nice guy," she said. "Different." She holds her gaze on me for what feels like a long time.

I move in to kiss her.

"Did you just go to kiss me?" She said, leaning back in her seat, denying me.

"I think I did," I said.

I know I did, so does she. I'm still shocked she wasn't up for it. She can't do better than me. Come on, she should be thankful.

"You're cute, but pity ain't attractive." She said, searching with her tongue for the drinking straw in her glass.

She holds the glass with her good arm. The other 'bad' arm was positioned on top of her right thigh. Her cute little face became etched with disappointment. Disappointed that I was pitying her. I must now take her rejection, live with the memory, and move on. It's probably best I pay for the drinks Amanda has poured and get back to the guys, return to the ghostly trio. They must be gagging for a drink, I know I am. I can't believe she wasn't accepting of my advances. I suppose my normal arm intimidated her.

I place the drinks tray on the table, sliding it toward the middle with a gentle, nudge from the side of my hip. All the guys grab for their glasses, we clink them together. Every round requires a new toast. The encounter with that mysterious woman will stay with me forever. I'm almost offended by her.

I'm getting more intoxicated. I can hear words from these guys, but I'm not able to respond. I don't know if they're talking to me. If I had my way, I would probably be less drunk, standing with Alyssa, her hand on my cheeks, gazing longingly into each other's eyes. Everybody in the bar would look on jealous at our blossoming romance. Instead, I'm having trouble resting my head on my hand and sitting upright. I seem to be sliding. I blame her. It's all her fault, everything is.

The bar is swaying with camp counsellors feet. There are 'Red Oak and Silver Wood Camp' T-shirts, hoodies and baseball caps everywhere, growing ever blurry to me. So many people standing at the bar. Arms wrapped around each other, laughing and joking. I can't engage in conversation. I can't understand or even articulate, not that I really want to. I'm confident I have the most interesting thoughts to share, but the puzzled faces around me don't share my slurred murmurings.

It's got quieter and quieter in my head. Everyone around me is dancing, enjoying themselves. This place has turned into a seedy, smoke filled American watering hole. I've indulged in one too many JDs. That's my call to have a piss. I broke the seal a long time ago. I jostle my way to the toilet through the crowd, using peoples' shoulders to keep myself from falling over. A group of men with Brylcreem swept hair styles, all wearing camp T-shirts, are sitting, drinking and smoking. I don't recognise any of them. I need a piss so I'm not getting into conversation and nor can I even hold one. I edge nearer to the toilet.

Handfuls of American dollar bills exchanging hands at the bar. Amanda is doing a great job harnessing tips from most of these male customers. She's using her breasts. She slides dollar bills into the back pocket of her denim shorts. She's rocking it. The sound of beer tops snapping off is almost rhythmic.

I make it to the empty toilet. It's so small in here, a pokey little room painted red. I swear my toilet at home is bigger than this. It has one cubicle and a metal trough urinal. I can't get my jeans undone, I do that little desperate for a piss dance. I don't quite shake but I'm close to it. I relieve myself, my piss is so yellow. I need to lean my head against the red wall as I fasten my flies back up. If that wall wasn't there, I'd be on my face, dribbling on the dirty floor.

I wash my hands in a small basin, leaning on the edge to stand up straight. I investigate my reflection in the mirror, my eyes blood shot. I move closer. I can't get over how much I've changed. I look so weird, even to myself. I can't stop sweating either. I dab my forehead dry. My heartbeat drumming in my chest. I rest against the mirror.

The toilet door opens. A guy I recognise from camp with an almost perfect, round, bald head. I'm looking at him in the mirror, he's looking back at me. My forehead has left an oily smudge on the mirror, almost obscuring my view.

"Hey, it's Dylan, isn't it?" he said.

I turn as he negotiates himself around the door to the urinal. I don't answer him. He finishes up doing what he came here to achieve and turns to use the sink.

"Jesus," he said. "You look awful. You OK dude?"

I concentrate not on his question but more on how weird it sounds to hear his South African accent and his use of the word dude.

"I'm good," I said.

That's the only response I can muster for this guy. I'm not in the mood or even capable of providing more than that. He nods, the toilet light shines off the crown of his head. I follow him out of the little toilet.

"Don't drink anymore." He said, manoeuvring through the crowd.

I'm not going to listen to that. I have every intention of just kicking back. I must have nodded as he's left. I'm squinting, it helps me focus.

Dan's sat back on his stool near the front door. Only this time he isn't alone. He's sat with one eye focused on the TV, kissing a young girl, sat straddling his lap. I hope she's getting free drinks. No idea what this song is. I'm usually pretty good with that sort of thing. It's loud though, I know that much. My head's banging. I make it to the bar. Do I have a drink at the table? Forget it, I'll get another. I squeeze, barging myself forward through all these people. I'm focused on getting another drink. Blurred faces around me.

Bobby, Carl Lee and Arnold all stand together, laughing. They've become a close little gang. Each one of them turning into a negative version of who they were before they arrived on camp. I used to hold some respect for Arnold, and even Carl Lee. Now, though, they're slowly becoming more like Bobby. I can see real evil in him. Bobby catches me out the corner of his eye. My neck's getting hotter. He enrages me so much.

"Hey sweet, what can I get you this time?" said Amanda. Now, she's not flaunting herself so much.

"Hey, can I get a whiskey and coke again," I said.

I'm surprised she had to ask. She winks, stepping over to the fridge, which is almost empty. She grabs for the bottle of Jack Daniel's. She flicks the cap off with her free finger, placing the half empty bottle in front of me. I almost have the urge to put my mouth on it and throw it down my neck. It could be a gift from her. She probably wants me drunk so she can have her wicked way with me. She pulls one red plastic cup from a stacked tower. All I can focus on is the tea-stained whiskey pouring from the neck of the bottle, filling the red plastic cup. No measure again, she just pours. Now for the little Coke squirt gun thing attached to the bar, she adds the smallest splash. She swigs from my cup and winks. She hasn't even charged me. I still whip out my wallet with an extroverted arrogance and remove a ten-dollar bill. I unfold it in my fingers, rolling it flat on the service of the bar. I lean forward, fold it in three and place it gently in between her breasts. She looks down, shaking her head.

"That's it for you." She said, plucking the bill from her fleshy crevice, screwing it up and throws it back in my face.

I flutter my eyelids as the greenback disturbs my ability to hold my eyes open. She hurries to the end of the bar. No smile, no flirt and no tits. She's such a tease, that one. I smile at her, she's not even looking. Playing hard to get, she wants me. Blame it on the alcohol, blame it on the boogie. Amanda will give me sex eyes in no time. I wonder where she lives. She'll drive me back to camp tomorrow morning, I'm gonna stay at hers. Such a tease. Can't wait to see her naked.

A heavy flat palm lands on my shoulder, distracting me from what would become erotic filled sexual fascinations, I mean fantasies. Oh, I don't know what I mean anymore. Perfect, it's Bobby, of course it is. His fat gorilla fingers, trusty sidekicks Carl Lee and Arnold, stand behind him like The Two Ronnies. I turn with my drink in hand to face them. Bobby, the ringleader, The Bash Street Kids, stands right in front of my face. He's taller than me, looking down into my drunk personal space.

"What's up Dylan, you havin' a good time?" Said Bobby with his smug little bitch face.

I look around the bar. I'm trying to grasp an understanding of these now unfamiliar surroundings. I don't really know where I am.

"Thanks, you?" I said, I really don't care for his answer.

He leans into my ear with hot breath.

"You fucked it up with Alyssa," he said. "I saw her storm outta here."

All these bodies around me, appearing as one, bumping and shoving into me. I'm a prizefighter, leaning on the ropes, my equilibrium shot.

"Great, well don," I said.

"Don't you worry, an attractive girl like that. I'm sure she'll get over ya." He said, patting me on the back.

One of those aggressive motions disguised as playful banter. I've interpreted it as he intends. He wants to intimidate me again. He's taken advantage of my worse for wear demeanour.

"No doubt she will." I said, squeezing my shoulder blades together. My way of getting him to remove his sweaty hand from my back.

"I'll make sure she's taken care of." He said, cracking his jaw.

"You do that," I said.

"Let me get you a drink. You could do with another one."

"Nah nah, I'm good. I've already got one."

Bobby reaches into his back pocket and pulls out a small metal credit card sized case. He pops it open with his thumb, as if he was going to share with me a bone white, black font embossed business card. Instead, there are four tiny white pills inside. He picks one up between his index finger and thumb and places it on the tip of his pointy tongue, then retracts it like a serpent. He hasn't broken eye contact with me once. I need to blink. Bobby plucks two more pills from the case and places them in Carl Lee and Arnold's waiting palms. They both glance over their shoulders and toss them into their mouths. Arnold fumbles and almost drops his. Bobby scowls. They swill the pills down with the drink they're carrying. They haven't said a word. Bobby picks up the last remaining pill, squeezing it between his fingers and drops it into my drink.

"You're up to bat," he said.

I have two choices now. I can put this cup down and leave, or I can put the cup to my mouth and swallow the contents. I go for the latter. He isn't getting the better of me. Whatever it is he's given me is now pulsing through my bloodstream. I suspect its ecstasy but I'm not about to ask. I'll see what happens. Bobby squeezes his massive fat hand down on my shoulder.

"Enjoy the fucking ride, little man," he said. "Abyssinia."

Arnold and Carl Lee follow him without question. The rat pack have merged into the crowd.

Where have I heard that before, 'Abyssina'? I can't think straight right now.

The lights have become blurry. Noise rattling in my head, sounding tinny, bouncing off every beat originating from the jukebox. What music am I listening to? I don't care if anyone's looking, judging me. I'm happy. I've never tried ecstasy, but I've heard you come up. Like a sudden rush of adrenaline, only it isn't adrenaline. Something sparks in your brain and a surge of happiness takes over. I'm not getting any of that. I'm just dizzy, feeling sick. Holding my breath will be the way to stop myself from vomiting. My arm's tight, I'm being tugged, my feet aren't touching the ground. I'm floating toward the front door, weightless. My head's heavy, I'm strong armed out through the door. What's going on?

Cool, fresh air smacks me in the nostrils, I swallow summer evening. I'm outside. I'm being pushed toward the road. I've lost my footing, on my hands and knees. My left palm has tiny stones embedded in it. Sparkles like gold. I sit up on my knees and flick them free with my other hand. My palms are white, with red indentations.

A honking horn from a white truck drives past, his headlights flashing. That's pretty. My chin drops to my chest. I wave in the general direction. That's nice of him. The yellow familiar school bus is parked in the train station car park, same place it was left, right by the train tracks. I push myself up from the pavement, planting my palms on the ground and pull my feet toward the curb, I'm standing. Nope, I've failed.

"Lord Jesus," I said.

My head's hanging over the curb. Beautiful vision of the dark evening sky, wow it's a starry night, so bright. Fuck me, it's almost too hard to keep my eyes open. I could be in Mexico, on a beach. Pina colada, perfection.

"I'll give you a tip on your next round," I said.

I can hear laughter, I like the sound of laughter. Who is that? They're laughing at me talking shit to myself. Makes sense.

The front door to the bar must have opened. Music thumps louder from inside, I feel it in my chest. The door shuts, and the noise disappears. I hear voices, soft-spoken voices. I think they're American, could be Dutch. I don't know any Dutch people, probably American then. The voices are still talking. I can't lift my head to see who it is. I'll lay here. I need to vomit. I launch myself forward. My throat burns, there it goes, yellow vomit leaving my mouth and funnelling from my nose. I'm a nomad. I'm tilting my head to the side, vomiting in the street.

Self-preservation must have kicked in, I crawl in the gutter. My aim, the end goal, is to get closer to the school bus. I can't focus on anything but my hands planted on the ground, as if I'm impersonating a dog. On my hands and knees I edge closer along the gutter to the pedestrian crossing, large white lines painted in the road. Clean trainers appear on either side of me, to my left and right. I vomit again, straight down into the road. It splashes up at me like pissing into a toilet bowl covered in cling film. The back splash, warm and sticky, on my cheeks and forearms. It covers my hands with its yellow tinted inconsideration. The trainers disappear from my peripherals. I'm guessing whoever it was has tried to avoid the splatters of vomit as it expels from my mouth.

I'm a mess.

24

Manifest Destiny

Am I safe? I'm sat down. Hopefully, on the bus. I think I'm on the bus. How did I get here? I must have had help. Someone has placed a large, brown, plastic bin on my lap. Faces of unfamiliar scary looking people board and shuffle past me, their faces swirling, pinching their noses. Eyes on me. I'm staring down at the bottom of this bin. There's scrunched up paper and cellophane. Could be a cigarette packet. Not to worry, I'm covering it in pools of my drink drenched vomit.

"You make sure you take care of him. If he messes my bus. He's off and you're cleaning it." Said a croaky woman's voice.

Must be the bus driver. Why else would she care?

We're moving, it's so disorientating. The jerking makes me want to vomit more. The bus is travelling through the night. Headlights illuminate the road ahead, the perpetual centre line rolling. I can't bear to look for too long. It makes me feel worse, that sensation of vomit waiting to be propelled from my stomach. I manage to breathe for a second, and the next bout of liquid wants to escape. It flows from my nose again. Surely, there can't be much left in my stomach. I lift my head, there's somebody sat next to me, they're brave. I don't know who it is. I can't focus. The bus driver is turning her head, looking at me. It must be the same frilly haired woman.

I'm conscious enough to know that we passed under the wooden sign for 'Red Oak & Silver Wood Camp'.

Where am I now? I can hear three male voices with distinct, different accents and one female. As far as I can tell, sounds like Alyssa.

Where am I?

"Shit Dylan."

That sounds like a panicked Alyssa. I recognise her voice, that teetering desperation. Her accent is a dead giveaway. I must be face down. I can't open my eyes, I can't move. I don't really want to either. I don't think I'm capable of doing anything.

"Hey, Everything OK?" Said a male voice.

Without doubt that sounds like the bastardised voice of Bobby. I'm assuming the other voices are Arnold and Carl Lee, since they follow him around like impressionable school children, waiting for their hand out of Pogs.

"He's in a right mess. I can't take him to the boys' side. Can you get him back to his cabin?" said Alyssa.

I can hear what's going on. I can't get up to protest.

"Don't worry, we'll take care of him." Bobby's voice sounds reassuring.

A soft hand touches the back of my head. It must be Alyssa, applying pressure. I can't open my eyes. My shoulders are stiff, and my neck may as well be made from concrete.

"Get him back, OK. I'm worried about him," she said.

"We've got this, no worries. Leave him with us."

"Thanks guys. Appreciate it. I've gotta go." She said, stroking my hair. "Get some sleep Dylan." Her voice getting quieter. Her steps become distant.

I'm still face down. How did I end up in the grass? I'm never gonna get myself to my feet. Am I dribbling?

"OK. Fuck him." Said Bobby, clearing his throat.

He hocks up some nasty phlegm with a thick rumble. He spits. A warm wetness slides down my neck.

"Abyssina bitch," said Bobby.

The sound of chuckles and laughter fades away.

Still, I lay here. Did I pass out, what would I do if I could stand? That expression 'Abyssinia', I know where I've heard it. That night, it was Bobby. Bobby fucked Lacey. Her bandaged wrist. I should have known at softball. He fucked her in the store shed, classy and romantic. If I could move, I might hit him. From what they were saying, they've done it before. Right now, I'm happy to revel in my perversion. I can't do much else. The sounds she was making echo in my head. I imagined myself in there, inside her. I thought I was just wanking to two people fucking. I can't move my feet. I might explore the darkness that has befallen me.

My eyes open, blurred. It feels like I'm drifting up from a riverbed to the surface of salt water. I'm so heavy. Then it comes with the cold. I shake and shiver. Followed by sweating. Is there any way to turn this off?

How long have I been here? I must have fallen unconscious. I'm still lying in the moist grass. Thick yellow bile near me and the taste of burnt salt on my tongue, acid taste in my throat. My nose is blocked too with whatever it is my body wants out of me. My shoulders are shuddering. Blades of grass tickle my mouth open. I open it and begin suckling at the grass like a kitten. I'm so thirsty that the moist grass is enough to suffice. It's so dark out here, I may as well have my eyes closed. I don't think they're closed, I'm sure they're open. I'm not in control of anything.

I can hear a male voice, soft, American. It's not familiar, at least I don't think it is. With the voice comes the intermittent flashes of yellow light burning at my eyes. It must be a torch. The voice is coming closer. I'm turned over on to my back in one powerful movement. The light blinds me as it's pointed at my face. My eyes shut tight, I cover them with my limp wrist, it flaps lifeless, like I have pins and needles. All I can see now is white, even with my eyes shut. The purest angelic white, the texture of an artist's canvas. My left hand still under my back. It's gone to sleep. Sleep would be such a luxury now. I could really do with a good sleep. I could do with some water. I can't move. The torch clicks off. Darkness. My hand flops from shielding my eyes.

"Shush, you're OK." The voice whispers.

Who is this?

There's this pressure on my navel, like I'm being leaned on. My belt buckle clanks. Quick and rough, my jeans unclasped. The buttons fling open like tearing at an envelope.

That hurts, I've got this intense pressure on my balls, like a twenty kilogram dumbbell. I can't get up. A warm hand cups my testicles inside my jeans, over my underwear. Shit. I can't muster enough energy to reach down. I flap my lifeless arm, it flops down to my crotch. He bats it away. I try to kick along the wet grass with the heal of my trainers, not going anywhere. I can't make any noise from my lips, I wanna scream.

My boxers and jeans are yanked down. My naked arse cheeks press against the wet grass, cold air, a wet warm feeling over the head of my dick. I can't lift off the ground. My eyes are darting over the night's sky, trying to focus. I can't move. Why can't I move? What the fuck is happening? I can't move.

Someone help me, someone please, help me. This is not happening.

Who the fuck is this?

Just get him off me, help me. Someone help. Please help me. Please.

A hand pushes down on my chest. I'm aroused. I don't wanna be. I'm pulsating in time with my heartbeat. Why is this happening? I don't want this. I'm not aroused. I'm not aroused. I want to fight this. I can't control myself. I'm getting harder and harder. Sloppy wet warmth gets warmer down my shaft. A pressure around the base and teeth on my left testicle, sucked and released with a loud pop.

I can't do anything.

I close my eyes. I just let it happen. I cough air. It's the only noise I can make. I'm close to coming. It's intense. I hate to admit it, pleasurable. I'm racked by inaction. I lift my head off the grass to see the top of a dark-haired man, his hair on my navel. He has a beard, a thick bushy beard.

I think of Laura, I imagine Laura. This is Laura sucking me off. It's Laura, no one else. Instead of black hair. Laura's long blonde hair. I see her familiar parting, she looks up at me, it's Laura. It's Laura sucking me off, that's it.

My mouth is open as I try to control my breathing and resist the need to come. I slide my hand down over my rib cage and scrunch my fingers through the black hair of this man's head. I'm weak. He clasps his hand on top of mine and entwines his fingers. I have no say in any of this.

I relax my body, my legs are forced open wide. A sudden, sharp burning sensation in my arsehole. A stiff hurt, stabbing pain. I clench. I could vomit. I release a loud breath, coupled with a submissive, high-pitched whiffled bird sound. My eyes roll back in my head. A finger deep inside me. It moves upward. I wince and everything tenses. Confusion rolls. My vision blurred becomes cloudy, my abs stiffen. My head arches, lifting from the grass. My shoulders crush into my neck.

I climax.

This man is swallowing my come. He continues sucking. I'm still hard. There's still an intense, pounding on my ring. It hurts. My eyes are watering.

I don't want this. I really don't. It's far too late now. I wanna cry, that won't help me either. I can only learn to forget.

25

Soft Focus Hardcore

I'm naked, on my back, not even covered by a sheet, in a strange bed. I have socks on my feet, yellow pus stains at the corner of my big toes. My head is pounding, my lower back tense and burning. My kidneys kicking into overdrive. It's light outside. This cabin is bright, painted clinical white. Am I in the medical centre?

This isn't my cabin.

There's no evidence of children ever being here. There's no sports equipment in cubbies. There are no clothes strewn around. There's nothing. One bed, a wardrobe and a desk with an iMac, stacks of DV tapes in plastic cassette cases. Who the hell does this cabin belong to?

A bright yellow T-shirt draped over the back of a desk chair. The words, those fucking words printed on it.

'Soft Focus Hardcore'

That inappropriate T-shirt slogan, on a camp full of kids. The only person I've seen wearing that is Max, the karaoke camp photographer, the videographer, the bearded man. Max has brought me back here, to his fucking cabin. He's taken advantage of me, taken advantage of his trusted freedom, he's treasured here, privileged and he knows it. He's afforded more independence, he doesn't report to anyone. That son of a bitch was hired to document the comings and goings of this camp. Max saw an opportunity, a weakness in me, and he took it. Last night, everything changed in me.

I sit up. I wanna find him, know why he's done this. My lower abdomen hurts, my back is throbbing needles. I'm scared and ashamed to look down at myself, to investigate. I almost don't need to. It's so sore. It's red and weeping with a clear liquid. I reach down between my legs as my arse hole is pulsating with a burning, fiery pain. My fingertips wet as I touch. I wanna cry. I want to hear my mum's voice, tell me it'll be OK. I need someone to tell me it's all right, this wasn't my fault.

If this is blood, I don't know what I'll do. I already know it is. I'm bleeding. I wipe my fingers on the bed sheet.

I thought I was safe here. I put my chin to my chest. Shake my head, close my eyes so tight my ears pop and shoulders shake.

I'm crying. I release a whimper. How has this happened? I do my best to conceal it, biting down on my index finger. It helps to avert my attention from the pain in the rest of my body.

Right. Pull yourself together, get the fuck up.

My jeans are crumpled on the wooden floor, caked in mud and grass stains. They're smeared with vomit. I can't see my shirt. I grab for my jeans, pulling them on. I see larger spots of blood on the bedsheets. I pick up the nearest T-shirt I can find and peel it over my head, covering my body. My Converse are by the door, organised among other trainers. I walk, my knees rubbing to retrieve them. It hurts, so painful with every step. I clench my butt cheeks, it helps. I'm sick to my acid stomach. My entire body is radiating heat. I have a horrible dust taste in my mouth, like smoked paprika or chilli chalk. I need a drink, I need some water.

I plunge my face under a running tap, water cooling my cheeks, open my mouth wide, filling it with water. Spit, the sink is covered in black speckles, I refill, spit it out, watered-down blood. I dive my head underneath the tap again filling my mouth. I swallow and repeat the same maniacal action. I snap down the tap lever and tread toward the door, checking I'm the only one here. The faster I try to stride, it hurts, the pain gets worse up through my lower back and feels like lobster pinches, clawing through my stomach.

I have no recollection of anything, apart from lying on my back in a field. I can almost cope with the blow job, I do remember that. The pain I'm experiencing, I'm not certain I can deal with. I can't tell anyone about this. I'm not even sure it happened. It must have. A minute ago, I was naked. How am I gonna confront Max?

It must have been him, he could tell me anything.

What the hell was that pill Bobby passed me? I'm sure as hell it wasn't ecstasy. I've never heard it knocks you out, it's the love drug. I didn't feel up for anything, and it wasn't the best feeling ever. I couldn't even gurney. I was paralyzed.

What am I gonna tell Doug?

In fact, what will I say to anyone?

I'm not even sure what to tell myself.

26

Depressed Depilation

Chillingworth's. It's indiscernible now. Every night since I can't sleep. Every time I try to close my eyes I'm in that white bleached cabin. I can't shake waking up in that room.

I haven't seen Max. It was him. As much as I'm trying to forget it. I haven't seen Alyssa. I haven't spoken to anyone. Not if I can help it. There's been no eye contact, no chat, no secret messages from friends, no smoke signals of apology from Alyssa. No one is interested in finding out how I am. Nothing, my fantasy with life is over.

It's like this whole thing I consider happy is nothing but a nightmare. All I know is I'm stood in this fucking baseball field, waiting for balls to be hit at me. These compressed corks, rubber filled cowhide, little white balls with that iconic red double stitching. They've become my life. I'm defined by them. Referred to, not by name but as the Baseball Counsellor. Even worse than that, 'The English Baseball Counsellor'.

I'm tasked with catching these balls and returning them to Bobby, like the bitch servant I've become. I haven't got the mental energy to confront him about anything that happened with Lacey. He's acting as the pitcher for this session. Not sure when and if I'll ever go back to softball. Alyssa will put a stop to that, if only for her own protection.

I can hear people's voices, I don't care what they're saying. It's been that way for days. Baseballs being hit off metal bats. Still, it doesn't register the reason I'm here. I came here to camp, to America for a once in a lifetime opportunity. All I know is pain. Everything hurts. Not only am I still struggling to walk because of that which I'm trying to ignore. Everything has become mere words, a category, a sketchy description. I'm putting my gravitas on it. Even now, both of my big toes hurt. I swear I want to cut them off. Down the edge of my toenails, both feet, they're puffy and red, crusty now too. It's really worrying me. I find it difficult to stand for too long and even walk without pain in my feet. The nails must be rubbing on my trainers. I'll have another look later; see if it's got any worse. With pain like this I hope the state of them is impressive.

If I could turn back time, I'm not even sure I would've come here. If I had that subsequent power, I'd make sure Alyssa was more interested in me, that she was on that bus with me, instead of being banged. She should have been in my company. I got what I deserved. I must have done something to someone. It helps I can't remember with any specificity, the actual attack. Is attacked the right word?

My life has changed. I don't know if it would be any better if I could remember any of it. Although, if I could remember, surely, I would have fought him off. I would have been enraged with desperation. Even if I was drunk, beyond drunk, I wouldn't have made it easy for him. I would have gone for his throat. I wanted it. Perhaps I needed to be abused. Too many thoughts flood to destroy me. I have these flashes of memory. I remember Alyssa being there. She sounded concerned. I was hoping she might try to find out if I was OK. Bobby's mentioned nothing. I think he's content in knowing that he broke me.

As I stand in this field. My mind wandering through all the faded brightness in me. From all that was good to all that is sordid. The baseball field is covered in a light, drifting mist. It mollycoddles the whole place, an enigmatic blanket. It's come from nowhere, eerily cold now too. I can't see the cabins, it's that misty. It's the height of summer, but cold. The weather seems to mirror my mind. It's nestled sweetly with my lost feelings, reflecting my own sense of shattered certainty. Why couldn't Chillingworth's be a positive night out? I was only looking to be free.

I try to focus on my reality. A baseball leaves Bobby's throwing arm, he's hit the ball foul.

That's it, I take off my glove and throw it to the ground. I'm out of here, stomping off the field. My head isn't here. I can't stomp, anyway my toes are fucking burning. I drag my feet on the gravel path toward the cabins. I can only wish for a different outcome. Warm my broken mind with Alyssa resting her head on my leg, sipping at alcohol as we sink into each other. A date by the lake. It never happened, never will. If only I paid more attention when people were telling me I looked rough. Whatever. I'm so lost. All I once had has now diminished. The dreams that I professed, the motivations for my travelling, gone.

I reach the steps to the cabin. Walk up, disturbed by the noise of my feet clapping on wood. As I ascend, my toenails cut against the leather of my Converse Weapons. The cabin door is wide open. It's silent, a kind of relief. I can't deal with anything disruptive right now.

I want to create my destruction. I walk to the bathroom, take a deep breath. I want to feel meditation. No one can see me. I'm creating my own lost drama. I can't bear to look myself in the eyes in the mirror. I muster the courage. I don't like what I'm seeing. My eyes are dark and puffy. There's nothing, not a frown, not a smile, nothing.

I grab for a nearby Gillette Mach 3 razor, it's not even mine. I don't care who's it is or where its been. I run the hot tap, steam billowing up like smoke from an ashtray. I tug on the plug lever and fill the basin, staring down, watching as it fills. I drag the razor blade from front to back, scrapping as it draws across my scalp, revealing egg white skin. The striped patch of bare skin like a combine harvester clearing a route through a cornfield. I want to make myself bald. I have no reason to use shaving foam. I don't care if it hurts. I pull the blade across my head, almost psychotically. I scrape, returning the razor to the sink, waggling the collected hair from the blade. I keep dragging the razor head through my hair and then back under the water, frantically swilling the blade to clean it. I'm almost done.

I hear the crash of the front door. Footsteps, voices and commotion. Wherever all the kids have been, they're back now. I can hear Doug's voice.

"Oh, shit dawg. You scared me." He said, shocked. Looking wide-eyed at me. "You ok?"

I think the question deserves my full attention. That was the intention. I want to be in control of something. I stop shaving my head and turn to face Doug like a pivoting lunatic. I nod, give him a slight smirk. I'm like a punk. I want to be violent. I want to destroy something, even if it's me.

"Yeah Doug. I'm fine, absolutely fine," I said.

I'm so deranged. My words sound empty. I mean it, I'm convincing myself I'm fine. I need to be in control. I can control this, and I will. My hair is floating in clumps on the surface of the water, it's decorating the white basin like scattered straw. I can own my uniqueness, my isolation. I'm better than most. This is where I can begin. I admire my fresh bald head in the mirror.

I'm trying to find myself in a world I don't belong. This place, this fucking camp, this hub for innocence, education and a pathway to adulthood. The institution of the American dream. This is far from those greeting cards or heart-warming notions. I'm lost in my own depressed depilation.

"Like the first monkey shot into space." Said Doug, investigating my head.

"I'll clean this shit up later," I said.

I pass Doug and climb on my top bunk. This little area I call my own. I grab for Malcolm X, the book by Alex Haley, my go to. Laura, as my bookmark looks back at me, nestled between the pages. I have the front page folded over the back, crushing the spine. I like to see books that have been read, even if the story is forgotten. I can identify the books I've finished, by the destruction of their covers. It's a sense of achievement. It's a spine bending applause of appreciation. I've absorbed the words, the book has lived. I'm no longer present. My eyes dart across the pages. I'm not taking in anything, only black blurs across the off-white page.

The back door screams open. I look forward to the crash, an uneasy, nurturing sound.

"Gentlemen." Said Rod, stomping in.

He grips his glasses, ripping them from his face. He stands by the edge of my bed, pinching his nose with his index finger and thumb. I catch his eye. He's said nothing. Instead replaces his glasses on his face and pinches the pages of my book. He's tilted his head, doing his best to read the front cover.

"I see," he said. "Plymouth rock landed on us. We didn't land on Plymouth rock."

"Almost." I said, humouring him. I need to try harder to hide my frustration. Fucking idiot. I can't hide my frowns anymore. Is he being sarcastic or ignorant?

"Go tell your nigger story to Joe." Said Rod.

None of the boys, not even Doug, have reacted.

He did just say that?

"Sorry, you what?"

"Joe, wants to see you," he said.

I can't move. I'm shocked. I don't feel anger. I'm just saddened, disappointed. I have no motivation to argue. Rod isn't looking at me now. Where the hell am I, how did I end up on this camp?

Rod's staring around the cabin like the T1000.

"Now." He said, slapping his open hand against my bald

head. He dashes out of the cabin the same way he came in.

There's no one to seek solace in. I'm on my own. If he had hung around. I'm too weak to fight. I thought Doug might get involved, he didn't. I can only rely on myself. Am I ever going to get out of here?

My head pounding, I'm filled with nervous anxiety. Why does nobody care, why am I being told to go see Joe?

Whatever the outcome of this meeting, it'll be like my life, negative.

I'd be happy to kill right now.

27

Call Me, Joe

I'm having to walk slow, it's not deliberate. Rod is moving too fast for me, too fast it makes my toes ache. I instead meander between cabins. The prospect of a meeting with Joe can't be good. I'm not sure why I'm worried, though. It's as if I know what's coming, knowing nothing. I'll cripple myself with worry. More tall trees, the distant rumbling of children's voices. Camp is still very much alive but dead in me.

The main door to the administration office is grand and intimidating. The building itself is one of the nicest on camp, with a huge veranda. It's like one of those antebellum homes. A grand white plantation sort of house, made of solid wood except for a stone-built chimney, two storey painted pearl white. Several wooden rocking chairs on the veranda, beautifully maintained, they rock on their own. The white grand front doors are wide open. It's bigger than I think it has to be. The parents would see this building when they first arrive. It makes an impression. Unlike the cabins, they'll see this for sure. I walk up the steps, so nervous. I've never been called to the office before, all very ominous.

At the top of the steps, in through the doors into a large open hallway with a grand fireplace set in grey stone. Decorating all the walls are camp pictures of years passed. Black and white group shots, kids with their arms around counsellors, action shots of children kayaking, playing baseball, swimming and dressed up in American football uniforms.

Ahead is an oak wood solid door. A sign with 'Director' adorns the entrance. The door reminds me of Regan's bedroom in The Exorcist. That impending doom, the horror held within. Just below is a piece of ripped white cardboard, pinned off-centre, that reads:

'Call me Joe.'

Underneath that is a hand drawn white feather again. The same thing tattooed on some of these girls. I open the door, entering the room. Joe sat behind his desk, two teenage girls standing in front of him. I notice the backs of their tanned legs. Both have their hair draping loose over their shoulders. I've interrupted whatever conversation they were having.

Joe looks up at me, beyond the girls with rage in his brow, as I enter his office, uninvited.

"What the hell are you doing?" Said Joe, glaring up at me with veiny eyes.

My dick shrivels in my pants, then wetness. The girls haven't reacted. Joe has never shouted before. He's never raised his voice. It scares me. He made me dribble with fear. I back out of his office, pulling the door closed. He hasn't stopped looking at me. I'm embarrassed but reeling with myself, that I even walked into his office without knocking. The sign implies that he's cool. That might not be the best start to what will be a pained meeting. The door clicks shut behind me. I shut my eyes, annoyed with my stupidity.

The door opens. The two girls, both seniors slide their bodies through the gap as I step aside to let them exit. They're both wearing crop tops, exposing their flat stomachs.

Joe's red face appears at the crack of the door. The girls exit into the lobby.

"Thank you, ladies." Said Joe, smiling after the two girls as they leave. "Right, get yer ass in here."

I follow Joe. He removes his glasses from his face, revealing a red indentation on the bridge of his nose. He wipes his right eye with the edge of his wrist and stomps around the other side of his desk, his heavy ankle boots banging on the wooden floorboards like a rhythm section. He slams his body down into his red leather office chair, like a house brick hitting pavement. He replaces his glasses on his nose, pushing them into place with his little finger. Joe sits hunched forward over the solid desk, resting his elbows on the edge. He flails a raised arm in the air, waving me to sit down in the much smaller and far less comfortable wooden chair opposite him. There's a hand knitted dog cushion, could be a Basset Hound. I take a seat. His office is nipple cutting, air-conditioned cold, far too chilly for me. Black and white pictures around the room, like those of the ones at the main entrance, mainly of him and his wife smiling bold toward the camera with cheesy faced children. It all looks fake. There are loads of pictures of Joe standing with all the senior girls from each successive year. Funny, his wife isn't in any of those.

If my toe wasn't hurting so much, I might tap the edge of his desk, see how much it's worth. The phone has one of those faded cream-coloured, curved plastic contraptions that lets you rest it in your neck. A plate with a half-eaten sandwich on it with the crusts cut off. Joe takes a bite from one corner, not looking at me or saying anything. I can hear his mouth clapping together as he eats, a metronome of annoyance. It looks like Joe sleeps in here, there's a red leather three-seater chesterfield sofa against the right-hand wall with four pink sheepskin blankets, all scrunched up on it.

The window behind him is massive, no curtains or nets, no blinds just a massive window. Wait, there are blinds, red Venetian blinds, they're pulled right up to the top. There's a Polaroid camera too. The windows provide a view of the whole of the girls' side of camp. You can see the entrances to their cabins. I can see off over his shoulder, through the open doors of the gymnasium building. Girls of about twelve, performing cartwheels, others throwing themselves into the air, tucking their knees up and landing graceful into a forward roll.

Every time a group of girls walks past the window or Joe hears a cackle of noises from female mouths, his eyes dart, he's immediately distracted from chomping on his sandwich, wiping his beard free of breadcrumbs.

"New look I see." Said Joe, as he bites down on another corner of his sandwich. "Quite confrontational." He continues, referring to my cleanly shaven head, as he pushes bread to the corner of his mouth with his tongue.

Has he really brought me here to watch him eat his fucking lunch?

The door to the office behind me snaps open. Rod walks through, scrunching his hat in his hands, followed by Bill and then Monte. The door closes behind them. The three of them stand behind me.

Nothing but silence, except for Joe breathing through his nose and distant female laughter coming from outside through the window.

I look back round, up at Rod, and then swing my head to Bill. This is a strange situation. They aren't saying anything. We all stare at Joe, the loud gum slapping noises with his mouth. I'm doing so well not to vomit.

"I'm very disappointed in you, Dylan." Said Rod, from behind me.

I turn in my seat to face him again. What does he mean?

"Don't look at me," he said.

Another slap on my bald scalp. It pops like a teaspoon breaking a soft-boiled egg.

I can't find the words to argue. Anger and shock envelopes within me. Keep it together, stay calm.

"I apologise for disappointing you, Rod."

I do my very best to sound sincere. I don't give too ounces

of shit if I've disappointed him or anyone. Now probably isn't the best time to announce how I think they, the camp has failed me.

"I'm sure you are." Said Rod, screwing up his cap "We've all been discussing your future here, and it's our decision that we want you to leave, today."

My eyes widen and my throats dry. My cheeks are red, heat pulsating from my neck into my ear lobes. My face falls slack, and my mouth opens.

"I'm not leaving." I said, shaking my head, trying to glare deep into their eyes.

"Oh, you're not, you think it's acceptable to be face down on the golf course?" said Joe.

"You only know half of it. Not a chance I'm leaving," I said.

"Do you know who you're talkin' to?" Said Joe.

I search for a glimmer of a soul in each of them.

"I'm not leaving, I won't. I've seen too much."

"What do you think you've seen exactly?" Said Joe.

I have all their attention now. I don't have to be specific. In a world of guilt, it's death by suggestion.

"I'll be quiet." I said and ponder for a moment "If you want nothing getting out." I lean forward in my seat, rest my elbows on the desk. "I'm not bluffing."

"This isn't a negotiation." Said Bill, pulling me back into the chair by my shoulder.

"Everything's a negotiation. I've got terms," I said.

Joe leans back in his chair, twiddling a yellow pencil between his fingers, pondering his options.

"I stay 'til the end," I said.

"That's it?" Said Joe, pointing his pencil at me, lead first.

"You leave me alone too."

"I don't know what you think you know?" Said Joe, clearing a fleck of crust from his cheek.

"Are we really listening to this shit?" said Rod.

"Grab a seat Rod, we all like a good nightcap." I said, winking.

"You're pushing it," he snaps.

"I'm not pushing it far enough. I've seen things here, you don't want the world knowing."

"Your words mean nothing. You have no evidence of anything," said Joe.

"I have a generation of evidence." I stand up, smiling "Leave me alone until the end and I leave. Nothing said, nothing printed."

"You're a very brave young man," said Joe.

"Joe, I've just got nothing left to lose."

The longest walk of my life. They follow me out of the office to the top of the steps, watching me walk down to the grass. As my trainers hit the ground, my toes burn. The Authority behind me, watching me leave. As corrupt as this camp is. It's their fear that set me free. This camp has consumed me. I want so bad to leave, but I'm scared to leave myself behind. I'm lost within the trees, the bent blades of grass. I'm locked in the wood of the cabins. My spirit held captive by the summer.

There was something nice about being naïve. Never having experienced anything. Being young and empowered. I may promise myself to be better. Life should be a process of constant evolution, continual improvement. Convincing yourself it can only get better makes you spend money.

I have a second chance, nestled in my pocket.

Joe might be proud of this camp. The world he and his wife have created. He can keep his well-oiled sales pitch. The smoke and mirrors, his grand illusion.

They can threaten me all they like. They're only worried about Civil War. This place is so screwed up.

Hypocrisy, darkness and no repercussions for anyone. Counsellors fucking campers. And I have nothing to pull me through my insanity but humility.

Now, I'm a marked man. It'll be worth it.

28

Rafters

The last few weeks are going to be hard. Nothing to look forward to but the end. I stretch my arms out along the side of my top bunk and rest my chin on the wooden slat, staring into the distance of the chipboard back wall.

What the hell is that?

I can see two bare feet sticking out of an unfolded sleeping bag. Who the fuck is sleeping in that bed?

The back door opens, Doug comes bowling through, slapping my shoulders in a friendly, unspoken greeting.

I'll leave him out of everything. He doesn't need to know all the threats from the authority. He'll be left alone, just as I will now.

"Wassup Dawg, missed you, man. Where you been?"

"Nowhere, mate." I said, distracted. "Who the hell is that?" I point toward the exposed bare feet.

Doug squints and peers over the top of my bunk, his neck like an ostrich. He screws up his face and pulls a weird side smile. He too has no clue who this sleeping bag stranger is. As much as he's trying to be quiet, his flip flops, flop disobediently, scuffing his feet across the wooden floorboards. Standing, staring for a second. He leans down, grabbing this mystery person's right big toe and tugs.

The body under the sleeping bag shuffles and squirms. A dark-haired head peers, weary eyed from underneath.

"Are you lost dawg?" Said Doug, with a slight chuckle in his voice.

I can't help but giggle, too. I've stepped closer to the human enigma.

"I'm Warren." He said, opening his eyes wider. "I arrived this morning." He said, in a thick broad Northern English accent. It's a Leeds accent, I recognise it straight away.

Despite his tired eyes, he swings his legs round and sets his t-bone steak feet on the floor. He recoils at the cold floor underfoot. He's wearing stylised underpants, Y-fronts with a comic book Batman emblem and words all over them. He stands up straight, stretches his arms out. This guy has the physique of a fitness cover model, tall too. He looks old. Doug used to have a goatee and looked old. This guy Warren looks in his mid-thirties, full of stubble, far older than all of us. His body is so toned with a stone, bench press, defined chest, covered with thick black hair. He must lift, bro.

"I'm Doug."

"I'm Dylan—, Where you from, sounds like a Leeds accent?"

"Spot on, mate. Well, I'm from Robin Hood," said Warren.

"Robin Hood?" said Doug. "That a real place?"

Warren smirks, nodding.

We're polite, shake hands, all very mature. Warren has dark hair with peppered sprinklings of grey coming through. Warren reveals under Doug's stiff questioning that he's twenty-one. He told us he never gets ID'd. That I can believe, no joke. This guy looks fucking old. We're gonna get on. He has a genuine vibe about him. I'm almost happy to know that he'll be a part of our cabin, an English friend.   "What is it you'll be doing here?" I said.

"I'm the new arts and crafts counsellor." He said with pride, shoulders back and chest out.

Right, I never expected that. He does not look like an artsy type of person. Half thought he would say he's gonna be a swim or basketball coach. That has thrown me completely. Doug's and my face say everything.

Warren is starting late at camp because of Civil War. The last event. They've mentioned how important it is to them, they bring in more staff to make it memorable and to help out.

We stand around for a little while longer. Not really saying anything. I'm thinking about how this might affect the dynamic of our cabin. Warren has to be better than Benedict, a simple task. Hopefully, it'll remain positive.

Doug and I pick up random pieces of clothes left on the floor of the cabin. The bathrooms are clean anyway, so that's a task we don't have to worry about.

"We should prob-lee show ya round, right dawg?" Said Doug.

"That'll be cool," said Warren.

It's good to be part of a trio, safety in numbers. Warren brings out my relaxed personality. I'm trusting him. Early days but I hope he has potential, like Doug, gonna be a friend or someone that'll have a similar ilk to my own. That's rare to find that sort of thing, rare for me anyway.

Warren's seen the camp, we approach the linen cabin. He needs sheets. There's a whole crowd of people standing outside again. Some have American footballs. Girls and guys are laughing, frolicking on the grass. Everything seems to have relaxed recently. People get close when the two sexes mix, it's like sugar being caramelised.

"Hey you," said Hazel.

A welcome encounter. Nothing but Hazel in my sight. A delightful surprise, in fact. I haven't seen her for ages. Not even to speak to. She's shimmering.

"Liking the new hair." She said, pointing at my bald, shaved head. "Hope you didn't do that for me." She runs her hand over my scalp. She grins, rips off her brunette wig from the crown of my head.

"Gorgeous," she said. Holding her hands out wide, as if admiring a piece of artwork.

It's good to see her bald and happy. She's not trying to hide it. I may not want to smile, laugh, or even talk. But Hazel is funny, different, playful and silly. I like that in her.

"What you been up to? We only seem to see each other at this glorious linen cabin," she said.

"All good."

I really should be honest with her. I think she deserves that much. Instead, I exaggerate my positive feelings to spare hers.

"I was worried about you the other night. You were out of your head."

"Yeah, it's a bit of a blur," I said.

"Bobby get you back all right?"

"Bobby, what d'ya mean?"

"I asked Bobby to take care of you," she said.

"Wait. That was you? I thought it was—, Of course, it was you."

"Yeah, who did you think it was?"

"It doesn't matter." I said. I can't shield my pleasant surprise. "Thank you." I adjust her wig on my head, fanning the fringe over my forehead. I'm so happy to hear it was her. That really means so much. "How do I look?"

"Divine," she said. "Right, I gotta help with our cabin and get clean sheets for these dirty bitches. Everyone's so stressed about Civil war. Gotta go. See ya real soon." She smiles as she bounces outta my eyeline, quickly returning. In a moment of slapstick comedy, she swipes her wig from my head.

"Almost forgot her," she said. "You do look cute though." She slides the wig back on her own head.

It's funny she refers to it as 'her'. I should have known it was Hazel. Bless her.

Warren and Doug beckon me over to the linen cabin. I assume they want my help. I didn't even see them leave my side. They must have left Hazel and me to it. Nice guys. I jog up the slope toward them.

"She likes you," said Doug with a smile as he passes me an armful of sheets and pillowcases.

"She's really nice," I said. "It's taken me a while to see it."

Hazel's always around when I wanna get lost. When I need to know there's someone to find happiness in. She makes me nervous. I like that. I haven't had that for a long time. Not like butterflies or any of that cliché stuff. I can see myself with her, happy. It's not even a sexual thing. Not like lust. Now wasn't the time to discuss anything I think happened the other night with her.

"Let's get all this shit back." Said Warren, clutching more sheets in his arms.

He's already cynical, he's funny. His attitude is subversive, and that's welcome here. His northern twang of an accent helps too.

The kids are getting briefed about this Civil War thing. We've been tasked with cleaning the cabins again and all that subservient jazz. There's a lot of speculation about what Civil War will be this year. Whether this will be like it was last year, with people arriving via helicopter. The only thing I know is that this camp takes the whole thing far too seriously. It's not an official night off tonight, but because the kids are being babysat on our behalf, we've got an informal free night. They've put on a bus to take those that want to go into town and watch a movie. See, I've started to use the word too now. I really can't be arsed and I'm kind of tired of having to act. It sounds like we're gonna need serious rest before this Civil War shit kicks off. If I was to go out and watch American Pie 2 or Along Came a Spider. I'd just be thinking about tomorrow anyway, having to mentally prepare myself. I wouldn't be able to relax. Plus, Hazel didn't mention she was going so, I'm not.

Laying on my back, staring up at the ceiling. The wooden cabin beams have writing all over them.

'Buzz was ere', 'Connecticut 97' and other tags. Words from over the years, all in different handwriting. The thickness of the pens in use change as you get higher to the pitch of the cabin roof. It's as if they encouraged this nostalgic graffiti. It's like a wall of fame for past kids and counsellors.

"There's some serious shit on this ceiling." I said out loud, not taking my eyes off it. "Look at it."

Doug's bottom bunk creaks as he shifts his body out from underneath.

"Shit dawg." Said Doug, his mouth open as he reads.

"It's mad innit," I said. "How have I never noticed that?"

Warren's sitting on his bed. He too, like Doug, is staring straight up at the ceiling. He's sat like a tiny child, despite being the oldest looking counsellor on camp.

"Not be possible," said Warren. "I have to die." He's reading from the cabin beams.

"Fuck off, dawg." Said Doug, walking over to Warren, not taking his eyes off the ceiling. Doug gets closer and lurches forward, almost on his tiptoes, to get a better vantage.

"Nah man, it doesn't actually say—, That's fucked up."

"Let me see that," I said.

I don't believe there shock. I swing my legs over the left side of my bed and hoist my bottom over. I land on Ben's bed next to mine.

"It does say that," I said. The words are intelligible as you like on the ceiling. Not even an attempt to cover it up.

"That's proper weird," said Warren.

"Shit. Check this one." I point at another piece of scrawling. This one is harder to read than the other.

"No light," I said. "The feathers. I'm writing in…" I pause, not sure if that says what I think it does. "Does that say—, Blood. I'm reading that right?"

"Yup," said Warren.

"What kind of shit is this?" Said Doug, in his soft southern drawl.

That's the reaction I'd expect, if he was to be stopped on a highway by a quivering light laden flying saucer.

"We should paint our names on that baseball wall," said Warren.

"What about this?" I said, pointing up. They're all too quick to dismiss my intrigue at this messed up writing.

Warren looks bored, shrugging his shoulders.

"It's bollocks, someone taking the piss." He said, pinching his left nostril. He looks down to examine whatever he's collected, rolling it between his fingers, and flicks it from the tip of his thumb to the floor. Nice.

Doug and I look at each other. Doug swallows and shrugs.

"So, you want to?" said Warren.

Seriously, what's he talking about now? I'm still trying to contemplate if this is a joke or not. I stare down at him sat on his bed. I'm almost at eye level with him. He really is tall.

"Paint our names." He said again, miming writing in the air.

"That's the home run wall. You only get to write your name on it if you hit a home run," I said.

"Balls to that," said Warren. "I've got the keys to the arts cabin. Get some paint, bish bash bosh. My names on that wall."

"Bish bash, bosh?" said Doug.

"Jobby done," said warren.

It could be fun though. We all nod.

"Not a home run in sight," said Warren. "We'll wait till later, let it get darker and go before the kids get back." Warren, flops back on his bed. His face aglow like a mischievous child, plotting to rob apples from a neighbour's tree.

It's not like I need more spice in my life. But, bring on the distractions.

It'll be worth it.

29

Spicy Finger Painting

Waiting for darkness to carry out our scheme and plot. Time drags on and on. The three of us haven't moved. Plenty of time to listen to tunes. I haven't heard Sally Cinnamon in so long. I'd almost forgotten how special to me that song is. I land on All Across the Sands, with its memories. That's a little too slow, especially in my current mood. I'm locked in this unfamiliarity. I can only rescue myself with sound. I'm enjoying the fact that Warren's here, and we all seem like a good bunch now. I can't even deal with the song Going Down, too much slow pain. Reminds me of weeping in my room at uni, sobbing along to the lyrics.

I gave Warren my Sean Paul CD to listen to. He's familiar with him, he's dancing one step, two step in the middle of the cabin, king monkey style. One hand raised, his body floppy and loose. I need some Tom Waits, he always has this way of stimulating my madness.

With these sounds, the time will soon be here for our sneaky spicy finger-painting fun.

The fact we don't have to deal with the whining kids tonight is a gift I'm thankful for. The three musketeers, Doug, Warren and me, hop from our beds. I dash my headphones to the side. The darkness is here. We exit via our favourite back door. I hold it securely in my hand, almost trapping my fingertips in the gap between the door and frame. If the thing that was to ruin this would be that whining door spring, that would be unfortunate. How I love that spring. Still cuts right through me, loving my regret.

The three of us are silent, not talking, not making any noise. I can almost hear my breath. We're tiptoeing, gliding across the grass. Hiding in the shadows of these white wooden cabins, they're providing cover for our clandestine path. We all scamper from trees to the next clump, doing our best to hide from what is a weirdly bright night. The moon is almost full. There's never much light pollution out here. I'll give it that. It's beautiful and peaceful. You could really explore the night's sky. I'm not a star gazer but I can appreciate all its sparkling wonder. It's not like those night skies you see in movies, with that unrealistic moon like saucer, crisp white, close enough to touch. This is just natural.

Warren leads the way, not taking in the sky. He's on a mission. He strikes me as a natural leader, it's probably his size. He's leading us into the fray. I don't think I've ever been, or even seen the arts and crafts hut. He's a couple of metres ahead of both Doug and me. He's peeking around the corners of cabins. They act like mirrors, reflecting white moonlight. It's a challenge not to be seen. We're cardboard cutouts bracing ourselves against this wood. To me, we're Navy Seals, hitching from helicopters and making our way behind enemy lines. We dart past the brightly lit laundry cabin. Through a window, Andy and Oxford Mark are standing talking with their arms folded. The churning of a struggling washing machine thunders round and round, as if it's rinsing bricks and tennis shoes. That noise alone will cover our movements. We skim along the wooden laundry cabin and out off toward the recreation hall. There's an open clearing from the rec hall to the arts cabin.

Warren bolts, running in a straight line, knees up, his hands like blades cutting through the air. It's like he's trying to be quick, like the flash, all very robotic. It's as if speed means no one will see him. He leaps toward the front door, the last step. He fumbles with the keys, dropping them to the floor. That disrupts our attempt at silence. Jingle jangle indeed.

"What's that?" Said Doug, looking over his shoulder in panic.

I follow his cue. There's a golf cart coming up the hill with its lights on, cutting through black. Pesky golf carts, ferrying around the privileged few, whilst the rest of us peasants, not worthy of battery-operated transportation, wear our legs out.

"Hurry," I said.

Warren shushes the pair of us, pushing the key in the lock, turning it wildly, dropping the bunch to the floor with a clank. The golf cart nears closer. The whirling motor giving off a louder and louder hum. Warren turns the key, the door pops open just enough for all of us to disappear into the darkness within. He nudges the door closed. The headlights of the golf cart illuminate the entrance foyer as we duck down, out of sight of the windows.

All clear. We've caught our breath back.

"Shit dawg, that was close." Said Doug, sucking in air.

"Right, let's get this done." Said Warren, slapping his palms on his knees. It's like we're grabbing a shopping cart of supplies, our Supermarket Sweep.

On the walls of this place are hand-painted, large murals of phoenixes in different forms, white feathers and stickmen pictures, much like the canteen. There are recreations of the Red Oak and Silver Wood Camp logo, tree lined baseball fields, childlike scrawling, capturing wooden cabins and papier mâché human figures. This stuff looks creepy to me. Bird like animals. Hopefully we won't invite Captain Howdy.

Warren pushes through a set of doors at the back, making Doug catch it before it swings shut.

"It's in the back." Said Warren with confidence, nodding in the direction he's walking. He wanders confidently through work benches to another cupboard in the workshop. He unbolts a narrow, tall cupboard. Inside are six or seven shelves from floor to ceiling lined up, full of large pots of paints. He grabs several cans, tilting them to read the label by the light of the moon. He's selected the white paint he wants. He heads toward the rear of the workshop, rifling loud through wooden drawers, the contents shifting loose as he jerks them open.

"They've moved the brushes," he said. "Help me look in here, Doug."

Doug joins him, looking through different drawers for paintbrushes. I'll try to join in too. Hopefully, my hapless glances around the room will make it appear like I'm getting involved. I'm not that committed to this whole premise as it is, anyway. The idea of painting my name on the home run wall has lost its excitement. Although, if we were to have the brushes in hand and make our way to the field, that may spark a little more fire in me. I can always write:

'Bobby is a cunt'

Even that may not lift me. I'm empty again. I've been getting this creeping emptiness that takes over me. I've never had a panic attack before, but I'd much rather stay in the shadows and catch my breath. It seems to get worse, growing more frequent since being on this fucking camp. I'm breathless and dizzy. Any light I can see expands in my eyes and my ears threaten to burst. Surely, this is learnt. I need to shake it. Warren and Doug are shushing each other, sniggering as they continue to rummage for appropriately sized brushes.

"Dylan, check in that cabinet by the taps." Said Warren.

The metal filing cabinet has a yellow and black Nirvana band sticker on it. I open the cabinet drawers from top to bottom. I'm trying to be delicate and deliberate in the same way Doug and Warren are behaving. It's almost melodramatic. How particular we're having to be. I open each drawer with a sliding metallic clunk. Nothing, no brushes. I open the bottom drawer and a black lock box slides forward. I'd love to find a gun. A cold, heavy gun. I lean down and flick the lid with my finger; it flings open. I can only wish for a bright, golden light illuminating my eyes. Through the darkness I want to see the outline of a firearm.

The box is empty.

If I was to find a gun, I'd have to use it. I don't think I'm capable. It would make me mighty. I'd be alive with power and the possibility of living. Good thing it's empty.

"We need a wallpaper brush. The bigger the better," said Warren.

"Dylan. We got 'em," said Doug.

It's one hell of a distance from the arts cabin to the lower baseball field. We're undercover, hidden by the backdrop of the dark woods, until we reach the main road. We do the customary looking left and right to make sure there are no vehicles or anyone silently roaming. We need to run down the hill to the main field. Along the back separating the field from the trees is the six-foot-tall green painted wooden perimeter, our blank canvas. It's covered in names of those successful in the endeavour of hitting that illusive home run. The honest pride in that must be pretty rewarding for these kids. It'd be good if I could manage it for real. I would then do myself proud. I would have at least achieved something. Despite none of us three, never hitting a home run. We're still gonna tag the wall.

"Shit. How we gonna open the paint?" said Warren, looking around him, as if the blades of grass are going to help.

"Use the keys." I said, like I'm B.A. Baracas. I'm that resourceful.

Warren nods in agreement, jamming a door key under the lip of the white paint. He jerks it, the key snaps in half. His eyes follow the broken half as it swirls through the air. We've all lost sight of it in the dark grass.

"Oops," said Warren.

He continues to use the broken end of the key, jerking at the lid. It pops open. He takes the brush and bangs it into the white paint, he slops the paint covered brush against the wall and sweeps his arm up and down. I step back to gain a better perspective. I can't tell what he's doing.

He's written:

'Big w In The House'

He's capitalised every letter except the 'w', odd choice. I assume 'w' is for Warren. That would be the one thing I would have capitalised. He passes the handle of the brush to Doug, who then writes his sonnet.

OK, so he's scrawled:

'Georgia Grillz'

Doug is sniggering to himself as he passes me the white paint tipped brush, droplets hitting the grass. He stands with his arms crossed. Next to Warren, they're both looking back over their shoulders, then back to their beloved artwork.

I let my arms move like Daniel Larusso, up and down - paint the fence, sand the floor. I don't end it with a full stop.

"All done." I said, as if Bob Ross has just added the finishing touches to a 'big old tree'.

Doug and Warren tilt their heads like they're trying to help themselves comprehend what I've written, you could say, a dog and card trick.

"The English are comin'." Said Warren, reading my words aloud.

"Nice," said Doug.

I'm still holding the brush.

Warren steps forward, snatching the brush from my hand.

"Right let's go," he said.

Warren takes the paint can, slamming the lid back on. He flicks the brush removing the excess white paint, splattering it like Jackson Pollock's, Convergence across the grass.

It'll soon be tomorrow. Every day used to become yesterday too quickly. Not now we're painting on fucking fences to entertain ourselves. I'm so impatient. This will all be over soon.

I want to get back to the cabin before these entitled bastards get involved in Civil War.

30

Civil War

The routine kills me. I'm not nervous about today. I am a little. I've heard rumours, but what use are rumours on a camp full of lies? I don't need to be involved with this anymore. I can't be onboard with this entire offering of a Civil War for kids. The country went through all that, the whole tainted history, for this camp to trivialise the whole thing and use it as entertainment for these privileged little kids, seems crazy to me.

With this passing of mediocrity, the sound of nothingness booms empty across the camp. Doug and Warren make their way to the cabin door. They look out through the fly screens, like a couple of caged animals. Doug even has his palm pressed against the material. All so well-timed.

The kids are stirring. I prefer the insular boys, the ones that don't bother me. I can't stand the needy ones. When did my attention become an endorsement for acceptance?

Does that mean they respect me? I'm not sure it does, I'm someone for them to use.

For the kids of this cabin, the ones that know what today will bring, they spout off to the freshman like they're ready to unwrap Christmas presents, the spoilt shits. They themselves are itching to share all their previous experiences and knowledge from last year. They must feel empowered over the newcomers. Even the three of us, Doug, Warren and me. We're no longer the adults here, only spectators. The kids, for Civil War, have all the power.

With an almost arrogant nod, I leave Doug and Warren to cajole the kids and get them ready for this disagreeably named event, Civil War. It's on for a fucking week, too. I'm not hanging around to offer help, I don't have to. They can cope.

Staff room it is then. I go up there. The TVs on. I've never seen it not on. Seems to be a lot of concentration on Timothy McVeigh. Bush standing at the White House podium detailing his last punishment. Other than that, not much else is being reported. Free PC, against the wall, perfect timing. Middle plastic blue school chair seat. The other seats are vacant. I Enter my email address and peer around to make sure no one's looking over my shoulder as I type my password: 'MichaelMyers1978'. Nothing, no eyes are bothered. I hope Laura has written to me by now, it's been ages.

I silently celebrate when the browser opens, click on the inbox. The number is low. The internet isn't the fastest here. It's not as if I'm waiting for a naked picture of the Dixie Chicks to open, but it always takes an age. I miss trying to find nude celebrities. I can't get away with that here. That black solid bar edging further, lower down the monitor screen, from head, shoulders, cleavage to nipples.

To my surprise and sour disappointment, Laura hasn't replied. I can't think what she's doing. My feelings of sweetness toward her are slowly diminishing, as if they haven't already dissolved. I'm convinced I know what she's doing. Charlie big balls. That's what she's doing, with his fucking royalist name. I've only tried to call twice. With the time difference and activities, it's hard to catch her. Harder still if she doesn't want to be caught. If I worry about it too much. I'll never be good enough. No email, no phone call. My life is making less and less sense. I could really do with talking to someone. I may even have to call my mum on my next day off. I only refer to her as mum when I'm desperate. I can't go into detail with her about what's happened to me and in fact I won't even think about it anymore. I can't. I don't want to be a victim. It's another reason to lose myself in this myriad of bleakness.

I press play on my CD player; it skips to track two, the distorted melody cranks out. Oh no, not now, Hot Hot Heat again, not a bad thing. I select emails, putting a tick in the box and then stab at the delete key, clearing down the screen. Random messages from people purposing to be female:

'My name is Jenny, and I'd like to meet.'

Marketing emails from MSN and the classic Viagra ones, all deleted. I'll go back over the old emails I've received from Laura. As I read, I try to ignore the content. I imagine her sat in front of her computer typing whatever it is and hearing her speak the words out loud. I'm depressed as I sense that even in these old examples of so-called love filled mails. She seems to be preoccupied or distracted. I don't think she must have been editing or re-reading what she's sent as she goes into detail about what happened at Tilly's house on Saturday, but then doesn't finish the story. Which means I'm tormented with paranoia, my mind all over the place. Filling in the gaps, making shit up, thinking Charlie is with her, filling in her gap. This is so fucking hard.

I need to crank up my CD player louder and louder until these thoughts disappear. As the synth kicks in for track three, Get in or get out, a blonde girl sits down to my right. I recognise her, don't know her name, I won't make eye contact. It's almost as if she can't be bothered with me either, which is fine. Now isn't the time for me to talk. I notice in the corner of my eye, looking over at her screen, that someone has clearly written a lengthy email to her, and she's opening an attachment of pictures sent to her. I'd assume it to be her boyfriend. It must be, I can see at the bottom there are like fifty kisses, not only kisses but that whole: 'xoxox'. What a load of fluff.

My chair tilts to the left, as if a beast of a person has sat down in the chair next to me with massive trainers and chunky calves. Bobby of all fucking people. There's my rage again. He's wearing his customary baseball hat and staring at the monitor. He hasn't even acknowledged me. I suppose he, like me, won't make the effort to talk. What would we say?

I'm so happy he hasn't tapped me on the shoulder or said a word. I'm not sure how I might react. I wonder how Lacey is, you fucker. He too is checking his email, logging in to AOL. I can see him tilt the screen away, as if to create a sense of privacy from my squinting eyes. He leans forward, reading, then whips round and belts me with his fist. It hurts. I stare down at his hand. Heat in my face. I'm holding it in, it'll bubble on up.

"Turn it down," said Bobby.

I can't really hear him over my sanctuary of music, but I can read his lips. Plus, he looks angry, his face filled with frustration.

I flick the power button off and remove my headphones from clamping down over my ears. I wonder if he'd have been so abrupt if I was a stranger.

"I didn't realise you could hear it," I said.

"Have some fucking consideration." Bobby said, with his teeth exposed, like a snarling Pitbull.

"Fuck you, Bobby. You don't get to tell me what to do anymore," I said.

"Don't talk to me like that." He said, his face tense like he was sniffing shoe polish.

The blonde girl shifts.

"Trust me. I'll talk to you however I want," I said. "Lacey sends her love."

I log out of Hotmail. Stand up, push my chair away from me with the back of my legs, all the while maintaining my stare on Bobby.

"Abyssina bitch," I said.

He looks surprised. He can't come for me anymore.

I hit the power button on my CD player. The song, In Cairo plays out over my headphones. If only it was a heavier track, it would have punctuated my exit better, with far more drama. Instead, a sweet-sounding piano chirps out.

I thump down the steps. I couldn't feel better if I tried. Maybe if I had whipped that plastic chair around his fucking head, knocking his hat off. I can only ever fantasise. I don't need to. He's captive in his own regret and embarrassment.

 I step down off the last wooden step. The grass has worn out to dry mud from all the staff room foot traffic, the dirt goes to a point like a pizza slice.

The bastard roaring bugle sounds out across the camp PA system. So loud, too loud. Heads turn and stare as if listening to instructions from a dystopian dictator. That's weird, it's the middle of the day, they rarely do this.

"All campers and counsellors to the main baseball field immediately." Said the deep coffee smooth, rich American accented announcer. It sounds like Joe, almost soft and suggestive with a mix of mischief. It's how he talks to the girls, sickly sweet.

"All campers and counsellors are to gather at the baseball field." The voice repeats.

On the hill, in the distance, all the cabins are spilling out on both sides, the boys and girls. Everyone making their way excited to the field, speculation filling the air. Some kids bounce and roll down the hill like peanuts on a baking tray. I'm more than apprehensive about all this. There's been so much strange shit going on, it's like being a part of a corrupt television show. I've only just realised that I'm not the star, merely a fading extra, dormant in the background. I wish I was more important than I am. Mediocrity has warmth but carries with it a chill of dark depression. My thoughts are permanently pernicious. I'm questioning my sanctuary of the escapism I find in my mind. I'm not convinced that I'm safe there anymore. I'm gaining an addiction to the longevity of isolation and tormented by my deliberate alienation. Life is a pickle. I'm far too honest and creative with my own deprecations.

"Hey you." A voice whispers in my left ear. A tug on my T-shirt sleeve.

It's Hazel, with a delightful smile. Her eyes are light, beaming beautifully. She's always smirking at me, whatever the situation, a delicious smirk. Her eyes almost sink down within her as she makes eye contact with mine.

"You good?" she said.

She moves her head, looking at me deep in my eyes, her pupils flicking across the whites with concern.

I can't answer. I'm not sure if I'm good?

She's being sincere. I know that much. I think I might break down if she tries to read me too hard. I wanna tell her I'm lost, tell her everything, to ask for her help. I'm not right. I can't burden her with my confusion.

"You're in a world of your own." She said, her smile now less excited.

I still can't answer her. She's maintaining her warm eyes. She may as well be flashing a doctor's light in my face to drag me from unconsciousness.

"Dylan." She said, placing her hands flat on my shoulders.

I can see her pupils darting, she's obsessed with having my full eye contact. I want to laugh. Her actions are melodramatic. I can't find my voice to chuckle.

"Dylan, talk to me," she said.

I hear her words through whistling distortion. She has panic in her voice, an urgency. Our feet in my eyeline, the green thick blades of grass tickling our ankles.

I lick my lips and look into Hazel's dark eyes. I don't want her to find loss in mine. I clear my throat.

"Hey," I said.

She opens her eyes, an abnormal, alien wideness. So much white in her eyes. It seems unnecessary.

"Is that it?"

I think I got that wrong. Her eyes are clearly trying to evoke some other reaction from me. Not sure I care. No, I think I do.

"Seriously. What's the matter with you?" She said.

"Me. Nothing. Why?" Hopefully, my beat like stuttering will convince her and she'll stop probing. I'm loving the attention.

"Right. Have I done something?" She asks, folding her arms.

Groups of people walk toward the baseball field, passing us either side.

"Nah. Not that I know of," I said.

"You look fucked."

"It's a pleasure to see you too." I said, I only hope she laughs.

"If you're gonna be a jerk about it." She said, shaking her head.

I thought she'd laugh. I thought she could take a joke. A little deliberate flirting.

In this situation, why would she choose to use a word like jerk? She bounces into my life and uses a cartoon word. I'm in a world of confusion. Is she crying? She doesn't really know me. Who the fuck is this girl? It's not like we've even communicated all that much. I know nothing about her. Why does she continue to converse with me? I mean, she's fucking bald, shiny bald. I've never considered she may actually like me. I can't think why she would. I only wish I could plough through this thought process faster. I clear my mind of distraction. She already has her back to me.

"Hazel," I said. "Hazel."

She flaps her left arm at me with dismissal.

I can't believe she's gonna make me run after her. She's made no attempt to slow down. I leap forward, jogging after her. Now the quandary, do I grab for her arm, her hand or clasp her shoulder, do I even touch her? She could always turn and take a swipe at me. That would be embarrassing. She's stopped dead on the spot. I avoid jogging into the back of her head.

"Woah," I said. "I'm sorry, Hazel. I really am."

"What are you sorry for exactly?" She asked, spearing me for more information.

She hasn't looked at me, trying to avoid my eyes, crossing her arms, gripping her own body. She's looking off over my shoulder into nothingness.

"I don't know what's wrong with me," I said.

Hazel lands her eyes on mine.

"I am sorry. I like that you're concerned, thank you." I said, rubbing my hand on her smooth cheek. It's a cliché, but she's appreciating it.

"I'm concerned. I want to know you're all right." She said, touching my fingers with hers.

"I feel a little lost," I said.

"I can see that. You're not alone here, ya know," she said.

"It's so hard."

"It can be tough. Find the positives in it."

"The only thing that's seeing me through this shit is that I can be free afterwards."

"Hold on to that."

"I am," I said.

"Good."

"I'm looking forward to the opportunity of getting to know you. I really am."

"I won't deny you that opportunity." She said, dropping her head, her wig fringe sweeps across her forehead.

I fall in love way too easily, any form of attention granted, I interpret as love. Hazel might be confused. That whole cabin fever thing. We're locked here, not literally, not yet. With limited people to indulge yourself, it's easy to understand that as soon as one person, just one, shows a snippet of attention to another, you wrap it up in the tightest of love laced ribbon and bury it down as far as you can to maintain that coupling.

I like the fact we'll build a relationship out of nothing. We're two people thrown together. It could be fate. We could be a talking point. People would think us lucky, even special. That, out of all these people, we were naturally brought together. It's that thing of movie love, a meet cute. Without the sickly moistness.

Hazel and I make our way down the hill, joining the other counsellors, kids and adult staff as some sit together on the grass, others fill the bleachers. Groups of girls perform handstands, failing and crumble to the floor in a heap of legs and contorted arms. Why is that the go-to move for bored girls, handstands?

A group of all blonde girls, with the same haircut and style, encroach onto the baseball field and are immediately shouted at and shooed off by Rod and Bill, as they flap and clap their hands, like they're ridding sparrows from a cherry tree. The girls shuffle off the grass and head behind the baselines. Rapturous noise from all sides, making my ears ring. Too many people talking, creating swelling, burrowing sounds in my head. American accents surround me. I used to like the accent, I like Hazel's, at least. American accents now sound obnoxious and obscene. I might be in the wrong country.

Sat down next to Hazel, crossed legged. It's comforting to pluck at the green, carpet thick grass, against the skin of my hands. Hazel's looking beyond the baseball field, sitting bemused with her chin resting on her hitched-up knees, her hands clasped over each other, running her fingers over my right arm in a subtle, concealed, comforting stroke. It's nice but giving me goosebumps. No one seems to pay any attention to us. This lack of attention always makes me realise how insignificant I am or, in fact, any of us are.

I'm looking at the crown of Hazel's hair. I don't think I'd be able to tell she's wearing a wig. She uses a technique of putting foundation powder down the middle of the parting to blend her scalp into the colour of her hair, looks natural.

The noise surrounding us lowers without influence from anybody standing along the lines of the baseball field. No Hitler arms have been raised.

Beyond the trees, a thumping rhythm. Silence falls across

everyone. Some people rise to their feet from impatient seated positions. The noise gets louder. Other kids and counsellors stand up. It sounds like heavy boot wearing feet, banging down on concrete. With it, the rasp of skimming drums and a lonely fluttering flute.

The noise then seems to come from behind too, the same thing, boots thumping on tarmac. The noise and rhythm growing closer. Kids and counsellors swing their heads around, looking off into the distance back round to take in the noise from behind with beaming smiles. All excited, spinning around on the spot, throwing their hands in the air. Impatiently trying to identify the noise.

Appearing over the brow of the hill, a line of men's heads wearing blue civil war attire march with straight faced determination.

I hear another flute tune from behind. A similar line of people, only wearing grey civil war uniforms. Everyone wide mouthed in awe.

A massive explosion rings out from a cannon, it's chaos. Plumes of white smoke fill the air. Uniformed men run on to the baseball field, shooting at each other with replica muskets, like that from Fort Sumter. They all have field gear, bayonets, scabbards, shoulder belts and canteens attached to their hips. They must be one of those professional re-enactment groups. More thick smoke fills the field, teasing the breeze. It's more difficult to see the home run wall now. I hope they're firing blanks. Men wearing historically correct uniforms drop to the ground, bodies turn stiff and tip over like rigid felled trees.

The kids clap and stomp their feet in agreement of people pretending to die, there's no other way of putting it. Everyone seems to react without consideration. Why must I be the only one to conjure an argument? It's ironic that these fucking people are celebrating a war that tore this country apart. I can't get Guns n Roses out my head.

These nutcases are using their fallen citizens to provide the opening to a sport filled week of competition, aptly named 'Civil war'. They've warned us about this. The camp is split in two, both the boys and girls, right down the middle into two opposing teams. One grey, one blue, and they compete against each other in pre-prepared events. I'm on the edge of my metaphorical fucking seat.

There is one rule, as soon as the kids get back to the cabin, all the competition is left on the field, the court or whatever. Otherwise, points are deducted.

Men are laying lifeless on the baseball field. Another explosion rings out. They've fired another canon.

"Civil War." Said Rod, with a guttural roar. His face red, veins popping out of his neck.

Kids jump up into the air, as if injected with amphetamines. They're completely free of all inhibition. Screaming at the top of their lungs and rushing the field. Grabbing hold of one another and shaking each other by the necks of their T-shirts.

These kids, whether through choice or indoctrination, have completely and soulfully subscribed to the sense of rivalry and competition. Competition is healthy, it's a cultural thing. Is that enough to excuse it?

I could be too reserved. Whatever I am, I'm not like these vapid pricks. I guess it's time for Civil War.

Oh, fuck me. Even Hazel looks excited. Deal breaker?

Rounded up like sheep at a rodeo. Somehow Hazel and I end up separated. I'm handed a grey branded shirt with 'Civil War' written on the front, the date on the back.

The dissolution continues.

31

Cannonball

I'm begrudgingly wearing my very own grey 'Civil War' T-shirt. It's game time, I'm the umpire. Now that the white talcum powder smoke has cleared. I endure this bullshit. Stood stiff behind home plate, being the umpire of all these fucking games of baseball to determine who wins Civil War. Like I give a fuck.

Hazel has long gone, rounded up. What with all the talk of Civil War and an undertone of misplaced conflict. This Sleepaway camp is like I'm a part of Andersonville. Beyond the deadline is my life.

So, it began with the re-enactment of the U.S. Civil War. I've only experienced anything similar from watching films like Glory and Dances with Wolves.

Bobby is blue, the opposite team. Now, we're real enemies, if we weren't already. We're going to experience intense internecine, no love lost there then.

The activities, the days, everything moves so much slower during a Civil War. My toes are heavy, my nails cutting deeper into the nail bed. I keep thinking about it without ever doing anything about it.

I hear Laura crying, I hear myself crying. I want out of here. I fall asleep with the thoughts of dying. I'm certain I won't just die, I'll have to kill myself. It's painful to be here. It hurts to be in my head. I'm tired of it. I wanna be free, to leave all my pain behind. I need to know what it's like to laugh again. I can't remember the last time I was myself. The day I last felt happiness. My mind is crusting over like my toes, inflamed and infected, the yellow pus protecting me. I prod at my toe with the edge of my trainer until it's red raw. I can feel again. It brings me comfort that I'm still producing something, it gives me back my reality, I'm still here, still alive, almost.

I don't have any idea how I'm going to stand up and umpire this last baseball game. It's the last game the cabin will play before the points are all tallied up and they announce the winning side. I think they mention the winner later tonight after everything ends, when the teams perform their fight song.

Warren's been going on and on about how great the grey team's coat of arms is, that'll be displayed alongside performing their fight song, another fucking Phoenix probably, rising from the ashes.

All my previously pristine white socks are dirty now, orange tinted around the top from all the dust from the baseball fields and the parching of the grass we've been experiencing. They all have two red spots from where my nails are oozing blood and pus. I could go to the medical centre, I suppose, but fuck that. Probably be given a Tylenol. My Converse Weapons are not helping. They fit OK, but I could be stubborn because of my commitment to the brand, that seems silly really.

The first kid gets up and stands at the plate with a bullshit stance, off balance. He's never gonna hit the ball like that. The ball is thrown right over the plate.

"Strike one," I said.

This kid is gonna be out in no time. With every shout of strike. He looks back at me as if I owe him something. I don't owe you shit.

"You gotta swing," I said.

"He ain't swinging at shit." Said the high-pitched catcher, crouching.

I drop my clenched hammer fist on top of his catcher's helmet. He's shut his mouth. No words are needed, and I don't give two shits if anyone saw me.

This will go on. Kids hitting baseballs, missing baseballs, arguing with me that it was the wrong call. Shielding their eyes from the sun, complaining it's too hot. I don't think I'd wanna be running around right now. I used to love this game. I can safely say I'm unlikely to ever play it again. I don't think I will even need to watch another game on Channel 5. It'll free up a videotape. Not sure what I'll record instead, Eurotrash or Sex and the City. This camp has tainted my appreciation of an American sport, which was once my favourite.

Frank, this little fat kid is on third base, he reminds me of myself. He, like me, will never make it to home plate without having to push it. He can't run. This kid at bat will have to hit a home run for Frank to relax and trudge his way to the plate. I want Frank to live what I did. I want him to know nothing is a given. In life, he needs to run like he's being chased.

The ball is thrown, slow motion in my mind, it floats down the middle of home plate. Lewis, the guy at bat with the baseball helmet on, swings and strikes the ball. He's hit it well enough that it makes the pitcher jump to one side to avoid it. He flings the bat, escaping his grip, it spins clockwise until it hits the dusty ground. I jump up and over it to avoid it hitting my feet. Lewis is off toward first base. He's quick, getting smaller as he runs away.

An outfielder, a tubby looking kid, grabs at the ball. He looks to his left at first base, thinks twice and notices that Frank is shuffling slow toward home plate. I identify with poor Frank, struggling with his prepubescent weight to run any faster. His belly jiggles under his shirt, he has fat boobs, man tits. This is it, that ball is propelled at us.

Frank's never gonna make it. He's only halfway between the bases. The outfielder looks up at the catcher, now shielding home plate with his left glove, hand outstretched. He's urging the ball to be sent in his direction. Here it comes, the ball now in flight. An easy out for them. The ball dips.

Crack.

I'm on my back in the dirt. The ball hit me on the right big toe, burning pain up through my legs.

The catcher scrabbles for the ball under my feet, fumbles with it as Frank is now almost at home plate. The catcher fumbles again. He jumps toward home plate and clips Frank's leg as he puts his foot down, he's out.

I can't bring myself to say it. I'm on my back with the pain. Wetness in my trainers. It must be bleeding. Eyes of the camp on me. They all want me to call the play. I don't care, he's out.

"Dylan, call it." Screams Bobby, his eyes bulging.

"Out. He was out." Bellows the catcher standing over me with his face mask under his arm.

"In. He was in." Said another insistent voice, off to the side.

I roll over onto my knees. I'm shorter than fat Frank. He looks at me with silent expectation. I see myself again.

"In," I shout.

Frank jumps in the air. His T-shirt lifts, revealing his fleshy, pale belly. He pulls it back down as boys run in and congratulate him for scoring the winning run.

I hobble toward the bleachers. I have kids voices at the side of my head, faces in mine, darting in from the left and under my chin. Another face, too many faces. Their eyes merging into one. They're screaming at me, right in my face. I can't focus on anything other than the pain in my toes and the taste of red wine on my tongue. Faces in mine, arms waving, gesticulation. I sit down on the bench, not listening, and lift my right leg over my left, resting my trainer on my knee and rip it off my foot. I drop it to the dirt. The end of my sock is soaked red with blood.

"Look at his foot," says a disgusted voice.

"Sick."

I peel my sock off.

Bobby jumps in front of the crowd, surrounding me as I remain seated on the bleachers.

"Right, guys. Dylan is fine." Bobby holds his arms outstretched, ushering the growing crowd away from this bloodbath. "Back up, back up."

A dark purple mess. My nail has sliced its way deep into the red infected nail bed. It's released the pressure, it doesn't hurt anymore. I'm not aware it's hurting. My ears pop. I can smell a pungent slimy cheese, a truly remarkable and disgusting smell, satisfying. That putrid stench is coming out of me. I created it.

I wanna vomit.

My head flops forward, I'm drifting back to the side.

I can't breathe.

White, now black.

I'm out.

32

Private Truths

A white ceiling above me. It's clean in here, professionally finished paint on roof boards.

Where am I?

I'm not naked. Please tell me I'm not naked. I'm covered in a paper gown, wrapped in a blanket.

This room is unfamiliar, small and clinical. There's a sink in the corner just behind a blue plastic curtain. I must be in the medical centre. I need to sit up. It smells sterile, a clean bleach smell. They've done well, whoever they are, to conceal my foot stench. I pull the soft, green blanket up to reveal my feet. Both my toes are massive with light bulb shaped bandages wrapped around my big toes. They're cartoon looking, as if an anvil has landed on my feet and caused them to throb in flashing red police lights. If I had my CD player. There's only one Hot Hot Heat song that would fit this moment. My toes are mummified, wrapped tight in cream bandages.

A female doctor walks in with her hands in her pockets. She isn't carrying notes, a stethoscope or any of that other doctor stuff.

She has a white jacket on. I'm perched on my elbows.

"You look familiar," I said.

"You probably recognise me from surgery. You came 'round a few times. You kept fainting." She said, still with her hands in her pockets, her thumbs poking free. She smiles.

"Have you taken my toes off?"

I'm joking, I think. Imagine if they had.

She laughs. "No, don't worry."

"Thank god."

"You still have both your toes. It's a simple procedure." She said, trailing off. Moving around the bed, looking out the window, distracted.

"Whatever hit your toe—,"

"It was a baseball."

"Well, it relieved some pressure, but left alone it would become far more infected."

"Was it already then?" I said. Knowing full well it was. There was too much crust. You don't have to be a doctor to know that. I could have stone baked it.

"It was yes, bad too."

"Was that the smell?"

She doesn't answer, just nods.

"It's a case of slicing down the nail bed, extracting it, then we typically apply a bandage."

"It hurts a bit," I said.

"It will. You'll find it hard to walk for at least a couple of days."

"I was finding it hard, anyway."

"I'm not surprised," she said.

"I thought it might sort itself out."

I'm trying to remember where I've seen her pale eyes before.

"These things rarely do. We'll have to change the bandages by the end of this—,"

"Hey—, You took Megan to the hospital."

The doctor's eyes focus on the point of my fingertip, pointing. Her face has changed. She looks tense. She's paying attention to me now, but still looks around the room, as if she doesn't want anyone to hear.

"I saw you in town with her too." I said, confirming my vivid memory.

"When?"

"Before Civil war."

She wants to shush me.

"Megan's my daughter." She whispers with a concealed pride, shaking off a smile.

"Why didn't you just say that?" I said.

"I can't just say that." She said, looking back over her shoulder.

"Why?"

"It doesn't matter—, You're lucky we're close to the end of camp, you won't be able to take part in anything."

"Seriously?" I said. I'm not even sure why I'm acting shocked. That's music to my ears. She removes her hands from her pockets. "That's all very interesting, but why tell me Megan's your daughter?" She can't change the subject that easily. "Why hasn't she come back?"

"She can't be here, she's not safe." She shakes her head. Looking at me with hope.

"Right. Why's that?" I said, noticing her wedding finger, no ring.

She studies the room, her head sweeping. She's got a small white feather tattoo on her wrist.

"That must be the fourteenth time I've seen a feather tattoo," I said. "What the actual hell does that mean?"

Doctor Dumbarton, if that's even her name, looks down at the tattoo. It's the same design I've seen everywhere. She rubs it with her right thumb as if it's Megan's rosy cheek.

"Joe's her father." She said, with empty emotion.

"Joe?"

So much fucked up shit here. I'm not even shocked, though. How can I be?

"Joe's married to Emma," I said.

"He is, yeah,"

"I assume then she knows nothing about Megan?"

"She knows, there's too many of us." The doctor said, staring at the corner of the bedside table.

"Do you love him?" I said, to shock her from her daydream.

"He loves us all," She said, smiling at the feather. "We're so lucky."

"Lucky?"

"Yeah, if you're chosen." She said, in lost hallucination.

What the fuck? Get me outta here. No idea what any of this means.

All this fucking drama. I can't think what I've learnt here. I used to be more convinced that I was a nice person. I don't feel content anymore. I wanna disappear, to be alone again. I just need a break. I have to understand this world. I can't help a Doctor's cry for help, if that's what this is. I can't help myself. That woman is lost in a stupor of nostalgic fantasy.

As soon as they say the word, I'm leaving here and not looking back.

They won't pluck a feather from my wings, time to fly.

33

Fight Song

American colonial church, that's all the Playhouse reminds me of. Pilgrims and Amish people, jars of blueberry jam. It scares me too. The entire camp cramped inside. Boys and girls, campers and counsellors. This is the last co-ed event. Then freedom to pay sales tax.

We're sat facing the stage. How did I get here? I've taken no interest in who's sitting next to me. I'm staring at the stage, rubbing my hand over the spiny bristles of my hair at the back of my head, it's growing back.

Each side of the hall, splitting the grey and blue teams. We've all been judged, points totalled. A fight song decides the outcome.

This whole place revolves on an axis of evil. It could have a mind of its own. It's like Amityville or The Overlook. The whole place is consuming me. I'm clutching to grasp tighter to the hope of my escape. My paranoia dangling over me. It overcomes all my positive feelings.

Why do these counsellors insist on singing?

One of the Australian counsellors with surf blond hair, all floppy and Cowabunga-esque, sings a shitty folk song, always with a guitar, that introspective self-obsessed tone. It's so middle class, vanilla. It's so white. I need some flavour. Take me to a free party, rave it up. This guy is trying to chirp artistically along to some song, he's failing. The room seems to know it, must be a popular song. The room gets louder, and a slow clap begins, followed by whooping. This must be the chorus, people joining along with an anthem. The room is singing along. I don't know this song.

Rod raises his Hitler hand. His raised voice gets our frightened attention.

"We have the fight songs to judge from each team. The winners will receive one hundred bonus points. We'll be looking for originality, heart and collective fire." He shouts into a microphone.

Collective fire? What the hell is that bullshit, how will they measure that?

"Up first are the blue team," said Rod.

The representatives and counsellors from the blue team appear from the right-hand side of the stage.

"The first song is called Phoenix rises." Said Rod, his voice pops, looking down at cards with handwritten notes.

A loud drumbeat booms out over the speakers. A guitar riff bangs. Sounds like Rage Against the Machine. No, they're using Audioslave's song Cochise as the backing track.

"We'll we've been fighting, while you've been losing." The blue team voices ring out in time to the music.

Half of the room. The blues, clap their hands. The other side, the Greys are all booing.

Such a pantomime.

"We've been hitting home runs, while you've been down and out. We say you're losers, while you just cry on out." The voices shout, droning.

Heavy clapping from the stage.

"The blue army rises, we'll count you out. Can't save the

greys, blue team'll take it out on you."

They're so proud of this rendition, it's not radical.

Grey, then are happy with their self-indulgent Foo Fighters inspired song. Ruined Learn to Fly forever for me. Bastards.

I don't even care who wins. I really don't. This is just distraction, like kids in slow motion.

The room fades to black. Chattering fills the otherwise uncomfortable dark silence. A green sweeping light shines out onto a large pulled down screen, above the stage. It splices across the screen like the opening to Alien.

The campers in the room gasp and falls silent as the first bars of AC/DC, Back in Black booms out over the surround sound system.

This is the annual camp video. A montage of moving images. Boys running with cheerful faces, the scenery of blurred trees. Boys running through lines of awaiting kids, high five after low five after high five. I've lost count as they go. Girls dancing, skipping, and running. The audience, laugh and clap at the screen, enjoying the female spectacle. They've all got smiling faces.

As much as they can put up pictures of young boys and girls with a thumping rock beat and guitar riff behind it, scenes of kids arriving on school buses, sitting on bleachers, hugging one another, laughing and that clean, friendly image of this camp. The entire video is contrived. Sheepish and quiet kids are made to appear like celebrities. Max or whoever produced this can add in dissolves and fades throughout. We all know the truth.

The film cuts to the Seniors, the girls of age. Every male counsellor nudges his mate to signal the bounce of ample breasts. Lacey's popular face flashes across the screen. There are naked navels, hot pants riding up crotches, low cut tops, hair brushed straight, tear drop faces, slender noses and pert round bottoms. I'd be one of the innocent ones, caught out by these girls, out on the street. We're all so depraved.

Vibrant bright colours aside, sun-drenched scenes, they won't disguise the underlying evil. Closeup of a girl with a mouthful of orange, juice and pith dripping from her chin.

"Shame that's not my cock in her mouth," said Warren.

Smiling faces, misplaced hatred, high fives and fist pumps, handstands and volleyball. Kill 'em all. Left to right, up and down, the room full of lost eyes dart.

More on-screen, full mouthed, straight white perfect teeth, another smile, another laugh, archery, running with a football, side eyed head tilts, the glimmer of personal expression.

As the music reaches a crescendo, the beats per minute slow. The smiling faces turn to hugs. The hugs dissolve to pensive faces and two fingered peace signs. Peace signs turn to kisses on the cheeks of girls in damp swimsuits.

Images unravel, pictures of boys posing in front of golf carts like gangsters pimping their ride, groups clutching basketballs, backward caps, boys sitting on laps, resting on the shoulders of counsellors gazing up at fireworks. Every day here is the fourth of July.

My faith in humanity is broken. Boys in trunks, boys posing topless. Am I clouded by perversion or is what I'm seeing not appropriate?

Max edited this video.

The connections these kids may have felt, the leadership from the counsellors. I'm surrounded by arm over arm smiles, as if they've experienced priceless self-discovery. I'll hide my hatred with a grimace and an overbite. Pout, pout, pout. I've been told my teeth are crooked. These kids remind me every day. Kids can be cruel.

If I reminisce, I can't describe this experience as favourable. It's certainly changed my life. I'm far worse, more alienated and acidic, like a prisoner. There's no security in my fear. I've contemplated suicide, just to have it end. I feel as if I'm sat alone, a single spotlight on me. Making me want to grab for alcohol, a cigarette or any dirty sleeved cut drug. That'll allow me to forget, to escape the hopelessness.

My body wants to fall inwards. This place isn't right for me. All around me, baseball caps of different states, Montana to New York. Basketball teams, hockey teams, all these American sports. I'm surrounded by a living breathing colour commercial. Gatorade, Cheetos and drooping cheese pizza, a dollar a slice from Sbarro.

The video is a deliberate misrepresentation of the realities of this camp. Kids with long hair, short basin cuts, wet looks, swish looks, unkept looks. The dirt box derby, carts made from sheets of chipboard. The boys steam it down a hill, slowed by counsellors holding plastic mattresses as a cushion of cessation.

This video almost convinces me, these kids have had fun. It's almost convinced me I have too. It's one of the greatest summers of their lives, not true. I don't know where I belong anymore.

Editing to slow paced music about growing and seeing each other again is too much of a predicable moist propaganda tool for me. The soundtrack rings out. I wonder if they have a back catalogue of bullshit songs that encapsulate the message they're trying to push?

Get me outta this place, please, once and for all.

The music fades out.

The images fade to black.

Arms waggle in the darkness, a cacophony of crashes, claps and noise. The excitement at the conclusion of the tape has slammed within the consciousness of these kids. That's it.

I'm done.

Grey won by forty points. Whatever that means.

Fresh air. I need to be outside. My chest tightens. As we exit the playhouse, we're each handed a VHS tape. What I'm going to do with this, no clue. It's NTSC too, my VCR only plays PAL. So, on a shelf next to I Spit on Your Grave and a white label Cannibal Holocaust this will sit, never viewed.

The kids are clearly gonna show their parents, it'll be an event. Chips and dip. If the parents care about their children, they'll watch this bullshit, not mesmerised by doing the right thing. Their kids are being conditioned into selfish little cunts. This symbolic gift of a videotape, to remind them how fucked up this whole fake experience was.

There're no bins around. I can't even get rid of it. I don't want it in my hands anymore. I don't need the memories; they'll haunt me forever, it's like voodoo. The evil object for Pinhead to be summoned and resurrected in the corner of your loft.

Everyone is being directed to the driving range. I'm not up for that. It might be the last night with the kids but I need to rest my feet.

I'm heading in the direction of the cabin. As I do, fireworks light up the sky. They're spending my wages on explosives to signify the end of Civil War and the end of camp. Pretty colours don't enthrall me, loud bangs are just loud, that crackle of gunpowder. It really won't ever excite me. If Tinker Bell was to fly down from a castle, it might make me stay and watch. I'd just worry then about having to leave at the same time with a sea of people.

I open the back door to the cabin. Bryan, a slight and quiet blond-haired kid, classically good looking, is standing staring back at me with a mortified look. I realise now why he looks so worried. He's holding a mascara brush and looking at me, I'm looking at him. He looks at the mascara.

This should be interesting. I can see now the black accentuation caked on his eyelashes.

"Bry, what you doing?"

It's the only thing I can say, it's obvious what he's doing, he's got thicker eyelashes on one side. It makes his eye pop, dark set against his blond hair.

I suppose he could be doing it to be goth or something. He does like Jimmy Eat World, sort of pop punk, not eyeliner music. I wouldn't say he was into all that Robert Smith stuff.

"Nothing." He said, holding the mascara brush, as his cheeks turn blotchy red.

"Well, you are."

I don't mean to sound argumentative, but how is he gonna get out of this one?

"I like how it looks." Bryan said, as he turns back to admire his eyes in the mirror.

"You carry on then, mate." I said, tapping his shoulder, walking into the main cabin.

"You're not like, gonna make me wash it off?" He said, his eyes soft and embarrassed in the mirror's reflection.

"No." I said, smiling back at him. "Besides, you shouldn't wash that with water. You need a cleanser. Stop thinking so much, don't worry what I think." I said.

Bryan smiles, relieved. He seems relaxed, loose.

"You're missing the fireworks," I said.

"I've seen it all before." Bryan mumbles from the bathroom.

"Me too, mate. Me too."

I'll miss some of these kids. A few of them. The ones that matter, they already know they're respected. I'll wish every one of them nothing but greatness in their life. No emails from me. I don't have the reason to catch up with any of them. I'm happy knowing we met, and that's where I'll leave it. Sharing too much with too many makes you weak. I won't be defeated. What would we talk about, anyway?

There's nothing interesting in having to be present when the kids leave. I begrudge having to be involved, standing around waiting for them to be collected, witnessing their happy or reluctant bored parents travelling to pick up their little darlings. Hugs for some, high fives and gestures of 'put your bags in the trunk' for others. Parents on chunky mobile phones, talking to their assistants. Discreet conversations with fingers in one ear. Some parents don't have time to listen to their kids' stories.

I'm not sentimental, no time for memories.

Tomorrow I can leave and this whole thing will be over.

Thank the lord or whoever gives a hooters.
    Shit.
    I'll be one catcher's mitt down too.
    You're welcome Josh, enjoy it mate.

34

Last Goodbye

Should I be sad, should I be thankful?

I'm happy, at the same time confused, almost emotional. They've all gone. End of camp for the kids, almost over for us. The chipboard cabins are empty.

Warren, Doug and my bed are all that's left still lived in. All the sheets gone, leaving bare green plastic mattresses. The cubbies with no lacrosse sticks poking out, American footballs, trainers or tennis rackets, nothing just dirt filled shelves and silence.

There's a vague sense of peace in me. I'm relieved. All the shit's out. The camp is growing smaller, in terms of staff still hanging around. Everyone's been saying how they'll remain here until morning, that's when the buses arrive, to take us from here to the station.

Some people with cars are already leaving. I can see them through the fly screen. Just like when the kids departed, I'm not compelled to say goodbye. I'm clearly unimportant to them, just as they are to me.

I pulled down my backpack from the top of my cubby, a thin

layer of dust on it. I haven't touched it since I arrived. Another task, emptying my chipboard shelves of shitty shit, discoloured clothes, soiled with summer memories. I don't need all this stuff anyway, it's more weight to carry. My Sanyo camera still wrapped in a towel.

I have my blood-stained Converse trainers, looking back at me with the pain they've caused my toenails. I'm in two minds whether I keep them or Chuck Taylor them away. I sniff the dust covered white leather, smells like dog chewed rawhide. I'm sad to throw these trainers away, more than I was to say 'laters' to the kids. I might miss Josh. My apathy divided by guilt, apathy will always win out.

The last evening here should be a good one. It doesn't matter how good it is, it'll soon pass. I take a picture with my disposable camera of my trainers, the blue emblem of the Converse arrows peeking from the bottom of the bin liner. Like the end of an era. I know they're only trainers, I have an affinity for the brand. It could be the connection to the history of the States, that whole 50s thing, or my love of Grease, seeing John Travolta roaming about, dipping his shoulders, learning to play baseball and running track.

I only need to get through tonight. Then I'll be catching a train, getting the hell outta Dodge, out of this fucking place, back to New York, which is now a lifetime away. I'll take the power back. Perhaps I've grown more distant from reality.

As I stand looking at Doug's disheveled bed, I'm not convinced I'm going to remain his friend either. I know we both said we would, I'm not sure that's realistic. I won't be going to Georgia to stay with him and his family. What a burden that would be for everyone, pre-planned or a surprise. Fake talk to stay in touch, it's never gonna happen. Friends, to me are episodic, sanitary towels, sopping up the discharge of indecision. If you need endorsement from others, you're weak. Like when you leave school, all those people with tight-knit cliques of friends always surround themselves with the same people, they never grow up. Just remain the same people they were as kids, same sensibilities, with no sense. Then they have kids of their own, that rely too heavily on others to think for themselves. It goes full circle, retards breed retards, and so the story shalt remain.

It's going to be good to be alone. I can have a bath, I can't wait for a bath. Something so simple, to feel weightless, warm and completely naked, that will be my divine pleasure. I've had nothing but standing in that claustrophobic narrow little shower with that mildew damp curtain hugging my leg, peeling it off my thigh. At the same time, humming to alert impatient ten-year-old boys that I am, in fact, naked. To be fair, no one ever disturbed me. I disturbed myself with the fear I'd be interrupted. There was no time for soapsud masturbation.

I can't get over how quiet it is here now the kids have gone. The only sound is the wind lashing at the trees, it's not wild, a light breeze. It would be splendid if a branch was to pop off and land on this cabin. I could emerge from the wreckage, peeling away shards of splinters from my face, the dust rising. I imagine a cluster of people standing before the cabin, crest fallen, realising it was only me, standing before them in my cheap JD sports red shorts and a white plain T-shirt. My head dusted like a muffin with icing sugar. That disappointment on their faces at my English unpopular ways. Probably wishing the branch would've killed me.

"Sup dawg," said Doug. He's chomping down on a soft pretzel as he enters through the front door of the cabin. The dough collecting around his gums like homemade paper mulch.

"You all packed?" He said, wandering into the cabin, forcing half chewed pretzel back between his lips.

"I've got most of it done. I really don't think I'll need any of it," I said.

"Where is it y'all planning on headin'?" Small soft dough leaves his wide mouth, like wallpaper paste lining his tongue.

"I think if we get the train. We'll all end up in New York." I said, poking at my backpack. "At least that's my understanding of how it's going to work, anyway."

"Yeah, I heard that. Me and Landon gettin' the train to Grand Central. Might stay in the city for a night, then fly out from Newark." Doug splutters with his mouth full.

"Just one night?"

"Once you've seen Yankee stadium, you've seen it all." Doug said, removing family Polaroids stuck to the chipboard wall by his bed. I believe him when he says that. I like Doug, but he's another example of a vapid individual. Other than being in this cabin, we really share no other similarities.

Warren arrives through the backdoor wearing a grey Superman T-shirt. He's spiked his speckled grey hair. His right hand down his shorts, adjusting his testicles. He's sticking his tongue out as if it's the most satisfying of scratches. Doug notices and spins away, back to concentrating on his photos. Warren makes a coughing, grunting noise. It seems to be an apparent attempt at encouraging both of us to question him.

"You all right dawg?" Said Doug.

Warren, with his arms stretched, circles his head on his neck. He produces a sound only fitting to that of waking up.

"I only fucked that Toni by the lake." He said, oh so proud and arrogant in a mocking American accent, as he throws his arms up in celebration.

"Which one is Toni?" said Doug.

I'm not interested. I'm not sure I really like Warren. He's too abrasive. His true personality is hidden in his accent.

"You know Toni. The gorgeous brunette girl."

If he was left in a room with your sister, he would lace her drinks with double rums and take advantage, fingering her as she drifts in and out of consciousness.

"Oh Toni, Toni—, Yeah, Toni we all know Toni."

His announcement of lakeside copulation isn't much of a surprise to me. Toni was probably asleep. I'm not sure why people decide to brag about having sex with women, that first they shouldn't be all that proud of sleeping with, but, as if me imagining their penis clambering, bewildered within another orifice is impressive and revered. I really don't care, keep it to yourself you wretched nob head. I suppose we've all got a story.

Warren lays back on his bed as if he's conquered the world. Toni is not worth celebrating, she's thin, perhaps too thin, lanky, her hair in a ponytail isn't flattering, it's almost thinning. She seemed nice enough, but I'll always associate her with Alyssa and that night, and everything else since; I'd rather not hear her name, much less think of her naked.

I then picture Alyssa, legs spread, being banged against that tree.

"Are we still getting food tonight?" Said Warren, staring at the chipboard ceiling.

"Yeah. Apparently, we do." Said Doug.

"Thank god. I always get so hungry after I fuck." Said Warren.

I turn to Doug and roll my eyes. I bet it was earth shattering. Must have really built up an appetite.

"The way you say that sounds like you haven't had sex for a long time." I said, with provocation in my voice. I want him to know how insignificant his story is to me.

Warren smirks.

"Well, ya see, people like me need sex more than once a year." He said with his mouth open in jest.

"I'm sure she won't be walking for a week, mate," I said. Only a couple more hours of this shit. I'll be able to sleep and I won't have to hear his bullshit anymore. Never again. It's about time we embark on our last journey from this cabin to the dining room. This will be our last meal. For whatever reason, we'll probably all sit at our designated cabin tables. We don't have to. It reminds me of an institutionalised habit. Taking up the same seats we did when the kids were here.

* * *

Dinner was one more task down before the evening could start. Now it's over, we can all kick back for one last time and get drunk until morning, with apparently no interruption from the dictators.

Cars arriving, male and female counsellors are stocking up boots, or trunks I should say with their filled bags and luggage. Most of the people staying tonight are retrieving plastic carrier bags full of beer from places hidden out of sight. Others are carrying brown paper bags and hoisting out the contained liquor bottles, holding them above their heads as if they're welcoming Simba to the world. Adulation from awaiting groups of guys wearing backwards baseball caps, ripped denim jeans and nothing on their feet, sharing swigs from whatever alcohol it is they're passing around. Looks like a cheap version of Jack Daniel's.

This will be the last time I'll stand here, atop these steps, looking out at the camp like an artist's pallet of colours. Mostly green splodges and white as people dip in and out of my eyeline. There's so much green. I should probably take it in, etch it into my memory. It's oddly overwhelming. I've only been here ten weeks, but I fear reality.

I step down on my heals, descending. I know I'm concentrating on my feet, they're enormous, like clown feet. A part of me will be left here. I won't forget anything that's happened. It's an experience that is carved deep into my memory, most of which I want to forget.

At the bottom of the steps are the three brother bears, Carter, Bedford and Herold. All with baseball hats on, pulled down low, almost covering their eyes. They tilt their heads back.

"You want some Dylan?" Said Carter, holding out a small hockey puck sized, open metal tin.

"What is it?" I said. It's like a dark brown, honey-soaked, sticky straw or something.

"Chewing tobacco." Said Carter, pushing his tongue against the side of his cheek. "Take a pinch and put it in the side of yer mouth."

"Alright," I said.

I like these guys, they might consider me rude if I don't take them up on the offer. Is that peer pressure? I'm not sure if I need to impress them.

"That enough?" I said. I don't want to take too much. I pinch a small amount between my thumb and fingers, probably only two teaspoons worth of parsley. I jam it into the right side of my mouth, between my teeth and my cheek.

"Shit. It tastes like a cigarette." I said, wincing, wanting so badly to spit.

The three of them laugh, their shoulders shuddering. They like seeing me disgusted. It tastes like I'm eating burnt cigarette ash, mixed with soured phlegm, thick and slimy. I hiccup uncontrollably. It's making me gag. I need to spit this out. The Trailer Park Boys keep laughing as Bedford grabs his tummy and folds over at the waist, he's loving it.

"We popped his cherry." Said Bedford, laughing and holding his fist up to his mouth so not to spit his own mouthful of tobacco out.

"Get this outta my mouth." I said, flapping my arms. "Seriously."

I spit it out, sweeping my tongue over my top teeth, scrape along the bottom, fold my tongue and feel for the gap in the back of my mouth, between the teeth and my gums. I need this shit out. I spit again, unashamed and frantic. I don't care who might be watching. Any of the guys sharing their drinks will probably hold fire for the time being. I'm trying to contain the dog like noises my mouth seems to make, like a maniac.

"That's disgusting." I said, looking up at them. I think it's all outta my mouth. The three bears haven't stopped laughing.

"That's hilarious." Said Carter, wiping his eyes and closing the tobacco tin shut. "Join us later, we'll have a drink".

"Cool," I said. "I can't really talk right now. Not with that rancid taste of death in my mouth."

"It's nuts, right?"Said Bedford, chomping on tobacco "You get used to it."

"Not sure I will. See you guys later." I said, saluting them with my index finger.

This might be my last walk along this grass route, under the tree canopy. Done this walk a lot, back and forth to the cabin. And now my memory of my last walk will forever be with the taste of warm burnt shit in my mouth.

The flagpole is quite an amazing sight to behold as I walk up the slight hill to the cabins. Perspective is so weird. Sometimes I think I should really open my eyes more. Out in the open, walking across this grass, the American flag waves in the wind, a gentle breeze to keep it flapping. I could count all the stars. It'll be strange not to see that every day, so unnatural not to pledge allegiance to it. It's become what I know. I don't even question it now. Will I want to continue that on my own in my hotel room? Give a little thought to the flag once I'm dressed, I doubt it.

It's going to be so nice to be on my own again. Waking up in a large hotel double bed, soft carpet under my toes, that hum of air conditioning, a TV and the remote within arm's length. I can be alone, silent. No instructions, no Hitler hand dictation, just exist. I'm really looking forward to that.

At the base of the flagpole, seeing the colours of the flag fluttering with the fading sky behind it, makes me think of living. Hollywood has hijacked my life. Seeing the flag like this is inspiring. The white flagpole is cold to touch. There must be symbolism there. My English hand, holding on to this flagpole, as if it's the hand of God. No idea what it would symbolise, the beginning of choices, the impetus for change. It will be a step forward, leaving here, one giant leap into my destiny. I can only hope for that much. It's getting a little darker out here. The evening is fast approaching. I'd better see who's around, see what the plan is. I should try to get involved.

It's dark. In the cabin, last time in this lighting, that murky crossover. Doug and Warren's bags all strapped up. They could be out the back,

I suppose. I can see some activity from the toilet window, people moving up the track.

A big green pickup truck parked close to the back of our cabin. It's not Doug's. Warren's English and so won't have a car. Not sure who it belongs to. There's mud splashes up to the windows, it's dirty, well used, looks more like an off-road vehicle, thick chunky black tyres and a massive spare wheel in the back with a pile of bags and a suitcase. Even a Gatorade water cooler. The driver's door crunches open, making me jump. It sounds as if the door wants to collapse off its hinges.

"Get in dawg." Said Carter from behind the wheel. The back door opens, Herold gestures with his head for me to get in. They're both chewing tobacco again, or it's the same tobacco. Carter closes his door, the hinge wailing as if in pain. I reach for the back-passenger door and climb up into the truck. Fast food cartons and cups strewn across both the footwells, maps, papers and pamphlets on the dashboard. I half expect to see some nude magazines, nipples peering back at me. No nipples in sight, unfortunately.

"Hey guys," I said.

Bedford is 'riding shotgun', as they say. Herold shifts over on the back seat. I nod, they all nod back simultaneously. They're good guys, I almost wouldn't have expected it from them. Oxford Mark is sitting leaning, squashed against the other passenger window. He's having to sit forward. I didn't notice he was there, Bedford is so wide, he blocks him completely.

"Hey, Oxford Mark," I said. I'm not entirely sure I've ever called him that to his face. His shocked reaction says I haven't. It's not offensive or anything.

"We're leaving early in the morning." Said Carter, unwinding his window, swiping at the rotating handle. The window clunks down.

"I didn't know you guys had a truck?" I said, kicking an empty burger box off my trainers.

"Oh yeah, we had to park it over on Longview Road, behind the catering cabins." Carter said, spitting tobacco out his opened window.

"This'll probably be the last time I see you guys," I said.

I imagine the flatbed truck with the bags and spare tyre, to be filled with moonshine barrels when these guys get back home, hidden under camouflage netting.

An opened bottle of Jack Daniel's is passed to me, they're drinking it neat, straight from the bottle. They've shared more than a bottle of booze before, going by some of their loose stories of sex with girls in the same hotel room. My life is in my own hands as I take a swig of alcohol.

Oxford Mark leans forward to Carter, whipping from his pocket a CD, like he's performing a magic trick, he's come prepared. Could be The Vengaboys I suppose. He passes the CD, pinching the outside of the disk with his fingers.

"Carter, put this on and skip to track three. You're gonna love it." Said Oxford Mark.

Carter grips his beard in his right hand and tugs. He clutches the CD like a Frisbee with his dirty fingers. Oxford Mark does not look happy. Carter shoves it heavy handed into the car's CD player slot. He fingers at the skip button, misses it the first time and then attempts to compress the button. He's successful. The lime green illuminated digital display skips from one, two, and then sets upon track three, silence. We're all sat waiting. I'm still holding the bottle, looking down at the contents. The intro to the track chimes out. It sounds like a wood saw wobbling in reverse, a simple bass line. Then the guitars. I recognise it, it's Jeff Buckley. I turn to Oxford Mark with warmth and sincerity. The bass kicks in.

"Last Goodbye." I said, with a smile.

He nods before he thrusts his head forward as the drums beat in, his eyes closed tight. He's enjoying it, as we all are. I know what he's experiencing. This song has a special place for him too, it's also living within me, I love it. It makes me favour Oxford Mark more. We have something, if only this song in common. As if this is his prayer time. It's soft drifting perfection. The words make me float. The world becomes a marshmallow haze. So beautiful, we all remain sat in this truck, completely still. We don't continue to pass the bottle, almost out of respect. Instead, we sit, our stiff heads pressing into the head rests, bolt upright. They all have their eyes closed, I close mine too. It's like we're each exploring our own souls. I can't speak for the others, but that's what I'm doing, feeling every word that Mr. Buckley is singing.

The three brothers and Oxford Mark all sing aloud with the music. I'm sitting with my mouth wide open in surprise. It's giving me goosebumps.

We all sing at the top of our voices, the veins in our necks popping, it's so good. A real memory is being created. The song regretfully finishes with Jeff's soft lingering fade. All four minutes, thirty-five seconds of it. Carter jams his thumb on eject. The CD spits out.

"Beautiful." He said, clapping his hands together in approval.

I feel dirty from being in the back of that truck. I've washed my hands in the cabin. Not only because of the filth from the truck, but I shook Huey, Dewey, and Louie's rough man hands. Stiff, heavy long hand shakes as we parted ways. No need to shake Oxford Mark's hands. He's not leaving early tomorrow morning.

I notice Doug's green prescription throat medicine sitting peacefully on his bedside table. He hasn't packed it yet. A swig of whiskey isn't enough for me. My hands grab out for the bottle, my green laced confidence, it's become a dastardly fiend playing with my addictions. Another way for me to forget. I push down the child lock, unscrew the cap as if my life depends on it. I wanna be unconscious. I swig down three thick mouthfuls. Despite it being minty, the taste burns my throat. My head's immediately clear. I steady myself, placing the bottle back down where I found it. I swear it's teasing me in the light, making itself twinkle.

I stagger on the loose gravel beneath my feet. Wandering, having to concentrate on my footsteps. I drift amongst the cabins. Flashes of cameras explode through the darkness, as group photographs are taken. I can only wish to be in their memories. I have my cigarettes, thank God. Time to light. It doesn't matter anymore if we smoke. At least I don't think it does, everyone else is doing it. There are no kids now, so we can get away with almost anything. Plus, it's the last night and what's anyone gonna do? We can't be fired now. They've handed us our last pay packets. Checks, paychecks I should say and that's that. No turning back now. I'm becoming more relaxed as this evening progresses.

Through an open doorway to one cabin, Oxford Mark holds an acoustic guitar, like a hippie, a drifter. A small crowd has gathered around him. No doubt I'll see him again in the future, riding a chopper push bike down the promenade of Exmouth beach, a real peddling nomad. I enter the cabin. Sit down on the first available bed. I hope I won't be noticed. Oxford Mark waves me over. That's kind of him.

He breaks into a guitar riff as I move closer to the group, his fingers dancing along the fret board with ease. People in the cabin turn to listen in, their eyes shut, and they sway in tune to the slow soft intro. I know what it is now. Ronan Keating. That one from Notting Hill. Seems like a strange choice to impress the ladies with.

Oxford Mark sings with a slight, impersonating Irish accent. He's got a pleasant voice, couldn't hear it earlier in the car, lost in all our volume. He's doing well to emulate the tone of Ronan, he really is. I only know the chorus, but Oxford Mark is singing it word for word. I have no reason to doubt his rendition. The cabin, all sing along with the beginning of the chorus. They look around with sentimental, soft smiles. The normal cronies are in attendance. Jimmy wearing yet another Manchester United shirt, Daniel and Andy stand clutching a red plastic frat party cup. They hang off Oxford Mark as if he's their leader. It's like its unified us at last. On the last night of camp, something positive, like a good old sing song. The tragic irony of everything. Why couldn't this have happened before now?

Oxford Mark is the lead singer in all of this. We sing along to the end of the song. As fast as it started, it's over. All the spectators clap their hands. I love this, it's so special.

I'm struck with a bout of confidence and gesture with a smile to Mark to pass over the guitar. He sees within me that this is something I wouldn't usually do. He's encouraging my bravery, nodding at me whilst he hands over the guitar, like it's a sacred cow. I hold it. It's majestic, tanned wood, clean cream-coloured strings, it's a gold briefcase moment. I'm honoured Mark has entrusted me with it, given it seems like an extension of him.

I sit down, adjusting my hands and rest the guitar on my knee. I don't wanna fuck this up. I sweep my fingertips along the fretboard. I have a guitar at home and whenever I pick it up, I sing the same words, a tune I keep coming back to. They're not new to me, the words are always there. The alcohol and I suppose Doug's throat juice may have given me more confidence, which I'm thankful for. I need it. I strum and sing aloud, my voice cracking with my eyes shut. I keep strumming, remembering the chorus. Building the anticipation, time it just right. I fill it with more chord changes. I take a quick, blurred glance around the room. Faces looking back at me, I want to give them the world.

Oxford Mark, being musical and having a good ear, starts singing along to my words. I did judge him too soon.

I finish the song, my song, and try my best not to smile. I don't wanna be thought of as arrogant. Oxford Mark has in this moment made me want to live again. Everyone around, sat on beds, opposite and alongside me, join in and sing my words, the words I wrote. This means so much to me, I almost want to cry. I stop moving my hands and the guitar chords finish ringing out. Everyone around, including the Canadian girls, are now closer to me. I didn't even see them move, but they're clapping and smiling too. They all seem to be well lubricated by the open beer cans they're drinking from. They make for fine looking audience members. I love it. I can't stop smiling. I'm attractive suddenly.

"Thanking you so kindly," I said.

"Encore. Encore." Saide Oxford Mark, clapping in genuine appreciation.

He's got a lit cigarette perched loose between his lips as he sucks his cheeks in, producing deep dimples as he inhales. The cigarette glows lava red. He looks like a rock star, completely cool.

"That's all I got, for now," I said.

I'd rather burn out than fade away. I could rock out a rendition of Jingle bells or Telstar if that would get the girls' panties moist.

Through the haze of this moment, we're all standing outside. I wrap my arms around three Canadian girls. Oxford Mark is holding my disposable camera and clicks down, setting off the bright white flash. Here I am, pursing my lips together as if air kissing the world, an unlit cigarette tucked behind my left ear. I'm proudly wearing one of the Goat Gear T-shirts I stole from one of the bigger kids, fits nice.

Oxford Mark hands back my camera. Everybody talks to one another, a rumbling of scattered accents. I'm not hearing anything specific. Instead, I investigate my camera as if it's new to me. I split from the crowd, escaping with makeshift distraction. Sometimes, it's nice to leave when it's good. Goodbye with words, it's always too final. Silent escape, open return.

Hazel is sitting patient on the bottom rung of the steps to our cabin. What a welcome surprise. I was wondering where she was. Hazel. Hazel Valentine. She's sat with her chin in her hands, resting her elbows on her knees. A black wig fringe, covering her face, she's scuffing with her foot at a cigarette butt in the dry, dusty dirt.

"Hey, you." I said.

She jerks her head toward me, smiling. She looks happy to see me.

"Sit with me." She said, slapping the bottom step with her hand.

I sit down next to her, my left jean leg touching the edge of her thigh. She's wearing a tight denim skirt and smells like cherries.

The skirts not too short, almost down to her knees. She looks; respectably pretty. And they say it's such a distracting word.

"What are you doing tomorrow?" She said, clasping her hands together in her lap, hunching her shoulders together. She looks cute. I'd almost do anything for her.

"Disappearing." I said, forcing fake enigma. I want her to talk to me.

"Disappearing?" She said, screwing up her face. Not literally, you understand. That's the reaction I was looking for.

"I certainly hope not," she said. "I was thinking we'd go for dinner."

"Dinner—, Sorry, the word dinner is so mature. It's an adult term. I wanna have fun with you. Dinner's too serious." I said. I can pretentious, I know. Uni's to blame, I swear.

"Oh." Said Hazel, shocked with my dismissal at her use of a word.

I'm afforded a new lease of life. It's like a fullness of contentment, a milkshake with a burger. Like getting back together with the love of your life, after twelve years of no contact. You carry on where you left off.

"I'm heading to New York," she said. "I think most of us are."

I need to articulate properly. I need to do it quick, say something reciprocal you idiot.

"Yeah, unless you're driving," I said.

"Exactly. Which I'm not. I'm catching the train to Grand Central." She said and flicked her black hair to the side.

"Ditto," I said.

When have I ever used the word 'ditto' before? By the look in her eyes, that went down like a ton of shit. She doesn't look happy with me.

"Well, if I won't be cramping your style. Perhaps we could sit together?"

Normally I'd consider this entire suggestion a complete

weakness. I've never understood why people feel the need to preplan seating arrangements, sit with friends. They can't experience the unknown, can't be talking to someone they don't know. I wanna sit with her though. It'd be superb. I'm flattered she's even interested in sitting next to me. We've come a long way since she got her wig off.

"That would be really nice," I said.

"Nice?"

"Yeah, nice—, What?"

"Sorry," She said. "Nice is a negative word, it comes in quick and pokes you in the eye. It's uncomfortable to hear it used too many times."

"Perhaps, but we'll have to see tomorrow if you live up to my expectations." I said. That's my attempt to save the moment.

"Perhaps, perhaps, perhaps," said Hazel.

She takes me by the hand and leads me up the steps into the cabin. She might be as neurotic as me with words. Could be interesting.

"Which one is your bed?" she said.

Jesus, she's being forward. I point to my bottom bunk. I've switched since Josh left.

"You mind if I stay with you tonight?"

Her question is innocent. I don't think of us having sex. That isn't on my mind. I think we're gonna sleep in the same bed. Doug's in his bed, so there won't be any naughtiness.

"That's OK with me," I said.

I slip off my jeans. I'm wearing black briefs. I wish I would've chosen boxers. I slide my half-naked body into the bed. For the first time in my life, for whatever reason, I'm self-conscious. Hazel unbuttons her denim skirt, wiggling it free from her waist, leaving her black thong on. I'm assuming it's a thong. She hasn't turned round, it's cut like a thong, high on the hip. She peels her black crop top off over her head, placing it on top of mine. Black and white polka dot bra. Her breasts are delicate. She jumps and slides her feet into the bed, kicking her feet under the sleeping bag to make room for her body next to mine.

"I haven't brushed my teeth," I said, into her ear.

"Me neither. You're fine," she said.

"I might be, but yours, well, my God."

I'm flirting with her. I'm at least trying. She laughs and graces her warm palm on my chest, nestling her head into my shoulder. She leans and kisses my nose. That's enough for me, that's all the intimacy I need.

"Night, Dylan." She said, looking into my eyes.

"Night, Hazel." I said, as she closes her eyes. "Night, Hazel Valentine."

She looks so serene. I only wanna hold her. It hasn't crossed my mind to try any moves. I can feel her soft skin on mine. It's a gentle connection of flesh, it's enough.

"Remember to breathe," she said.

She's so sweet. She must've been listening to my lack of breath. I was holding it. Concentration maybe. She's left her wig on. I nuzzle my nose into the top of her head and sniff. She has an amazing aroma, it's a fresh wholesome scent, kind of like cherry blossom mixed with vanilla.

I'm falling asleep. As I do, I squeeze her. I'm drifting into slumber as my body is with her heartbeat.

Thank you, Hazel. Thank you for saving me.

35

Escape To New York

"I'll never know," said Doug.

His southern accent wakes me up. I'm expecting to see Hazel. She isn't here. Her clothes gone from laying on top of mine. I'm filled with the empty, unfulfilled realisation that I may have dreamt the whole thing. I can't have. Doug would have seen her, she was here.

"Hey Doug," I said.

He's folding his remaining clothes, giving me some of his loose, distracted attention.

"Sup dawg."

"Where's Hazel?"

"Who's Hazel?" He said, looking up at me, now giving me his full attention.

That's exactly what I didn't want to hear. I kick off my sleeping bag and swing my legs round, my fleshy feet tickling the floor, almost forgetting about my bandaged toes, reminded only by burning heat.

"You being serious?" I said.

He must be joking. Please tell me you're joking. There's no way in hell I imagined last night. I can't have been that fucked up. Doug nods toward the bathroom.

There she is, standing backlit by the morning sun, illuminating her angelically. My relief, she's real. Why would I ever imagine meeting a girl with alopecia? I'm glad she's now the object of my infatuation. Hazel is pure to me, she's what I need. Not that her only inclusion in this world is for my benefit. I hope I'll be a positive influence in her life. I can see her in my future. I imagine her in my arms. I hope too that I empower her as much as she has restored me to normality.

"Hey," said Hazel. So simply.

I already like the intimacy of the way she utters 'hey', for me and only to me.

"Morning, little lady."

"I have to pick up my stuff before the bus arrives." She said, adjusting her denim skirt.

"OK." I nod, not breaking my gaze from her beautiful eyes.

"I'll meet you down there." She said, as she walks on by, stroking her hand through my hair. She taps Doug on the shoulder as she leaves. It's nice that's she's even social and accepting of him. She looks back at me through the fly screen door, smiling again. What have I done to deserve her?

"She seems nice, dawg." Said Doug, nodding with approval, continuing to fold his clothes in a pile.

"I know, she's lovely." I said, half in a daydream. My mind wandering through scenarios of emotion.

I want to escape with her. I haven't thought as far ahead as meeting her parents, but it could be a possibility. One thing at a time. I seem to put too much emphasis on other people, relying on them to provide me with an ounce of happiness. I'm not sure it's even fair of me to burden Hazel with that. She seems like someone I could love. She can't be the one to save me, no one can. I need to save myself.

* * *

Our bags are packed. It's customary to check around the cabin, make sure I've not left anything. I have all my CDs. I have everything I need. We're all itching to leave. Warren is talking loud. I'm not listening. Doug's the first to push the front door open for the last time, he's gone. The fly door slams shut. I'm not waiting for Warren either. I've left my copy of Malcolm X on the bookshelf. This camp needs it more than I do. I'm out, down the steps, onto the grass. My old beautiful trainers will sit for eternity in that bin. I look back at the cabin, I certainly won't be coming back here. I won't be a returning counsellor. I'd need counselling myself if I did.

Doug and I don't speak. There's a slight feeling of sentimentalism in me. It won't last long. I hum the bass line to Walking on the moon by The Police. We're heading toward the yellow school buses parked off the main road. There's a group of people, fellow counsellors, all with their packed bags. They all have different intentions to mine, some will probably travel around in groups, others will disappear back to their families. Most of them, I'll never see again. Most of them, I don't want to.

Doug turns to me. He looks back at the cabin, then at the buses, a gentle nod. He puts his arms around me. We hug. A long hug. It probably isn't long enough. We pat each other on the back and loosen our grips. We both know this is it.

"You're a good guy, Doug," I said. Trying not to make too much eye contact, I might cry if we do.

"I know. You too, Dawg."

I hold out my hand, our thumbs interconnect. A poignant and meaningful handshake. He pulls me into his shoulder and he rests his chin. A genuine sign of mutual affection. We break away from this, our last embrace. We retreat back into our own personal space. I nod and smile. We've exchanged email addresses, that's covered. As much as Doug and I have maintained this friendship whilst we were here. He and I both know, almost like an unspoken agreement, that we're very unlikely to maintain any form of contact. I might drop him an email now and again, but other than being here, what would we discuss? It won't be a friendship of longevity. I wanna get on the bus. I need to find Hazel. Doug's helped me through to the end of this, that much I know. He knows that too, I hope he does. He walks beside me and high fives Landon, he's got his real friend now. Landon smacks me on the shoulder and smiles.

That's it, done. I'll forever associate balls with Landon, said in that loud Bama accent. They both get on one of the yellow school buses. I won't see them again, that I'm certain of.

Back up the hill, the long grass punctuating my time here. I can't stare for too long, otherwise Warren will think I'm waiting for him. I don't want him cramping my style and tagging along. He's got his own crew and he'll stick with that lanky, tall girl, Toni. Good luck to him.

I refuse to look back at the cabin or the rest of the camp with emotion, instead with misplaced satisfaction that I've survived and now my journey can begin, I can travel.

I'll travel with Hazel. I haven't really prepared myself for that possibility. No idea what I'm gonna do if I'm with Hazel, and I need to speak to Laura on the phone. I should probably call again, or at least try. I might have to lie to Hazel or prewarn her or something. She hasn't asked if I'm single, I haven't told her. I don't know if she has a boyfriend. I know I'm far more comfortable lying to Laura than I am to Hazel. I wanna give us the best chance of a beginning.

There she is. Blonde wig now. The anxiety in the pit of my heart has disappeared. She's making her way up the hill from the girls' side of camp, the middle girl of three. I don't recognise the other two, no need to care. Oh wait, White Russian. She's not tagging along, is she? They stop, they all seem to say their goodbyes, hugging and standing close to each other. Thank god, they're all going their separate ways. Hazel heading toward me. A glare of disapproval from White Russian. I can see Hazel's been crying as she gets closer. I'm jealous she seems to have had the type of experience here, that means she can shed a tear for this place. That's nice for her. I wanted that, too. For now, I'm accepting of waiting to welcome her into my life.

"Hey," she said.

I wipe at her cheek, absorbing a teardrop.

"Hey you," I said.

This is all different, genuine. I know it, she knows it.

"Shall we?" She asked, cordially, holding out her hand.

We step up onto the bus.

I can't believe I'm leaving here alive. A lot has happened, too much I wanna forget. I have no room for emotion, although I'm attached. They can't take my soul.

Rod, Bill and Joe are standing arms crossed surveying the buses as the engines kick over. Their expressionless faces. I can't give them any more of myself, they've stolen too much.

I'm not seeing anyone on this bus, although it's almost full. It's all a blur as I follow Hazel. She's smiling back over her shoulder at me, her eyes rich with life. She dives into a free seat, resting her bag on her lap. I slide the shoulder straps of my bag off and sit down next to her. The door shuts, the bus roars, jerking forward.

The white cabins on the hill reduce in size. The three figures of arm crossed authority soon become mere dots, punctuated by the shadow of the misguided flagpole. Good luck to them.

One last look at the totem pole.

'Red Oak and Silver Wood Camp'.

I thank you, for all the hurt.

Hazel and I share my foam headphones from my CD player. I skip the track to Toad the Wet Sprocket, Crazy Life.

"I like this song. I've not heard it before," she said.

"It's a little obscure. I only know it from Empire Records."

"Never seen it,"

I'm disappointed by that.

"Don't worry, I'll show you it. It's also the film that introduced me to AC/DC," I said.

"I've heard of him."

"Them, they're a band."

Hazel shrugs her shoulders. I like that. She doesn't care.

The tempo of this song fits with us travelling through the English-looking countryside of New York State. Hazel sways to the music, her head bopping. I can see my reflection in the bus window, as trees outside provide shade. Hazel catches my eye and smiles into the reflection back at me. Hazel Valentine. I can't hide my happiness.

Dover Plains, a train station in the middle of nowhere. What was I expecting? There's literally a train track and an elevated platform, nothing else. Everyone bundles off the yellow school buses the moment we arrive and head toward the platform. A queue forms at a red ticket machine, people inserting monies to purchase a ticket to Grand Central Station. Some people are panicking getting impatient as the queue is only getting longer. There are shit loads of us. Luckily, Hazel and I are relatively close to the front, so we're certain to get a ticket before the train arrives.

"Don't worry. We can always pay on board." Hazel said, rubbing my shoulder.

It's like she sensed my anxiety. I needed that reassurance from her.

I count out eighty-six dollars, mostly fives and one-dollar bills. I insert them into the ticket machine. The machine gobbling them up like a hungry paper shredder. The sound of huffing and impatience coming from behind us. Hazel keeps turning and cutting her eye at those stood waiting. I like how her glare is enough to defend me. That seems to avert their attention for a while. Although, we all worked on the same camp for as long as we did. Some people with their backpacks on, I don't even recognise. The machine spits out two, large Amtrak one-way tickets, 'Grand Central Station' printed through the middle. I'd like to keep this, it's like something out of a movie. Naturally, I paid for Hazel's. That goes without saying. Why is she surprised? She rests her head on my shoulder in what I'm interpreting as voiceless appreciation.

The silver Amtrak train doors slide closed behind us. We find a set of four seats together, all empty. Two facing the direction the train is travelling, the other two facing the wrong way. Hazel sits in the seat opposite me. We sit on the aisle, our bags in the seats next to the window.

"Well, we made it." She said, zipping up an open pocket on her backpack.

I feel empty. I try to conceal it, it's hard. I can't get the cliques and packs of friends out of my head. For an itching second, I'm not sure I want her sitting opposite me. I'm not sure of anything anymore. She's so beautiful, so genuine, so different.

We maintain conversations of growing old, the way we should act our age, succumb to life and our responsibilities. The pair of us laugh off the seriousness of any chat with the ignorance it deserves. We filled the journey with flirtation, playful mocking of each other's accents, changing seats uncomfortably, bathroom breaks, avoiding familiar faces. Hazel runs circles with her fingers on my right knee as she gets lost in the view from her window seat. We listen to my CD player until the batteries die, mostly Hot Hot Heat; the album of the summer; well, this experience. Summer makes it sound more enjoyable than it was, more film noir than coming of age.

The surroundings from the window are familiar, a massive metropolis. After this solid, three-hour journey. This is now over too. I'm thankful Hazel is with me. It makes it so much easier.

The train penetrates the historic station of Grand Central and we get off on yet another platform. It reminds me of the one Mick Dundee proclaims his public love for whatever her name was in Crocodile Dundee.

From losing myself in her eyes to wanting to just lose myself. We seem to pace up the sloping platform. We round a corner and there are faces from camp lining the walls by a hexagon shaped wooden newspaper stand. A shop selling flowers on the right.

Hazel squeezes my hand. We run up the main steps until we reach the grand, magnificent arrival's hall. It's like all the movies. I used to have a poster in my room at uni, with shafts of light coming through these very windows. It's like I've been here before.

We head out through bronze-coloured doors to the familiar streets of Manhattan. Warm, dusty smell, chalky dirt. It's almost as if I've never left.

It's good to escape the crowds of people, the ones forced upon us. I kind of want to escape Hazel now, too. How do I disappear? I need a chance to have a bath, to relax, be alone. I want to think again. There have been too many murmurings all around me, for too long.

It would be nice if amongst the native New Yorkers. I got separated from Hazel, lost in the bustle. I think though with the pressure she's applying to my hand, there's never a chance of that happening. Was this, like so many, a fleeting relationship? I'm forever indecisive. Do I want to humour this or even pursue it further? I really would like to be alone, camp's over now. I'm not a sociopath but sometimes I need silence. I don't wanna act anymore. I don't think of these people we've left behind as family, I don't think that of Hazel either. Why have I become so disingenuous? What are we even gonna talk about now? It's been easy so far, but I can't commit to her. Why would I? I'm with Laura, anyway.

Right, my plan is simple. I'll lose her, somehow, I'm gonna lose her. As we stroll along the pavement, a group of people I recognise, clearly Hazel recognises them too, are standing on the corner of East 45th Street. The sign flashing:

'Don't Walk'

One girl with a pink sleeping bag wrapped tight to the top of her backpack turns around, almost with a subconscious knowing, that Hazel was approaching. They both scream, arms flapping to fly.

"Oh, my god. Oh, my god." Said Hazel, clapping her hands.

"What are you doing here, babe?" Said the girl to Hazel.

"We just arrived a second ago." Said Hazel, throwing her

arms around her. She's not holding my hand anymore. She's turned into a mall rat. This could be my chance to bolt.

"You're kidding, me too."

"This is Dylan." Said Hazel, pointing at me for the benefit of this girl.

"Hi Dylan. The pleasure is all mine." She said with a smile, not loosening her grip on Hazel.

"Hi," I said.

That's all she's getting from me.

"Where you guys heading?" The girl asked.

"Well, we're gonna get a hotel, right, sweetie?" Said Hazel, looking at me.

I nod. Hazel grabs for the girl's hand, she knows her very well. They must be old friends, or from the same town. I still don't care enough to ask.

This group of fifteen people walk. I prepare myself for repetition and the conversations of spending a summer working on a children's camp, monotonous, soporific chatter. I can't get away, it would be far too obvious. I expect to slip away into the distance of the future. I can't be listening to the same old shit.

We end up at the Crowne Plaza, Times Square. This group of people, random fuckers. They all enter the hotel through the automatic glass doors without discussion. Hazel's near the front of the group as they filter inside. Gone out of sight.

I turn without hesitation, the hotel doors behind me. I walk brisk, north on Broadway, darting between people as they dip their shoulders to avoid me. I may as well be running. I turn left on 49th street. Up 8th Avenue, until I reach the Howard Johnson. From outside, this is as good as any hotel. I'm not a sheep, I'm a wolf. The orange and blue signage entices me. Howard Johnson is a name I trust. I go to reception, drop my massive travel backpack off my shoulders, thumping it down at my feet, making sure I don't rest it on my big toes. They're still giving me trouble, these bastard toenails.

The pencil-thin moustached gentleman behind the counter provides me with his salutation.

"Afternoon. If you want a room, go 'round the corner here." He said, pointing, "Pick up the receiver and book." He mimes using a phone handset.

That must be a joke. Why would I?

"It works out cheaper for you." The receptionist insists.

That's nice of him.

I get a rate of seventy-nine dollars for one night. A spacious enough room. It beats the cabin. I need a bath. I want to be clean, relaxed. Why is the first thing I turn to the remote control? The TV pings on, opening on a still picture of the hotel exterior, yellow NYC cabs. The message:

'Welcome home, Mr. Nemerov.' Written in Big Apple Red font.

Bath time. Seriously, I need a bath. I searched my bag for the last fully charged batteries I have in my possession. I listen to the Long Beach Dub All Stars whilst soaking. The entire album, chilling. Only when settled in my mind and pruned by the water, am I safe to venture out again into the city outside?

To Times Square. That's where I'll roam. There's a public computer in the lobby. I should check my emails. It's two dollars for fifteen minutes. I don't know why I need to torture myself. I know Laura won't have messaged me. Am I bluffing? It's like I want to load the page with one eye open. I really wanna see one of her subject lines, her email address, anything.

Fuck her. Again, nothing. What is she doing? She's making me insane.

There's a strong smell of sausage links in this lobby, fatty sausages.

I walk on my own, never safer, through the city. People jostling past me. Noise left, right, here and there. I've never been more confident, never felt more me. I enjoy being alone, fading into the shadows. American flags flapping everywhere.

McDonald's on the corner, four guys appear from the entrance. It's Daniel, Jimmy Wickwar, Andy and some other guy. I don't recognise him. Strange that Oxford Mark isn't with them. I hope he's got lost, like me. Daniel is giving Jimmy a piggyback. Andy laughs as he puts a Filet-of-fish in his mouth. I'm not up for getting involved in that shit. I dart across the road to avoid them, doing my best not to make any eye contact or draw attention to myself. I need to move on from this. I need to grow up.

I spot an Applebee's restaurant and wade my way over, swinging my body from side to side to avoid the impatient people of this, their Manhattan. I haven't eaten since the poxy brown paper bag breakfast from camp this morning, a turkey sandwich. My legs trudge as if stuck in lethargy, slow motion. I shift my shoulders like a downhill skier to avoid barging into people as I cross the street. I'm vegetarian but need chicken, I really want to eat something naughty, Applebee's will do.

Classic combo to start, mozzarella sticks, chicken quesadilla and wings. I don't even wipe my sauce covered fingers. Next, medium rare bourbon steak. All washed down with a large frosty glass of root beer, this is bliss. I've been eating nothing but aubergine with cheese and marinara sauce for weeks, all because I kept up the pretence that I'm veggie. More for Laura than for me. I need the fat now.

The City has become personable to me, flexing its fingers around my mind. The smell of warm pretzel dough rummages amongst my nostrils. As I stand with my eyes shut, my senses are aroused. Car horns in time with my heartbeat. Steam from the street. A forceful hand reaches into my jacket pocket and grabs for my wallet. A heavy and sustained poke in my back like a gun.

"Give it over." A voice demands, uttered with a familiar American accent. It's female. Immediately, I know it's Hazel. I turn, and our eyes collide.

"Oh, my god." I said, acting surprised.

"What the fuck happened to you?" She said, with disbelief in her eyes.

"I lost you."

"I noticed. Was it deliberate?"

"No, of course not," I said. "One minute you guys were there, and then, gone. I was looking up at the Empire State building."

"We were nowhere near the Empire state."

"Whatever that tall building is," I said.

"I'm not letting you out of my sight." Hazel said, grabbing my hand.

"I don't want you to."

Tell me, why am I so conflicted? I want so much to be with her, but I have nothing to offer.

"You're taking me to your hotel room," said Hazel.

She pulls our clasped hands to her chest. She's serious. She won't let me out of her sight. I like that. I think we're gonna engage in exactly what we've been putting off for nine weeks.

Let me be happy for once.

36

Hazel, Hazel Valentine

The door clicks shut behind us. I nudge it into place with my shoulder blades. Hazel on my lips, cupping my face in her hands, she's breathing heavy. Her eyes are tight shut. I'm conscious the curtains aren't closed. If anyone was to spy on us, they'd see everything. That excites me.

Hazel's undoing my belt, fingering for the buttons on my jeans. She's looking up at me with her eyes wide. She bites down on my lip and tugs me toward her, sitting on the edge of the bed, sliding her back across the surface of the crisp white sheets. I pull my shirt off and drop it to the floor, kick my unravelled jeans from my ankles. They clank with the metal buckle on carpet. I slide on my hands and knees, catlike, and lay over Hazel, looking down into her eyes. She's wearing a candy floss pink bra and black lace knickers. Now is not the time to judge her underwear, not matching. I stroke her face.

"Can I take my wig off?" She said, looking up at me with these expectant eyes.

"You don't have to ask." I said, kissing her on the cold tip of her nose.

I want her to be comfortable. I really do like her. She slides her blonde wig off. For a moment, I see Laura's face. With the wig now gone, Hazel's back with me, only now with a glistening bald head.

"You're so beautiful," I said. "I mean that."

She smiles and sits up to meet my lips. This isn't a moment for oral sex I know she doesn't want that. I don't need it to become aroused. I place my fingers over her black underwear and press my fingers between her lips, she's already wet. I straddle over her, she sits up and unclasps her bra from behind her back. I do like how toned she is, not emaciated. She looks delicate and athletic, the right amount of muscle and just enough fat to cover her bones, she looks healthy. I need to take her in, really appreciate her. Her head is moulding into the pillow. I peel down her underwear, over her tanned thighs, clip her delicate knees and gather them together over her ankles. I bunch them between my fingers and sniff, sweet citrus.

"My feet are tingling." She said, placing her hands over her nipples, as if trying to conceal them.

"I want to see you," I said. She lays her arms flat, like on a crucifix. There it is again, a white feather tattoo on her right breast, in the crease of her chest.

"How long you had that tattoo?"

She tugs on my hard erection. "Don't talk now." She said, pulling me toward her.

"Seriously," I said. I circle my finger over it. The familiar design.

"Couple of years."

"Have you been to Red Oak before?"

"Of course, we all have."

Before I can think, she pulls me into her lips by the back of my head. White feathers have fluttered free from my mind.

I slide my knees in between her legs. Desire flashes through me. Lust cripples my thinking. I stab blindly at her pussy. I wanna be inside her. I need to be with her.

"I want you." She said, guiding me inside her, around my shaft. She leans back into the pillow, accepting slow, deep thrusts. I'm gentle. I need to go slow. I wanna respect her. I need to stay cool. Make this moment last. Our mouths meet again. I'm conscious the TV has come on. I must have hit the remote, the volumes loud. I can feel her heat. I'm not stopping now. This spark is dreamlike. Her breath is quick. She draws her fingers through my short hair and pulls my head closer to hers. A sharp slap on my right butt cheek, she's digging her nails in. It hurts, it's a surprise, I like it. It encourages me. I thrust faster, our naked bodies together. Her skin soft. I wanna kiss her head, I can't. It might ruin the moment. I need to stop thinking.

It was over not long after it started. It was passionate, worth remembering. I'll think about it again and again. Finally, I'm not guilty. I didn't think of Laura once. I get the impression she hasn't thought about me either.

"I never know what to say." I said, turning to Hazel.

"As long as it's not thank you. We're all good." She said, as I rolled over onto my side, my semi flopping and slapping on my thigh.

"I won't say it was amazing." I shift, leaning on my elbow, circling her nipple with my left finger. "Of course, it was."

"Good save," she said.

"You know what I mean." I said, kissing her on the shoulder as she strokes her stomach with her fingertips. "It was more than special. Amazing seems so arbitrary."

"You really know how to ruin a moment, don't you?"

"Well, it's been said. Too late now, you can't take it back."

"I don't wanna take anything back." She said, curling her lips. She looks sincere.

I'm kind of guilty that I almost left her. What is this, post sex madness? I still think I intend to leave. I wanna hold her though. I'll make that my priority. All I need is to hold her. I might think differently in the morning, we'll see.

* * *

With Hazel in my arms, the city sun piercing through a hairline crack in the curtains. The TV's on. Has it been on all night? As my eyes adjust to the blurry light. Hazel's wrapped up, resting on my chest again. She rolls off beside me. She has no wig on. She really is so beautiful.

We've planned to meet up again later this morning. All the details were contained within what you might call pillow talk. I'd love to say that we woke throughout the night, made love to the soundtrack of sultry saxophones and soft dissolves until the sun came up, we didn't. It was right, just the way it was. Her eyes closed soft, right arm tucked back behind her head, elevated on the pillow. She looks cute, kind of fetal. The plan is, she'll head back to her hotel, get her stuff and tell the others she'd be leaving with me. I bet none of them sharing that room had a bath or even had sex last night.

I stand at the bedroom door, my foot holding it open with the corner of my trainer.

"I won't be long," said Hazel.

"I'll be here, little lady." I lean down and kiss her on the forehead. Her wig is tucked behind her ears. "Be good." I say with ephemeral intention.

Hazel scrunches her nose.

"Bye."

I hold up my hand as if to signal a wave. My hand motionless and stiff. Hazel smiles, spins on her heal and walks away down the hallway of the Howard Johnson. I close the hotel room door behind me, my shoulders pressing it closed. I rest my spine against the cold wood. I need to take a moment.

Bryant Park was where I should have been at 10.30am. Hazel had said how much she wanted to head toward Allentown, Pennsylvania. I didn't know until last night that she had a thing for trucks and wanted to see the Mack Trucks Historical Museum. I know 10.30 has come and gone. My destination is out of this city, alone. I need to break ties and start all over. I care about Hazel, Hazel Valentine. I'll certainly never forget her, I really won't.

I've cheated on Laura, but deep down, I think she knew it would happen. The way she kissed me goodbye and wrote that good luck letter with hand-drawn hearts and ladybirds. She worded it in such a way, that either she didn't expect me to return at all or she innately knew something like this would happen and I'd be unfaithful. She was right. I always seem to fuck up everyone else's lives. It's time to find myself.

I'm out. 41st and 8th, Port Authority. Twenty-one dollars later, Greyhound. I'll head for DC. I have Tom Waits and Hot Hot Heat for company. Mule Variations is the choice for now. It'll have to entertain me on repeat until I reach the capital and distract me from thinking about Hazel, wondering what I've done with my life.

I can't bear thinking of Hazel, on her own at the fountain, if she keeps her promise she was getting coffee on the way. I can't think what her reaction will be when she realises I'm not coming, the coffee going cold. Life moves on. She's the only connection I have left to that camp. I'm so sorry Hazel.

Regardless of any heroic action I could have taken, holy intervention or misguided revenge. A bullet to the head would all be irrelevant to those people. Bill, Rod and Joe, can't be stopped. Red Oak and Silver Wood Camp is too big, too prestigious. They'll welcome more innocence next year. Think for a second, there could exist another counsellor, more vengeful than me. Now, leave your kids with a stranger for nine weeks.

As much as I'll forever wonder, I'll never forget. Time for me to be selfish and I don't even wear a watch.

With certainty, I don't know myself anymore. I don't have all the answers, I'm not secure and most of the time evil wins.

All I know is, I can recite the declaration of independence without hesitation.

For all the good it'll do me.

* * *

The books:

Shattered Vanilla
Flagpole
Autumn in Georgetown

About The Author

Neil Hall was born in England.
He is a writer.
Simple as that.

tallbluemidget.com

Flagpole

Neil Hall

Printed in Great Britain
by Amazon

82488813R00202